DEATH *of a* BLACKBIRD

A DI MATTHEW STANNARD NOVEL

C.K. Harewood

This is a work of fiction. Names, characters, businesses, events and incidents are the products of the author's imagination. Any resemblance to actual persons, living or dead, or actual events is purely coincidental.

This work may contain a few instances of language and sentiments representative of the novel's historical setting that some readers may find offensive and which do not reflect the author's views or opinions.

ISBN (Hardback): 978-1-912968-54-1

ISBN (Paperback): 978-1-912968-53-4

ISBN (eBOOK): 978-1-912968-52-7

DEATH OF A BLACKBIRD

C. K. HAREWOOD

Chapter One

Monday, 5th May 1930

Josiah Clough's weather-beaten face screwed up in anger as he raised the spade above his head and brought the flat of the blade down hard.

The wooden post shuddered. He banged it three times more, forcing it deeper into the ground with each blow, then grabbed the top of the post with a gnarly, crabbed hand and wiggled it, making sure it was secure. Tossing the spade to the ground, he used both hands to set the painted sign nailed to it straight.

Heedless of the rain bouncing off the brim of his hat and slipping under the collar of his oilskin overcoat, he stepped back to examine his handiwork. Clough nodded with satisfaction. The Blackbird Farm sign was as it should be once more, how it had been for decades. And how, he'd decided, it was going to stay.

Closing the gate behind him, he picked up the spade and made his way along the path to the farmhouse. He propped the spade against the outside wall, then stepped into the hall, taking off his hat and coat and throwing them over the rickety settle. Muddy footsteps marked his way to the kitchen, where he filled the kettle and banged it down on the gas ring. The match he used to light the gas was shaken out and thrown on the floor, where it joined a multitude of others.

As he waited for the kettle to boil, Clough thumbed through the bills he'd tossed aside earlier in the day. Bills for chicken feed, for hay, for cow ointment from the vet. His lips curled in disgust. A tidy sum was owing and some of the bills were stamped with OVERDUE and PAY NOW in bright red ink. He turned to the shelves above the kitchen cabinets that were laden with tins, jars and packets of food, reaching up to take down a tin of OXO stock cubes.

Carrying it to the table, he sat down and pulled off the lid, tipping out the contents. Not stock cubes, but rolls of banknotes held together with thick rubber bands. Clough pulled off one band from a roll and, licking his filthy thumb, counted out six five-pound notes. These, he set to one side and rolled up the remaining notes, snapping the rubber band back on.

There was a loud click behind him and Clough twisted around in alarm. The back door opened and Father James Pettifer stepped in.

'What do you want?' Clough demanded.

Pettifer's wrinkled face fell. 'Is that any way to say hello, Josiah?'

'Why are you coming in the back? I've got a front door, you know?'

'This way is closer. I didn't think you'd mind.'

'You don't bother knocking either.'

'My apologies. May I come in?'

'You're already in, ain't ya?' Clough muttered, rising to lift the whistling kettle off the gas. He poured the boiling water into the teapot and banged on the lid. 'What do you want?' he asked again.

Pettifer shook his umbrella out and propped it against the wall.

‘I was taking my evening constitutional and I thought I’d pop in and see how you are.’ He looked around the kitchen, shaking his head at the mess, then saw the banknotes on the kitchen table. His eyes widened.

Clough followed his gaze. With a snort of annoyance, he grabbed the rolls and stuffed them back into the tin. ‘You don’t be looking at that,’ he said, replacing the OXO tin on the shelf.

‘You have all that money just sitting there on your kitchen shelf, Josiah? That seems a little reckless. Shouldn’t you put it in the bank where it will be safe?’

‘It’s safe enough where it is.’ Clough stirred the leaves in the teapot. ‘What do you mean, see how I am?’

Pettifer pulled out a chair from the table and sat down. ‘You’ve been out of sorts of late, even more so than usual, and I wondered if something was troubling you?’

Clough snatched up two chipped mugs from the draining board and banged them onto the table. ‘I was thinking about doing something, but I’ve decided against it,’ he said, pouring out the tea.

‘What were you thinking of doing?’

‘Never you mind.’ Clough splashed milk into the tea and pushed a mug towards Pettifer. ‘It ain’t going to happen now and I’m telling ’em so.’

‘Telling who so?’

‘I told you, it don’t matter now. Stop asking questions. It’s none of your business.’

Pettifer held up his hands. ‘Very well, I shan’t ask again. But there’s no need to be so defensive, Josiah. I only have your best interests at heart, and besides, your mother would never forgive me if I failed in my duty. She made me promise I would keep an eye on you and I intend to keep it.’

‘I don’t want you here.’ Clough slurped at his tea. ‘I’ve had enough of pests bothering me day and night. Coming round here uninvited, telling me what to do. Trying to make me turn my back on everything my family's done.'

'What are you talking about, Josiah?' Pettifer cried indignantly. 'I've never said anything against your family.'

'Trying to push me into things,' Clough went on. 'I'm fed up with you all interfering. You can all bugger off.'

Pettifer rose, pink lips pursed, chin in the air. 'I can't think what I've done to deserve being spoken to like this, Josiah. I really can't.' He picked up his umbrella and left the kitchen, letting the door slam behind him.

Unmoved, Clough finished his tea. *Pests,* he thought. *Why can't they leave me alone?*

Chapter Two

The first thing Matthew Stannard sensed when he awoke was pain.

Somewhere above his left eyebrow, it felt as if his skull had been cracked open and lightning bolts were striking the exposed, spongy matter of his brain. He didn't want to open his eyes, certain they would hurt, too.

The second thing he sensed was noise. Unfamiliar sounds. Strange voices. Rolling trolley wheels. Rubber heels on wooden floorboards.

The third sensation he experienced was smell. Carbolic. Starch. *I'm in hospital*, he worked out, and then tried to work out why.

'I think he's awake,' someone whispered, and Matthew felt a bony hand squeeze his. 'Mattie?'

'Mum?' he croaked.

'Yes, Mattie. It's me.'

Matthew pulled his eyelids apart. Everything was blurry, and he had to wait for his eyes to focus on Amanda sitting beside the bed. She was smiling at him, but her eyes were full of worry. Then his other hand was grabbed, and he turned his head, slowly, because the movement jostled his brain and made black spots dance in his vision.

'Pat?'

'I'm here,' his sister said, and patted his hand reassuringly.

'My head hurts.'

'You were hit on the head, Mattie. You're in hospital. Do you remember what happened?'

'Don't make him talk, Pat,' Amanda chided. 'Go and get someone. The nurse said they wanted to know if he woke up.'

Pat's hand slipped away from his as she obeyed. He closed his eyes; they hurt too much to keep open.

'How bad is it?' Matthew asked his mother.

'Oh, Mattie, you look awful,' she said. 'Your head's all bandaged up and you've got a big bruise over your forehead and your eye's all black and blue.'

He heard footsteps approaching, two pairs this time. Someone leaned over him and peeled back his eyelids. He caught the faintest whiff of perfume. A nurse, then. Not a doctor.

'How are we feeling, Mr Stannard?' the nurse asked.

'He said his head hurts,' his mother supplied.

'I'd be surprised if it didn't. That was quite a blow you took. I'll let the doctor know you're awake.' The perfume drifted away.

The mattress dipped as Pat hitched herself onto the bed and took his hand once more. 'The nurse said you're going to be all right, so there's no need to worry. You've got a bit of concussion, that's all. There won't be any permanent damage.'

'But look at the state of him, Pat,' Amanda cried loudly, making Matthew wince.

'They're only cuts and bruises, Mum,' Pat snapped. 'They'll heal and he'll be back to normal again.' He felt her body turn as heavier footsteps came towards the bed.

'Well, Mr Stannard,' a male voice said above him, 'quite the adventure you've had tonight. How are we feeling?'

'My head hurts,' he said. 'I can't keep my eyes open.'

'Headache?' the doctor asked.

Matthew groaned in answer.

'Let's check your vision.' Matthew's eyelids were pulled apart. 'How many fingers am I holding up?'

'Three?' Matthew guessed.

'Is everything blurry?'

'Yes.'

'Can you follow my finger?' The doctor moved his hand from side to side and Matthew tried to follow the multiple pink blobs in his vision.

'Feeling queasy?'

'A bit.'

'Yes, I'm afraid you're going to feel this way for a few days. Your skull took quite a crack. The blow broke the skin and the left side of your face is bruised, but all in all, I'd say you've been very lucky. It could have been a lot worse. Do you remember what happened?'

'Someone was in my flat,' Matthew said. 'Standing behind the bedroom door.'

'That's right,' Pat said. 'That's where I found you. You were lying on the floor with blood all over you. It gave me such a fright, I can tell you.'

'Don't keep going on, Pat,' Amanda said.

'I've hardly said a thing!' Pat returned indignantly.

It hasn't taken them long to start arguing, Matthew thought wryly.

'Anything else?' the doctor asked.

'White-blond hair,' Matthew said, and then it hit him. He opened his eyes and lifted his head off the pillow, ignoring the pain. 'It was Wilfred Gadd.'

'That's what the police said,' Pat nodded. 'I told them what he looked like and—'

'You saw him?' Matthew cried in alarm, trying to sit up.

'Calm down, Mr Stannard,' the doctor said, pushing Matthew back onto the pillow. 'You mustn't get excited.'

Amanda prodded him gently to stay where he was. 'The police said Pat frightened him off.'

'He pushed past me in the hallway,' Pat said. 'I went flying into the wall, but I got a good look at him.'

'Did he hurt you?'

'Don't you worry about her,' Amanda said sharply. 'She's all right. You're the one in hospital.'

Pat smiled sadly at him. 'I'm fine, Mattie. Really.'

'Well, your memory seems to be intact,' the doctor said, 'so that's good. We're going to keep you here for a day or two, just to keep an eye on you. The best thing you can do now is rest,' he added with a pointed look at Amanda and Pat. 'I'll be back to check on you later.' He left, passing Fred and Georgie as they came in.

'He's awake, is he?' Fred asked. 'Hello, Matt. Back in the land of the living?'

Matthew gave a weak smile to his brother-in-law. 'Just about.'

Georgie stood beside Fred, staring down at Matthew with wide, frightened eyes. 'Are you all right, Mattie?' he asked quietly.

'The doctor seems to think so. It probably looks worse than it is,' he said, hoping to comfort his brother.

'It was that burglar you've been looking for, wasn't it?' Fred said. 'He nearly got Pat as well, you know?'

'I'm sorry,' Matthew said. 'I didn't mean to put her in danger.'

'It weren't your fault,' Pat said. 'It's a blooming good thing I went to yours, otherwise you might have been lying there for days with your head bashed in. Or worse.'

'All right, love,' Fred said, putting his hands on her shoulders, 'Matt don't need to hear all that. I heard the doc say he needed rest, so now we've seen him and know he's going to be all right, we should leave him alone.'

'I don't like leaving him,' Amanda whined as she reluctantly rose from the chair. 'Maybe they'll let me stay.'

Matthew shot Fred a look.

'He needs to sleep, Mother,' Fred said, understanding his silent plea. He gently guided Amanda and Pat towards the door. 'See you soon, Matt,' he promised and winked. 'Come on, Georgie.'

'I'll be in to see you tomorrow, Mattie,' Georgie promised and followed after the others.

Matthew's eyes closed and he was asleep before Georgie was out of the door.

Wilfred Gadd wasn't sleeping. He was too angry to sleep.

He, too, was lying in bed, but he was alone, no concerned, loving family clustered around his bedside. His bed was in a damp, rented room in a boarding house with decades-old paper peeling off the walls, staring at the large crack in the ceiling and cursing the bitch who had stopped him from doing what he had wanted to do.

And he'd come so close. Stannard had gone down like a sack of spuds, had been unconscious at his feet and at his mercy, and then that stupid bitch had come into the flat, calling out 'Mattie!' and he'd panicked, running away without a second thought. And it had only been when his lungs were about to burst and he'd come to a stop, doubling over to catch his breath, that he realised he shouldn't have legged it. He should have whacked Stannard again, finished him off, and then done the bitch, too.

Tears pricked his eyes and Wilf let them fall. He'd let his mother down; he hadn't got her the justice she deserved. She was probably looking down on him now, shaking her head at his balls-up, muttering 'Typical'.

'I'll get him, Ma,' Wilf promised, speaking aloud to the empty room. 'I'll get him.'

Chapter Three

Charlie Woods snapped off the twig that was poking his hair and stripped the leaves from it, crushing them between his fingers. He took a surreptitious look at his wristwatch, then glanced at his friend leaning against a tree trunk nearby. 'Shouldn't we be going?' he asked.

'There's plenty of time,' Nathan Jowett said, sucking on his cigarette and trying to make a smoke ring.

'Not really. They'll ring the bell in ten minutes.'

'We're not going to school.'

'Aren't we?'

'Well, *I'm* not. I thought you said you weren't, either.'

Charlie shrugged. 'I've got PE this afternoon and Mr Goodwin said he was going to let me go in goal.'

Nathan snorted. 'What do you want to go in goal for? It's boring.'

'I like being in goal,' Charlie muttered, picking at a hangnail. 'So, you coming in or not?'

Nathan held out his cigarette packet. Charlie looked at it uncertainly. 'Go on, take one,' Nathan said, shaking the sticks at him.

Charlie teased a cigarette out and put it between his lips. Nathan drew a silver lighter from his blazer pocket and lit it for him. Charlie drew the smoke down and coughed, bending over double.

'Pathetic,' Nathan laughed.

Charlie straightened, wiping his mouth with the back of his hand. 'Where'd you get the lighter?'

Nathan held it out in the palm of his hand. 'Nice, eh? I found it in Mr Collins's pocket.'

'You stole it?'

'Course I stole it. Why pay for stuff when you can nick it?'

'But what if Mr Collins finds out?'

'And how's he going to do that? You going to tell him?'

'Course I ain't.' Charlie took another look at his watch.

Nathan noticed. 'So, you're going in?'

'I suppose so.'

'You worried about your dad finding out?'

'No,' Charlie said sulkily. 'It's like I said. I want to play football. But Dad will wallop me if he finds out I'm bunking off.'

'He won't find out. And even if he did, everyone hops the wag some time or other. My mum couldn't care less.' Nathan took another drag, watching Charlie out of the corner of his eye. 'I should have known you'd let me down.'

'I don't want to let you down.'

'Don't go in then.'

Charlie toed a pebble that was stuck in the mud. He really did want to go to school and play football that afternoon, but that also meant having to sit through History and Geography, and he wouldn't mind missing those one little bit. And he had promised Nathan to spend the day with him.

'Nah,' he said, kicking the pebble away. 'I won't bother. I can play football another day.'

Nathan slapped him on the shoulder. 'You know what, Charlie? You're a real pal.'

Father Pettifer closed his study door on his housekeeper banging with her mop and bucket in the hall.

Sitting down at his desk, he picked up the envelope that had arrived during his breakfast and which he had put off opening as soon as he had seen the company stamp on the top left corner. But he couldn't ignore it forever and he ripped open the flap, knowing what it would say. He was proved right. "Despite several reminders," he read, "we are sorry to write that your account is still in arrears. Kindly pay the outstanding amount stated below within the next 14 days to avoid legal action being taken."

Fourteen days! It wouldn't matter if they'd given him fourteen weeks, or fourteen months, come to that. He didn't have the money. It was his own fault. If only he hadn't made that stupid investment last year. If only he'd listened to advice and not gone near it with a barge pole. But no, he had known best and sunk all his savings into a stocks and shares scheme that had failed almost as soon as it had begun. And now all he had was his stipend, an income that barely covered his outgoings.

Where was he going to get the money from? He couldn't go to his own bank because he was in the red with them. Another bank? He supposed another bank might be prepared to listen to a man of the cloth, but they'd want to see his accounts, they'd make enquiries and find out his state of affairs and refuse him a loan.

He could appeal to the diocese, perhaps. Explain to the bishop his parlous state of affairs, ask for the church to help him out. Yes, he could do that. The bishop was an old friend of his; he'd be sure to understand. It was worth asking, at least.

Pettifer picked up the telephone receiver and asked the operator to put him through to Bishop Lancey.

Matthew opened his eyes and started in surprise when he saw a blurry Superintendent Mullinger standing at the foot of the bed, the glinting silver buttons of his uniform hurting his eyes.

Wondering how long he had been there, Matthew tried to lift his head off the pillow, but Mullinger held up a hand.

'As you were, Stannard. The superintendent at Victoria Park Square informed me of your attack early this morning. He telephoned me at home.' His lips tightened and Matthew guessed Mullinger had not appreciated being disturbed, especially to hear news about him. 'From the description your sister was able to give the police, I understand the man who attacked you was Wilfred Gadd, the burglar we've been looking for. Is that correct?'

'Yes, sir. I saw him just before he hit me.'

'Why the devil should he come after you?'

Matthew thought for a moment, trying to get his brain to work. 'It could be he blames me for the death of his mother. She collapsed while I was questioning her, if you remember, and died later in hospital.'

'Yes, that was most unfortunate, But it is sheer nonsense to blame you for it. The woman had advanced heart disease. She could have died at any time.' He huffed in irritation. 'Did Gadd mean to hurt you or kill you?'

Matthew summoned the last image he had had of Wilf into his tired mind. He remembered the cosh in the raised hand, the tombstone teeth behind the ugly grin, and the glint in the light-blue eyes. 'He meant to kill me,' Matthew decided.

'Then it's possible he may try again. Well, that settles it. You can't return to your home until he's caught. Is there anywhere else you can stay until then?'

'I suppose I could stay with my sister,' Matthew said reluctantly. 'If you think that's really necessary.'

'I do. I will issue an alert for all stations to be on the lookout for this Gadd. He won't remain at liberty.'

'He's stayed hidden this long, sir,' Matthew said, not at all certain Gadd would be apprehended as quickly as Mullinger seemed to think.

'You should have more faith,' Mullinger said. 'I shall also give the Press a statement. Once the public knows to keep an eye out for him, Gadd won't be able to walk down the street without someone realising who he is and turning him in.'

'If you say so, sir,' Matthew muttered, wishing his superintendent would leave so he could go back to sleep.

But Mullinger continued. 'And, of course, I will update CID about your condition. Your doctor has told me you've got a concussion but that you will make a full recovery. So, that's good news.'

It doesn't sound to Matthew as if he was pleased. He could imagine what his colleagues would say when Mullinger told them what had happened. Lund would say he was a silly sod not to have seen Gadd coming and that he might have actually knocked some sense into his head, Barnes and Denham would express some little concern, and Pinder would say he deserved everything he got. 'The doctor said I should be discharged in a few days, sir.'

'Did he? Good. And then, plenty of rest. You'll be on a week's leave, Stannard, when you are discharged.'

'That's not necessary, sir,' Matthew protested.

Mullinger held up his hand again. 'Certainly, it is.'

'But the cases I'm working on…'

'Can be handled by DI Lund and the others. They can manage without you for a few days, I'm sure. They did before you arrived.'

'Yes, sir,' Matthew agreed, not missing the note of sarcasm in Mullinger's words. 'Thank you, sir.'

Mullinger put his cap on his head. 'I must be off. Remember to let the station know your change of address.' He nodded, and turning on his heel, strode out of the ward as a nurse came over, bearing a tray.

'Breakfast, Mr Stannard,' she said brightly. 'Sit up.'

'I'm not hungry,' Matthew protested.

'Now, now, none of that,' she said, putting the tray on the table at the end of the bed and tucking in the bedclothes. 'You've got to eat. Was that your boss just leaving?'

Matthew nodded as he sat up. His head swam, and he groaned as he fell back against the pillows the nurse plumped up for him.

'Headache?' she asked.

'Yes. Can I have some aspirin?'

'When you've eaten,' she said, taking the cover off the tray to reveal a bowl of porridge. 'You've got to keep your strength up. Do you need me to help you eat?'

'No,' Matthew said irritably, snatching up the spoon. 'I'm not five years old.' He sighed at the look she gave him. 'Sorry. I didn't mean to snap.'

'That's all right,' she said, giving him a kindly smile. She checked over her shoulder and leaned a little closer. 'Are you really the detective who caught all those murderers?'

Matthew dipped his spoon in the porridge. 'That's me.'

She gave a little shiver of delight. 'You must be awfully brave to chase after people like that.'

'Look where it's got me,' he said ruefully.

Dickie Waite was yawning as he entered *The Chronicle*'s office. He had slept badly, his grumbling stomach keeping him awake for most of the night. He'd shaken his head at the boiled egg and toast his wife, Emma, had offered him and drunk only a cup of black coffee, hoping it would wake him up. But it hadn't helped; he still felt dead on his feet.

His editor called him into his office as he hung up his hat and coat. 'You look rough,' Bill Edwards said as Dickie shuffled in.

'I feel rough,' Dickie said, rubbing his stomach and falling into a chair. He took out his pipe, pressing the tobacco already in the bowl down with his thumb. 'What's up?'

Edwards threw a box of matches across the desk to him. 'I received a summons last night.'

'And what did our esteemed proprietor want?' Dickie asked, throwing the spent match into the ashtray.

'He's not happy. Apparently, we're not competing with the other local rags. And he reckons we should be, considering the stories we've had to cover lately.'

Dickie puffed on his pipe. 'I thought we were doing all right.'

Edwards made a face 'He showed me the figures. Sales are down. We're doing worse than *The Graydon Heath Gazette* and even *The Trentwood Mercury*.'

'But we're reporting the same news,' Dickie protested.

'That was his point. They're the same stories, but they're the ones with the higher circulation. So, what are we doing wrong, I hear you ask?' He raised his eyebrows at Dickie.

'What are we doing wrong?' Dickie asked.

Edwards took a deep breath. 'Our writing isn't good enough.'

Dickie stared at him. 'Not good enough?'

'Not exciting enough,' Edwards corrected. 'Now, there's nothing wrong with your copy in the main, Dickie. It's factual, it's tight. It tells the reader what they need to know. The problem is,' he glanced nervously at Dickie, 'it's dull.'

Dickie puffed on his pipe and said nothing.

'If you compare the language of the other locals,' Edwards hurried on, dropping copies of the *Gazette* and other newspapers before Dickie, 'you'll see the difference. Look at this headline about the Empire Club Murders from the *Gazette*. "SHOCKING MURDER IN CLUB BEDROOM". And look at ours.' Edwards showed Dickie the front page of *The Chronicle* from the same date. 'Ours says "DEATH AT EMPIRE CLUB". You see the difference?'

'Of course I see the difference,' Dickie snapped, his temper finally breaking. 'But that's their style. *The Chronicle*'s never been sensationalist in the same way as the *Gazette*.'

'And that's why our sales are down,' Edwards said. 'Now, I'm like you, Dickie, an old-fashioned fella. I don't want to change our style, but we can't ignore facts. Compared to our competition, *The Chronicle* is dull and readers don't want to read dull stories.'

'So, what do they want to read?' Dickie asked sulkily.

'Sex. Violence. They want to be titillated over their breakfast. Excited and shocked by what they're reading, yet unable to stop themselves. They want to read about terrible things but feel safe knowing it's happening to someone else. That's what they want.'

Dickie shook his head. 'I never thought I'd hear this from you, Bill.'

Edwards laid his arms on the desk and leaned forward, lowering his voice so the secretary just outside the door wouldn't hear. 'I want to keep my job, Dickie. And if this is what it takes, then from now on, this is exactly what you're going to hear from me.'

'And if I refuse to write trash like that?'

Edwards tilted his head to one side and shrugged.

Dickie understood. He rose, grimacing as his stomach grumbled, and headed for the door. 'I'll have to see what I can do, then, won't I? I'm making no promises.'

'I have faith in you, Dickie,' Edwards called after him.

'I'm glad someone does,' Dickie muttered as he grabbed the telephone ringing on his desk. 'Waite,' he barked into the mouthpiece.

'Hello. Mr Waite?' a female voice said, and Dickie frowned as he struggled to place it. 'It's Pat Harris here. Matthew's sister.'

'Oh, of course. Mrs Harris, hello. How are you?'

'Oh, same as ever. But I thought I better give you a bell to tell you about Mattie.'

'What about him?'

'He's in hospital. Some rotter bashed him over the head in his flat last night.'

'Bloody hell. Was he badly hurt?'

'Well, he looks blooming awful to me, but the doctor said he'll recover. But I'm ringing you because I thought you could pop in and see him? Cheer him up a bit.'

'Yes, of course I will,' Dickie said. 'Which hospital is he in?'

'The Queen Mary in Bethnal Green. He's in Gardiner Ward. He'll be there for a day or two. Well, that's all. I won't keep you. I hope you don't mind me calling you at work?'

'Not at all. Thank you for letting me know.' Dickie said goodbye and replaced the receiver in the cradle. He turned to see Edwards standing in his office doorway.

'What was that?' he asked, nodding at the telephone.

'Personal,' Dickie said, too angry with Edwards to tell him Craynebrook's famous detective was in hospital after being violently attacked in his own home. *That's not a dull story, is it?* he thought rebelliously as he pulled on his hat and coat. 'I'm popping out for a bit. Be back later.'

Matthew was trying to read. A nurse had given him a magazine left behind by a former patient, but the words kept getting jumbled up and his brain didn't seem able to put them in order. He was on the point of giving up when Dickie walked into the ward.

'This is one hell of a way to get out of buying a round,' Dickie grinned.

Matthew threw the magazine to the end of the bed. 'How did you get in? Visiting hour's not until four.'

'Don't tell anyone,' Dickie said, putting a finger to his lips. 'I told them I was a copper.'

'And they believed you?'

'What can I say? They'll let anyone in the Force these days.'

Dickie's expression became serious. 'If only we'd had that drink at yours last night.'

'I know,' Matthew agreed. Dickie had been outside his flat when he arrived home, offering a bottle of stout to celebrate the capture of the Craynebrook Strangler, and Matthew had turned him away. If he'd accepted, the night might have turned out very differently.

'Do you know who it was?'

'Wilfred Gadd. The burglar we've been looking for.'

Dickie's eyes moved to the bandage around Matthew's head. 'You look bloody awful. Why did he come after you?'

'Because he blames me for his mother's death, I think. How did you know I was in here, anyway?' He didn't think there had been time for Mullinger to alert the Press.

'Your sister called me,' Dickie explained. 'She thought I would want to visit and cheer you up.'

'Oh, did she?' Matthew rolled his eyes.

'Well, you look like you need cheering up. What's wrong? Apart from the obvious.'

Matthew made a face. 'Nothing. It's just that I'm under orders not to go back to my flat until Gadd's caught. Mullinger reckons Gadd will try again to kill me.'

Dickie's eyes widened. 'You really think he meant to kill you?'

Matthew shrugged. 'Pat disturbed him. I reckon he would have finished me off if he could.'

'In that case, Mullinger's right, for once. Don't be daft, Matthew. There's no sense in putting yourself in danger.'

'I know,' Matthew agreed reluctantly. 'It's just that I'll have to stay at the pub with Pat and Fred.'

'What's wrong with that?'

'It's a bit small for five adults.' Matthew didn't want to admit he wasn't relishing being cooped up with his family for days.

'You're welcome to stay with us,' Dickie offered.

'I don't know how long it's going to be for,' Matthew said,

doubting Dickie's wife would be as ready to offer him a bed as Dickie supposed. 'It's not just until Gadd's caught. Mullinger's making me take a week's leave once I'm discharged, and Pat doesn't trust me to look after myself.'

'Everyone's looking out for you, Matthew. You should be grateful.'

Matthew looked away, mindful of Dickie's disapproval. He hadn't meant to sound ungrateful, but he knew he'd managed it.

'So,' Dickie went on in a lighter tone, taking out his notebook and pencil, 'seeing as how you can't run away. How about an interview?'

'You are joking?'

'I'm not. Craynebrook's finest hospitalised, and you expect me not to make a story out of it?'

'I don't think Mr Mullinger would want to advertise the fact that policemen are targets for criminals.'

'Mr Mullinger doesn't dictate what goes into the 'paper,' Dickie said, adding in an undertone, 'even if our proprietor does. So, what have we got here?' he said, pointing at Matthew's bandaged head. 'Cracked skull? Black eye?'

'Both of those.'

'Broken ribs?'

'No. Just the head.'

'Will you have any scars?'

'I don't know. What does it matter?'

'It matters to our readers, Matthew. They'll want to know if you'll be pretty again.'

'Sod off,' Matthew said, trying not to laugh. It made his head hurt more.

Dickie chuckled, then gasped and pressed his fingers to his side.

'What is it?' Matthew queried.

'Indigestion. I had it all last night. Didn't get a wink of sleep.'

Matthew gestured at a nurse who had just walked in. 'Shall I ask her to give you something?'

'No, it's all right. I'll get some bicarbonate of soda at the chemist's. There. It's going away now.' He glanced at the nurse, who was looking at him with suspicion. 'I think she might have tumbled I'm not a copper. I'd best be off.' He rose, putting his note-book and pencil back in his pocket. 'Anything you need?'

Matthew shook his head. 'Pat's sorting me out, thanks.'

'Fair enough. I'll try to pop in tomorrow.'

'You don't have to.'

'I know I don't,' Dickie said. 'Get some sleep, Matthew. You look like you could do with it. And let people help you, will you? Don't be your usual stubborn self or I'll send in Matron to tell you what for. And trust me. You don't want to mess with her.'

Chapter Four

Alfred Duggan reached the bottom of the basement steps, adjusted his bowtie and smoothed his fingers over his moustache. When he was ready, Alfred nodded at the doorman, who opened the unassuming, black-painted door and allowed Alfred through.

Warmth, smoke and the hubbub of conversation immediately hit him, and the nervous half-smile he'd fixed on his face as he crossed the threshold developed into a full grin. This was where he had wanted to be for years now, mixing with the kind of people who were at home in basement nightclubs, sipping cocktails and smoking expensive cigarettes.

Realising he was standing like an idiot in the entranceway, looking around the dimly illuminated room with its tiny round tables and glittering glassware, Alfred stepped tentatively forward, putting his left hand in his dinner jacket pocket, assuming the air of a sophisticated gent about town. He knew he had failed when a twenty-something woman turned from her male companions to look him up and down and then slid her gaze away, her expression dismissive.

Alfred swiftly changed direction and searched in earnest for the man he had come to meet. He started to sweat when he couldn't find him; what if he hadn't turned up? He'd look such a fool because he couldn't linger without a companion, not in a place like this, and he wasn't brave enough to attempt an introduction with a complete stranger.

Then the door marked 'Gentlemen' at the rear of the room opened and Richard Bagley walked out. Breathing a sigh of relief, Alfred raised his hand and waved.

'Richard!' he called, hoping to be heard above the noise of the club.

Standing almost a head taller than most of the people around him, Richard Bagley raised his head and caught sight of Alfred. His greeting was not as effusive as Alfred would have liked, just a nod of acknowledgement, but at least he was coming over.

'Duggan,' Richard said, holding out his hand. 'So, you found it all right?'

Alfred shook the hand, hoping his own wasn't clammy. 'Yes, no problem at all,' he lied. It had, in fact, taken him twenty minutes longer than he'd planned to find the basement nightclub, walking past it twice.

'Come and have a drink.' Richard led the way to the bar. 'What will you have?'

'Let me,' Alfred urged, already reaching into his jacket pocket for his wallet. He'd stuffed it with five-pound notes earlier that evening and he let Richard get a good look before tugging one out and laying it on the counter.

'I'll have a White Lady,' Richard said.

'Make that two,' Alfred told the barman, wondering what he was going to end up drinking. He leaned one elbow on the counter and looked around the room. 'Nice place, this.'

'Yes, not bad,' Richard agreed, lighting a cigarette. He selected a green olive from a small bowl and popped it in his mouth. 'So, what news do you have for me?'

The question disappointed Alfred. He had hoped they wouldn't get down to business so soon. 'Making progress,' he said with a confident nod. 'Things are moving.'

Richard frowned. 'That sounds a little vague. What exactly is happening?'

The drinks came up and Alfred gained some thinking time as he handed over the fiver and waited for his change. He wondered if he'd made a faux pas as the coins were handed over. Should he have told the barman to keep the change? Would that have been the sophisticated thing to do? He didn't have time to wonder, however, for Richard said, 'Well?'

'I've made the farmer an excellent offer for his land,' Alfred said.

'And he's going to accept?'

'He'd be a fool not to, wouldn't he? The land is too small for the farm to be profitable in this day and age, and he's not going to get a better offer. He's old and he wants a comfortable retirement.' Alfred took a sip of the White Lady cocktail. It tasted foul to him, but he did his best not to show it.

'That's good to hear,' Richard said. 'When I didn't hear from you, I was starting to worry.'

'No need, old chap,' Alfred assured him. 'I promised you the land and I always deliver on my promises.'

'Excellent,' Richard said, finishing his drink with a smack of his lips.

Alfred tugged at his earlobe, unsure how to phrase his next question, 'I say, Richard, old man. When this deal is done and Bagley Bros. are underway, will you have something else for me? I remember you saying you're keen to expand. I'm your man for that, just so you know. You can rely on me.'

'I'll keep that in mind,' Richard said. 'You've done well for us so far, what with the office and the houses. I'm sure there will be other projects we can put your way. No promises, mind. We'll have to see how things go.'

'Of course, of course,' Alfred nodded understandingly. 'But do keep me in mind, if and when.'

'I will,' Richard promised, turning his attention to the female singer approaching the microphone on the small dais by the dance floor.

Alfred watched him out of the corner of his eye. He'd blown his own trumpet enough, he thought. If he did any more, he'd be pushing his luck with Richard. But what to talk about next?

'How's the packing going?' he decided on. 'All ready for the big move?'

Richard made a face. 'I never want to move again in my life. It's nothing but boxes and wrapping things up in newspapers. I can't find a thing. And then there's all the letters you have to write, giving a forwarding address, the bills you have to settle.' He shook his head. 'It's never-ending.'

'Surely your wife is writing most of the letters?'

'She's doing all the personal ones, of course,' Richard nodded, 'but the business ones are down to me and Roger. And Verity is... well, she still hasn't quite come round to the move.'

Alfred decided he wouldn't ask about Richard's wife. She seemed a sensitive subject. 'Yes, it will take a while to settle in. Everyone complains about living out of boxes. But it will be worth it, I guarantee you. Craynebrook is a lovely place to live, and your street one of the best. I'd like to move there myself.' He felt his last sentence was a mistake when Richard glanced at him and said nothing. Alfred wasn't quite of the class that could move into a house on Craynebrook's St Jude's Avenue. Not quite. At least, not yet.

He quickly took another sip of his White Lady as the three-man band played the opening notes of *Nobody Knows You When You're Down And Out*. He tapped Richard on the arm. 'I love this song.'

Chapter Five

Roger Bagley stood before the mirror and knotted his tie with a smile on his face. Reflected in the mirror was his wife, sitting up in bed with her peach bed jacket draped around her still lovely shoulders and a breakfast tray across her lap. She looked comfortable and content, and for the first time in months, Roger felt they were putting the past behind them. He pushed the knot up against his top collar button and turned towards the bed.

Hettie looked up, her coffee cup halfway to her mouth. Her brow creased, and she smiled as she said, 'Why are you looking at me like that?'

Roger put his head on one side in contemplation. 'I was just wondering what I've done to deserve such a beautiful wife.'

'Oh.' Her cheeks dimpled with pleasure. 'You silly thing.'

Roger leaned across the bed. 'Give us a kiss, old girl.'

Hettie pressed her lips to his. 'Love me?'

'Always.' He pushed off from the bed and took his jacket from the valet stand. 'So, what do you have planned for the day?'

'Oh, packing, packing and more packing.'

'I thought we were all packed up.'

'We are, mostly. There's just the bathroom things and a few bits from the kitchen. But Verity wants me to help her. She's still got lots to do.'

'Why is she so behind? It's not like her.'

'I don't know. Just putting it off, I suppose. You know what it's like when you don't want to do something. You say to yourself 'I'll do it tomorrow', and then tomorrow comes and you don't feel like it.'

Roger frowned, wondering if that was the real reason. 'She's not still complaining about moving, is she?'

'Not to me.' Hettie pulled out the newspapers sitting in the compartment at the side of the tray. 'We seem to have more of these than usual.'

'I added the local rag from Craynebrook,' Roger said. 'Thought it might be interesting to see what's going on there. I expect it's all jumble sales and WI meetings and teas with the vicar, but you never know. It might be worth a look, all the same.'

Hettie unrolled the newspapers and threw Roger's *Financial Times* to the end of the bed, setting her *Daily Express* to one side as she picked up *The Chronicle*. 'Oh dear,' she said.

'What is it?'

Hettie turned the front page around so he could see.

'DETECTIVE BRUTALLY ATTACKED IN HOME,' Roger read. 'What's that all about, then?'

Hettie held the newspaper at arm's length and read aloud. '"Detective Inspector Matthew Stannard of Craynebrook CID was viciously assaulted in his Bethnal Green flat on Monday evening. The renowned detective had returned home from concluding an exhausting murder investigation in which he captured the Craynebrook Strangler. The Strangler had been assaulting women in the local and surrounding areas for almost three weeks. Inspector Stannard's dogged pursuit of the villain and his subsequent arrest put an end to the fear felt by many women in Craynebrook who had been afraid to walk alone lest they be attacked. Inspector Stannard was beaten about the head and knocked unconscious. It was only the arrival of Mr Stannard's sister that prevented the villain from carrying out his dastardly plan to kill the celebrated detective. The attacker took to his heels and fled the scene. Inspector Stannard was taken to Queen Mary's Hospital in Bethnal Green, where he is expected to make a full recovery. The assailant is understood to be a Mr Wilfred Gadd, a convicted criminal whom the Craynebrook Police have been looking for in connection with a series of local burglaries. A London-wide search is now underway for this most dangerous of felons and police advise members of the public that Gadd is a highly dangerous individual and should not be approached. It is believed the motive for the unprovoked and violent attack on Inspector Stannard is a misplaced sense of revenge. Gadd's mother, Mrs Edna Gadd, was helping the police with their enquiries when she collapsed. She was taken to hospital, where a previously undiagnosed heart problem was determined to be the cause of her collapse. Her condition was so severe that recovery was ruled out by the doctor, and she died in the hospital a few days later. Police believe Gadd blames Inspector Stannard for his mother's death, though the inquest exonerated the police of endangering Mrs Gadd's life, and indeed, complimented the detective for his swift action in ensuring Mrs Gadd received the medical attention she required. Mrs Gadd will be buried at the City of London cemetery on Friday, 9th May at 11 o'clock. Anyone with information regarding Wilfred Gadd's current whereabouts should contact their local police station immediately. All information will be held in the strictest confidence." Oh, Roger, isn't that awful?'

'Pretty bloody,' Roger agreed. 'But I suppose that kind of danger goes with the job.'

'But to be attacked in your own home where you should feel

safe. I mean, imagine if someone was hiding in here,' Hettie looked around the bedroom a little fearfully, 'just waiting to jump out at me.'

'You mustn't worry about such things,' Roger said sternly. 'I wouldn't have taken the damn rag if I'd known it was going to make you think like that. Here, give it to me.' He reached for the newspaper, but Hettie clamped it to her chest.

'Don't,' she said, slapping gently at his hand. 'I want to read it. And I'm not worried about myself. I'm thinking of the poor policeman.' She pointed at the picture of Matthew that accompanied the article. 'Isn't he handsome?'

Roger glanced at the photograph. 'If you say so.'

Hettie glanced up at him and smiled. 'I think you're handsome, too, silly.'

'With these grey hairs and grizzly old face?'

'You're handsome to me,' she insisted.

He grinned. 'I must be off. And listen to me, old girl. Don't let Verity wear you out. We've got a big day tomorrow, and...'

'And what?'

'And I want you looking your loveliest this evening because we're all going out for dinner uptown.'

'Oh, darling, are we?'

'A last-night celebration. We might as well go out in style. So, my dearest dear,' he sat down on the bed beside her, 'I want these lovely auburn locks curled and gleaming. I want this delicious neck on show and ringed with sapphires, and I want these lips plump and red and just waiting to be kissed. So, can do?'

'Can do,' she nodded. 'Just for you.'

'I'll be the envy of every man in the restaurant,' he said. 'No, forget that. Of every man in London.'

'Oh, go to work,' she said, pushing him away, 'before you say any more ridiculous things.'

Roger got up from the bed with a grunt. 'But we do need everything ready before we go out tonight. The removal men will be here at eight in the morning.'

'We'll be ready,' she said.

'I suppose you'll be walking round the house, patting bits of woodwork fondly.'

Hettie tutted. 'Not a bit of it. I'm looking forward to going. It's exciting.'

Roger smiled back at her. 'I'll be back by five.' He blew her a kiss as he left the bedroom. He didn't see his wife take her nail scissors out of the bedside drawer and cut out the picture of Matthew from the newspaper. He didn't see her smile as she looked upon his face nor her putting the clipping carefully in her diary.

Verity Bagley nibbled at a corner of toast as she watched her husband across the breakfast table. He looked tired and a little frazzled, and he hadn't paid her a moment's attention since he'd sat down.

'Oh, bugger,' Richard muttered, and banged down his cup in its saucer. He grabbed his napkin from his lap and wiped the coffee he'd spilt from his tie. He looked up at her. 'Has it stained?'

She shook her head. 'You won't see it when it's dried.'

'Thank God for that. I don't know where all my other ties are. You didn't label the box.'

'You could have packed them yourself.'

'When have I had the time?' he demanded. 'I'm up to my ears at work.'

'Well, you know who you have to thank for that.' Verity poured him more coffee.

'Don't start. Please.'

'I'm not starting.'

'We're moving, and there's an end to it.'

'I know.'

‘Then could we please have an end to this sulking?’

‘I haven’t said a word—’

‘You don’t have to. It’s there, all the time.’

‘Can you blame me? I have plenty to sulk about, Richard,’ Verity went on. ‘As well you know.’

‘Yes, and I am sorry, but you agreed, Verity.’

‘What choice did I have?’

‘You had a choice. If you had said you wanted to stay here, we would be staying.’

‘Without Roger and Hettie?’ she cried.

‘There you have it,’ he cried victoriously. ‘You moan about leaving, but don’t want to stay without them.’

‘I just don’t see why we can’t stay as we are, that’s all.’

‘You know why. We’re not going over all that again.’ Richard gathered up the post he had been sorting through and handed it to her. ‘You’ll have to deal with all these. I don’t have the time.’

Verity set the pile of envelopes down beside her plate. ‘What time will you be home?’

‘By five, I should think. Roger’s taking us out for dinner.’

‘He is? Why didn’t you tell me? I had Jenny buy lamb.’

‘Because I can’t remember everything. And give her the lamb if you’re worried it’ll go to waste. I daresay she’ll be glad of it.’

‘I don’t think I’ll go.’

‘Oh, for heaven’s sake.’ A car horn sounded from the street. ‘That’s Roger,’ Richard said, rising from the table and brushing himself down. ‘You are going tonight and you will do your best to enjoy yourself, Verity. If not for your own sake, then for Hettie’s.’

‘Oh yes. God forbid Hettie should be upset.’

‘I mean it, Verity. Now, I know you have reason to be like this, but we’ve said our apologies, and it’s all in the past. Time to move on.’ He bent to kiss her cheek, but she jerked her head away. He sighed. ‘I’ll be back by five.’

He left, and Verity listened to his receding footsteps and the opening and closing of the front door. She sat at the table for some little while more, drawing spirals on the white linen tablecloth with her knife. With a heavy breath, she picked up the first of the envelopes and ripped open the flap.

Chapter Six

Pinder looked up as Barnes entered the CID office. 'What did I tell you?' He held up his copy of that morning's *Chronicle*. 'Stannard's plastered all over the front page. Again.'

'I've seen it,' Barnes said. 'I thought it was a good article.'

'Is that what you call it?'

'Why? What do you call it?'

'Propaganda.' Pinder pointed to the byline. 'Dickie Waite wrote that, and you know he's hand in glove with Stannard. Stannard probably told him what to write. Listen to this. "Renowned detective." "Celebrated detective." "He caught the Craynebrook Strangler".'

'Well, he did.'

'With our help. But where are we in the 'paper? No bloody where. Stannard saw to that. I don't even get a mention.'

'Why should you be in the 'paper? You hardly did a thing.'

'What the bloody hell do you know?' Pinder sneered and thumbed his chest. 'I did plenty.'

'Course you did, Gary,' Barnes said, his voice dripping with sarcasm. He was about to sit down when Lund came in and he straightened. 'Morning, sir.'

'Morning, Barnes,' Lund jerked his head at Pinder. 'What's the matter with sulky drawers?'

Barnes smirked. 'DC Pinder is unhappy about this morning's *Chronicle*, sir.'

'You seen it, guv?' Pinder asked, handing him his newspaper. 'It's all about Inspector Stannard. There's nothing about you, sir,' he added maliciously.

Lund scanned the text. 'Very interesting,' he said, handing the newspaper back. 'Any progress with Gadd?'

'There's nothing from local stations,' Barnes answered. 'All their patrols are keeping a lookout, but there's no sign of him. They did say they've had a few members of the public call in saying they've seen Gadd and they're following them up, but they're not hopeful.'

Lund made a face. 'And we've had nothing?'

Barnes shook his head. 'I'm ringing round all the local boarding houses and hotels. I might get lucky.'

'You might,' Lund acknowledged. 'And what are you doing, Gary?'

'This and that,' Pinder shrugged.

'You mean nothing?'

'I'm working on stuff, guv,' he insisted.

'I don't know why we bother,' Lund muttered and headed for his office.

'What's up with him?' Denham asked Barnes as he entered CID.

'He's annoyed we haven't found Gadd yet.'

'We will.' Denham threw the files he was carrying onto his desk. 'Whitechapel nick have sent me everything they've got on Gadd. I'm going to plough through those. See if I can find any known associates who might be hiding him.'

'Good idea,' Barnes said. 'I'm on boarding houses.'

Denham looked across to Pinder. 'What are you working on, Gary?'

'Jealousy,' Barnes murmured.

'You what?'

'He's sore he hasn't been mentioned in the newspaper.'

Denham rolled his eyes. 'You can take the calls we're going to get from the public,' he said to Pinder.

'What calls?' Pinder asked.

'The calls from people who reckon they know where Gadd is once they read that article. Someone's got to sort the wheat from the chaff.'

'And why is that me? Why can't Barnes do it?'

'Because I'm telling you to do it,' Denham said. The telephone on Pinder's desk rang. 'There you go, Gary. Pick it up. "Craynebrook CID. How can I help?"'

Pinder's lip curled as he snatched up the receiver. 'Craynebrook CID,' he barked.

'So, Stephen,' Bishop Henry Lancey began, handing over a cup of coffee, 'to what do I owe the pleasure? You were a little vague on the telephone.'

Pettifer sipped at the coffee. It was far too hot and he burnt his tongue. He set the coffee cup down and wiped his mouth with a napkin. 'I'm afraid I need to ask a favour, Henry.'

'Oh, my dear chap, ask away. Anything I can do.'

That sounded promising, Pettifer thought, as he mentally framed his next sentence. 'I've been a little unfortunate, Henry, with my finances this year. I made a silly investment. Lost quite a bit. The Crash, you know.'

'Many people did,' Lancey nodded, biting into a shortbread biscuit. 'I didn't know you speculated in stocks and shares.'

'I don't. At least, I didn't until a few years ago. But I was told the only way to increase one's income was to invest it, that simply putting it in the bank yields very little. So, I decided to dip my toe in the water, so to speak. And came a cropper, as the saying goes. So, you see, I could do with a little help. I was wondering if the diocese—'

Lancey held up a hand. 'Let me stop you there, Stephen. I feel for you, I really do. But what you're asking isn't possible. The diocese has no spare funds, and even if it did, if you were to be helped out, then others would ask the same. Unfortunately, you're not the only clergyman with money problems. If I agreed to do it for you, an old friend, while turning others down, I would be accused of nepotism. You understand?'

'Of course,' Pettifer nodded, staring down into his cup. 'I just thought I'd ask. I wonder, Henry, if perhaps you could personally see your way to…'

Lancey shook his head sympathetically. 'I'm afraid not, Stephen. I, too, am not in a position to lend money.'

'Not even a few hundred?' Pettifer pleaded. 'That would get me out of a hole.'

Lancey held up his hands. 'I'm economising as much as the next man. I'm sorry, Stephen. I really cannot help you.'

Lenny Gibbs stuck one roll-up behind his right ear and put the second he had made in the corner of his mouth. Lighting it, he leaned back in his armchair, stretched his legs out and picked up the newspaper he had bought that morning. Lenny didn't normally bother with newspapers — he had little interest in the world beyond the few streets he considered his territory — but the front page of *The Chronicle* had caught his eye as he stood at the newsagent's counter waiting for his change.

He read the article, studying the grainy photographs that accompanied it, then looked up at the ceiling, picturing the occupant of the room above. He finished his cigarette, then climbed the stairs to the first floor and banged on one of the doors.

'What d'ya want?' came the angry reply.

'I want to talk to you,' Lenny said. 'Let me in.'

A grunt, footsteps crossing the floor, and the door was yanked open. Wilf glared at Lenny. 'What about?'

Lenny held up the newspaper and pointed to Wilf's mugshot. 'That's you, ain't it?'

Wilf snatched the newspaper from his hand and peered at the photograph. His lip curled as he looked back at Lenny. 'What if it is?'

'Rozzers are looking for you, that's what.' Lenny grinned, showing the gaps in his teeth. 'So, what do I call you from now on? Sidney Parker or Wilfred Gadd?'

'You stick to Sidney Parker.' Wilf crossed his arms over his chest. 'So, come on. What do you want?'

Lenny rubbed the back of his hand under his nose. 'Fifty quid.'

Wilf snorted. 'You're 'aving a laugh. If I had that sort of money, do you think I'd be in this dump?'

'You can get it.' Lenny snatched the newspaper back. 'It says here you're a burglar. So, getting the money shouldn't be a problem, should it?'

'I ain't working. And if I start doing jobs, I'll get noticed. I can't get rid of the stuff anymore.'

'So, don't take anything you can't move on,' Lenny shrugged. 'Take money. Seems to me you need money more than anything.'

'And what if I don't give you anything?'

'Then I might find myself calling the rozzers,' Lenny said. 'I don't want to do that, Mr Parker, so don't make me.'

Wilf considered for a moment. 'I'll get the money,' he said, and slammed the door in Lenny's face.

Chapter Seven

'How can a man just disappear?' Lund cried as he slammed his telephone back into its cradle.

Barnes, sitting at Matthew's desk, reading a file, looked up. 'You all right, sir?'

'No, I'm not bloody all right. Three days since everyone's been on the lookout for Gadd, and what have we had? Not a bloody thing. I mean, how is that possible? Someone must have seen him.'

Barnes sighed and tapped the file. 'All of his known associates have been questioned and they all say they don't know where he is. None of them have any reason to cover for him, and from what the coppers in his old haunts have told me, their snouts reckon Gadd's crossed a line by going for the inspector. They'd turn him in if they knew where he was.'

Lund grunted unhappily. 'What about you, Pinder?' he asked the detective as he came into the office.

'Nothing, guv.' Pinder held up a thick wad of envelopes. 'But look at this lot.' He snapped off the rubber band holding them together and read the names on the front. '"Inspector Stannard." "DI Stannard." "DI Matthew Stannard." Most of them are for him.'

Lund held his hand out and Pinder passed the envelopes to him. Lund flicked through them as Pinder had done, his eyebrows rising. He slid one pale blue envelope out and sniffed it. 'Perfumed. And look.' He turned it around to show the lipstick on the flap. 'She's sealed it with a kiss.'

'Open it,' Pinder urged, grinning.

'You can't do that,' Barnes said, shocked. 'They're addressed to the inspector.'

'They're not marked Private and Confidential,' Pinder said. 'Unless they're marked like that, we're supposed to open them. Right, guv?'

'Right.' Lund ran his thumb under the flap of the perfumed envelope and took out the letter. Something fell onto his blotter.

'What's that?' Pinder said, craning his neck to see.

'A photograph.' Lund turned it round to show them. 'Not a bad looker. Let's see what she has to say for herself.' He read, then chuckled.

'What's she written?' Pinder asked, curious.

Lund handed the letter to him. Pinder read, his lips curling in amusement.

'What does it say?' Barnes asked, annoyed at being left out.

'Listen to this,' Pinder said. '"Dear Matthew, I was so sorry to read about your terrible ordeal and hope you're feeling better." Blah, blah, blah. "If ever you are in need of a little company and comfort, do please call round any time after ten o'clock. I'll be waiting." And she's given him her address, look.'

Barnes snatched the letter from Pinder's hand and read it for himself, his eyes widening. 'I didn't know women wrote things like that.'

'Don't you believe it, Barnes,' Lund said. 'I've known women who would put a docker to shame.'

'Open the others,' Pinder said, grabbing a lavender-coloured envelope.

Lund ripped open another. 'This one's just commending him and wishing him better.' He tossed it onto his blotter. 'This one's a bit more interesting. "Wishing you well and if there is anything I can do for you, please don't be shy. Let me know. Anything at all."' He chuckled and passed it to Barnes to read. 'What does that one say?' he asked Pinder.

'The same,' Pinder said, disappointed. 'Hoping he's all right and offering him comfort.'

'I notice none of them are signing themselves Mrs.' Lund shook his head. 'Women.'

Pinder suddenly whistled. 'Look at this one!' he cried, showing Barnes and Lund a photograph of a middle-aged, rather plump and very naked woman reclining suggestively on a chaise longue. ''ere. She looks like your missus, guv.'

The smile dropped off Lund's face. 'That's not funny, Pinder.' He snatched the photograph from Pinder's hand and jerked his head at the door. 'Get back to work.'

'It was only a joke,' Pinder muttered as he slouched out.

'He didn't mean it, sir,' Barnes said quietly when Pinder was back at his desk.

'Don't you stand up for him, Barnes,' Lund warned, picking up the previous day's *Chronicle* from his In tray. He reread Dickie's article and looked up at Barnes. 'Gadd's mum's being buried tomorrow. They were close. Chances are Gadd will turn up at the cemetery.'

'I doubt it, sir,' Barnes said. 'He must know we're looking for him. He wouldn't risk it.'

'Would you miss your mother's funeral if you could help it?'

Barnes considered. 'I don't know. Maybe. If there was a chance I could get caught and end up in prison.'

'Still,' Lund drummed his fingers on the desk, 'I think it might be worth one of us going and keeping a watch. Just in case.' He glanced through the partition window at Pinder and his lips curled. 'I think I'll send Pinder.'

'Got everything?' Pat asked as Matthew finished tying his shoelaces and got gingerly to his feet.

'I think so,' Matthew said, reaching for the suitcase at the end of the bed.

Pat snatched it up. 'I'll take that.'

'I'm not an invalid, Pat.'

'You're as good as. The doc said I had to look after you, and that's what I'm doing.'

'By carrying my suitcase?' he smirked.

'You'll get a clip round the ear if you're not careful,' she retorted, trying not to smile. 'Come on.'

Matthew thanked the nurse who had looked after him and followed Pat out of the ward.

'You're sure you don't want to go straight to the pub?' she asked as they approached the hospital's exit. 'I can pick your things up later. There's no need for you to bother.'

'You're doing enough as it is,' Matthew insisted. 'I'm not making you go out again. And besides, you won't know what to pack.'

'I just don't know if it's a good idea. I mean, what if that fella's there again?'

'Gadd won't be there. But that's even more reason why you shouldn't go on your own.'

'Oh, you're going to fight him off if he's there, are you?' Pat said, raising her eyebrows at him.

'Too right, I am,' Matthew said.

She shook her head. 'The way you are at the moment, you couldn't fight your way out of a paper bag.'

'I'm fine,' Matthew said through gritted teeth, and pushed past her and out into the open air. He started down the steps, too quickly, he realised, as his vision blurred and he had to clutch the handrail to stop himself from falling over.

'Mattie!' Pat cried in alarm and grabbed his arm.

'I'm all right,' he said, keeping his eyes closed as he waited for his head to stop swimming.

'I'll get someone.'

'No,' he said, grabbing her hand and pulling her back to him. 'I just got a bit dizzy. The doctor said I might.'

'Maybe you shouldn't be out of hospital yet. You're not well enough.'

'I'll be all right. I've got you and Mum and Georgie looking after me.' He took a deep breath. 'There. Better now.' He smiled at her. 'Really, Pat, I'm fine.'

'You're sure?' Pat didn't seem convinced.

He nodded. 'Come on. We don't want to miss the bus.'

It had been an uncomfortable journey from the hospital to his flat. Matthew had been pressed up against a rather large man who took up most of the seat and stared with unashamed curiosity at the large bruise on Matthew's face. Matthew had pulled his hat as low as it would go to hide it. He'd also had another bought of dizziness, which made him worry he was going to be sick right there on the bus. He'd forced the feeling down and done his best to hide it from Pat, but he doubted he'd fooled her. When they got off the bus, Pat took hold of his arm in a gesture that could have been sisterly affection, but which Matthew suspected was her way of making sure he stayed on his feet.

It took effort to climb the stairs to his first-floor flat, and Matthew's heart beat faster as he put his key into the lock. It wasn't only the exertion but what he knew was a stupid, irrational fear that

Gadd was still in his flat, waiting to strike. He gritted his teeth, forced himself to turn the key and opened the door.

Something screeched at him, and both he and Pat cried out in alarm.

'Oh my gawd,' Pat said, clutching him tight. 'What's that?'

Matthew laughed with relief. 'It's all right. It's the cat.'

'What cat?'

'I forgot all about him.' Matthew pushed the furry creature back into the flat with his foot.

'Since when have you had a cat?' Pat demanded, moving past him into the bedroom.

'Since Monday.' The kitten was reaching up and scratching at his knee, its claws as sharp as needles through his trouser leg. He bent slowly, mindful of his swimmy head, and picked it up. 'It must be starving.'

Pat put her head around the bedroom doorway. 'It's been eating something. There's half a mouse in here on your floor.'

'I must have left a window open.' Matthew went into the kitchen, and putting the kitten on the worktop, opened his cupboards, hoping to find some food. There was a tin of beans, half a packet of stale digestives, and a jar of marmalade. Nothing else. 'I don't have anything for him. I'll have to pop down the shops.'

'We don't have time for that,' Pat snapped. 'I've got to get back to the pub and help Fred. You know how busy it will be this time of day. Can't you ask that fella downstairs if he's got a tin of sardines or something?'

'Mr Levitt?' Matthew made a face. 'He won't give me anything.'

The kitten meowed insistently and dug its claws into his arm.

'Well, it's got to have something or it'll be making that noise all the way home on the bus,' Pat said. 'That is, if you're going to bring it with you?'

'Do you mind?'

'I suppose not. Go and ask him. I'll start packing and you can come back and make sure I've done it right.'

Matthew gave the kitten a quick tickle behind the ears, then went down to the ground floor and knocked on the door of 47A.

It opened and Mr Levitt scowled at Matthew. 'You're back, then? I heard you got bashed up?'

'I did,' Matthew said, thinking the massive bruise on his face made that remark unnecessary. 'I've been in hospital.'

Mr Levitt offered no sympathy. 'I had people all over the place. Going up and down the stairs for hours, they were. Asking me questions. If I'd seen anybody going into your place. As if I've nothing to do but watch who's going upstairs. And not a bit of concern for me. I mean, I could have been killed, couldn't I? But did anyone worry about that?'

'I'm sorry you were disturbed, Mr Levitt,' Matthew said, gritting his teeth in irritation. 'I need to ask a favour. Do you have a tin of sardines you could let me have?'

Mr Levitt frowned at him. 'You what?'

'Or any tinned fish?' Matthew pressed. 'I wouldn't ask, only it's an emergency.'

'How can a tin of fish be an emergency?'

'I've got a very hungry kitten upstairs and—'

'Who said you could have a cat?' Mr Levitt demanded angrily.

Matthew sighed. His head was throbbing and he really could do without having to beg his cantankerous neighbour for cat food. 'Do you have something you can let me have?'

'It's all very well asking me for this and that, but I ain't made of money, you know?'

Matthew felt in his trouser pockets but they were empty. His wallet was in his jacket pocket, back in the flat. He turned at the sound of footsteps on the stairs. Pat was coming down. 'Have you got any money on you?' he asked.

Pat joined him at the door. 'Is he asking you for money?' She glared at Mr Levitt. 'You want money for a piddling tin of sardines?'

'I was just saying—' Mr Levitt protested.

'I heard you,' Pat cut him off. 'You've got the cheek to moan about the police being here when my brother was nearly killed a few feet above your head. He'd just caught a murderer. Did you know that? That's what my brother does. Puts his life in danger every time he walks out that door, and what does he get for it?' She looked him up and down contemptuously. 'If I was him, I wouldn't blooming bother, not for people like you. And then, when he's asks you for a favour, you want to make him pay for it? You nasty little bleeder. That's what you are, you know.'

''ere,' Mr Levitt cried, shuffling his feet, 'you can't talk to me like that.'

'I'll talk to you anyway I want,' Pat declared. 'Now, what about those sardines?'

'I got a tin,' Mr Levitt nodded.

'Then get it,' she ordered, folding her arms over her chest and huffing.

'All right, I will.' Mr Levitt turned into his kitchen and returned a moment later, thrusting a tin of sardines into Matthew's hand. 'You can have it.'

'Thank you very much,' Pat said, pushing Matthew up the stairs. When they got to his flat, she slammed his front door shut. 'And what do you think you're grinning at?'

'Nothing,' Matthew said, trying not to laugh. He was touched by his sister's defence of him.

Pat grunted and went off into the bedroom, muttering about ungrateful sods. The kitten jumped up onto the counter again as he opened the sardine tin, sticking its head inside and nipping small bites of the oily fish. 'Let me do it,' Matthew said, pushing the little head out of the way so he could tip the fish onto a saucer. The kitten ate hungrily, making little grunting noises.

Matthew went into his bedroom. His suitcase was open on the end of the bed and Pat had already packed a couple of his shirts, a jumper and a spare pair of trousers. He opened a drawer and threw in underwear, socks and handkerchiefs.

'Is that it?' Pat asked.

'You haven't put my cricket stuff in,' Matthew said, moving past her to the wardrobe. 'The season starts a week on Sunday. If I'm still at yours then—'

'Oh no,' Pat shook her head. 'You're not well enough to play cricket.'

'I might be.'

'You leave it here, Mattie. And we'll see nearer the time.'

There was something in her voice that convinced Matthew to relinquish the cream trousers he had grabbed hold of from the wardrobe. Maybe he was being foolish, but he'd been looking forward to playing. Still…

'You got something to put the cat in?' Pat asked, snapping the suitcase locks.

'There's a box in the front room.'

'Let's get it, then, and be off,' she said with an encouraging nod.

Chapter Eight

Roger pressed a five-pound note into the palm of the head removal man and closed his new front door. He heaved a sigh of relief and turned to look around the hall.

He liked it; he had been worried he wouldn't. The move to Craynebrook had been decided in something of a rush, and he and Richard had only looked around the house once before deciding to buy. But it had been a good deal — a bigger house than their Balham one and it had been got at a great price. But most importantly, Hettie seemed happy.

She had had a busy day, directing the removal men where to put the furniture, probably driving them mad with all her changes of mind, and talking to him endlessly about the colours of the curtains she wanted to hang, the wallpaper she wanted to redecorate with and the paintings she wanted on the walls. She had worn him out with all her talk, an excited little girl with a new toy to play with, but it made him happy to see her so happy. Even so, he was relieved when she decided to test the plumbing, as she had put with it with a girlish giggle, and gone off to take a bath.

Time for a drink, he decided, and hoped Hettie had found the box with the booze and glasses. He had taken one step towards the sitting room when the doorbell rang.

He sighed and opened the door. 'Oh, it's you,' he said.

'That's a charming welcome,' Richard said, stepping in.

'I thought it might be a neighbour wanting to get to know us.' He made a face. 'I'm too exhausted for all that.'

Richard nodded. 'I know the feeling. It's been a long day.'

'Drink?'

'I won't say no.'

Richard followed his brother into the sitting room. 'How long will we be living out of boxes, do you think?'

'Hopefully, no more than a week,' Roger said, delving into a box and giving a cry of satisfaction as he pulled out a bottle of whisky and two crystal tumblers wrapped in newspaper. 'But we're going to have to leave the unpacking to the ladies, Rich. We'll have our hands full at the new office.'

'I know,' Richard said, accepting the glass his brother held out. 'I think we should pop down there tomorrow. Give it the once-over.'

Roger took a mouthful of his drink and moaned in appreciation. 'Christ, I needed that.'

'Did you hear me?'

'Yes, you said we should go to the office in the morning. Agreed.'

'And we could go down to the farm on Saturday,' Richard suggested. 'We won't be able to go in, of course, but Duggan said you could see quite a bit from the lane. Just to take a look.'

Roger nodded. 'Why not? It'll be interesting to finally see this farm.'

'What farm are you talking about?'

Roger and Richard turned to see Hettie standing in the doorway. She was wearing a silk dressing gown, the belt tied loosely and barely covering her nakedness beneath. Her skin was flushed, the result of the hot bath water, and auburn curls were sticking to her temple and neck. Richard turned away, his cheeks reddening.

'The farm we're buying, darling,' Roger said with a smile. He gestured at her dressing gown and Hettie looked down. With a smile that made her cheeks dimple, she tightened the belt. 'Rich and I are going to take a look at it on Saturday.'

'Oh, can I come?' she asked eagerly.

'I don't think so. We're only able to see it from the gate, so there won't be anything of interest to you. Besides, you'll be busy, won't you?'

'Will I?'

Roger gestured at the boxes dotted around the room.

Hettie looked at them forlornly. 'I suppose so. But unpacking isn't nearly as much fun as putting the stuff in.'

'Got to be done. Did you want a drink, darling?'

'Not just yet. I came down to ask you what you wanted to do about dinner?'

'Oh, Lord,' Roger frowned, 'I hadn't thought. I don't know what restaurants there are here. I suppose I could go out and look—'

'But I don't want to eat out,' Hettie said. 'I want to cook something here.'

'You want to cook?' Roger looked at her doubtfully.

'Well, needs must, darling, until we get a maid,' Hettie said. 'And besides, I can cook. I used to do it all the time when we were first married.'

'I remember,' Roger said, remembering too what a hash she had made of their meals. 'But you don't want to do that. Rich, I daresay Verity has something for tonight?'

Richard caught his brother's meaning. 'Of course. You know Verity. She's planning lamb chops, I think. I'm sure there's enough for all of us.'

'There, darling,' Roger said, gesturing grandly at Richard. 'We'll go back with Richard.'

Hettie pouted. 'But I wanted to cook. It's our first night in our new house and I wanted to cook for you.'

'Well, if that's what you want, Hettie,' Roger said, relenting with a smile, 'then that's what we'll do.'

Hettie's face brightened immediately. 'I'll see what we have,' she said, and disappeared. Roger heard her heels clacking on the parquet floor and the kitchen door opening and closing. He breathed a quiet sigh of relief.

'It's probably just as well,' Richard said. 'Verity wasn't in the best of moods when I left her. One of her boxes got dropped and the removal men got a flea in their ear.'

'You better get back before she sends out a search party.'

Richard nodded and downed the remains of his drink, handing the empty glass to Roger. 'See you in the morning, then. What shall we say? About ten?'

'Yes, ten. Good luck with Verity,' he grinned as he showed Richard out.

As he closed the front door, the sound of singing reached his ears. Roger smiled. Hettie was happy, and all was right with the world.

Matthew's head felt like a hammer was being knocked against his skull when he stepped into The Fiddler's Retreat. The kitten had been quiet on the journey to his sister's pub and had curled up in its box, but it started mewing when the box was knocked by Ruby the barmaid in her hurry to wrap Matthew in her arms.

'Oh, I've been so worried about you,' Ruby declared. 'When I heard what had happened, my stomach turned over. It really did.' She pulled a little away and stared into his face. 'Oh, you poor thing,' she said, running a red-taloned finger down his bruised cheek. 'Does it hurt?'

'Of course it hurts,' Pat said grumpily. 'And you poking it won't help. Leave him alone, Ruby. Mattie needs to have a lie down.'

Ruby made a face and planted a kiss on his other cheek. 'If you need anything, you will let me know?'

Matthew promised he would and carried the box to the counter. He set it down as Fred came over.

'What's in the box?' he asked.

'He's got a kitten, would you believe?' Pat said. 'I'm going to see him settled, then I'll be down to help. Go on up, Mattie.'

Matthew did as he was told, and picking up the box once more, climbed the stairs behind the bar to the first floor, Pat following. As he neared the top landing, Amanda leaned over the bannister.

'You're here,' she cried delightedly. 'How are you?'

'He's tired, Mum,' Pat called. 'He needs to go to bed.'

'I've got it all ready,' Amanda said, leading the way into Georgie's bedroom. She gestured at the neatly made bed against the far wall, seeking approval.

Matthew put the box down on the bed and looked anxiously at the Put-You-Up in the corner. 'I don't like putting Georgie out of his bed,' he said. 'I can sleep on that thing.'

'No, you can't,' Amanda said briskly. 'You need to be comfortable. The doctor said so.'

Matthew had a feeling he was going to hear "The doctor said so" a lot over the next few days. 'Georgie doesn't mind?'

'He offered,' Pat insisted, setting his suitcase down. 'Now, does that thing need anything more to eat?'

Matthew opened the box flaps and the kitten meowed at him to be picked up. He lifted it out and held it to his chest. It closed its eyes and purred. 'Looks like he's tired. He just wants to sleep.' He laid the kitten on the end of the bed and it curled up, tucking its head under its tail.

'You follow his example, then,' Pat ordered. 'No argument.

You're tired. Don't pretend you're not. I saw you nodding off on the bus. Come on, Mum. Let's leave Mattie alone.'

Amanda reached up to cradle his face. 'I'm so glad you're here, Mattie,' she said, kissing his cheek.

Matthew met Pat's eyes, and she rolled them, half in amusement, half in irritation. 'Thanks, Mum,' he said.

Pat tugged at Amanda's cardigan sleeve and they both left. Matthew took off his jacket, hung it on the bedpost, and put the now empty box on the floor. He stretched out on the bed and laid his head on the pillow. He was already asleep when the kitten uncurled itself and settled on his lap.

Chapter Nine

Alfred pushed open the gate to Blackbird Farm and let it fall shut behind him with a bang. He frowned at the muddy track and wished he'd thought to wear galoshes; his brogues were going to get filthy.

I can buy a new pair, he thought happily as he made his way to the farmhouse. *Once I get this deal sewn up, the Bagleys will want me to get all their land for them. And then I'll be back to my twelve per cent commission. And that will buy a lot of brogues.*

He reached the farmhouse. The front door was open and Alfred poked his head inside. 'Mr Clough?' he called.

'Who's that?' a voice came from the end of the hall.

'Alfred Duggan.' Alfred headed towards the kitchen and found Clough by the sink. 'I said I would call in today.'

Clough shook the water from his hands and grabbed a dirty tea towel to dry them. 'I forgot.'

'Well,' Alfred said, pushing the dirty mugs and plates on the kitchen table out of the way to make room for his briefcase, 'here I am, as promised. So, who do I make the cheque out to?' Clough leant against the sink and studied Alfred for a long moment. So long, Alfred grew uncomfortable. *What is the oaf playing at now?* he wondered. 'Mr Clough?' he pressed.

'I ain't selling,' Clough said.

Alfred tilted his head and frowned. 'I'm sorry?'

'I said I ain't selling.'

'But we had an agreement. You agreed to sell.'

'No, I didn't. I said I'd think about it. Well, I've thought about it, and I'm saying no.'

'That's not how it was, Mr Clough,' Alfred said, hearing his voice rise a little in desperation. 'I made you an offer, and you were impressed — yes, that's what you were — you were impressed by the amount. You said you never thought the farm would be worth so much and that you'd be mad to turn it down.'

'I didn't say that,' Clough insisted.

'You did,' Alfred said sharply, then put a finger to his lips at Clough's raised eyebrows. 'I'm sorry, Mr Clough, but you did.'

'Well, what if I did? That don't mean nothing.'

'It means everything. We had an agreement.'

'Didn't shake hands.'

'A gentleman's agreement,' Alfred said, knowing full well to call the farmer a gentleman was ridiculous. 'That's what we had.'

Clough snorted a laugh. 'So what? Whatever I said, then, I ain't selling now.'

Alfred felt sweat prickling on his forehead. 'Is it the money? Do you want more?'

'You offering more?'

'It's possible,' Alfred said carefully, wondering how the hell the price going up was going to play with Richard Bagley. Would he refuse to pay more? And if he did refuse, and Alfred had committed to the price, would he have to cough up the difference? 'Not a great deal more, mind. The offer I made you was extremely good, as you know.'

'It's up to you,' Clough shrugged again.

'An extra five hundred pounds,' Alfred said quickly, wanting to get the words out before he thought better of it. 'But that's my absolute limit.'

Clough put his head on one side and seemed to consider it. But then he grinned and clapped his hands together. 'I ain't selling,' he cried with delight. 'I don't care how much you offer. I'm staying put.'

Alfred's blood boiled. The oaf had had no intention of considering another offer. Clough had just wanted to make him wriggle. Well, he wasn't having this.

'Now, you look here, Mr Clough,' Alfred said, moving forward and wagging a finger at him. 'An agreement is an agreement. You agreed to sell this farm and you are damn well going to sell it.'

All humour left Clough. He straightened and set his shoulders. 'And you listen to me, you little toerag. You're not getting your hands on my farm and that's that. Now, get off my land before I really lose my temper.'

There was something in Clough's eyes that made Alfred think twice about grabbing the farmer by the collar and giving him a shake. Alfred backed away, banging into the kitchen table and knocking his briefcase onto the floor. He scrabbled to pick it up.

'You're making a mistake,' he said, edging towards the door as Clough came towards him. 'You'll be sorry.'

'The only thing I'm sorry for is listening to you in the first place,' Clough shouted after Alfred as he hurried down the muddy track.

'I am the resurrection and the life,' the vicar intoned, and Matthew bowed his head as the plain pine coffin was lowered into the ground.

Matthew was thinking it had been a mistake to come to Edna Gadd's funeral. Not only had he had to explain to his family why he wanted to attend and knock back their endless protests, but he'd spotted Pinder about a hundred yards away, lounging against a tree, smoking a cigarette. *Keeping a lookout for Wilfred Gadd or keeping an eye on me?* Matthew wondered. He had hoped his attendance at the funeral would go unnoticed, and he kicked himself for not realising that someone from the police would be present, just in case Wilf showed up. Now Pinder would go back to the station and inform the others that Matthew had gone to the funeral, and then he might get a telephone call or even a visit, perhaps from Mullinger, demanding to know why he deliberately put himself at risk in that way.

He felt guilty, that was why, but no one seemed to understand. Matthew knew Edna had been ill and that it had just been a matter of time before her heart gave out, but it had happened right in front of him, when he was pressuring her to answer him. Matthew had even thought she looked unwell when he began questioning her and still he had ploughed on. It didn't matter what anyone said to him; he couldn't help but feel responsible for her death.

Pat had insisted on accompanying Matthew — 'Just in case you have a funny turn' — and despite his protestations that he couldn't put her out like that, he had been grateful for his sister's presence. Wilf might be at the cemetery for his mother's funeral, and Matthew wouldn't be much good if it came to a fight between him and Wilf, but he would still have to attempt to apprehend him. With Pat there, Wilf might think twice about showing his face.

'Mattie?' Pat whispered in his ear. 'You all right?'

'Fine,' he whispered back. It was the third time Pat had asked him. 'Stop worrying about me.'

'As if I can ever do that.' She sighed. 'How much longer?'

'You didn't have to come,' he reminded her.

'I couldn't let you come on your own, could I? You'd probably keel over and fall in the 'ole.'

Matthew laughed, and that set Pat off. They were giggling like naughty schoolchildren, and the vicar gave them a reproachful look. They stared at their feet, trying not to snigger.

'Shush,' Matthew whispered, getting himself under control.

'All right,' she tutted back and sniffed. 'Sad, ain't it? Just us here. I hope when I go, I won't have strangers standing around my grave.'

'Don't talk like that,' Matthew chided.

They fell into silence as the vicar finished the service and closed his bible, nodding to them solemnly before walking away.

'Can we go home now?' Pat asked.

Matthew nodded. 'Yes, we can go home.'

Pat threaded her arm through his and they turned away from the grave. 'Who's that fella over by the tree?'

'DC Pinder. I expect he was sent in case Gadd turned up.'

'Don't you want to go over and say hello?'

Matthew shook his head. 'Not particularly.'

Pinder flicked his spent cigarette onto a mound of freshly turned earth and watched Matthew and Pat walk away from the grave.

What a silly sod Stannard is, he thought. *Fancy going to a funeral for an old lag's mother. You wouldn't catch me doing that.*

He wouldn't have been caught wasting his time at the cemetery either if it had been up to him. As he pushed away from the tree, Pinder cursed Lund for sending him. Gadd wouldn't be stupid enough to turn up here, not even for his mother. And even if Gadd did, if Pinder had spotted him, there was no way he was going to try to arrest him all by himself. He wasn't paid enough to grapple with a nutter like Gadd, especially not one who had already proved he wasn't above bashing a policeman's head in.

Pinder checked his wristwatch. Lund had reckoned the funeral would take an hour, at least, but as it was a council funeral, no one else stepping forward to bear the cost, and Gadd the only known relative, there had been no service, just the internment, and that had taken less than twenty minutes. *Time for a drink at the boozer*, Pinder thought gleefully, and headed for the cemetery exit.

If Pinder had done as Lund instructed and stayed in the cemetery for another fifteen or twenty minutes, he would have seen Wilf standing over his mother's open grave.

Matthew had gone to bed after the funeral, lying down on his bed fully clothed. He meant only to have a nap, but he was out for almost four hours, and he was shocked how much his actions of the morning had worn him out.

He had wandered into the sitting room just in time for afternoon tea and found Amanda already pouring him out a cup. He'd sat and had tea with his mother, not having to make much conversation because Amanda did most of the talking, but was still a little relieved when Pat came in. She was annoyed because Ruby had telephoned she was unwell and now she would have to work in the pub and so wouldn't be able to take Amanda to the pictures as planned.

Matthew volunteered to take Ruby's place, and Pat reluctantly accepted. Amanda wasn't happy about it, either. She declared Matthew would be lowering himself to work behind a bar, but she also wanted to go to the cinema and so agreed, extracting a promise from him that he wouldn't work himself too hard.

Matthew hadn't pulled pints since before he joined the police, when he'd worked Saturdays in the pub at the end of the street to earn a little extra money, but he found it all coming back to him as he stood behind the bar and pulled on the pumps. It was a relaxing job, in its way, nothing to do but ask the customer what they wanted, deliver their drink and take their money before moving on to the next. No responsibility, no one to tell what to do and make sure they were doing it, no one's life in his hands. For perhaps half an hour, Matthew fantasised about chucking in the police and pulling pints full time, but as the pub filled up and the demands for drinks became constant, he found himself wishing for his desk and the intellectual challenge of crime-solving.

Fred sent him to bed as soon as the last of the customers had gone and the pub doors had been locked. Matthew didn't argue and wearily climbed the stairs to the bedroom. He entered as quietly as he could, thinking his brother would be asleep, but Georgie switched on his bedside lamp and sat up, the Put-You-Up squeaking noisily beneath his weight.

'I wasn't asleep,' he assured him.

'Where's the cat?' Matthew asked.

'She's here.' Georgie pulled back the covers to reveal the kitten curled up beside him.

'She? It's a boy.'

'It's a she, Mattie. Definitely.' The kitten stretched, and Georgie picked it up and held it before his face. 'Bella.'

'You've named her?'

'You said I could. Do you like it?'

Matthew nodded. 'Bella, it is.'

The kitten wriggled to be free, and Georgie released her. She got down from Georgie's bed and crossed over to Matthew, jumping up onto his lap. He tickled her behind the ears, then set her on the end of the bed.

'I would have helped Fred behind the bar when I got home,' Georgie said as Matthew got into his pyjamas. 'You didn't have to do it.'

'It's all right. You'd already done a day's work. And besides, I had nothing else to do.'

'But you're not well enough.'

'Pulling pints for a few hours won't kill me, Georgie.' He got into bed, sighing wearily as he put his head on the pillow. Bella settled herself on his chest and promptly fell asleep.

'Mum said you went to that woman's funeral today.'

Matthew murmured an affirmative.

'Why? She was nothing to do with you.'

'I just felt I ought to. I owed it to her.'

'You didn't owe her anything. And you didn't kill her, either.'

'Georgie,' Matthew said patiently, too tired to have a conversation.

'You shouldn't have gone. What if that Gadd had turned up? He could have killed you.'

'Well, he didn't. So, no harm done.'

'You're such a selfish sod,' Georgie muttered.

Matthew looked up. 'I'm what?'

'You never think about us, do you? When we got the telephone call that you were in hospital, you should have seen Mum. She nearly had a fit. She thought you were going to die, and she didn't stop crying for ages. And Pat was sick with worry. Said she'd been waiting all these years for something horrible to happen to you. And I was... Oh, it doesn't matter, does it? You don't care.' He switched the lamp off, and turning his back, slammed his head into the pillow.

Matthew stared into the darkness, taken aback by Georgie's outburst and totally at a loss for what to say in reply.

Wilf had watched the street for almost half an hour, hiding in a clump of trees, to see which of the houses were occupied and which were not. There were lights on in most of them, and even if the owners went out for the night, there would probably be a maid or two inside. It would be a big risk to burgle any of these houses, but he had no choice. If he was going to get the cash Gibbs demanded, he needed to get inside a rich man's house.

He craned his neck as a front door about twenty yards away opened and a man and woman, he in evening dress, she wrapped in a silver mink, stepped out onto the pavement and into a waiting Rolls Royce. A maid watched them drive off, then nipped back inside to reappear a moment later with a woollen shawl around her shoulders. She pulled the front door shut and scurried away to skip down the area stairs of another house a few doors away.

While the cat's away... Wilf straightened, stretching his back, aching after crouching for too long, realising he'd got lucky. He made his way around the back of the houses, counting them until he reached the one he'd been watching. Another spot of luck. A window on the ground floor was open and he pushed up the sash gently, testing to see if it squealed. There was nothing and he climbed inside.

It was the work of a few minutes to search the room. It was a lady's sitting room and he found no cash there. He moved quietly out into the hall. He needed to find a study. That was where money was most likely to be. Two doors later, he found one, and he moved to the large desk by the window. The drawers were locked, but that was no obstacle to a man with Wilf's skills. The large bottom drawer yielded a small cash box. This too succumbed to his lock-picking tools and opened to reveal a wad of notes. He flicked through them. There had to be close on to a hundred pounds in his hands. He smiled to himself. He had been right to try his luck in Mayfair.

Wilf pocketed the notes and returned the cash box to the drawer. Moving out into the hall, he fought the temptation to see what silverware he could lay his hands on. There was no point. He had no way of getting rid of it.

But then he caught sight of the large mirror hanging on the wall and he stopped in his tracks. *Don't do it*, he told himself. But his hand was twitching, and the urge was growing, and he picked up the bronze replica of a Trafalgar Square lion sitting on the console table beneath and, his breath coming fast, hurled it at the glass. A shudder of pleasure ran through him as the glass shattered and fell, tinkling musically onto the table.

Someone screamed somewhere in the house and Wilf pulled himself together, leaving through the window at the back where he had entered and hurrying away.

Chapter Ten

'Thanks. Let me know if you get anything else.' Barnes hung up his telephone and grabbed the note he had just made. He rushed into Lund's office. 'I think we've got something, sir.'

Lund looked up with a sigh, annoyed at being disturbed. 'What is it?'

'I just had a call from Boyle Street station in Mayfair. They had a break-in reported last night and they think it might have been Gadd.'

'Why'd they think that?'

'A large mirror in the hall was smashed. That is Gadd's MO. But no silverware was taken, just a wad of cash. Gadd normally goes for silverware, so it's possible the mirror might just be a coincidence.'

'Hell of a coincidence.' Lund threw down his fountain pen and leaned back in his chair, frowning. 'It could be Gadd's in need of ready money. He knows we'll be on the lookout for anyone fencing silverware, so maybe he's steering clear of it.'

'It's a bit stupid to smash a mirror, then, if it is him,' Barnes said. 'That's put us straight onto him, hasn't it?'

Lund scratched his chin. 'From what Stannard told me, breaking mirrors is a compulsion with Gadd. He can't help it. Trauma caused by the war, or some such rot.'

'If it is Gadd, then it proves he's still in London, though.'

'Is that because Stannard's still here?' Lund wondered. 'Doesn't want to leave until the job's done and Stannard's dead? Pinder!'

A chair was scraped back and Pinder came lazily into the office. 'Yes, guv?'

'You went to the funeral, yes?'

'That's right.'

'And you didn't see anything? Gadd didn't turn up?'

Pinder leaned against the door frame, hands in his trouser pockets. 'Not a dicky bird. Other than Stannard and a woman he had with him.'

'Stannard was at the funeral?' Lund cried in astonishment. 'What the bloody hell did he think he was doing?'

'Do you think we should warn him, sir?' Barnes asked. 'That Gadd's still around?'

Lund snatched up his telephone. 'Yes, I do. And I'll tell him not to be so bloody stupid in future. The idiot. It's almost as if he wants Gadd to get him.'

Roger turned off the ignition and the car's engine fell quiet. He looked through the window at the houses on Blackbird Lane.

'These are a little on the shabby side,' he said to Richard sitting in the passenger seat. 'Your man Duggan didn't mention these. They'll bring down the price of our houses.'

'Well, he did say it wasn't the best area of Craynebrook.'

'I know, but still…,' Roger shrugged, disappointed by what he was seeing.

'Unless,' Richard turned to him with a smile, 'we buy the houses, too?'

Roger laughed out loud. 'Can we get the farm before you go buying up half of Craynebrook?'

'You've got to think big,' Richard said. 'Come on. Let's take a look at the farm.'

They got out of the car, and Roger locked the doors, joining Richard on the pavement. 'Nosy neighbours,' he murmured, nodding towards a face peering out of a front window. He smiled at the woman and she stepped away from the window, letting the net curtain fall back into place. 'How much do you think each of these houses would cost to buy up?'

'Ah,' Richard wagged a finger, 'now you're thinking about it, aren't you?'

'Like you said, we've got to think big.'

They reached the farm gate, and Roger leaned on the gatepost. 'It's a big plot.'

'It has to be to take the five houses,' Richard reminded him. 'There's this... what do you call it? Field? Paddock? To the left. That stretches quite a way, all the way to the end. To the right here, there's another field. I think he's got chickens on it. There's the house, but that'll be coming down, of course. And beyond that, there are a couple of outbuildings. Cowsheds, I think Duggan said.'

'It's incredible to see a farm here,' Roger said, shaking his head. 'In a place like Craynebrook.'

'It's a relic. A hangover from the last century. The farmer probably only scratches a living. I mean, he can't be making a profit, can he? It's a big plot, as you say, but not for a farm. And it's an eyesore. Best thing for the area, us building houses here.'

'And Duggan's got it for a good price?' Roger asked. 'You realise you haven't actually told me how much?'

'You left it to me, Rog,' Richard reminded him. 'I told Duggan what we were prepared to go up to and left the rest to him.'

'So, how much?' Roger pressed.

'I don't know yet,' Richard admitted. 'I'll find out,' he promised at his brother's disapproving look. 'Let's get the office up and running and I'll have a meeting with Duggan. Get it all settled.'

Roger nodded, then his eyes narrowed as he looked into the distance. 'That's the farmer, I suppose.' He pointed at Clough, turning into the muddy track from the right, carrying a basket of eggs. Clough had stopped and was staring at them.

'I expect so. Duggan says he's not the friendliest of chaps.' Richard touched his brother's arm. 'Let's go.'

Roger nodded and straightened. With one last look at the farm, he followed his brother back to the car.

Wilf slapped the notes down on the table. 'Fifty.'

Lenny picked up the notes and took his time counting them. 'Fifty,' he nodded when he'd finished. 'Spot on.'

'So, we're all right?' Wilf asked.

'Yeah, we're all right. For now.'

'What does that mean?'

'It means it'll do for this week,' Lenny grinned, folding the notes and putting them in his trouser pocket.

Wilf's fists clenched at his sides. 'I just got lucky last night. I can't get that much every time I turn a place over.'

'Fair enough. I can be reasonable. Let's say you give me half of whatever you pick up. How's that?'

'And what if I only get a fiver?'

'Then I get half of the fiver. I ain't greedy, Mr Parker. I'll take half of whatever you get. But I have faith in you. I know you'll do your best to pick up more than that. Won't ya?'

Wilf took a deep breath and nodded, letting his fingers uncurl. 'Whatever you say.'

'Good boy,' Lenny said as Wilf left his room. He chuckled as he heard the door upstairs slam.

'He's just coming.' Mrs Gould held out the telephone as Father Pettifer came into the rectory. 'It's your sister, Father. She sounds a bit upset.'

Pettifer took the receiver with a mouthed thank you. 'Alice?' he said into the mouthpiece. 'Is something wrong, my dear?'

He listened patiently, but with a mounting sense of frustration, as his sister told him about the letter she had received from the bank that morning threatening to foreclose on her cottage. It was a letter he had been expecting, but he had expected it to come to him rather than to his sister, and he chided himself for not contacting the bank before they had had a chance to upset her.

'Yes, I know, Alice,' Pettifer said when his sister paused for breath and heard the catch in her voice that presaged crying. 'It's very upsetting… It's the money, yes. I'm afraid I've had a little money trouble this month and haven't been able to make the payment…. But it's all in hand… Yes, yes, I promise I will sort it out... No, of course you won't be thrown out onto the street… And even if you were, Alice, my dear, you would come here, wouldn't you? I'd never allow you to be homeless… I know you like it in the village, but… Yes, now, don't you worry. I'll have it all sorted out by next week… Yes… Yes. Goodbye.' He dropped the receiver onto the hook with a heavy sigh.

'Miss Alice worried, is she, Father?' Mrs Gould asked, poking her head around the kitchen door.

'Only a little. There's been a mix-up at the bank. Nothing I can't sort out.'

She was looking at him doubtfully. 'I can understand her worrying about money. I don't like to mention it, Father, but you haven't paid my wages for two weeks, if you remember.'

'Good Lord,' Pettifer cried, 'has it been that long? You should have reminded me, Mrs Gould.'

'I didn't want to bother you. But the truth is me and my husband are feeling the pinch a bit now, so if you could…?' She put out her hand expectantly.

'Yes, yes, of course,' Pettifer nodded, pretending not to notice. 'I'll get it to you, Mrs Gould. Certainly I will.' He gave her an encouraging smile and headed into his study, closing the door so she couldn't follow.

If only Lancey hadn't been so unhelpful, he thought resentfully as he leaned back in his desk chair and stared at the cracked ceiling. Pettifer didn't believe the bishop was as hard off as he'd made out, nor that it would have got around if he'd leant him some money from the diocese. Those had just been excuses. Oh, if only he had the money!

And then it came to him. He'd been a fool not to think of it before. He could ask Josiah. Josiah was a friend, of sorts. Josiah would help him out, Pettifer felt sure. After all the times he had been a support to him, Josiah couldn't, in all conscience, turn his back on him in his hour of need.

Yes, he would ask Josiah for a loan. He had all that money in the OXO tin, doing nothing. There must be a couple of hundred pounds bound up in all those rubber-banded rolls. That was plenty to get him out of trouble for six months or more. And Josiah wouldn't charge him any interest like a bank would, so he might actually have a chance of paying back every penny.

A little cheered by this simple solution to his problems, Pettifer opened his desk drawer and took out one of the Belgian chocolates given to him by a grateful parishioner that he had been trying to make last. He felt he deserved a little treat. Chocolate was, after all, the only vice he had these days.

Hettie's culinary experiment on their first night in Craynebrook had been a failure. So had breakfast the next morning, and despite

Roger's assurances she had done a jolly good job, she had made it her first task that day to engage a maid. She had telephoned the local domestic agency, who said they would send a candidate for her consideration. Daisy had arrived within the hour, and Hettie, taking to her at once, engaged her on the spot, installing her in the servant's room at the top of the house that very evening.

Daisy set the tray down on the table and stepped back, her hands clasped before her starched white apron. 'Will there be anything else, madam?'

Hettie glanced up. 'No, that's lovely, Daisy.' She closed her magazine and reached for the pot to pour herself a cup of coffee. 'How are you finding it here? Settling in all right?'

'Oh yes, madam, thank you,' Daisy nodded. 'It's quite like old times. Only better, if you don't mind me saying.'

Hettie smiled up at her. 'Really? Were your former employers so awful?'

'I don't like to speak ill of the dead, madam,' Daisy protested insincerely, 'but Mr Ballantyne could be rather too free with his hands, if you know what I mean.'

'I'm afraid I do,' Hettie sighed.

'Mind you,' Daisy went on, 'I reckon I got off lightly considering what he did to other girls.'

Hettie sipped at her coffee. 'I read a little bit about the scandal in the newspapers. So, you were still here, working for the Ballantynes, during all that?'

'Oh, yes, madam. I only left a few weeks ago when Mrs Ballantyne moved out. I never thought I'd be back here.'

'Oh, you don't mind, do you?' Hettie asked. 'I'm afraid it never occurred to me this house might hold terrible memories for you.'

'It doesn't, madam,' Daisy assured her. 'None of what was in the 'papers happened here. And, if I'm honest, I thought it was all rather exciting. People wanted to know all about the Ballantynes.

They were always asking me to talk. I even made a scrapbook of all the newspaper articles. I like looking back on things like that.'

'Oh, so do I,' Hettie said. 'A scrapbook, you say? How interesting.'

'Would you like to see it, madam?' Daisy offered, pleased by Hettie's interest. 'I have it upstairs in my bedroom.'

'I'd love to. Do fetch it, Daisy.'

Daisy disappeared and returned a few minutes later with a large, very well-stuffed scrapbook. She passed it to Hettie. 'My mum said I shouldn't be interested in what Mr Ballantyne and his friends got up to, that it ain't good for a young girl to know, but I say to her it's like reading about history.'

Hettie was flicking through the pages as Daisy spoke. She stopped at one page and Daisy craned her neck to see what had caught her mistress's eye.

'Oh, that's a picture of the inspector what caught the woman who killed Mr Ballantyne and the others.'

'Matthew Stannard,' Hettie breathed, stroking the photograph. Had he received her letter? she wondered.

'Yeah, that's him. Nice-looking, ain't he? He caught the Crayne-brook Strangler, too, only a few weeks ago. And there was another murderer before he came here, but I can't remember the name of that one.'

'The Marsh Murderer,' Hettie said dreamily. 'May I keep this to read, Daisy? I promise I'll take very good care of it.'

'Of course, madam,' Daisy said, taking Hettie's engrossment in the scrapbook as a cue for her exit.

Hettie kicked off her shoes, lifted her legs onto the sofa and set the scrapbook on her lap, smiling as she turned the pages, looking for articles about Matthew.

'Are you sure this is a good idea?' Charlie asked as he watched Nathan launch himself over the farm gate. 'What if we get caught?'

'Stop whining, will you?' Nathan snapped, kicking the gatepost to knock mud from his shoes. 'I told you, I almost got a barrel before but I couldn't move it on me own.'

'But the farmer—'

'He'll be in bed by now. Come on.'

Charlie reluctantly climbed over the farm gate and followed Nathan, keeping a wary eye on the farmhouse as they passed by. 'Where are we going?' he whispered.

'To a shed over there,' Nathan said, pointing. 'That's where he keeps it.'

'How do you even know about it?'

'The farmer sells it. It's his own brew. Me dad used to buy it from him.'

'And it's strong?'

'So strong it'll blow your brains out,' Nathan promised as they reached the shed.

'It's locked,' Charlie said, pointing to the padlock on the door.

Nathan whipped out a leather roll from his back pocket. 'Not for long, it won't be.' He unfurled the roll to reveal a range of lock-picking tools.

Charlie's mouth fell open. 'Where'd you get that?'

Nathan tapped his nose and fitted one of the tools into the padlock.

Charlie watched in fascination as his friend fiddled with the lock and gave a quiet laugh of surprise when it sprung open. 'Can you show me how to do that?'

'Maybe,' Nathan said, flinging the door open. 'And there they are!' Like a showman, he made an elaborate gesture towards the barrels stacked three high inside the shed.

'That's all beer?' Charlie asked, his eyes widening at the sight.

'What did I tell you?' Nathan stuffed his lock-picking set back in his pocket. 'Come on. Help me get one down.' He stepped into the shed and reached up to grab the nearest barrel.

'How are we going to get it out of here?' Charlie wondered as he took the weight of it against his chest.

'We'll roll it.' Nathan grabbed the base, and between them, they set it on the ground. Nathan pushed it onto its side and Charlie backed out of the shed so it could be rolled out.

He glanced over his shoulder and froze. 'Nat,' he whispered.

'Don't just stand there. Help me roll it out.'

'Nat,' Charlie said again, not moving.

'What?' Nathan poked his head around the shed door. 'Oh, bugger.'

Clough was standing perhaps twenty feet away. 'Come out of there,' he barked.

Nathan nearly fell over the barrel to get out of the shed. He pushed at Charlie, but Charlie was frozen to the spot. 'Move,' he snarled.

'He's got a gun, Nat,' Charlie said, a tremor in his voice.

Clough cocked the shotgun he held and raised it to his shoulder. 'Think you can take my beer, do you? I'll teach you a lesson to trespass on my land.'

Charlie found his legs and bolted, surprising Clough, who jerked the gun at the fleeing boy only to bring it back round to Nathan.

'You the brave one, are ya?' Clough sneered.

'Put the gun down, you stupid old git,' Nathan said, edging the same way as Charlie. 'You'll do yourself a mischief.'

Clough took a step forward and stumbled, almost keeling over into the mud. Nathan took his chance and ran past him, back towards the farm gate. As the gate came into view, a shot rang out and Nathan yelped in alarm. He reached the farm gate and hooked a leg over it. Another shot rent the air and Nathan cried out in pain.

He tumbled over the gate and fell to the ground. Looking back through the bars, he saw Clough walking towards him, reloading his shotgun.

'Jesus,' Nathan gasped and scrambled to his feet. He ran as fast as he could down Blackbird Lane, clutching his bleeding arm.

Chapter Eleven

Nathan hissed in pain as Charlie unbuckled the belt he had used to secure the dishcloth to his arm. 'Watch it,' he said, sucking hard on his cigarette.

'I can't believe he actually shot you,' Charlie said as he peeled the dishcloth away.

'I told you the bloke's a nutter.' Nathan twisted his arm around to see the damage. The top half of his left arm was smeared with blood and there were nine dark-red spots where the gunshot had penetrated his flesh. 'Bloody hell,' he breathed. 'He nearly killed me.'

'We shouldn't have gone there, Nat. What if—?' Charlie broke off at the sound of footsteps outside in the corridor. Both boys held their breath, only breathing again when the footsteps passed on.

'What if what?' Nathan asked.

'What if he goes to the police?' Charlie unrolled some toilet paper and wet it. He dabbed it over Nathan's arm, wiping away the dried blood.

'What, and admit he shot me?' Nathan sneered. 'He won't go to the rozzers.'

'But if he does?'

'What can he tell 'em? He don't know who we are. So, stop panicking.'

'It's all right for you,' Charlie muttered. 'You don't have a dad who'll kill you if he finds out.'

Nathan's face hardened. 'You shut up about my dad.' The two boys glared at each other until Charlie looked away. 'Look in my pocket,' Nathan instructed. 'There are tweezers in there.'

Charlie fished out the tweezers. 'What are these for?'

'You've got to get the shot out.'

'I can't do that.'

'Well, I can't go to a quack, can I?' Nathan angled his arm towards Charlie. 'Get on with it.'

Charlie took hold of Nathan's elbow gingerly and pushed the point of the tweezers into one of the dark-red holes. Nathan's face screwed up in pain and he kicked at the nearest lavatory cubicle as the shot was tugged out. Charlie dropped the shot in the basin. 'Eight more to go,' he warned. Nathan nodded and pressed his lips together in readiness. Charlie removed the rest of the shot and gave the tweezers back with a sigh of relief.

'Now, bandage me up,' Nathan instructed.

Charlie took out the bandage he had bought in the chemist's that morning. He wrapped it around Nathan's arm. 'I'm staying in school today.'

'All right,' Nathan tutted, 'you don't have to say it like that. So am I.'

'And for the rest of the week,' Charlie said, emboldened. 'I think we should lie low.'

Nathan snorted a laugh. 'Listen to you. Lie low. Anyone would think we're gangsters.'

'We were trespassing, Nat, and trying to steal. You might be used to it, but I'm not.'

'You're such a mummy's boy.'

'No, I'm not.'

'Prove it, then. Come back with me to the farm.'

Charlie stared at him. 'You're mad. We can't go back there.'

'Yes, we can. Well, *I* can,' Nathan shrugged dismissively. 'If you're too chicken—'

'I ain't chicken,' Charlie burst out. 'But if we go back there, he'll kill us.'

'He won't even know we're there.'

'You said that last time. It's not worth it. Not for a barrel of beer.'

'I ain't talking about going back there for beer.'

'What are you talking about, then?'

'I'm talking about getting that nutter back, that's what.' Nathan rolled his sleeve down over the bandage and buttoned the cuff.

'How are you going to do that?' Charlie asked warily, not sure he wanted to know the answer.

Nathan pulled on his school blazer. 'I don't know yet. But whatever it is, it'll be good. You in?' He looked Charlie up and down contemptuously. 'Or are you a mummy's boy, after all?'

Charlie's fists curled. 'I'm in.'

Alfred tugged on his collar, convinced he could feel fleas crawling all over him. The Lamb and Flag public house was just about the lowest establishment he had ever had a drink in and he had rather hoped he would never have to visit it again. But needs must and so here he was, trying not to be noticed. Not an easy thing to do when he was the only man in a suit and tie, and he wished he'd had the foresight to wear something more appropriate.

He took a hesitant sip of his whisky. Ordering a short had been a mistake, too. All the patrons he could see were holding pint jugs. God, he loathed the working class, and his mind turned to the club where he had met Richard Bagley. A little sordid though that place had been — he had found out later it was frequented by high-class prostitutes and card sharps — it occupied a certain milieu he so wanted to move in. Richard Bagley was Alfred's way in, and he was prepared to do anything to keep that avenue open, even if it meant paying another visit to the Lamb and Flag.

Alfred had been keeping an eye on the pub's door and had decided he would wait only twenty minutes more before calling it a bust and leaving. He half hoped the man he was waiting for wouldn't show. After all, it wasn't as if they had an appointment. Alfred had come to the pub only because he knew this was the man's regular watering hole.

But he had to endure only a few more minutes' wait, for when the pub door next opened, Alfred recognised at once the bright red hair of David Cotton. He raised his hand, hoping to attract his attention.

Cotton caught the strange movement of a man waving at him and frowning, lurched over to Alfred's table. 'Hello, Alfie,' he grinned. 'What you doing here?'

'I have a little job for you, David,' Alfred said, speaking in a low voice so as not to be overheard. 'Sit down, won't you?'

'I need a drink,' Cotton said, glancing at the bar.

Alfred got his meaning. 'A pint?' he offered, and at Cotton's nod, went to the bar and ordered one. He brought it back to the table and set it before Cotton.

'This job,' Cotton said, taking a mouthful. 'Like the other one, is it?'

'The same, yes,' Alfred said. 'You're going to need to show the man you mean business.'

'I did last time,' Cotton protested. 'He got the message, didn't he?'

'No brick-throwing this time. You'll be face to face with him,' Alfred explained, raising his eyebrows meaningfully.

The side of Cotton's mouth twisted up. 'You mean you want me to get rough with him?'

Alfred nodded. 'If you have to. He's old, but he's a tough little sod. Just make sure he can still use his hands when you're finished with him. I need him to be able to sign his name.'

'No problem. Where?'

'Craynebrook. He lives at Blackbird Farm.' Alfred drew out a map and pointed. 'You see?'

Cotton examined the map and nodded.

'His name's Clough,' Alfred went on, putting the map away. 'He lives alone, so you don't have to worry about anyone else being there. Now, when you've got him, you tell him he has to sell or else.'

'Or else what?'

'Or else you'll beat seven shades out of him, David,' Alfred snapped, incredulous he had to explain. He knew Cotton wasn't that bright, but for God's sake! 'That should be enough to convince him. And if it isn't…' He nodded at Cotton's hands.

Cotton curled his left hand into a fist and pumped it a few times with a smile. 'Gotcha. Money?'

Alfred delved into his pocket and withdrew his wallet. Hiding it beneath the table, he took out four five-pound notes and slipped them into Cotton's lap. 'As soon as you can. Just let me know when you've done it.' He rose.

'You haven't finished your drink,' Cotton said, pointing to Alfred's half-full glass.

Alfred buttoned up his jacket. 'I don't want any more,' he said, trying to ignore the curious stares of the men around him. 'I must be getting back. My wife's expecting me.' He hurried to the door without another word.

'Be seeing you, Alfie,' Cotton called after him.

Turkel wandered into CID and tossed a bundle of post onto Pinder's desk. 'Wakey wakey, Gary,' he grinned as Pinder opened one bleary eye.

'Sod off,' Pinder muttered.

'The inspector's not in, then?' He nodded at Pinder's feet up on the desk, knowing not even Lund would put up with that.

'In court today.' Pinder spied the post. 'There's a lot there again.'

'Probably more love letters from the inspector's admirers,' Turkel grinned. It had been all round the station that Matthew had been receiving letters from women keen to bestow their affections upon him. By all accounts, Mavis Halliwell, Mullinger's secretary, had been quite put out.

Pinder grunted as he pulled off the rubber band holding the envelopes together.

'Getting anywhere with Gadd?' Turkel asked conversationally.

'What?' Pinder murmured, distracted by a lavender-coloured envelope. 'Oh, no. Nothing but rubbish from people who claim to have seen him. They've all turned out no good.'

'Ah well, he's got to turn up sooner or later. How's Inspector Stannard getting on? Better, is he?'

'How the hell would I know?'

'All right, you touchy sod. Be like that,' Turkel said, walking out huffily.

Pinder glanced around the office to make sure no one was looking. Satisfied, he ripped open the lavender-coloured envelope and took out the letter and read.

Dear Matthew,

I've been reading about you in a scrapbook my maid has put together. I had no idea you were such a clever detective as well as a handsome one. How lucky the women of Craynebrook are to have a man like you looking after them. I hope they appreciate you and that you have someone who treats you the way you deserve. If you haven't, and I hope you don't think me forward, I'd like to be that someone. I would treat you the very best you've ever been treated if only you'd let me.

Will you let me? Oh, please say yes. I so long for you. I mustn't say more or you'll wonder what kind of woman I am to write such things. And I don't want you thinking badly of me.

Goodbye for now, darling Matthew.

Yours forever, Henrietta.

What a trollop! Pinder thought, grinning. He wondered how old she was, what she looked like. Whether he would give her a go? Whether—

'What you got there?'

Pinder jumped and looked up. Barnes was standing by his desk, looking down at the letter. 'Nothing,' he said, tucking it hastily back into the envelope. 'I thought you wouldn't be back for ages.'

'We got through quicker than expected. Anything from the Yard in that lot for me?' Barnes pointed at the untouched mail on Pinder's desk.

Pinder sorted through the pile. He found a large brown envelope addressed to Barnes and handed it over. Barnes took it to his desk. Pinder tapped the lavender-coloured envelope against his chin, thinking it was time to have a little fun.

Pettifer found Clough shovelling manure into a wheelbarrow. 'Good morning, Josiah,' he said.

Clough turned to him. 'You here again?'

'I hope you don't mind.'

'Don't seem to matter if I do. What is it this time?'

Pettifer cleared his throat. 'I'm actually here to ask a favour, which I hope you'll be kind enough to grant.'

'Get on with it.'

'Well, you see…' Pettifer sighed and shook his head at the manure. 'Do you think you could stop that for a moment, Josiah? I would rather like to know you're listening.'

'Cowshed needs mucking out.'

'I'm sure it can wait a few minutes.'

'Or you can,' Clough tipped another load of manure into the wheelbarrow.

'Very well,' Pettifer said. 'I shall wait.'

And wait he did, growing surer with each passing second that asking Clough for a favour hadn't been such a good idea after all. He had hoped to find the farmer in a good mood, but he should have realised that had been unlikely. Josiah Clough was never in a good mood.

'There,' Clough said, leaning the shovel against the barn wall. 'Didn't kill you to wait, did it?'

'No, it didn't,' Pettifer acknowledged.

Clough walked past him out into the daylight and headed for the farmhouse, forcing Pettifer to follow.

'Are you prepared to listen now, Josiah?' he asked, picking his way through the mud.

'I'm listening, ain't I?' Clough said, banging open the farm-house front door and stomping through to the kitchen.

'Barely,' Pettifer snapped, following. He watched as Clough cut himself a slice of bread from the loaf on the table, stopping himself from commenting on how unhygienic it was to not wash one's hands after shovelling excrement. 'The favour I would like to ask is rather…' he paused.

'Rather what?' Clough asked, chewing on the bread.

'Delicate,' Pettifer said. 'You see, I've found myself in a rather unfortunate situation. I am, as they say, embarrassed.'

'About what?' Clough asked, unfamiliar with the term.

'My finances are in a rather desperate state, Josiah,' Pettifer ploughed on. 'The fact is, I have several bills that require settlement with all haste and I don't have the means at the present time.'

'You mean you don't have any money?'

'Not at the present time,' Pettifer reiterated, keeping his eyes on the flagstone floor rather than meeting Clough's. He imagined they would be twinkling with delight at his predicament. 'It's just a temporary situation, of course. Cash flow. But I was wondering if you would be so good as to extend to me a loan? Just to see me over this rough patch.'

'You want me to give you money?'

'Not give, no. A loan, Josiah. I will pay you back every penny as soon as my situation improves.'

Clough pulled out a chair and sat. 'I ain't got no money.'

'Yes, you do. I've seen it.'

'You've what?' Clough's face darkened.

'I saw you had plenty of money the other night. Possibly hundreds. Now, if you could just let me have—'

'You been spying on me?'

'Of course not. What an absurd thing to accuse me of. I saw the tin the other night when I called.' He pointed to the OXO tin on the shelf. 'You have at least three rolls of banknotes in there. I saw them.'

Clough jumped up from his chair. 'All right, so you saw them. Now, you can forget about them.'

'There's no need to be so defensive.'

'You'd be defensive if you had to put up with what I've had. People coming in here, demanding this and that, gadding about all over the place. Spying on me.' He glared at Pettifer. 'I'm sick of it. I'm sick of you.'

'Josiah, will you loan me the money or not?'

'Not.'

'Not even out of friendship?' Pettifer asked desperately.

Clough grabbed the OXO tin and held it protectively to his chest. 'It's my money and it's staying where it is.'

Pettifer felt rage surge within his chest. 'You really are the most unreasonable man I've ever had the misfortune to know. I can't think why I ever troubled with you.'

'Nor can I,' Clough yelled, chasing Pettifer out of his house. 'And don't bother coming back. I'm finished with all of you.'

Mrs Doris Askey squinted up at the grey sky and opened her umbrella with a mild curse. Making a dash for it, she hurried across to the end of the lane, yanking open the telephone box door and hurrying inside, shaking out her umbrella before pulling the door shut. She lifted the receiver and told the operator she wanted to be put through to the police. She waited impatiently for the line to connect.

'Is that Craynebrook Police?' she demanded before the person at the other end of the line could speak.

Sergeant Turkel replied, 'Yes, madam. How can I help you?'

'I want to make a complaint,'

'I see, madam.' There was the sound of paper shuffling. 'May I take your name?'

'You know me, sergeant,' she tutted. 'It's Mrs Doris Askey.'

'So it is. Who's upset you today, Mrs Askey?'

'Don't you take that tone with me. I'll tell you who's upset me. All these people coming and going along the lane, that's who. There's been people walking up and down outside my house for weeks and all hours of the day and night and I've had enough.'

'Blackbird Lane is a public right of way, Mrs Askey. People are allowed to come and go.'

'I don't like the look of 'em,' she declared.

'Why's that?' Turkel asked, amusement in his voice.

'Kids running up and down here. Businessmen in suits. They

don't have any business down the lane, so why are they parking their cars right outside my house, blocking out all my light? And then there's the other fella tonight.'

'What other fella?'

'I didn't like the look of him,' Mrs Askey said, shaking her head. 'Horrible-looking brute. What's he doing here? That's what I want to know. I wouldn't be surprised if he was looking to murder me in my bed.'

'I'm sure he wouldn't dare.'

'That's what you say.'

'That's all I can say, Mrs Askey, unless they actually committed a crime. Did any of these people commit a crime?'

'Well… I don't know… but—'

'Then, I'm afraid, they're perfectly at liberty to walk down your road. There's nothing we can do unless they are breaking the law.'

'So, you're not going to send anyone round?' Mrs Askey cried indignantly.

'Regrettably, no, Mrs Askey,' Turkel said. 'But I will make a note of your complaint in my book. So, if that's all, Mrs Askey?'

'Well, if you're not going to do anything, I suppose it is. But let me tell you, the moment one of them puts so much as a toe out of line, I'll be on to you again. You hear?'

'I do, Mrs Askey. Goodbye.'

The line went dead, and Mrs Askey stared at the mouthpiece for a long moment before hanging up the receiver. With a loud tut, she opened the door and her umbrella and made another dash back to her house.

Chapter Twelve

There was a knock on the door and the secretary came in. 'There's a man here to see you, Mr Duggan,' she said, looking nervously over her shoulder into the main office.

Alfred frowned at her. 'A man, Miss Watson?'

'Well,' she said, pushing the door to and stepping closer, 'I wouldn't call him a gentleman, if you know what I mean.'

'He wants to buy?'

She shook her head. 'He wants to see you. Wouldn't tell me what about.'

Duggan rose from his desk and opened the door an inch. He looked out and saw a crop of bright red hair. 'Show him in, Miss Watson. It's quite all right,' he added when she opened her mouth to protest. 'I know him.'

'Well, if you're sure.' She went out and returned a moment later, showing David Cotton into the office. 'Will you be wanting tea, Mr Duggan?'

'No, thank you, Miss Watson. That will be all.' Alfred waited until the door had closed before demanding, 'What the hell are you doing here?'

'You said to let you know how I got on,' Cotton said.

'I meant for you to telephone me,' Alfred said. 'Not turn up here.'

'What's wrong with me coming here?'

'You stick out like a sore thumb, David,' Alfred explained. He gave a heavy sigh. 'But as you are here… how did you get on?'

Cotton fell down into the visitor's chair. 'I went there last night. Found the old duffer in a cowshed. I told him what you told me to say, that he had to pay up or else.'

'Yes? And?'

'Well, he got a bit mouthy. Shouting at me to bugger off his land and all that sort of stuff. So, I hit him, thinking that would shut him up. It didn't. He went on. So I hit him again. You said that was all right. You wanted that.'

Alfred nodded. 'So, you roughed him up and he agreed to sell?'

Cotton made a face. 'I couldn't say. I mean, I asked him one last time if he was going to sell, like you said, but he wasn't making much sense. I couldn't really work out what he was saying. He had blood in his mouth, you see.'

'Yes, I see. But he got the message?'

'Oh yeah. He got the message all right.'

'And nobody saw you?'

'Nah,' Cotton waved the idea away. 'It all went sweet as a nut. He was a tough fella, though. I'll give him that.'

'You wouldn't if you had to deal with him as I've had to,' Alfred muttered. 'Good. You've done well.'

'Anyone else you want duffed up?' Cotton asked hopefully.

'No, thank you, David,' Alfred replied dryly. 'That's all I needed you for.'

Cotton sniffed and got up from the chair. 'I'll be off then. If you do need me again, you know where to find me.'

Alfred watched Cotton leave his office, sincerely hoping he wouldn't have need of his particular talents ever again.

Chapter Thirteen

Alfred had let Clough stew for a day. Now it was time to meet the old duffer and get his agreement. As Alfred parked his car on Blackbird Lane and got out, he patted his briefcase affectionately. The contract for the sale of Blackbird Farm was inside, just waiting for Clough's signature.

He pushed open the farm gate and walked along the muddy track, thinking yet again he hadn't remembered to wear galoshes to protect his shoes and the bottom of his trouser legs. Alfred glanced towards the chicken coops to his right; no sign of Clough. He carried on towards the farmhouse, wondering if Cotton had done his job so well the farmer was confined to his bed. He hoped not. That would make this even more difficult.

But then he saw the cows were out in the field and knew Clough must be up and about. He came to the farmhouse and saw the front door was open. He stepped inside.

'Mr Clough?' he called.

'What you doing here?'

Alfred whirled around. Clough was behind him, and his face appeared to be one whole bruise. Cotton had certainly done a number on him. He cleared his throat, his heart banging in his chest. 'I've come to see if you're prepared to be reasonable, Mr Clough.'

Clough pointed to his face. 'I know this is down to you. Sending your bullyboy round to beat me up.'

'You gave me no choice,' Alfred said, growing a little braver. 'If you'd stuck to our agreement… But never mind.' He tapped his briefcase. 'I have the contract in here. If you're ready to sign, we can—'

'I ain't signing,' Clough said.

Alfred put a hand to his ear. 'I'm sorry?'

'I said I ain't signing. You can do what you like to me. Send your bullies round. Send your men in suits to look me over.' He shook his head. 'But you ain't never going to get your hands on my farm.'

Alfred's mouth went dry. He stared at the mud at his feet, his breath coming fast, his frustration mounting. 'Don't be silly, Mr Clough. This farm is an albatross around your neck. Just think of what a comfortable retirement you can have with all the money you'll get for it.'

'This farm has been in my family for generations,' Clough snarled. 'And no one's going to throw me off it.'

'Be sensible. We don't want things to get even more unpleasant, Mr Clough,' Alfred said, his voice harsh.

'What you going to do? Send your bullyboy back to finish me off? Try it and I'll have the law on you. And if that don't work, I know how to protect what's mine. I've got my shotgun and I know how to use it.' He took a step towards Alfred. 'Now, get off my land before I really lose my temper and fetch my gun.'

Alfred took off, almost running towards the farm gate. He clambered back into his car, his hands shaking as he gripped the steering wheel. He'd lost, he realised, as he rested his head on his hands. He'd lost the farm, he'd lost the money he would have earned in commission, and he'd probably lost the favour of Richard Bagley to boot.

Roger heaved a box onto the desk and opened the flaps with a heavy sigh. This was the tenth box he had unpacked that morning and the novelty of setting up the new office was wearing off. He glanced around the room, seeing at least six more boxes waiting to be unpacked. He sighed again.

'Let's take a break,' Richard said, shoving his own box aside and putting his hands on his hips in resignation. 'Leave this until later.'

Roger shook his head. 'I'd rather get it all done today. The longer we leave it, the longer it will be before we can open.'

'I don't see the need to rush,' Richard said, propping himself on the table and taking out his cigarette case. 'The Balham office is still open for the time being.'

'I know, but this is important, Rich. This has to work.'

'It will work. What are you worried about?'

'What am I worried about?' Roger asked incredulously. 'How about everything?'

'But it's all gone smoothly,' Richard said, not understanding. 'The house moves, this office...' he shrugged. 'I don't get what's wrong.'

Roger sighed and pushed the box aside. 'It's the money. I was looking through the accounts last night and I didn't realise before just how much we've spent on this. I know we got the houses at a good price and this office, too, but all the money we've spent on the business.' He shook his head. 'And then there's Hettie.'

Richard took a drag of his cigarette. 'But that's all over now. You don't need to worry. I promise.'

'It's not you I'm worried about,' Roger said with a shake of his head.

‘Verity will keep an eye on Hettie. And as for the money. That will all sort itself out.’ He moved to his brother and put a hand on his shoulder. ‘You need to relax, Rog. Let me take some of the burden. You try to do everything, that’s your trouble.’

Roger patted his brother’s hand. ‘I know. I can’t help it.’ His gaze travelled past his brother to the shop front and his eyes narrowed. ‘Who’s that?’

Richard turned. ‘It’s Duggan,’ he said in surprise, and opened the door. ‘What are you doing here?’

Alfred stepped in sheepishly. ‘I thought I’d pop down, make sure you’re settling in all right.’ He glanced over at Roger.

‘Rog,’ Richard said, ‘this is Alfred Duggan.’

Roger extended his hand. ‘Pleased to finally meet you, Mr Duggan.’

‘And you, Mr Bagley,’ Alfred said, shaking Roger’s hand. ‘So, are you happy with the office?’

‘It’s fine,’ Roger nodded. ‘Good of you to check.’

‘Oh, not at all,’ Alfred said with a smile that didn’t reach his eyes.

Roger frowned. ‘Is something wrong?’

Alfred swallowed and turned to Richard. ‘There’s been a hitch with the farm. You see, Clough is refusing to sell.’

‘What?’ Richard roared, taking a step towards Alfred.

Alfred shuffled backwards in alarm. ‘I know. I can only apologise.’

‘But you said he’d agreed. You said it would only be a matter of days before the land would be ours.’

Alfred held his hands up. ‘I know what I said, and I honestly thought it would be. Clough gave me every reason to believe he was prepared to sell, but I’ve taken the contract to him today and he’s refused.’ He swallowed. ‘He threatened me, actually. There’s nothing more I can do.’

‘So, let me get this straight,’ Roger said to Alfred. ‘You told my brother you would make the sale of Blackbird Farm. You assured him you could get it. And now you're saying it's impossible? You've had nothing in writing? Nothing legal we can throw at him for breaking a contract?'

'It was all done verbally,' Alfred said, a tremor in his voice. 'But that's quite normal for me. I work like that often.'

'It's not how we work,' Roger said.

'For Christ's sake, Duggan,' Richard said. 'Do you realise how much we've spent because I trusted you when you said you could deliver the farm?'

'I'm sorry,' Alfred burst out. 'I've tried my best. I even sent someone round to beat him up to get him to sell. Nothing's worked.'

'You did what?' Roger yelled. 'You sent someone to—' He broke off, shaking his head at Richard. 'Bloody hell, Richard, what have you got us into?'

'I didn't know he was going to do that,' Richard protested. 'We'll get this sorted out, Rog. I promise.'

'You make too many promises.' With a sudden burst of rage, Roger shoved the box he had been unpacking spinning across the desk to tumble onto the floor, spilling its remaining contents.

'You better go,' Richard said to Alfred, keeping his eyes on Roger. Alfred hurried out. 'Rog?'

Roger took a deep breath to calm himself. 'We'll talk to this farmer,' he said. 'See if we can persuade him to sell.'

The doctor pressed the cold end of his stethoscope to Matthew's chest.

'Breathe in,' he ordered, and Matthew obeyed, taking a deep breath. 'And out. Breathe in. And out.' The stethoscope moved to the other side of his chest. 'Breathe in. And out. Very good.' He pulled the earpieces out of his ears and folded his stethoscope into its box. 'You can get dressed now, Mr Stannard.'

Matthew pulled his shirt on. 'Is everything all right?'

'There's nothing wrong with your heart or your lungs,' the doctor said, scribbling on Matthew's notes.

'So, I can go back to work?'

'Patience, Mr Stannard,' the doctor smiled. 'Have you experienced any vomiting? Nausea?'

'I sometimes feel a little queasy.'

'But you have an appetite?'

Matthew shrugged. 'Not much. But I eat when I'm supposed to.'

'And you manage to keep it down?'

'Yes.'

'What about headaches?'

Matthew hesitated. 'A few.'

The doctor's eyes narrowed. 'How many is a few?'

'A couple a day,' Matthew admitted. 'Sometimes, all day.'

'Are they all over or localised?'

'They usually start here.' Matthew pointed to the spot on his skull where Wilf had hit him.

The doctor nodded. 'That's not unusual. Your brain took a severe shock. It's feeling bruised and your skull is healing. There will be some pain. Are you taking painkillers when you get these headaches?'

'A couple of aspirin if I need to.' Matthew didn't tell him he'd got through two bottles of aspirin in the last week.

'The headaches should lessen over the next week or so. You must let me know if they don't or if they worsen. And what about tiredness? Have you been more tired than usual?'

'I suppose so. But I reckon that's because I've got nothing to do.'

The doctor smiled. 'Eager to get back to work, are you?'

'Just a bit,' Matthew said dryly, knotting his tie.

'Well, tiredness is also to be expected. On the whole, though, your wounds are healing and I would say you are making a good recovery.'

'So, I can go back to work on Monday?'

'Yes, you may. Providing,' the doctor held up a finger, 'you are on light duties. I will be writing to Superintendent Mullinger and insisting your return is conditional upon that. I don't want you chasing after murderers for a while.'

Matthew smiled. 'That's fine by me.'

Roger pulled up the handbrake and switched off the engine. 'Let me do the talking.'

'What are you going to say to him?' Richard asked.

'I'll increase our offer. See what he has to say to that.' Roger opened the door and nodded to Richard. 'She's watching again.'

Richard turned to the window of No. 7, where Mrs Askey had her nose pressed to the glass. 'Ignore her,' he said, and followed Roger into the farm.

They found Clough by a section of fence near the far end of the farm. One of the fence posts had tipped over, threatening to pull the rest of the fence down with it, and Clough was repairing the post hole. He didn't seem to notice Roger and Richard approaching.

'Mr Clough?' Roger said.

Clough whirled around. His face was shiny with sweat. 'What do you want?'

Roger was taken aback by the purple bruises on the farmer's face, understanding they were evidence of Alfred's attempt to get him to honour their verbal agreement. 'I'm sorry to have startled you.' He held out his hand. 'I'm Roger Bagley.'

Clough stared at the hand. 'So?'

Roger drew back his hand. 'You've been talking with a Mr Duggan.'

‘That bastard. He did this.’ Clough pointed to his face. ‘Sent a bloke round to do it. Didn’t want to get his own hands dirty.’

‘We’re not involved with Duggan anymore,’ Roger said, sending Richard a warning glance to keep quiet. ‘We want to deal directly with you.’

‘I ain’t selling.’

‘You haven’t heard our best offer, Mr Clough.’

‘I don’t need to. I ain’t selling.’

‘We are very keen to buy your land.’

‘You’re very desperate.’

Roger’s jaw tightened at the jibe. ‘We’ve invested a great deal in expectation of buying your farm.’

Clough chuckled. ‘Landed yourself in the muck, have you?’

‘Only because you’ve gone back on your word,’ Richard snapped.

Roger put a hand on his brother’s arm to silence him. ‘I’m sure you wouldn’t want to see my brother and I go under because of a misunderstanding, Mr Clough. So, I’m going to do all I can to persuade you to sell. I’m going to up our offer by another five hundred pounds. Now, how does that sound?’

‘That’s generous of you,’ Clough mocked. ‘You, with all your money. Think you can buy anyone, don’t ya?’

‘I’m not trying to buy you, Mr Clough. I’m offering you a great deal of money for land that could be put to better use than your farm. I can’t believe this is a profitable enterprise for you—’

‘What the hell do you know?’ Clough burst out angrily, taking a firmer grip on the spade he’d been using. ‘Coming here, telling me my business. I ain’t taking nothing from you. Now, get off my land. You’re trespassing.’

‘Mr Clough,’ Roger said, taking a step towards the farmer. ‘We must have this land. Now, we’ve made a more than generous offer. You won’t get a better one. You’d be wise to take it.’

'Wise, would I?' Clough snarled and brought up the spade, the flat of its blade aimed at Roger's head.

Roger reacted quickly, grabbing the shaft and wrenching it from Clough's hand. The old farmer almost lost his footing, but righted himself, just as Richard moved to stand between him and his brother.

'You get out,' Clough roared, gesticulating wildly.

Roger threw the spade to the ground. 'You're making a mistake, Mr Clough.' He tugged at Richard's sleeve. 'Come on, Rich. Let's go.'

Chapter Fourteen

Pat gave the trousers a few vigorous whips, unhappy with the creases that had appeared during the journey to the cricket ground, then held them out to Matthew. 'Here you go.'

'Thanks.' Matthew pulled them on.

Pat watched him and shook her head. 'I don't think this is a good idea.'

Matthew buttoned up the flies. 'The doctor said I can go back to work tomorrow. If I'm well enough for work, I'm well enough to play a game of cricket.'

'You're supposed to be on light duties when you go back to work. That means sitting behind a desk, drinking tea and writing reports, or whatever it is you do. It doesn't mean running around a field for hours.'

'It's a pitch, and I'm not missing the first game of the season.'

She took up the trousers he had taken off and folded them neatly. 'You won't listen, will you? You won't be happy until you've worried me into an early grave.'

'Oh, shut up,' Matthew said, pulling on the jumper his mother had knitted him for his birthday a few months earlier.

A man poked his head into the changing room. 'We're starting, Matt.'

'Can you talk some sense into him, Pete?' Pat called. 'Tell him he's not up to playing.'

Pete grinned. 'I can't do that. Matt's the best batter we've got.' He looked Matthew up and down. 'Besides, he looks all right to me.'

'See?' Matthew said, nodding to Pete that he was coming. Pete ducked back out.

'Go on then,' Pat waved him towards the door with a roll of her eyes.

Matthew grinned, squeezed her hand, and hurried out. Pat put his trousers on the slatted wooden bench beneath the hook where his shirt and jacket were hanging and followed after him. She sat down in a deckchair next to Amanda.

'How is he?' Amanda asked, watching Matthew as he walked up to the wicket, bat in hand.

'He says he's well enough to play.' Pat reached down to the wicker basket by the side of the chair and took out a bun. 'You know what he's like, Mum. You can't make him listen when he wants to do something.'

'Especially if it's cricket,' Amanda smiled.

'Especially if it's cricket,' Pat nodded.

Fred and Georgie came out of the pavilion. Fred had two pints of beers in his hands; Georgie held two half-pints. He handed one each to Pat and Amanda.

'Is Matt opening the batting?' Fred asked, shielding his eyes against the sun.

'He's the team's best batter,' Georgie said proudly. 'He always opens.'

'Yeah, but I thought they'd ease him in.' Fred pulled up a deckchair beside Pat and bent his body into it carefully. 'Considering.'

'He says he's all right,' Pat explained with a sigh.

Amanda twisted in her deckchair. 'There's a lot of people here today,' she said, nodding towards the netting that enclosed the cricket ground. People had stopped on the pavement and were watching the players assemble through the netting.

'Maybe word has got out Matt's playing,' Fred laughed.

Pat twisted in her chair as her mother had done, her attention caught by one of the spectators. He stood alone, intent on the players, and seemed vaguely familiar. She couldn't quite place him.

'Got another bun in there, Pat?' Georgie asked.

She delved into the basket and handed Georgie a bun. She looked back at the netting, but the strangely familiar man had gone.

Wilf had been watching Matthew's flat ever since reading the hospital had discharged him, and he'd seen Matthew and Pat come out, Matthew carrying a pair of cream trousers and a jumper over his arm. Wilf had followed them to the cricket ground, staying outside the netting with the other passers-by.

When the match started, Wilf made his way inside, using the back door to enter the now empty pavilion. He went into the changing room, delving into the pockets of the clothes hanging from the hooks and helping himself to any cash he could find. When his own pockets were full, he looked for a place to hide.

There was a slatted door at the far end, and he opened it to discover a small storeroom full of cricket equipment, broken and discarded, probably hoping to be mended one day. Slipping inside, he pulled the door to.

Matthew stretched as far as he could and managed to touch the tip of his bat to the crease a second before the umpire called 'Out'. He was panting, trying to catch his breath, and he ran his sleeve over his brow to wipe away the sweat. His head was throbbing and there were black spots dancing before his eyes.

The umpire stepped forward. 'Are you all right, Mr Stannard?'

'Just give me a minute,' Matthew nodded, taking a few deep breaths. He looked across to the scoreboard and saw he'd got seventy-eight runs so far. Taking a few deep breaths, he moved back into position and got ready for the ball.

The bowler started his run and Matthew saw the ball leave his hand, saw it arc through the air… and then lost sight of it as his vision blurred. He swung his bat, hoping for the best. But he didn't hear leather hitting willow, only the sound of the stumps being knocked off behind him.

'OUT!' the umpire called, and Matthew straightened with a groan. He walked back to the pavilion, a little unsteadily, to the sound of applause.

'Well done, Mattie,' Georgie said.

'Nice one, Matt,' Fred agreed.

Pat struggled out of the deckchair and put her hand to his forehead. 'You're all flushed.'

'I'm a bit dizzy,' Matthew admitted. 'Maybe you were right. This mightn't have been such a good idea, after all.'

'I knew it,' Pat muttered. 'Let's get you sat down.'

Matthew shook his head. 'I'll get changed first and come back out. Stay here and watch the rest of the game.'

'I'll have a beer ready for you,' Fred said.

'Make it a cup of tea and something to eat,' Matthew said, heading into the pavilion.

Wilf heard footsteps and tensed. Someone had come into the changing room. He peered through the slats of the door and his breath caught in his throat.

It was Matthew. Wilf put his hand in his pocket and drew out the cosh.

Matthew sat down on the wooden bench and closed his eyes, willing the dizziness away. Pat had been right; he shouldn't have played. He looked up at the sound of footsteps.

'Pat said I was to come in and see if you're all right,' Georgie said. 'She thinks you're going to keel over or something. Are you?'

Matthew bent down to unbuckle his shin pads. 'I don't think so. I just got a bit dizzy.'

Georgie crouched and unbuckled the other one for him. 'Are you really going back to work tomorrow?'

'Yes, I am.'

'But is it safe to go back?' Georgie wondered. 'With that nutter still on the loose?'

'I can't hide forever,' Matthew said, changing into his grey flannel trousers.

'I know, but wouldn't it be better to wait for him to be caught?'

'I've no idea how long that will be. We may never find him. And apart from that, I want to go back to work. I'm going mad with nothing to do all day.'

'Is it so bad at home?'

There was something in Georgie's voice that made Matthew meet his brother's eye and hold it. 'The pub's not my home,' he reminded him.

'It could be. You could stay.' Georgie smiled shyly and shrugged. 'It's better with you there. Mum doesn't go on at me.'

Not knowing what to say, not wanting to give Georgie any false hope, Matthew pulled his jumper on and grabbed his jacket from the hook. 'Let's go out to the others. I want to see the rest of the match.'

He gestured Georgie towards the door. As he was closing it, he thought he saw the door at the far end of the room open, but when he looked again, he saw it was shut.

'You're seeing things now,' he muttered to himself, and followed after Georgie.

Chapter Fifteen

'Really, you two.' Hettie shook her head as she refilled Roger's wine glass. 'You've both been like bears with sore heads. What on earth is the matter?'

Roger glanced across the dining table at Richard and gave him an almost imperceptible shake of the head. 'It's just the move, darling,' he said, patting Hettie's hand. 'Sorry if I've been a grump.'

'I've enjoyed moving,' Hettie said, shrugging. 'It's exciting being somewhere new. Don't you think so, Verity?'

Verity sipped at her drink. She'd seen the nod between Roger and her husband and was watching them both carefully. 'I wouldn't say exciting. Stressful. And I can't bear not being able to find anything.'

'Are you still unpacking?' Hettie asked in surprise. 'We've done all ours.'

'That's because you've got a maid to help you. And I daresay Roger has helped.'

'Not much, I'm afraid,' Roger said, seeing Richard shift uneasily in his chair and knowing Verity was having a dig. 'Hettie and the maid have been very busy.'

'And isn't the house lovely?' Hettie breathed dreamily. 'So much better than our old place. Or at least, it will be, once we've redecorated. I've been looking through catalogues, darling, and I've found all the fabric I want for curtains for the entire house.'

Roger took hold of her hand and squeezed. 'Let's not rush into deciding details like that, Hettie.'

'I haven't rushed. Why can't I have what I want?' she whined.

'I think we should wait to make sure. It's a lot of money to spend on a whim.'

'It's not a whim. And I wanted to put an order in tomorrow.'

'No, I don't think so,' Roger said a little more firmly. 'Not tomorrow.'

'But darling—'

'Hettie,' Richard cut in, 'best hold off for a while.'

Hettie looked from Richard to Roger, frowning. 'But I want the curtains. Verity, tell them it's not fair.'

Verity caught Richard's warning eye. 'I agree with them,' she said. 'You change your mind so often, Hettie, it would be best to wait. Besides, I haven't seen what you've chosen. Don't you want my opinion?'

Hettie pouted. 'I suppose so,' she said reluctantly. 'Though I think you're all being mean to me.'

'Mean to you,' Verity muttered under her breath.

'So, Verity,' Roger said airily, wanting to change the subject, 'have you much more to unpack?'

'Quite a bit,' Verity nodded. 'In fact, we won't stay after lunch. We need to get on.'

'We can stay for a bit,' Richard protested.

Verity glared at him. 'No, we can't. Hettie and I are out tonight and I can't do everything by myself, Richard.'

'I'm not asking you to—'

'You might as well, seeing as how you haven't lifted a finger to help me so far.'

'I have been busy.'

'At the new office?' Verity's voice became a little shrill. 'That's just one room you have to set straight. I have a whole house to put in order. But that's all right. You just sit around here or go off to one of your clubs and leave it all to me. I can mânage. I always do, don't I?'

The table fell silent, Roger and Richard exchanging glances, Hettie still pouting, Verity fuming.

'I think you ought to go home after lunch,' Roger said after a minute or so. 'Verity's right. You can't expect her to do it all.'

'Fine,' Richard said, throwing his napkin onto his dirty plate. 'I'll do the bloody unpacking.'

'All those need unpacking.' Verity pointed Richard to the stack of four boxes against the wall on his side of the bed. 'They're all yours from the wardrobe.'

Richard nodded and lifted the topmost one onto the bed, pulling the flaps apart.

'What was all that about at lunch?' Verity asked. 'Why doesn't Roger want Hettie spending?'

Richard shrugged. 'Because it might be a huge waste of money. You said it yourself. She changes her mind so often, she'll spend a fortune on the curtains this week and next week decide she wants something different.'

Verity came into the room and sat down on the corner of the bed. She shook her head. 'That wasn't it. We all know she's like that and Roger's never complained before. So why make a fuss this time?'

'Because it's been a big expense,' Richard said, tipping the box upside down and spilling the contents onto the bed. 'These houses, the new office.'

'I thought you got these houses cheap.'

'We did. Cheap for Craynebrook, anyway. But it's still a lot of money. And there's the legal fees, removal costs…' He shrugged. 'And last year cost a lot of money.' He glanced over at her and met her eye.

Verity's eyebrow rose. 'You and Roger haven't overreached yourselves, have you?'

'Money's going to be a bit tight for a little while,' he admitted, gathering up an armful of socks and dropping them into the top drawer of a chest of drawers. 'We can't afford to spend a lot getting this house the way you want it, V. Not just yet.'

'We wouldn't have to spend anything at all if it wasn't for Hettie,' Verity said angrily. 'We wouldn't have had to move.' Richard said nothing, and she took a deep breath to calm herself. 'Is it just us personally, or is it the business as well?'

'It's everything,' he said, tossing the now empty box aside and picking up the next. 'We just need to get through this rough patch, and then we'll be all right.'

'Do you have the finances to buy this farm you and Roger have been talking about?'

'The farm is key,' he said, almost to himself. 'We just have to get the farm and we'll be in clover.'

'You're talking as if this farm sale isn't certain.' He wasn't looking at her and Verity clicked her fingers to get his attention. 'Richard? What's wrong?'

With a sudden burst of anger, Richard grabbed the clothing he'd taken out of the box and threw it all against the opposite wall. 'I should have known everything was going too well. We got the houses for a song and the office, too. The farm was going to be the cherry on the cake.'

'Going to be?'

'The farmer is refusing to sell,' he sighed. 'He was just stringing us along. No, stringing Duggan along, and the bloody fool fell for it. So, it's not all my fault. Duggan promised he could get the land. He assured me the deal was as good as done. If he hadn't said so, I would never have talked Roger into ordering all the building materials. Christ, we've even commissioned an architect to draw up plans for the houses and he's charging us an arm and a leg.'

'So, you don't have the money for all the materials and the architect?' Verity asked. 'That means you could end up bankrupt, doesn't it?'

Richard dragged another box over and bent back the flaps. 'It won't come to that. Roger will think of something.'

'Oh, yes, leave it to Roger,' Verity said sarcastically. 'Like you always do. Let Roger sort out your mess.'

Richard glared at her. 'That's right. Rub it in, why don't you? It's all my fault.' He rummaged around in the box angrily.

'Well, it usually is,' Verity muttered.

But Richard barely registered the jibe. His attention had become suddenly focused on an item his fingers had brushed against in the bottom of the box.

Verity rose and smoothed her skirt over her thighs. 'I'll make a pot of tea,' she said, and left the bedroom.

Richard waited, listening for her to reach the bottom of the stairs. Then he reached into the box and lifted out the object that had made his heart skip a beat. He peeled the cloth away and studied the gun as it lay heavy in his hand.

Chapter Sixteen

Mullinger looked over the top of his half-moon spectacles at Matthew. 'And you're feeling quite well?'

'Yes, sir,' Matthew nodded, glancing down at the doctor's report lying on Mullinger's blotter, wondering what the doctor had written about him to make the superintendent ask. 'Very well, in fact.'

It was only a little lie. He'd recovered well enough from the cricket the day before, and though he still felt a little dizzy if he got up too quickly and he had a headache he couldn't seem to shift, he knew he could cope. What he couldn't cope with was being stuck inside with nothing to do any longer.

Mullinger appeared satisfied. He closed the report and eased back in his chair, taking off his glasses and rubbing the bridge of his nose. 'Well, I daresay Lund will be glad you're back. He's been run rather ragged, and I understand he has to be in court for much of this week. I appreciate the doctor insists on light duties only—'

'I'm up to anything, sir.'

'Glad to hear it. I suppose you want to know about Gadd?'

'Has he been found?'

'Regrettably, no. He is still in London, by all accounts. There have been burglaries in Mayfair that bear his stamp, but he is yet to be apprehended.'

'Someone must be hiding him.'

Mullinger nodded in agreement. 'But he will be caught, sooner or later. It's only a matter of time. However, I must say I was disappointed to learn you attended the mother's funeral.'

Matthew recalled Lund's telephone call to him after the funeral to tell him to stop being a bloody fool. 'In hindsight, it was a stupid thing to do.'

'It was. Very. And I believe your sister was with you. If you had no thought for your own safety, you should have, at least, considered hers.'

Matthew's breath caught in his throat. It hadn't occurred to him he had put Pat in danger. 'Gadd wouldn't attack her,' he protested, but realised even as he said it that Wilf had hospitalised an old woman for merely getting in his way during a burglary. Why should he have any scruples about harming Pat? Georgie's words came back to him: 'You're a selfish sod', and he felt suddenly sick.

'Well,' Mullinger said, picking up his spectacles again, 'I think that's all. I shan't keep you.'

'Thank you, sir.' Matthew rose and buttoned his jacket. He headed for the door.

'It's good to have you back,' Mullinger said in a quiet voice.

Matthew halted, his hand on the doorknob. 'Thank you, sir,' he said, surprised by the remark. 'It's good to be back.'

Dickie pressed his fingers into his side as pain stabbed through him, thinking he really must go to the quacks and get himself looked at. The pain had been going on too long to be mere indigestion or a stitch.

The pain ebbed away a little, and he watched Teddy Welch as he manoeuvred the shopkeeper into position, intent on getting the best photograph possible for the newspaper. The young man had fallen in love with his new toy, a brand new Ikonta camera, and had been playing around with it for the past three days. It had been Teddy's suggestion *The Chronicle* do some features on local shops in Craynebrook to fill the pages, and Dickie suspected it had been only so he could use the camera. But Dickie was not so enamoured with photography, and he mentally urged the young reporter to hurry up.

'Is the article going to be on the front page?' the shopkeeper asked, trying not to move his lips as Teddy stared down the camera lens and held up a hand for him to be still.

'Page three or four, I should think,' Dickie replied, seeing no point in getting his hopes up. The shopkeeper looked disappointed, and Teddy tutted as he pressed the shutter button.

'I need you smiling,' he said irritably. 'Let's try one more, shall we? And this time, a big smile!'

Dickie checked his wristwatch. They had spent almost an hour in the shop. His interview with the shopkeeper had only taken about fifteen minutes; Teddy had taken up the rest. He watched as Teddy finally took a decent photograph and clapped his hands. 'Right. That's it. All done.' He glared at Teddy not to contradict him. 'Thank you,' he smiled at the shopkeeper. 'We'll be off now.' He opened the shop door and stepped out onto the pavement. Teddy joined him, putting the camera back into its box.

'Had your fun?' Dickie asked sarcastically.

Teddy grinned. 'It's not a bad little camera, this.'

'I don't know what was wrong with the old one.'

'It took forever to set up. I can take ten pictures in the time it took the old camera to take just one.'

'Exactly. And while you're taking your ten pictures, I'm left standing around like a lemon.'

'Mr Edwards wants more pictures in the 'paper,' Teddy reminded him.

'I know what Mr Edwards wants,' Dickie snapped, and turned at the sound of raised voices behind them.

'What's all that about?' Teddy shaded his eyes with his hand and looked down the road.

A man came up to them. 'There are cows on the high street,' he said, gesturing the way he had come.

'You what?' Teddy cried.

'Cows walking down the high street,' the man repeated incredulously.

'They must be from Blackbird Farm,' Dickie said.

'What are they doing on the high street?' Teddy asked.

'I don't know, Teddy. Why don't you ask them?' Dickie turned to their informant. 'Has anyone called the police?'

'I don't know,' the man shrugged and hurried away, seemingly not keen to get involved.

Teddy pulled the camera back out of its bag. 'I'm going to get some pictures.'

'You do that,' Dickie called as the young reporter dashed away. 'Then meet me at Blackbird Farm.'

The junior detectives got to their feet as Matthew walked into the CID main office.

'Good morning, sir,' Denham said. 'How are you?'

Matthew nodded. 'I'm better, thank you, Denham.'

'It's good to see you up and about, sir,' Barnes said.

'Thank you, Barnes.'

Pinder muttered something Matthew didn't catch, but Lund came out of their office at that moment and raised his eyebrows at him.

'Decided to come back, have you?'

'I had to see the mess you've got into without me,' Matthew returned with a smile.

Lund's eyes narrowed as Matthew walked past him into their office and hung up his hat. 'You are all right, then?'

'I'm fine. I wouldn't be allowed back if I wasn't, would I?' Matthew added at Lund's dubious expression.

'Suppose not.' Lund poked his head out of the office. 'Barnes. Get the inspector a cup of tea.'

'Just doing it, sir,' Barnes called back.

'So, what's been happening?' Matthew asked, noticing his In tray was full of envelopes.

'Same ol', same ol',' Lund said. 'We haven't had any luck finding Gadd.'

'I heard.'

Barnes came in and put a cup of tea on Matthew's blotter. 'There you go, sir.'

'Thanks.' Matthew took a mouthful and pointed at the envelopes. 'What's all that?'

Barnes grinned. 'Your post, sir.'

Matthew looked from him to Lund, who was smiling too. 'What's so funny?'

'Shall we tell him, Barnes, or let him find out for himself?' Lund said.

'Up to you, sir.'

Intrigued, Matthew reached for the topmost envelope and pulled out the letter, feeling both detectives' eyes upon him. He felt himself colouring as he read the contents.

'Look at him. He's blushing,' Lund laughed and clapped his hands delightedly.

Matthew tossed the letter aside. 'Are they all like that?'

'Most of 'em.' Lund rifled through the envelopes. 'Oh, this one's a corker. "My dear Inspector Stannard, I was so sorry to hear of your terrible ordeal. That you should be so wounded in the despatch of your duty is just awful. If there is anything I can do, and I do mean anything, to make you feel better, please do get in touch.

You will always find me in after 2 p.m. when we won't be disturbed. Yours in admiration, Jessica." I wonder what she means by 'anything'.' He wiggled his eyebrows at Barnes and snatched up another envelope. 'And I remember this one. This lady, and I use the word loosely, wants you to give her a good seeing to. And this one—'

'Yes, all right.' Matthew snatched the letters from Lund's hand and threw them in the bin. 'I get the gist.'

'You can't throw 'em, Stannard,' Lund said, taking the letters out of the bin and dropping them back into Matthew's In tray. 'They have to stay on file.'

'Why do they?' Matthew demanded.

'It's the rules. Aren't you interested in what you're being offered?'

Matthew shook his head.

'Oh well. Waste not, want not.' Lund scooped the envelopes out of Matthew's In tray and carried them over to his desk. 'I remember there's one in here…' he sorted through them. 'Yeah, here it is.' He held up the photograph of a naked woman lying on a chaise longue. 'I'll keep this one.' He winked at Matthew. 'Just don't tell the missus.'

The gate was wide open at Blackbird Farm.

Dickie frowned at it, seeing the churned mud at its base, evidence of the cows having passed that way. He turned as he heard running footsteps behind him.

'I got the pics,' Teddy, red-faced and sweating, panted. 'The gate's open.'

'I noticed,' Dickie said. 'I take it the farmer wasn't on the high street with his cows?'

Teddy shook his head. 'Didn't see anyone that looked like a

farmer. One of the shopkeepers was telephoning the police as I left. So, we going in or what?'

'We're going in,' Dickie said. 'Come on.'

Teddy removed his camera once more from its box as they headed up the track towards the farmhouse. 'Do you know the farmer?'

'I've seen him around a few times,' Dickie said. 'He's a bit of a character. Doesn't leave the farm often, so he should be around here somewhere.'

'I can't see anyone,' Teddy said, craning his neck left and right. He gestured at the farmhouse as they drew near. 'Shall we go inside and shout for him?'

Dickie nodded in agreement, and they went up to the front door. It was ajar and Dickie peered into the hall. 'Hello?' he called. There was no answer. He called again. Still nothing. He turned to Teddy, shaking his head. 'He's not in there.'

'I should have brought my wellies,' Teddy moaned, knocking his shoes against the boot scraper on the doorstep. 'God knows what I've stepped in.'

'Mud and manure. What else do you expect on a farm?'

'I don't know. I've never been on one before.'

'Come on,' Dickie said, 'let's carry on looking for him.'

They moved off, heading for the outbuildings towards the rear of the farm. The doors of one barn were open and Dickie looked inside. This was the cowshed. The hay racks were empty and there was no sign of Clough.

'Let's go down by the large field,' Dickie said and set off, Teddy following, fiddling with his camera. After about a hundreds yard, Dickie suddenly stopped, causing Teddy to barge into him.

'Steady, Mr Waite,' he began, but Dickie cut him off.

'What's that over there?' he said.

Teddy followed Dickie's finger to a heap of something lying

against a fence about a hundred yards off. 'I can't make it out. Sacks of wheat, maybe?'

Dickie hurried over to the fence. 'Oh, God,' he cried, as he got near enough to see what the heap was. 'No.' He thrust out his arm to block Teddy from coming closer.

'Is that—' Teddy swallowed. 'Him?'

'I think so,' Dickie said.

'Look at the blood,' Teddy said, waving his hand at the red-stained mud. He tutted loudly. 'I'm such an idiot,' he muttered, and aimed his camera.

'You can't take pictures,' Dickie cried, appalled.

'I'm not missing this,' Teddy shook his head at him. 'This'll be the front page of every newspaper you can think of once we've printed it. Now, come on, Mr Waite. Move out of the way.'

Dickie stepped away to the side, not liking what Teddy was doing but knowing he couldn't stop him. And Teddy was right. If Edwards wanted sensational, you couldn't get more sensational than a picture of a dead body on the front page.

'We have to get the police,' Dickie said. 'I passed a telephone box on the lane. I'll call them.'

'I'll stay here,' Teddy called as Dickie set off, his camera clicking away.

Dickie ran as fast as he could, which wasn't that fast, and he was struggling for breath when he picked up the receiver and demanded to be connected to the police.

Chapter Seventeen

Matthew climbed out of the police car, wondering if he was the victim of some elaborate wind-up. His first morning back at work and the first call he had was to a crime scene that sounded like a suspicious death? But Denham, sitting beside him in the car, had behaved as if it was serious. And there was Dickie leaning on the farm's gatepost, grey-faced, and an excited Teddy Welch talking ten to the dozen by his side while PC Rudd kept the gawpers back. It couldn't be a joke, Matthew decided. *The Chronicle* reporters wouldn't be in on a station leg-pull.

Dickie straightened as he saw Matthew and Denham approach. 'I'm glad it's you,' he said to Matthew. 'I don't think I could face Lund.'

'This isn't a joke, then?' Matthew asked.

'No, it isn't a bloody joke,' Dickie snapped. 'He's lying there with his blood soaking into the ground.'

'The farmer?'

Dickie nodded. 'I think so. I've only seen him a couple of times, but from what I remember, it looks like him.'

Teddy stepped up to Matthew, elbowing Dickie out of the way.

'Is this your first day back at work, inspector? I reckon Crayne-brook must save its murders up for you.'

Matthew raised an unamused eyebrow at the young reporter. 'Is that what you reckon, Mr Welch?'

'You'll have to excuse Teddy,' Dickie said, with a glare at his fellow reporter. 'He's what you might call eager.'

'He's what I'd call impertinent,' Matthew said.

The grin dropped off Teddy's face. He reddened and stepped away, pretending renewed interest in his camera.

'Did you both find the body?' Matthew asked.

'We were together,' Dickie confirmed. 'We saw the cows on the high street and made our way here.'

'Then I need you both to stick around.' Matthew gestured to Rudd to open the gate. 'Don't go talking to the neighbours,' he warned Dickie. 'And nothing goes in your 'paper that you haven't run by me first. Understand?'

'All right, inspector,' Dickie said, a little indignantly.

Matthew realised he had spoken unnecessarily harshly to his friend, having it confirmed a moment later when he heard Teddy say, 'Full of himself, ain't he?' as he and Denham made their way up the track.

'Mr Waite told the desk sergeant the body's by the fence beyond the outbuildings,' Denham said, peering ahead. 'Yeah. There he is.'

Matthew followed Denham's pointing finger and his stomach lurched. Another murder! Maybe there was something in what Teddy Welch had said, after all.

'I can't see any footprints, sir,' Denham said, studying the ground. 'But the cows must have come this way, so—'

'If there were any, they're gone,' Matthew nodded. 'Stay there while I take a look. Let's not mess the scene up more than it already is.'

He stepped closer until he was only a few feet away from the body. Clough was lying face down in the mud. The blood seemed to have come from the top half of his body, and Matthew peered closer at his head, seeing what looked like the tail-end of a throat wound. A wave of nausea and dizziness struck him and he felt his body sway. He put out his hands to steady himself, his fingers sinking into the mud.

'Sir?' Denham called worriedly.

'I'm all right,' Matthew called back. 'Just lost my balance.' He got to his feet gingerly. There was still concern on Denham's face and it irritated him a little. 'Throat wound, from what I can see.' He looked around and nodded at a spade lying on the ground. 'Is that blood on the blade?'

Denham studied the blade. 'Looks like it. Murder weapon?'

'Looks likely. I want that fingerprinted and bagged for evidence as soon as the photographer has taken his pictures.'

'Both he and the police surgeon are on their way, sir,' Denham said, pre-empting Matthew's next question.

'Cowsheds are over there,' Matthew pointed behind Denham. 'Why were the cows out?' he wondered aloud.

'A deliberate attempt to mess up the crime scene?' Denham suggested.

'Maybe.'

They made their way to the cowsheds, but there was nothing to suggest there was anything amiss. Nevertheless, he told Denham as they emerged back into the sunlight that he wanted the door handles dusted for prints. As they walked back towards the body, Matthew saw two men approaching, and he recognised the photographer and doctor.

'Morning, Dr Wallace,' he said in greeting and held out his hand.

Wallace took it. 'Inspector. Back on your feet, I see.'

'Just about. It's my first day back.'

'And you have a corpse to contend with. What a welcome.' Wallace gestured at the body. 'May I?'

Matthew nodded. 'Please.'

Wallace bent down by the corpse, taking care not to muddy his trousers. 'From the colour of the skin and the quantity of blood that appears to have soaked into the ground, I would say the cause of death was exsanguination. I can't say more without turning the body over.'

'Not until the scene has been recorded,' Matthew said, nodding to the photographer to begin as Wallace stepped to the side. 'If you don't mind, we're going to continue our investigation.'

'Oh, you carry on, inspector,' Wallace said, waving him away.

Matthew and Denham made their way to the farmhouse. The front door was closed to but not shut. Matthew nudged it open with his toe, feeling his heart bang in his chest. *Gadd's not in there*, he told himself.

'Going in, sir?' Denham asked, wondering why Matthew wasn't moving.

'Yes,' Matthew said, and stepped into the hall. There was an unpleasant smell, an accumulation of dust and dirt. Thankfully, not the smell of something rotting. *No more dead bodies in here, please*, he begged.

'What a dump,' Denham muttered, stepping in after Matthew.

'I'll do down here,' Matthew said. 'You check upstairs.'

Denham mounted the stairs. Matthew watched him go up, heard the floorboards creaking beneath his feet, and waited, holding his breath for a cry of alarm that didn't come. He shook his head. *Pull yourself together*, he chided himself, and turned the knob of the nearest door.

The room was dark; the curtains drawn. Matthew felt for the light switch on the inside and flicked it on. The unshaded lightbulb hanging from the ceiling illuminated piles of newspapers stacked haphazardly on the floor and on the few items of furniture. An old-fashioned painting in a heavy, dark wood frame hung skew-whiff on the opposite wall. It didn't look like the room had been used in years. Matthew turned the light off and stepped back into the hall, heading for the door at the end.

Pushing it open, he caught his breath. There was blood on the flagstones. He stared at it, unable to move.

Denham came thumping down the stairs. 'It's a mess upstairs, sir, but—' he broke off as he joined Matthew at the door. 'Oh. Blood. Sir?'

Matthew took a deep breath. 'Watch where you tread,' he said, forcing himself to move into the kitchen. 'Bloody footprints here.'

Denham followed his pointing finger around the table to the back door. 'But none in the hall,' he said, looking back.

'They look like ordinary shoes to me,' Matthew said, peering at the footprints. 'Not boots. No ridges in the sole. The farmer had boots on.'

'So, these could belong to the murderer?'

'Possibly. You were saying? About upstairs.'

'It's a mess. Doesn't look like he's cleaned or tidied up for years. I couldn't tell if anything had been disturbed.'

'It's the same down here.' Matthew took a last look around the kitchen. 'When the photographer's finished with the body, I want him in here. I want everything photographed. The blood, the prints, the table, the shelves. Everything.'

'Yes, sir,' Denham said, and hurried out to instruct the photographer. Matthew followed at a slower pace. As he drew near the crime scene, he saw the body had been turned over onto its back and Wallace was snapping his medical bag shut.

'Time of death,' Wallace said when he saw Matthew, 'is anywhere between ten and fifteen hours. The mortal wound is the one to the throat. It's been sliced through.'

Matthew pointed to the bloodied spade. 'Could that have done it?'

'It's a thin wound, and that blade looks quite sharp. Yes, I should say so.'

'How messy would it have been? What I'm asking is whether all the blood is in the ground or would the killer have been covered in it too?'

Wallace considered. 'No arteries were cut, so there was no arterial spray. If the spade is the murder weapon, which seems likely, it has a long handle and so the killer may have been a couple of feet away when the wound was inflicted. The blood may not have reached them. I will be able to tell you more after the post-mortem, of course. Will you be attending, inspector, or are you sending a deputy?'

'I'll be there,' Matthew confirmed.

'I'll book you in for one o'clock, then.'

Matthew walked with the pathologist to the farm gate. Dickie and Teddy were still there.

'Well?' Dickie asked when Matthew had said goodbye to Wallace and he had climbed back into his car. 'Is it him?'

'Won't know for sure until the body's identified, but it seems likely.' Matthew noted Teddy was keeping back, evidently not keen to receive another rebuke. 'Do you know if Mr Clough has any family?'

'I think it's just him. It was him and his father here, but he died years ago.'

'Mother?'

'Don't know anything about her.' Dickie tapped his notebook with his pencil. 'What else can you give me?'

'Just that it was a brutal attack. It's too early for anything else.'

'You will let me know?'

'There will be a statement. You know the procedure.'

Dickie stepped closer. 'You know, Matthew,' he said, quietly so Teddy couldn't hear, 'it's supposed to be an advantage to a reporter having a friend in the police, but it's like getting blood out of a stone with you. I'm better off with my other contacts.'

'Really? And who are they?'

Dickie grinned. 'Like I'm telling you.' His face suddenly screwed up, and he sucked in his breath, pressing his fingers into his side. 'Bugger me.'

'What's wrong?' Matthew asked.

'Got a bit of gyp. I'm going to see a quack about it.' He took a deep breath. 'It's a bit better now.'

'You don't look better.'

'You're a fine one to talk,' Dickie said, looking into Matthew's face at the yellow bruise that a week earlier had been a deep purple. 'You look tired. Are you sure you should be back at work this soon?'

'Don't you start,' Matthew said, distracted by Barnes running up the lane towards him. 'What is it?' he asked the detective constable.

'Message from Sergeant Turkel, sir.' Barnes glanced at Dickie, and Matthew gestured for him to step to one side, out of earshot. 'There was a call from one of the neighbours on Blackbird Lane about shots being fired at the farm around nine-forty-five last night.'

'Was it followed up?'

'The sarge made a note of it in the report book,' Barnes said, 'and he was planning to get the morning shift to pop in to have a word with the farmer. But he thought it was a low priority, just the farmer shooting at foxes, and Uniform haven't got round to it yet.'

'Who was the neighbour?' Matthew asked.

Barnes consulted his notebook. 'Mrs Doris Askey at No. 7.'

'I'll see her now. As you're here, I want you to go to all the newsagents on the high street and question the owners. Find out what they can tell us.'

'Sir?' Barnes queried, not understanding.

'There was yesterday's newspaper on Clough's kitchen table. It didn't look like it had been read and there wasn't an address written on it, so I don't think he had it delivered,' Matthew explained. 'I want to know where the farmer bought it, what time, if he said anything, how he looked. Understand?'

'Yes, sir. Understood.'

Barnes hurried away and Matthew went over to Rudd. 'You're in charge of seeing the body gets to the mortuary and securing the farm,' Matthew told him. 'No one goes in.'

'Yes, sir,' Rudd said.

'You off, then?' Dickie asked, as Matthew turned away.

Matthew nodded. 'Things to do.'

Chapter Eighteen

Pettifer pulled his eyelids apart as his front door banged shut. The force of it resounded through the wall, making the glass doors of his bookcases rattle.

He blinked a few times, letting his eyes adjust to the darkness. As they focused, he tried to work out where he was. It definitely wasn't his bedroom. He registered the bookcases, the desk in the corner, the clock ticking on the mantelpiece, and realised he was in his study. He pushed himself up onto his elbow and saw that his bed had been the settee and that he was still in the clothes he had been wearing the day before. His head was pounding, and he put a finger to his temples and rubbed, trying to ease the pain. It didn't work. His tongue felt furry, and his lips were dry and crusty, and he worked up saliva to wet them with the tip of his tongue.

Someone was singing in the hallway; the under-stairs cupboard was opened, something taken out and shut again. Who was out there? He tried to get his brain to work. Of course. It was the housekeeper. Mrs Gould was out there, banging mops and buckets and making his head hurt even more than it did already.

Pettier jolted upright, his head spinning. If Mrs Gould was in the house, then it must be past nine o'clock. And him in his study, probably looking the worse for wear and...

The study door opened, and Mrs Gould entered the room. 'Oh, my gawd,' she cried, putting a hand to her chest in fright. 'I didn't know you were in here, Father. The curtains are still pulled and...' She broke off to sniff, then looked at him reproachfully.

'I... er...' Pettifer fumbled for a reply but couldn't find one. He dusted himself down to cover up the silence. 'I think I must have fallen asleep reading,' he said with a little embarrassed laugh. 'What a silly thing to do. Very uncomfortable, the settee.'

'I imagine it would be,' she said, examining the settee and the floor around it with suspicion.

He followed her gaze and noticed the absence of any reading material. Her expression, when he looked back at her, suggested she didn't believe his story and he brushed past her into the hall, staggering a little.

'Careful, Father,' Mrs Gould warned.

'Just got up a little too quickly, I expect,' he said, making his way to the stairs.

'I'll make you a cup of tea,' she called up after him. 'That'll put you right.'

'Excellent idea, Mrs Gould,' he called down as he reached his bedroom. 'Just the thing.'

He closed the door and locked it. Sinking down onto the bed, Father Pettifer put his head in his hands.

Roger had been watching the cows for almost a half hour. People had come out of their shops and homes to watch the animals as they moved carelessly down the high street as if they had every right in the world to be there. He was leaning against the doorframe when Richard came hurrying along the pavement.

'What's going on?' Richard asked, staring at the cows.

Roger shook his head. 'No idea, but the chap next door says they can only have come from the farm.'

'Why are they out?'

'How the hell would I know?' Roger cried irritably. 'Maybe Clough wanted them to have a walk.' He pushed away from the doorframe and went back into the office.

Richard followed and closed the door. He stared at his brother.

'Sorry,' Roger said. 'I didn't mean to snap.' He threw a box file onto a shelf. 'I've been awake most of the night trying to work out how we're going to get out of this hole we've got ourselves in.'

'You mean the hole I've got us in,' Richard corrected miserably.

'I didn't say that.'

'You didn't need to. But I know it's all my fault. If I hadn't let Duggan convince me the farm was a good idea—'

'If it wasn't for Duggan, we wouldn't have the houses,' Roger reminded him. 'He did well on those. But we shouldn't have taken his word on the farm. We should have waited until the sale was made before moving ahead. That was our mistake. Ours, Rich, not just yours. I was all for it, too.'

'I tried to make things good, Rog,' Richard said. 'I swear, I did it for the best.'

'I know you did,' Roger smiled. 'It's just the way our luck's going. But we'll get through it. We stand together. That's how we do things. Right?'

Richard nodded, unconvinced. 'Right.'

Verity stepped into the hall and drew off her gloves, handing them to Daisy. 'Is your mistress in?'

'Yes, madam,' Daisy said. 'She's in bed. I just took her breakfast up. Shall I tell her you're here?'

'No need,' Verity said, already mounting the stairs. She rapped on Hettie's bedroom door and entered without waiting for a response. Standing at the foot of the bed, she stared down at Hettie. 'Well?' she asked, putting her hands on her hips.

Hettie pulled the bedclothes up to her chin. 'I'm not feeling very well, Verity.'

'You're going to have to pull yourself together,' Verity said sternly. 'If you give any sign that something's wrong, then everything will be ruined. Did you say anything to Roger?'

Hettie shook her head. 'No. You told me not to. Did you say anything to Richard?'

'No. Of course not.' Verity stole a slice of Hettie's toast and bit off a corner. 'Richard wouldn't be the slightest help and Roger has enough to worry about at the moment.'

'What is he worrying about?'

'Oh, the business, that's all. It's always a strain setting up somewhere new.'

Hettie cracked the shell of her boiled egg. 'I think I would like to tell someone about it, though, Verity. Unburden myself.'

'Don't be so selfish,' Verity said sharply. 'Stop thinking of yourself for once. I won't let you spoil everything again. Now, promise me, Hettie, that you won't say a word to anyone.'

Hettie dug her teaspoon into the yellow yolk. 'I promise,' she said sulkily.

Chapter Nineteen

Mrs Askey ushered Matthew and Denham into her front room enthusiastically. 'Have you arrested him?' she asked as they took a seat on her rickety settee.

'Have we arrested Mr Clough?' Matthew asked, surprised by the question.

'For making all that noise last night,' she nodded. 'I won't be a minute. I've got tea all ready in the pot.'

'Does she really not know he's dead?' Denham said in a low voice to Matthew.

Matthew raised an eyebrow in similar disbelief as Mrs Askey bustled back into the room with a large tea tray. She set it down on the table and fell into a hardback chair. 'I'm glad to see I'm being taken seriously at last.'

She poured out the tea, adding milk and two teaspoons of sugar to each cup without asking. A Garibaldi biscuit was propped in each saucer before being handed over.

'I understand you called the police station last night to complain about shots being fired at the farm,' Matthew said, setting the saucer on his knee.

'That's right,' she declared. 'He was off again, making all that noise.'

'You called the station at a quarter to ten last night. That was when you heard the shots?'

'Around then.'

'I need you to be exact. What time did you hear the shots?'

Mrs Askey stared down at her lap as she considered. 'Well, I heard them after I saw him at the farm gate when I was putting the bin out. I know that because if I'd heard them before then, I would have given him a piece of my mind.'

'You saw Mr Clough at the farm gate?' Matthew said. 'What time was that?'

'That was just before nine. I know because the news on the wireless started a minute or two later. I listened to that. Then I listened to the music that came on until half past. When that had finished, I got up to turn the wireless off and it was then I heard him shooting.'

'But you didn't call the station until fifteen minutes later. Why the delay?'

'Well,' Mrs Askey shifted uncomfortably in the armchair, 'I don't like to say.'

'To say what, Mrs Askey?' Matthew pressed.

She tutted. 'I was in the lavvie, if you must know. Busting, I was. I couldn't wait. So, I did my business and then I telephoned your lot.'

'I see,' Matthew nodded understandingly. 'And how many shots did you hear?'

'I don't know.' She shrugged, still annoyed at having to admit to urgent bodily functions.

'Try to recall, Mrs Askey. It is important.'

'Well, I think actually last night it was just the one shot I heard. But,' she wagged her finger at Matthew, 'other nights, it's been loads of 'em. One after the other.'

‘But just the one last night?’ Matthew asked. ‘The policeman you spoke to thought Mr Clough might have been shooting at foxes? Does that sound possible to you?’

‘I don’t know, do I?’ she cried indignantly. ‘And I don’t think it matters why he was doing it. He was doing it, and that’s bad enough. And I called because I’m fed up with him. All this coming and going and what-have-you.’

‘What coming and going?’

‘Over the last few weeks,’ she cried, gesturing at the window behind Matthew and Denham. ‘Girls singing and dancing down the lane. Men in suits, parking their cars out there. Right outside my window, blocking out my light. I mean, I find it hard enough to see at the best of times. In low light, I’ve got no chance.’

‘Can you describe these men?’ Matthew asked.

‘There was a bald bloke who was out there a lot. Three or four times at least. He had a moustache. Shifty looking fella, if you ask me. And then there were two other men. They arrived together in the same car twice.’

‘What did they look like?’

‘One was short, stocky, had grey hair. The other one was taller, dark hair, a bit thinner.’

‘You didn’t know them?’

Mrs Askey shook her head. ‘Don’t know any of them.’

‘Do you know what cars they drove? Or,’ Matthew asked hopefully, ‘got their registration numbers?’

‘I don’t know nothing about cars,’ she said. ‘One was black, the first fella’s. The other one was blue.’

‘Did you see any of these men last night?’

‘Not last night, no.’

‘But would you recognise them if you saw them again?’

‘I think so. You want me to identify them?’ she asked eagerly.

Matthew smiled. ‘I’m not saying that’s necessary just at present.’

'Oh,' she said, disappointed. Then she clicked her fingers. 'There was another fella, the other day. He didn't have a car, but I saw him going in the gate. He weren't like the others. He weren't wearing a suit.'

'What did he look like?'

'Had a carrot-top,' she said, 'and a face like the back end of a bus.' Mrs Askey watched as Denham scribbled in his notebook. 'So, have you arrested the old so-and-so?'

'Mrs Askey,' Matthew said solemnly, 'Mr Clough appears to have been murdered last night.'

Her mouth fell open. 'You what?' she breathed.

'I'm afraid so. Did you know Mr Clough?'

'Only to nod to, you know,' she said. 'The old bugger wasn't one to have a chat with. Oh, I shouldn't have said that, should I? Talking ill of the dead. But,' she went on, 'he never had any time for anyone. I told Father Pettifer he shouldn't waste his time on him, but he said it was his duty.'

'Father Pettifer?' Matthew asked.

'He's the vicar at St Benedict's.'

'Mr Clough was one of his parishioners?'

'I never saw him in church, so I don't know how Father Pettifer knew him.'

'I see.' Matthew smiled. 'Well, this has been very helpful, Mrs Askey. Thank you.'

'Oh, you're going?' she asked as Matthew and Denham rose.

'We have all we need for the moment,' Matthew said, opening the front door and seeing Barnes coming down the lane. 'If we need to speak to you again, we'll be in touch.' He felt Mrs Askey watching as they walked down the path onto the pavement. Barnes came to a halt a few feet away. 'Well?'

'Mr Clough bought his Sunday newspaper from Taylor's on the high street yesterday morning, sir,' Barnes said. 'Called in just after nine.'

'And how was he?'

'Grumpy, as always, Mr Taylor said. But he did say Mr Clough had bruises on his face and he asked him about them. Mr Clough got upset. Told him to mind his own business.'

'He doesn't know how Mr Clough came by the bruises?'

Barnes shook his head.

'All right,' Matthew nodded. 'You and Denham make the house-to-house enquiries along here and the next nearest street. I'm going over to the rectory to talk to Father Pettifer.'

Matthew knocked on the rectory door, noticing how close it was to the rear of Blackbird Farm. He had thought the farm was enclosed all the way around, but, in fact, only a row of trees and a low brick wall separated the two. Anyone could gain access to the farm that way and he realised with irritation he would have to get Rudd securing the rear of the farm as well as the front.

The door opened, and Mrs Gould appeared, wiping her hands on a tea towel. 'Yes?'

Matthew showed her his warrant card and introduced himself. 'I'd like to see Father Pettifer, if he's in.'

'He's in, but I don't know if he's up to seeing anyone,' she said, and gestured for him to step inside. 'You all right?'

He frowned, then understood as she pointed at his bruised face. 'I'm fine. They were done a while ago now.'

'I know. I recognise you. You're that copper from the 'paper. You go in there and I'll see if he'll come down.'

Matthew went into the sitting room, wondering why the vicar was still in bed at this time of the morning. He heard steps on the stairs and turned expectantly to the door.

Mrs Gould entered. 'He's coming down.'

'Is he ill?' Matthew asked. She hesitated before answering, and Matthew wondered why.

‘I think he’s just tired,’ she said, screwing her face up. ‘He didn’t have a very good night.’

Matthew filed this piece of information, nodding as he heard another set of footsteps on the stairs.

‘Inspector Stannard?’ Father Pettifer said, coming a little bleary-eyed into the sitting room.

‘Yes. I’m sorry to disturb you if you’re not well,’ Matthew began.

‘Oh,’ Pettifer said, buttoning up his jacket, ‘I’m just a little tired. What can I do for you?’

‘Have you heard the news?’ Matthew asked, looking from Pettifer to Mrs Gould. ‘About Mr Clough?’

Pettifer’s face hardened a little. ‘What has he done?’

‘I see you haven’t. I understand he was a friend of yours?’

‘I hardly know,’ Pettifer said, then frowned. ‘Was, did you say?’

Matthew nodded. ‘I’m afraid Mr Clough was found dead this morning at his farm.’

Pettifer fell into an armchair, his face ashen.

‘What was it? Heart attack?’ Mrs Gould asked.

‘He was murdered,’ Matthew said. Mrs Gould gasped and put a hand to her mouth. Father Pettifer stared at the carpet. ‘Are you all right, Father?’

Pettifer looked up at him, a strange, confused expression on his face. ‘Oh, yes. Well, no. It’s rather a shock. Who?’

‘We don’t know yet. I’ve been told you knew Mr Clough well?’

‘I suppose so.’

‘Can I get you a cup of tea, Father?’ Mrs Gould asked, bending over the vicar. He didn’t answer, and she looked up at Matthew.

He nodded and sat down on the settee as she left the room. ‘Did he have any enemies that you know of?’

‘Enemies? Good Lord, what a word.’ Pettifer sighed. ‘No, I know of no enemies, but Josiah wasn’t a well-liked man. He was difficult, cantankerous. I suppose he may have upset a few people in his time.'

'Anyone in particular?'

'I really couldn't say, inspector.' Pettifer frowned and toyed with the fraying arm of his chair. 'When did it happen?'

'We think between nine last night and eight-thirty this morning.'

'Good Lord,' Pettifer muttered and bent his head.

Matthew rubbed his forehead. His headache was getting worse. 'We've had a witness say there have been visitors to the farm over the past few weeks. Men in suits? A red-haired man? Any idea who they might have been?'

'No idea at all.'

'When did you last see Mr Clough?'

'Oh,' Pettifer raised his eyes to the ceiling, 'some days ago. Tuesday, I think it was.'

'And how was he then?'

Pettifer shrugged. 'The same as ever he was. Unpleasant.'

'Forgive me, Father,' Matthew said, 'but if he was so unlikeable a character, why did you bother with him?'

Pettifer frowned at him. 'Because it was my pastoral duty, inspector.'

Matthew nodded, not really understanding. 'Do you know Mr Clough's next of kin?'

'Josiah didn't have any family. Not since his father died.'

'Then I'm afraid I'm going to have to ask you to identify the body.'

Pettifer started half out of his chair. 'No, I can't do that. I don't want to see a dead body.'

'I'm sure you've seen dead bodies before,' Matthew said, a little taken aback by the vicar's vehemence.

'You can't ask that of me,' Pettifer whimpered.

'I'm afraid there doesn't seem to be anyone else I can ask. I'm sorry.'

Pettifer slumped in the chair. ‘When?’

‘After the post-mortem,’ Matthew said. ‘I’ll let you know.’ Pettifer nodded, and Matthew rose to leave. ‘I’ll see myself out,’ he said, and left the vicar in the sitting room, closing the door.

Mrs Gould tiptoed into the hall. ‘Is he all right?’ she whispered, jerking her head at the sitting room.

‘He seems a little shocked,’ Matthew smiled. ‘Maybe you could give him a little brandy with his tea.’

To his surprise, Mrs Gould rolled her eyes. ‘He don’t need no more,’ she muttered and reached for the door to open it for Matthew. ‘I’ll see to him,’ she said as he stepped out onto the front step. The kettle whistled in the kitchen. She said a hasty goodbye to Matthew and closed the door.

Chapter Twenty

Matthew got to the mortuary just before one o'clock and Clough's body was being wheeled out on a trolley. The pathologist was only a step behind.

Matthew leaned against the worktop and rubbed his temples, trying to ease the ache. He was feeling tired and a little weak. Amanda had made him promise he would eat regularly during the day after he had waved away her offer of a cooked breakfast that morning, and he thought ruefully he'd already broken his promise and it was only lunchtime.

'Let's see him,' Wallace said to his assistant, who whipped off the white sheet covering the body.

An odour of damp and manure wafted over Matthew and his head swam. He put a hand over his nose and mouth, closing his eyes.

'Get the inspector a chair, Andrew,' Wallace said.

Matthew straightened. 'I'm fine,' he said, holding up a hand to halt the assistant.

'A chair, Andrew,' Wallace insisted. 'I'm mindful of your recent head trauma, inspector, and it doesn't take an expert like me to see you're still not fully recovered. To be perfectly honest, I'm surprised you've been declared fit for duty.'

Matthew wasn't about to tell Wallace he'd been cleared for light duties only; he doubted a murder investigation fell into that category. He was grateful for the chair Andrew placed behind him.

Andrew grabbed a clipboard from the work counter, and pencil poised, nodded to Wallace he was ready. Wallace cleared his throat and began.

'The subject is a white male, approximately fifty-five to sixty-five years of age. Height is five foot seven. Weight is fifteen stone, six pounds. Well-nourished. There is bruising to the right cheek-bone. Judging by the colour, the bruises are between five and ten days old. There is a one-inch wound above the left eyebrow, similar to the throat wound, but much shallower. The wound to the throat measures four inches. No artery was severed, but the throat wound bled severely, possibly leading to death caused by excessive blood loss. That is to be determined. Right, Andrew, we'll remove the clothes now.'

Matthew watched as Clough's clothes were cut from his body. As the shirt was removed, Matthew saw a bandage on Clough's upper arm. Blood had stained the crepe fabric. He resisted the urge to ask about it, knowing the pathologist would get to it in his own good time.

'Well, it's not just the face,' Wallace said as Clough's vest was cut away.

'What is it?' Matthew asked, rising.

'Bruising to the torso, inspector. Two bruises to the ribs. I'd say he was punched at least twice.'

'Are those bruises as old as the ones to the face?'

'Yes,' Wallace said. 'The same discolouration.'

'So, he was beaten up days before he was killed?'

'I would say so.'

Matthew frowned. 'Both sets of bruises are on the right of Clough's body. That means a left-handed person?'

'Probably.'

'But the murder wounds are on the right?'

Wallace murmured an affirmative. 'It is possible the killing wounds were made by a right-handed person. But it's also possible that a left-hander swung the spade, which we think was the murder weapon, from the right to the left. I will need to check the angles of the wounds.'

'The head wounds.' Matthew went over to the slab and pointed. 'Which came first? Can you tell?'

Wallace bent over Clough's face and studied both wounds. 'I would say the one above the eyebrow. There are streaks down the face. That means he was upright when that was inflicted. With the throat wound, he would have collapsed very quickly, and if that had been done first, the blood from the face would have flowed sideways rather than down.'

'What about this?' Matthew pointed to the bandage on Clough's arm.

Wallace grabbed a pair of scissors and cut the bandage away.

'That's a bullet wound,' Matthew declared.

'Very good, inspector.' Wallace probed the wound. 'It is.' He lifted the arm and examined the rear. 'It's gone straight through the flesh. The bone wasn't penetrated.'

'How fresh is that wound?'

'Very. Yesterday, I'd say.'

'So, he was beaten up five to ten days ago, shot yesterday and murdered with the spade last night?'

'Rather a lot for one man to endure in so short a space of time, wouldn't you say, inspector?' Wallace said ruefully.

Matthew nodded. 'But he had time to bandage the bullet wound, so some little time at least must have passed between being shot and being killed.'

‘That makes sense.’

‘But he didn’t report the shooting. Why wouldn’t he report it?’ Matthew shook his head in bewilderment. ‘Just how many times did someone try to kill him? What the hell had he done?’

Dickie was waiting outside the mortuary when Matthew left.

‘I overheard Denham telling Barnes the post-mortem was at one,’ he explained apologetically as Matthew gave him a look of disapproval. He followed Matthew’s gaze over his shoulder to where Teddy was loitering near the entranceway. ‘I told him to stay out of your way.’

‘I can’t tell you anything about it yet, Dickie,’ Matthew said, lighting a cigarette.

‘All right,’ Dickie nodded. ‘But you can tell me what it’s like coming back to another murder. It will make great copy.’

Matthew made a face. ‘Oh, come on.’

‘I know,’ Dickie held up his hands. ‘But that’s the sort of thing my editor wants and I’ve got to deliver.’

‘What do you mean you’ve got to deliver?’

Dickie put out a hand to lean on the wall. ‘My writing’s dull, apparently. He told me I need to spice it up.’

‘He didn’t say that,’ Matthew shook his head disbelievingly.

‘Oh, he did,’ Dickie assured him. ‘It’s a sign of the times, Matthew. I’m told it’s not enough to report the facts anymore. Readers want to read about people and how they feel and that sort of rubbish.’

‘Well, they’re not reading about how I feel,’ Matthew said firmly. ‘And you should put your foot down. Say you’re not doing it. There’s nothing wrong with your writing.’

‘If I refuse, I’m out of a job. He made that very clear.’

‘Better to be out of a job than you become the gutter press.’

Dickie snorted. 'Easy for you to say. You're not as old as me and you haven't got a wife to support.'

'You really have to do this?'

'I really have to,' Dickie nodded and took out his notebook and pen. 'So, can you give me something for the 'paper? Please?'

'All right,' Matthew sighed. 'I'm glad to be back at work, but sorry that I've come back to a murder. Craynebrook's had more than its fair share of late.'

'Are you concerned Gadd's still at large?'

'No, I'm not concerned. He will be caught. It's just a matter of time,' Matthew said, echoing Mullinger's words.

'But he might come after you again,' Dickie said. 'Surely, that plays on your mind? Aren't you worried you'll be distracted because Gadd is still on the loose? Would it be better if Lund was put on the case? Are you up to the job of solving this murder?'

'Of course I'm up to it,' Matthew snapped.

Dickie sighed. 'That was me asking, Matthew. Not my editor.'

'Sorry.' Matthew held up his hand. 'I'm a bit tired and it's making me touchy. I'm fine, Dickie, really.' He took a deep breath. 'This is for your editor. I'm confident Gadd will be caught soon. In the meantime, my attention will be focused entirely on solving this murder. Now, that's it. That's all I'm saying.'

'It'll do.' Dickie put his notebook away.

'I've got to get back,' Matthew said and moved around Dickie, making for the exit. But Dickie suddenly cried out and he turned back to see his friend doubled over, clutching his side. 'Dickie! What is it? What's wrong?' He heard running footsteps and Teddy was by his side.

'What's wrong with him?' Teddy cried.

'Get help,' Matthew ordered, struggling to hold onto Dickie and stopping him from falling headlong onto the pavement. 'Get the doctor. Quick!'

Matthew was pacing the hospital corridor, waiting for the doctor to come out of the examination room and tell him what was wrong with Dickie.

The door opened and a trolley was wheeled out. Dickie was lying upon it, writhing with pain. His face was coated with sweat and his eyes were screwed up tight. He was rolled away down the corridor without even seeing Matthew.

A doctor followed the trolley. 'Mr Stannard,' he said.

'What's wrong with him?' Matthew asked, watching the trolley turn the corner.

'His appendix has burst. It must have been troubling him for weeks. We're taking him to the operating theatre now. There's no time to lose. We have to get in there and take it out.'

Matthew's stomach flipped. 'He is going to be all right, though, isn't he?'

The doctor raised an eyebrow and shook his head. 'I won't deny there is a very great risk. The infection may have got into his blood, in which case…' He didn't bother to finish the sentence. 'Do you know Mr Waite's next of kin?'

'His wife,' Matthew said.

'Then she should be here,' the doctor said portentously. 'Can you arrange that?'

'Yes, of course.'

The doctor clapped Matthew on the shoulder. 'He's in the best place, Mr Stannard. We'll do our best for him. Try not to worry.'

Matthew took the police car to Dickie's house and told his wife what had happened. Emma had been shocked and, Matthew sensed, feeling a little guilty, for she kept saying on the journey to the hospital how she had dismissed Dickie's claims of feeling ill, telling him he just had indigestion. Matthew tried to console her, but she was close to tears as he left her in the hospital waiting room. He promised he would visit later to see how Dickie was, privately hoping his friend would still be alive later.

He got back to the station and walked into CID to find Pinder with his feet up on an open desk drawer, reading a newspaper. He saw Matthew and hastily dropped his feet to the floor and stuffed the newspaper into the drawer. 'We expected you back a while ago, sir.'

'I got held up at the mortuary,' Matthew said, nodding at Barnes who was holding a large brown envelope expectantly. 'What do you have there, Barnes?'

'Crime scene photographs, sir.' He handed the envelope to Matthew.

'Good. And where's Denham?'

'He's arranging sending the murder weapon to the mortuary for Dr Wallace to examine. He'll be up in a minute.' Barnes looked at Matthew keenly. 'Can I get you anything, sir?'

Matthew was about to give his customary refusal, but he remembered his promise to Amanda and nodded. 'Get me something from the canteen, would you?'

'Of course, sir. What would you like?'

'Anything they've got left. Sandwich, cake. Anything.'

'Will do.' Barnes hurried out as Denham came in.

Matthew gestured for him to follow him into his office. 'House-to-house complete?' he asked.

Denham nodded and flipped open his notebook. 'We spoke to everyone on Blackbird Lane. A couple of them, the owners of numbers three and four, confirmed what Mrs Askey told us, that they heard a shot last night around nine-thirty. They didn't think anything of it. Clough was well-known to have a shotgun and they thought he was shooting at foxes trying to get at the chickens. They do have a fox problem, they said.'

'What about the men Mrs Askey told us about?'

'A lady at number six also said there had been cars parked on the lane that didn't belong to any of the residents. She couldn't say what models they were or their registration numbers. But no one else reported any strange men, in suits or otherwise.'

'Any of them know Clough?'

Denham shook his head. 'They all said he kept to himself, didn't encourage visitors or make efforts to be sociable. They left him alone, and he left them alone, it seems.' He turned as Barnes came in with a tray.

'Here you go, sir,' Barnes said, setting it down on Matthew's desk. On the tray was a plate of chips, two slices of buttered bread and a mug of milky tea. The smell of salt and vinegar was strong and made Matthew's mouth water. 'Will that do?'

'It's fine, thanks.' Matthew made a chip sandwich. He took a large bite and washed it down with the tea. He waved the two detectives into chairs. 'Dr Wallace promised he would send the full post-mortem report by the end of the day. His preliminary findings confirm Clough died from the throat wound, but he had other injuries. There was a deep cut to his forehead just above the left eyebrow, possibly caused by the same weapon, which for the moment we are assuming is the spade, but also bruising to the right cheekbone and to the ribs. The bruises, though, are days old, at least five, possibly as many as ten. And,' Matthew stopped to take another bite of his chip sandwich, 'he had also been shot in the arm.'

'Bloody hell,' Denham said.

'Yep,' Matthew agreed. 'So, someone definitely had it in for him. We need to find out what Clough had been up to over the past week, and we need to find these men who kept bothering Mrs Askey. We don't have a motive for this murder. We need to find one.'

'And why were the cows out?' Barnes wondered aloud.

Matthew had forgotten about the cows. 'Did the murderer let

them out?' he suggested. 'Or was Clough disturbed putting them away in the cowshed? Cows get locked up at night, don't they?'

'I expect so,' Denham said. 'But I don't really know about farms.' He looked at Barnes, who shrugged and shook his head.

'What happened to them, by the way?' Matthew asked.

'The RSPCA were called to deal with them, sir,' Barnes said. 'They've been taken to another farm in Essex to be looked after.'

'Give this other farm a call,' Matthew said, 'and ask them what time is normal for cows to be put away for the night. If it's before nine o'clock, then we should assume Clough put the cows away and that someone else let them out, possibly to mess up the crime scene and destroy evidence.'

'Do you think the murder was planned, sir?' Barnes asked.

Matthew finished his sandwich. 'It doesn't look that way. Assuming the spade was the murder weapon, the killer used what was to hand. If it was premeditated, I would have expected him to have taken a weapon with him. Were there any prints on the spade?'

'Clough's were all over it, as you'd expect. But there were also a set of prints near the base of the shaft that aren't his.'

'Anything on the cowshed door?'

'No definable prints. All smudged, so we weren't able to get anything from them.'

Matthew nodded. 'Well, you know what you have to do. Check all fingerprints on file and go through the mugshot books. Anyone who bears even the faintest resemblance to the men Mrs Askey described, we want to talk to.'

'Yes, sir.' Both Barnes and Denham rose.

'And I want the farm thoroughly searched.' Matthew looked through the partition window at Pinder. 'Pinder can do that. He obviously has nothing to do.'

Chapter Twenty-One

Matthew decided to call it a day once he had given the junior detectives their orders and read their reports from the house-to-house enquiries, making sure they had told him everything they'd found out. The men Mrs Askey had told him about seemed the most likely suspects for Clough's murder and until they were identified, there was little to be done. Besides, he felt he'd done enough for his first day back and found himself yearning for the relative peace of his temporary home at The Fiddler's Retreat. When the clock on his office wall showed quarter past five, Matthew put his hat on his head, said good evening to the others and made his way out of the station.

He was halfway to the bus stop when he remembered his promise to Emma Waite, and instead of getting on the bus that would take him home, climbed aboard the one that would take him to the hospital. Home would have to wait for another hour.

He breathed a sigh of relief when the hospital receptionist told him Mr Waite was in a recovery ward and he could go through as long as he only stayed for five minutes. Matthew promised he would and made his way to the ward.

As he walked down the corridor, he saw the doors at the end open and Bill Edwards come out. Remembering what Dickie had told him about *The Chronicle*'s editor, Matthew pulled his hat a little lower and attempted to walk past without Edwards realising who he was. But luck wasn't on his side.

'Inspector Stannard?' Edwards called, thrusting out his hand as Matthew stopped. 'Bill Edwards. Editor of *The Chronicle*.'

'Of course,' Matthew said, taking the hand. 'Mr Edwards.'

'I've just been in to see Dickie,' Edwards said, jerking his head at the ward doors. 'I couldn't believe it when Teddy told me what had happened.'

'It was quite a shock,' Matthew agreed.

'You were there, weren't you? Teddy said.'

'I was, yes.'

'You've come to see Dickie?' There was a note of surprise in Edwards' voice.

'Yes, I said I would pop in on my way home to see how he is.'

'That's good of you. I don't know many coppers who would bother about us reporters. Especially when you've got another murder to investigate.'

He was fishing, Matthew knew, and said nothing.

'Going well, is it?' Edward went on. 'The investigation?'

'It's progressing,' Matthew said smoothly.

'I'm going to have to get Teddy to cover the story now. Dickie's going to be out of action for weeks.'

'I'm sure Mr Welch will do an adequate job. If you'll excuse me…'

'Yes, yes, of course. But remember to keep us informed. You scratch our back, we'll scratch yours, yes?'

'I'll certainly keep that in mind, Mr Edwards. Good evening.'

Matthew walked on before Edwards could detain him any longer. He found Emma sitting by Dickie's bedside and she gave him a sad smile as he came up to the bed.

'The doctor said he should be fine,' she said, 'although there is always a chance of him getting an infection.'

'I'm sure they'll keep an eye on that,' he said, hoping to reassure her. He was shocked at how grey Dickie seemed. His pallor reminded him of the exsanguinated Clough lying on a slab in the mortuary and his stomach lurched at the comparison. Dickie wasn't dead, he told himself. He was trying to think of something to say to Emma when Dickie's eyes fluttered open.

'Dickie?' Emma said, grasping his hand. 'Can you hear me?'

Dickie grunted. He smacked his lips a few times, and Emma rose, reaching for a glass of water on the bedside cabinet and tipping his head forward so he could drink. Water dribbled down his chin, but he licked his lips and nodded he'd had enough. His head sank back upon the pillow and his eyes found Matthew.

'You here?' he said.

'Had to see how you were,' Matthew said, smiling.

'Well, I'm not dead, so that's a start.'

'Oh, Dickie, don't,' Emma groaned.

'I thought I was a goner.'

'I think you came close,' Matthew nodded. 'You are an idiot. The doctor said you must have been in pain for a week or more. Why didn't you get it looked at, not wait for it to nearly kill you?'

'I was just hoping it would go away, I suppose.' Dickie sighed. 'It was a good thing you were there, Matthew. I hate to think what would have happened to me otherwise.'

'Don't be daft,' Matthew said, growing embarrassed. 'Welch would have seen you all right.'

Dickie made a face. 'I wouldn't bet on it.'

'Mr Stannard was kind enough to fetch me and bring me here, Dickie,' Emma said.

'Did he? That was good of you, Matthew.'

'It was the least I could do. Well, I'm only allowed in here for five minutes, so I better be off. I'll try to drop by tomorrow.'

'Don't feel you have to,' Dickie said. 'I know you're busy.' He gave a sad smile. 'I suppose Teddy will cover the murder now I'm out of action. I dread to think what he'll write. It will probably come out like a penny dreadful.'

'You're not to worry about the newspaper,' Emma ordered. 'All you've got to worry about is getting better. Isn't that right, Mr Stannard?'

'Absolutely,' Matthew agreed. 'Well, I'll say good evening, Mrs Waite. Dickie.'

'Good evening, Mr Stannard,' Emma said. 'And thank you.'

'So, how was your first day back?' Pat asked as she ladled out gravy from the saucepan onto the mash.

All eyes turned expectantly towards Matthew. 'I had a murder,' he said, and waited for the room to erupt.

'Another one?' Pat cried.

'You're kidding?' Georgie laughed.

'But you're not up to investigating a murder,' Amanda moaned.

Matthew held up his hands. 'Can everyone just calm down, please?' The noise quietened. 'Yes, it wasn't what I was hoping for on my first day back, but it's fine.'

'How is a murder fine?' Fred wondered as he chewed on a sausage.

'I mean, I can cope,' Matthew said. 'I think it's going to be fairly straightforward. This isn't the start of a lot of killings. It's just a one-off.'

'You can't know that,' Pat said.

'That's how it feels.' Matthew dug into his mash, hoping that would be the end of the conversation.

'Who was killed?'

'A farmer.'

'There's a farm in Craynebrook?' Georgie asked in surprise.

'I know,' Matthew nodded. 'It was the last thing I expected. But apparently, it's been in Craynebrook for generations, and the man who was killed was the last of a line. He didn't have any family, so I'm having to get the local vicar to identify his body tomorrow.'

'Oh,' Amanda made a face. 'Isn't that awful? Not having anyone to even miss you.'

'So,' Pat said, 'apart from having a murder to solve. Again. How was the rest of your day?'

'Well, Dickie's in hospital,' Matthew said. 'He collapsed right in front of me with a burst appendix.'

'Blimey!' Fred cried. 'It was all go for you today, wasn't it?'

'Poor Mr Waite,' Pat shook her head. 'Is he going to be all right?'

'He came through the operation well enough. The only danger is infection, but fingers crossed, he'll be fine. I visited him before coming home and he was awake and talking.'

'But that must have been awful, having that happen before your very eyes, Mattie. Do you feel all right?'

'I'm a bit tired,' Matthew admitted. 'It's been a hectic day.'

'There, I knew it,' Amanda declared. 'It was too early for you to go back. You need to rest for another week at least, Mattie. Why won't you listen?'

'I'm fine, Mum, really. And I can't stay off work forever. I wouldn't get paid, for one thing.'

'But you don't have to worry about money,' she cooed. 'Not while you're here with us to look after you.'

'I'm not sponging off you.'

'It's not sponging when it's family, Matt,' Fred said, reaching for the brown sauce bottle. 'And Mother's right. It's one thing going back to work and sitting behind a desk all day, drinking tea. It's another chasing after a murderer.'

Matthew swallowed down a sigh along with his mash. 'It's fine. I'm fine. Now, please, can we drop the subject?'

They did as he asked, and for a few minutes, the only sound was the sound of cutlery scraping on china. Matthew sensed an air of resentment that he had dismissed their concerns, and he finished as much of his dinner as he could manage quickly.

'That's me done,' he said, laying his knife and fork together on the plate. 'Do you mind if I leave you to the washing-up and go to bed?'

'But you've hardly eaten anything,' Pat said, looking at the remains on his plate.

'You gave me loads, Pat,' Matthew said. 'I swear you're trying to fatten me up.'

'You need fattening up.'

'I can't eat any more. Georgie can finish it.' Matthew passed the plate to his brother. 'I just want to get my head down for a bit.'

'It is just tiredness, isn't it, Mattie?' Amanda asked worriedly.

'That's all it is, Mum,' Matthew said. 'Promise.'

'Off you go then. If you're awake later, I'll bring you in a cup of tea.'

Matthew got up, then turned back to the table. 'Has anyone fed Bella?'

Georgie nodded. 'I gave her some liver I brought home from work.'

'Thanks.' As Matthew crossed the landing to his bedroom, he heard Fred say, 'We need to keep an eye on him. He'll kill himself if we let him work so hard.'

Chapter Twenty-Two

Matthew had only just walked through the station door when Sergeant Turkel called out to him.

'Morning, inspector. Got someone wants to speak to you.' He nodded towards a middle-aged man with a moon face and thin brown hair sitting on the bench on the far side of the lobby. The man looked expectantly at Matthew.

Matthew mentally cursed. He had been hoping to have a cup of tea at his desk before taking Pettifer to identify Clough's body, wanting to take a couple of aspirin to help ease the headache he'd had since waking. His mother had caught him on his way out and demanded to know if he was better that morning. Matthew had lied and said he was much better, but Amanda had gone on and the only way he had been able to get away from her had been to promise to be in by seven that evening. He hadn't had to tell her what time he would be home for years and doing so had made him feel sixteen years old again. Matthew didn't like the feeling one bit.

He went over to the man. 'Yes, sir? What can I do for you?'

'I'm not sure if I'm wasting your time or not,' the man said awkwardly. 'It's about the murder up at the farm.'

'Please come in here,' Matthew said at once, opening the door to the lobby's waiting room. He gestured for the man to sit at the table and took a chair himself. 'Can I take your name, please, sir?'

'Dennis Clarke.'

'And you have information regarding the murder?'

'I think so. I was on my round.' Clarke began. 'I'm a milkman, you see, and Blackbird Lane's one of my roads. Anyway, I was dropping two bottles off at No. 11 when two boys came running down the lane, calling out to each other and laughing.' He shrugged. 'It just seemed a bit strange.'

'Were they coming from the farm?' Matthew asked.

'From that direction. I don't know if they actually came out of the farm.'

'Could they have been coming from another house on Blackbird Lane?'

'I suppose they could have done. But I know everyone on the lane and they don't live there. And there's no one usually about at that time of the morning.' He laughed. 'I'm the only silly sod up then.'

Matthew smiled. 'So, what time was this?'

'About six, six-thirty. No later.'

'And you say they called to each other? Did you hear what they said?'

Clarke frowned. 'I think one of them said something like, "I can't believe we did that".'

'Any idea what he was alluding to?'

'No idea.'

'Can you describe these boys?'

'The dark-haired one was thin. Skinny, really. Was in his shirt sleeves, but had a pullover tied around his waist. I don't know him.'

'Age?'

'Thirteen?' Clarke suggested.

'And the other boy?'

'Oh, I can tell you who he was,' Clarke said with assurance. 'I know him right enough. It was that nasty little sod Nathan Jowett.'

'Have you seen the 'paper this morning, sir?' Denham asked as Matthew walked into CID.

He held up *The Chronicle*, and Matthew took it from him. The front-page headline read GRISLY MURDER AT BLACKBIRD FARM. But it wasn't the headline that grabbed his attention; it was the photograph that accompanied it. *The Chronicle* had printed a picture of Clough's body lying on the ground as Matthew had seen it. Only the fact that it was black and white prevented the reader from making out the blood that had soaked into the ground around him.

'What the hell are they thinking?' Matthew said. 'Printing a picture like that?'

'I know,' Denham said. 'I reckon it's a good thing Clough didn't have any family who might see it. It would upset them, I'm sure.'

Matthew turned the pages. The second and third pages were filled with photographs — of the cows on the high street, the farm cowshed, chicken coops and the inside of the farmhouse. Welch must have had a good look around and taken the pictures while Dickie was calling the police. He handed the newspaper back to Denham and told him about his chat with Mr Clarke.

'We're going to the school to talk to this Nathan Jowett and the other boy, if we can find out who he is. But I'm supposed to be taking Father Pettifer to identify the body.' He looked around and saw Pinder idling by the tea things. 'Pinder,' he called, and the detective turned round, eyebrow raised. 'You can take the vicar to identify the body this morning. Pick him up at nine.'

'Yes, sir,' Pinder sighed and stirred his tea noisily.

'Did you search the farm?' Matthew asked, irritated by the young man's insouciance.

'Yes, sir,' Pinder said, taking his mug to his desk.

'And?' Matthew demanded impatiently.

'I didn't find anything unusual,' he shrugged. 'Just a lot of mess all over the house, but it looked like it had been that way for years. Made me itch just walking round it. I'm sure I've picked up some fleas.'

'Just make sure your report is on my desk when I get back,' Matthew said testily. 'And don't be late for Father Pettifer. Denham. Barnes. You're with me.'

Mr Seabrook, the headmaster, seemed alarmed by the presence of policemen in his office. He hovered around his desk, not knowing whether to sit down or remain standing, and called the secretary back as she was closing the office door to make tea for his visitors. He only let her go when Matthew said tea wasn't required.

'Well,' he said, resuming his seat and glancing across the desk to where Matthew sat, 'what is all this about, inspector?'

'I understand you have a pupil here by the name of Nathan Jowett?'

'Oh,' Seabrook sighed and fiddled with his fountain pen. 'Nathan. Yes, we do.'

'What can you tell me about him?'

'He's what we call a wrong 'un, inspector. A truant, more often than not. Not very bright. Always in trouble.'

'What kind of trouble?'

'Oh, all sorts. Deliberately spilling ink over exercise books, writing rude words on the blackboard, smoking in the lavatories. The usual. You name it, Nathan has a hand in it.'

'Schoolboy pranks?' Matthew was disappointed. 'Is that all?'

'It's bad enough, I can tell you. Nathan is a disturbing influence in the school. I've had reason to talk to his mother on at least three occasions about his behaviour, though that proved to be a waste of time.'

'Why was that?'

'She wasn't interested, inspector. Nathan's father isn't around anymore. I've heard some talk he ran off with another woman, and I suspect there is a lack of discipline at home as a result. His mother won't hear a word against Nathan.'

'What about his friends?'

'I couldn't really say, although other teachers have mentioned he's become friendly with Charles Woods, which is a pity, as Woods has always been a good boy. Never had any problems before he got mixed up with Nathan. He has become a truant as well, and I am intending to speak to his parents about him. His work has been suffering, too.'

'Are both boys in school today?'

'I'll have to check the register.'

'If you could do that,' Matthew said, 'and if they are here, I'd like to see them both.'

Seabrook buzzed the intercom on his desk and asked his secretary to bring in the school register. 'What do you want to see them about, inspector?'

'About an incident last night,' Matthew said evasively as the secretary came in with the register.

She handed it to Seabrook, and he ran his finger down the column of names. 'Yes. They are both in today. Miss Hill, have Nathan Jowett and Charles Woods brought here at once.'

The secretary departed and Seabrook closed the register. To pass the time until the boys arrived, Matthew made small talk with the headmaster about the school. Barnes and Denham talked quietly between themselves. It was almost ten minutes later when the door opened once again and Miss Hill showed two boys in. Matthew could immediately tell which was which. The dark-haired boy was

Charles Woods, and he looked terrified. The other, Nathan Jowett, looked ready for a fight.

'Jowett, Woods,' Seabrook addressed the boys sternly. 'These gentlemen are from the police. They want to ask you some questions.'

'Police?' Charlie cried.

Nathan shot him a silencing glare.

'Barnes,' Matthew said, 'take Master Woods into the other office for the moment, please.'

'Yes, sir,' Barnes said, and putting his hand on Charlie's shoulders, turned him towards the door and pushed him out.

'Sit down, Nathan,' Matthew said, gesturing to an empty chair opposite.

Nathan stared at the chair for a long moment as if wondering whether to obey, then slouched over and fell down onto it, spreading his legs wide.

'Behave yourself, Jowett,' Seabrook warned, 'and get your hands out of your pockets.'

'Nathan,' Matthew began when Nathan had dragged his hands out and folded his arms over his chest, 'can you tell me where you were last night from around 9 p.m.?'

'Why?'

'Because I want to know.'

'What for?'

Matthew met Nathan's eye. He wasn't in the mood to take any cheek from a schoolboy. 'Where were you?' He waited for Nathan's response. None came. 'If you don't tell me where you were, Nathan, I'm going to wonder what it is you've got to hide.'

'I ain't got nothing to hide,'

'You don't have anything to hide, Nathan,' Seabrook corrected him irritably.

'So?' Matthew said.

‘I was with Charlie at his house,’ Nathan said sullenly. ‘I stayed over at his from eight o’clock.’

‘Until what time?’

‘I don’t know. Until it was time to get up this morning. Seven-thirty, I suppose.’

‘You didn’t go out during the night?’

‘No.’

‘So, if I ask Charlie’s parents, they’ll confirm you were in their house all night until seven-thirty this morning, will they?’

‘Yeah. Course they will ’cause that’s where I was.’

Matthew nodded. ‘Do you know Blackbird Farm, Nathan?’

Nathan shifted in his seat. ‘Yeah, I know it.’

‘Have you been there?’

‘No.’

‘What about Blackbird Lane? Ever been there?’

Nathan shook his head.

‘So, explain to me how you were seen there this morning around six-thirty, running away from Blackbird Farm?’

Nathan jerked up, grabbing the sides of the seat. ‘Who says I was?’ he demanded. ‘They’re bloody lying.’

‘Watch your language, Jowett,’ Seabrook snapped.

‘I weren’t there. You ask Charlie. We was at his house, like I said.’

Matthew studied the boy for a long moment. He’d met his sort so many times before. A criminal in the making. Nathan was lying, he was sure of it, but he doubted he would get anything out of him, not without some very good motivation. Charlie Woods, on the other hand…

‘All right, Nathan,’ he said. ‘You can go.’

Nathan seemed surprised. He looked from Matthew to Seabrook as if expecting there to be a catch, then he jumped up and strode to the door, yanking it open and going out.

Matthew nodded at Denham to bring in Barnes and the other boy.

'Come and sit down,' Matthew said, pointing Charlie to the chair Nathan had vacated.

Charlie did so gingerly, sitting with knees together, swallowing nervously.

'Is it Charles or Charlie?' Matthew asked kindly.

'Charlie,' came the whispered reply.

'Charlie,' Matthew nodded. 'Can you tell me where you were last night around 9 p.m.?'

'I was at home.'

'From what time until when?'

'From around five o'clock until this morning.'

'What time this morning?'

'Seven-thirty.'

They have their story down pat, Matthew thought. 'Do you know Blackbird Farm, Charlie?'

'No,' Charlie shook his head vehemently. 'I've never been there.'

'What about Blackbird Lane?'

'No.'

'Have you heard what's happened at Blackbird Farm, Charlie?'

'What's happened?'

'The farmer who lives there has been murdered.' He studied Charlie's face for his reaction, but the boy just stared at him. Out of the corner of his eye, Matthew saw Seabrook's mouth fall open. 'Do you know anything about that?'

The veins were standing out on Charlie's neck, but he shook his head. 'Can I go now?' he asked in a broken voice.

Matthew didn't answer straight away, wanting the boy to sweat a little, hoping he would blurt out something of interest, but the boy continued to stare at him and he nodded. 'Yes, Charlie. You can go.'

Charlie bolted out of the chair and headed for the door. He yanked it open as Nathan had done and ran out.

'I'd like the home addresses for both Charlie and Nathan, please,' Matthew said.

'Miss Hill will get them for you,' Seabrook nodded. 'But you don't really think the boys had anything to do with a murder, do you, inspector?'

Matthew rose and picked up his hat. 'Thank you for your time, Mr Seabrook.'

Chapter Twenty-Three

Mrs Gould threw open the door of Father Pettifer's study, muttering under her breath. For all his promises, Father Pettifer still hadn't paid her, and she was asking herself what kind of fool she was to still be working for him. Her husband had asked the same question only that morning. 'He might be a man of the cloth,' Bill had said, 'but we can't live on thin air. If he's not going to pay you, you need to find an employer who will.' Mrs Gould knew her husband was right, but she didn't like to walk out on Father Pettifer without giving him another chance to make good.

She banged the broom into the corners of the room, sweeping beneath the desk and the sideboard and even running it over the coving to get down the cobwebs she had noticed earlier in the week. Thrusting the broom beneath the settee, something came skidding out across the floorboards and struck the skirting board. Propping the broom against the wall, she picked it up and frowned. What was an OXO tin doing under the settee? It wasn't the one from the kitchen; that tin was half the size, and besides, she'd seen it there that morning when she'd made the vicar's breakfast. Mrs Gould pulled the lid off and her eyes widened in surprise.

Rolls of bank notes greeted her, and she jammed the lid back on, her lips pressing tightly together in annoyance and indignation.

She heard a key turn the lock in the front door. Mrs Gould was about to put the tin back beneath the settee, but then thought again. Instead, she put it in the middle of Father Pettifer's desk, and snatching up her broom, went out into the hall.

'Everything all right, Father?' she asked.

'Yes, thank you, Mrs Gould,' Pettifer said, hanging up his hat. 'I identified Josiah for the police. So, that's that.'

She nodded and went into the kitchen, leaving the door ajar. With her ear to the wood, she heard him go into his study. He couldn't miss the tin. He'd see it and know she'd seen it too. And then he would have to pay her.

And if he doesn't, she thought, *I won't be coming back.*

Someone was shouting as Matthew and the others climbed the stairs to CID.

'That sounds like Old Mouldy,' Denham whispered to Barnes.

Matthew opened the door and discovered Denham was right. Mullinger was standing in the middle of the office, looming over the police photographer seated at one of the desks. He was waving a copy of *The Chronicle* in the man's face.

'How did they get them?' he bellowed.

'I don't know, sir,' the photographer said, cowering. 'They didn't get them from me.'

'Don't lie. These photographs were taken at the crime scene. Only you had access to the scene. So, come on. How much did the newspaper give you for the pictures? Tell me. I want to know.'

'I didn't get anything.'

'You gave them away for free?'

'No. I mean I didn't give the photographs to the newspaper.'

'What's going on?' Pinder, who had also just come into the office, whispered to Barnes.

'Old Mouldy thinks Bob sold the crime scene photos to the newspaper,' Barnes whispered back.

Matthew heard Pinder laugh.

'I won't have my men selling photographs to the Press,' Mullinger went on. 'It's disgraceful. And I won't stand for it. I—'

'Sir,' Matthew interrupted, 'if I may say something?'

Mullinger rounded on him. 'What is it, Stannard?'

'I don't believe Mr Mayhew has sold anything to the newspaper. The body at the farm was found by two reporters from *The Chronicle*. I expect they took the pictures before calling us. So, they are their photographs, not our police ones. And if anyone's to blame, it's me. I should have confiscated the camera.'

The room fell silent. *I'm for it now*, Matthew thought as he saw Mullinger's lips tightening and a purple tinge creep up his neck.

'I see,' Mullinger said calmly, surprising him. 'Well, that puts a different complexion on the matter, doesn't it?' He gave Mayhew a sideways glance, then looked quickly away back to Matthew. 'It was remiss of you not to confiscate the camera, as you say, Stannard. Although I'm not sure legally you would have been in the right to do so.' He grunted unhappily. 'Very well. Carry on.'

Mullinger strode out and Pinder whistled after he closed the door. 'I thought he was going to burst a blood vessel. Shame. I'd have paid to see that.'

'Are you all right, Bob?' Denham asked.

'Bet you nearly shit yourself,' Pinder grinned.

'Watch your language, Pinder,' Matthew said sternly.

Pinder made a face behind Matthew's back as he headed for his office. Mayhew jumped up and blocked Matthew's way.

'Thank you, sir,' he said, his cheeks still blotchy from his humiliation.

Matthew shook his head. 'Don't mention it.'

'You didn't have to say anything,' Mayhew insisted. 'I'm grateful.'

'And you're welcome,' Matthew said, turning back to Pinder before Mayhew could go on. 'Did Pettifer identify the body?'

Pinder nodded. 'He said it was Clough, all right.'

'Good. I want you to check on the schoolboys' alibis. Get the addresses from Denham.'

Pinder tutted loudly. 'Why can't Denham check their alibis?'

'Because I've told you to do it,' Matthew said with an edge to his voice that didn't go unnoticed by the others, who pretended interest in their paperwork. 'And if you question my orders again, I'll put you on report. Is that understood?'

'Yes, sir,' Pinder replied sulkily, and went over to Denham, snatching the paper the sergeant held out from his hand. 'Sure sign he's back,' he muttered.

Matthew sat down at his desk, watching Pinder through the partition window storm out of the main office. He was fed up with Pinder. Always arguing, always moaning. A poor excuse for a policeman. If Pinder carried on the way he was, Matthew thought he might just get him transferred and make him somebody else's problem.

Barnes came in. 'The post-mortem report has just arrived, sir.' He handed Matthew a file.

Matthew scanned the text. Much of it was confirming what he already knew, but a sentence caught his eye. 'Dr Wallace found an indentation in the bruise on Clough's cheek. Says it could be the mark of a ring. He wasn't able to make out if there was any design, though. Still, could be useful.' He frowned. 'I didn't notice either of the boys wearing a ring, did you?'

Barnes shook his head. 'Can't say I did, sir.'

Matthew grunted and set the report aside. 'Any progress with the mugshots or the prints?'

'We haven't turned anything up yet, but we've still got quite a lot to go through.'

'Keep on it.' Barnes went out and Matthew opened his top drawer and took out his bottle of aspirin, tipping two pills into the palm of his hand. *Sod this headache*, he thought as he threw them down his throat.

Pinder knocked on Mrs Woods's door and shoved his hands into his pockets while he waited for it to be answered. He'd already been to the home of Nathan Jowett and got a flea in his ear from the boy's mother. 'Nathan's a good boy,' Mrs Jowett had screeched at him, and went on to say that all these interfering people badmouthing him should mind their own business and leave her boy alone in very colourful language. Nathan had been with his friend Charlie at his house on Sunday night and Pinder could bugger off if he didn't believe her. He expected he would get the same kind of treatment from Mrs Woods.

'Yes?' A thin, pinched-face woman was hanging onto the front door. He flashed his warrant card. 'Craynebrook CID. Are you Mrs Woods?'

Her eyes widened fearfully. 'Yes. What's wrong?'

'I need to ask you a few questions about your son, Charlie,' he said, taking out his notebook.

'Oh my God,' she cried, her hand going to her mouth. 'Has he been hurt?'

'Not as far as I know,' Pinder said irritably. Why did women always assume the worse? 'We're investigating the murder at Blackbird Farm and need to check your son's whereabouts.'

Mrs Woods frowned. 'What's Charlie got to do with that?'

'He's told us he was here on Sunday from 5 p.m. until seven-thirty the next morning. Can you confirm that?'

'You've questioned him?'

‘My colleagues did this morning at the school.’

‘Why?’

‘He was seen near the farm yesterday morning.’

‘So what?’

‘We have to follow up leads, Mrs Woods,’ Pinder explained with a sigh, seeing the next-door neighbour come out of his front door with a rubbish sack. ‘Now, is what he’s told us correct?’

Mrs Woods watched the neighbour warily as she answered. ‘Yes, he was here Sunday night.’

‘And what about Nathan Jowett? Was he here, too?’

‘Yes, he stayed the night.’

‘The boys didn’t go out at all?’

‘No. They had their tea and then they went up to Charlie’s bedroom. They didn’t come down again until breakfast.’

‘Right. That’s all. Ta.’ Pinder tucked his notebook away as he walked down the path. He heard the front door close behind him.

The neighbour leaned over his wall. ‘You from the police?’ he asked.

‘That’s right.’

‘Asking about Charlie, are you?’

‘Might be.’

The neighbour grinned. ‘What’s he been up to, then?’

‘What makes you think he’s been up to anything?’

‘You wouldn’t be here asking questions if he hadn’t. Go on. Tell us.’

Pinder drew his packet of cigarettes out of his pocket and shook out a stick. ‘I’m making enquiries into the Blackbird Farm murder,’ he said, lighting a cigarette.

The neighbour’s eyes widened. ‘And young Charlie’s mixed up with that?’

‘He and a friend of his were seen near the farm the next morning.’

‘Nathan Jowett,’ the neighbour said knowingly. ‘I’m not surprised he’s involved.’

‘Why’d you say that?’

‘He’s a nasty little sod if ever there was one. It’s a pity young Charlie’s fallen in with him because he’s always been a nice boy. That’s what happens, though, isn’t it? They fall in with the wrong crowd.’

Pinder shook his head. ‘It’ll probably turn out to be nothing to do with them. Mrs Woods says the boys were both here the night of the murder.’

The man grinned. ‘That’s what she says, is it?’

‘Yeah. Why?’

‘I’ve seen young Charlie climbing out of his bedroom window, night after night. Charlie’s parents, they’ve got no idea what he’s up to. Mind you, that’s no surprise. They’ve got a lot on their plate with the other kid. Terminally ill,’ he whispered. ‘Poor little sod. But I’ll tell you something for nothing. If Charlie is in trouble, it’ll only be because Nathan Jowett’s got him into it.’

It was lunchtime when Pinder finished checking on the boys’ alibis and he didn’t feel like going straight back to the station. He went to The King George instead, ordering a pint and a pork pie for his lunch, taking them over to a table and picking up a discarded *Daily Express* from the stool beside him. He’d finished his pie when a voice said, ‘Not reading me, then?’

Pinder looked up to see Teddy Welch grinning down at him. ‘What do you mean you?’

Teddy sat down. ‘I got my first front-page byline this morning. Didn’t you see?’

‘The murder piece? Yeah, I saw it. I thought Mr Waite wrote the crime articles?’

'He's in hospital. Didn't Inspector Stannard tell you? I thought he would have said, him being there when he collapsed.'

'He didn't.' Pinder threw the newspaper aside. 'Bit of luck for you, then. Mr Waite being out of action.'

'You're telling me.' Teddy pointed at Pinder's half-drunk pint. 'Want another?'

Pinder checked his watch. He really should be getting back, but what the hell. 'If you're buying, yeah.'

Teddy went to the counter and brought two pints back. 'There you go. So, how's the investigation going?'

Pinder took a mouthful of beer. 'Reckon we know who did it.'

'Already?' Teddy's eyebrows rose almost to his hairline. 'That was quick.'

'We got a tip-off.'

'Who did it, then?'

Pinder gave Teddy a deprecating look. 'Like I'm telling you for nothing.'

'Ah, so, you'll tell me for something?' Teddy wheedled.

'I might. Not names, mind. Just who we're looking at.'

'How much will it cost me?'

Pinder considered. The most Dickie had ever agreed to pay him was a pound a time. 'Couple of quid will do it,' he chanced.

Teddy shoved his hand in his trouser pocket and pulled out his wallet. He took two pound notes out of the flap and pressed them into Pinder's waiting hand. 'Well?'

Pinder tucked the notes away. 'A couple of schoolboys. They were seen by a milkman running away from the farm. And they're known troublemakers, so...' he shrugged. 'No point looking for anyone else, is there?'

'You can't give me their names?'

Pinder shook his head. 'No can do. Not until they're charged.'

'And when will that be?'

'When I tell Stannard what I've found out. In my own good time.'

'It sounds like you don't like him.'

Pinder made a face as he raised his glass to his lips. 'So, are you taking over from Mr Waite from now on? Because he and me, we had an understanding.'

'Is that right?' Teddy nodded. 'Well, I don't see why not. Mr Waite's going to be off work for a couple of weeks, and between you and me, there's a rumour he ain't coming back.'

'You've got to make it worth my while. That little snippet I've just given you. That was me being nice. Ordinarily, that would have cost you a fiver.'

'That's a bit steep, ain't it?'

'It's my rate. If you can't pay it—'

'I didn't say I wouldn't, did I? All right.' Teddy held out his hand and Pinder shook it. 'You're on.'

Pinder rapped on Matthew's office door. 'I'm back, sir.'

'About time. And?'

'Nathan's mother confirms he spent the night at Charlie's house. Charlie's mother confirms the boys were there all night. But…' he paused for effect.

Matthew bit. 'But what?'

'But the Woods's next-door neighbour said Charlie regularly sneaks out his bedroom window and the parents never know.'

Matthew nodded. 'You and Barnes bring both boys in.'

'Will do,' Pinder said and clicked his fingers at Barnes to follow him.

Matthew lit a cigarette and sank back in his chair, watching the smoke waft towards the ceiling. With any luck, he would have closed the case by the end of the day.

Nathan was drumming his fingers on the table when Matthew and Denham entered the interview room. He looked up at Matthew defiantly as he sat down. 'You've got no right to drag me in here.'

It was half-past six and Matthew was annoyed. He had hoped to have wrapped the case up by five, but the boys had proved elusive, and it had taken Barnes and Pinder two hours to track them down, finding them in the front row of the cinema on the high street. Nathan had been asked if he wanted his mother present when being questioned and he had said no. Charlie, however, had cried when he arrived at the police station and refused to say a word until he saw his father. Matthew had sent Barnes to bring Mr Woods in, but no one was home and a message had been left with the neighbour, telling the Woods to contact the police.

'Nathan,' Matthew said, 'we've spoken to your mother and to Charlie's mother, and they both believe you were in Charlie's house all night on Sunday.'

'Like I said I was.'

'We've also been told it's usual for Charlie to sneak out of the house from his bedroom window, and that you've been seen doing the same. Apparently, Charlie's parents aren't aware he and you do this and they think you're in his bedroom.'

Nathan looked from Matthew to Denham and back again. 'We are in his room. We don't climb out any window.'

'You've been seen,' Matthew reminded him.

'Oh yeah? Who by?'

'That's not important.'

'I want to know who's telling lies about me.'

'It's not a lie, though, is it?' Matthew said. 'Now, we have two witnesses who both claim they've seen you doing things you say you haven't.'

'And you're going to believe them rather than me,' Nathan sneered. 'But you ain't arrested me, have ya? So, I don't have to stay here and listen to this rubbish. I'm going.'

He jumped out of the chair and moved around the table. Denham grabbed at him, taking hold of his left arm.

Nathan cried out in pain as Denham shoved him back into the chair. 'You hurt me, you bastard.' Blood was seeping through his shirtsleeve.

'I hardly touched him,' Denham said to Matthew in alarm.

'Nathan, what is that?' Matthew asked.

'It's nothing.' Nathan turned to the wall, hiding his arm.

'It doesn't look like nothing. I'm going to get a doctor to take a look at you.'

'I don't want a doctor. Just let me go and I'll be all right.'

'Sergeant Denham will take you down to the medical room, Nathan,' Matthew said. 'Go with him, please.'

He could tell Nathan wanted to argue, to stand his ground and refuse, but when all was said and done, he was a kid and a kid in some pain. When Denham held out his arm, Nathan looked at it for a long moment, then walked out without another word.

Matthew lit a cigarette. So much for getting home by seven. His mother would give him hell.

The police surgeon arrived at the station forty minutes later and examined Nathan. Matthew waited impatiently in his office and jumped up out of his chair when he saw the doctor enter CID.

'How is he?' he asked.

The doctor put his medical bag on a desk and raised his eyebrows. 'He's got a gunshot wound to the arm, inspector. Not severe, but it should have been properly treated. There is a slight infection which is causing him some pain. I recommend he is taken to the hospital so the wounds can be cleaned.'

Matthew swore. 'Did he tell you how he got shot?'

'He didn't say, and I didn't ask. That's your job.'

'How old is the wound?'

‘Six or seven days, judging by the look of the wounds and the infection.’

‘Not only a couple of days?’ Matthew asked.

‘No, inspector. If that’s all?’

‘Yes, that’s all. Thank you.’

The doctor left and Matthew called to Denham. ‘Take Nathan to the hospital and get his arm seen to. Stay with him until it’s done and then bring him back here. He’ll have to spend the night in a cell. Tell Copley to inform his mother.’

‘Yes, sir. What about Charlie? We still haven’t located his father.’

‘Put him in a cell, too,’ Matthew said, rubbing his forehead. ‘Assuming we’ve found his father by then, I’ll question him in the morning. I’m calling it a night.’

Before Matthew left the station, he telephoned the hospital and left a message for Dickie that he was sorry but he couldn’t visit that night. He hoped Dickie would understand.

Chapter Twenty-Four

Matthew sat down at the table, wondering if he was going to have a good day after all. He'd gone to bed confident he had the killers of Josiah Clough in custody, but a halfway decent night's sleep, a proper breakfast and one look at Charlie's face was making him doubt himself. Was this boy, this pale-faced, terrified boy, really a killer?

He nodded at Charlie's father sitting beside his son. Derek Woods looked half dead. When Denham had told Matthew the father had been found and was waiting in the interview room with his son, Matthew had expected this to be followed up with a remark that the father was creating merry hell at his son being treated as a criminal. That would have been normal. But Denham had lowered his voice and told Matthew he wasn't sure Mr Woods fully understood why his son was in custody.

'We finally tracked him down at the hospital,' Denham said. 'It turns out the other boy, Charlie's younger brother, has a terminal illness and took a turn for the worse yesterday afternoon. Both parents were with him at the hospital and didn't even know we had Charlie here.'

So, now Matthew had to interview a terrified boy with his worn-out, worried father sitting beside him while his mind was on the other son dying in hospital. There were some days when Matthew really hated his job.

'Charlie,' he said, giving the boy what he hoped was an encouraging smile, 'you know why you're here?'

'I didn't do it,' Charlie blurted out. 'It wasn't me.'

'What wasn't you?'

'I didn't kill the farmer. I wouldn't do that. I couldn't. Dad,' he turned desperately to his father. 'It wasn't me.'

Derek Woods nodded but said nothing.

'We've been speaking with Nathan,' Matthew went on. 'He's been shot in the arm. According to the doctor, that happened about a week ago. Do you know anything about that?'

Charlie's mouth opened and closed. Then he shook his head and looked down at his hands, picking at the cuticles.

'We know you sometimes sneak out of your bedroom window without your parents' knowledge,' Matthew said. 'Did you sneak out on Sunday night?'

'You do?' Mr Woods said in surprise.

'Sometimes,' Charlie admitted to his father. He turned to Matthew. 'But not Sunday night. Not then.'

'When then?' Matthew asked.

The boy's chest was heaving. 'Nat said I wasn't to tell you anything.'

'Do you always do what Nathan says?'

'No, not always,' Charlie said defensively. 'But he's my friend.'

'He's not much of a friend if he lets you get into trouble for something he's done,' Matthew pointed out. 'If he was a proper friend, he'd own up, wouldn't he?'

Charlie shrugged. 'I dunno.'

'Inspector,' Mr Woods said. 'Charlie's a good boy. He's never been in trouble before.'

'I know that, Mr Woods,' Matthew nodded. 'Charlie's never come to our notice before this. His friend, Nathan Jowett, has, however. Nothing serious as yet, but enough to get the odd clip round the ear from a constable on patrol. Mr Seabrook, the headmaster at Charlie's school, says Nathan's a troublemaker and a bad influence. And I think that's true. I also think, Charlie, that Nathan's involved you in something you didn't want to be involved in. Is that right?'

Mr Woods elbowed his son in the ribs. 'Answer the inspector, Charlie.'

'I didn't want to do it,' Charlie burst out. 'It was all Nat's idea.'

Matthew's heart beat a little faster. 'What was Nathan's idea?'

'He knew the farmer had barrels of beer at his place and he said we could take one. So, we went there the other Sunday. Not when he was murdered,' he added hastily. 'The one before. Anyway, we'd got into the shed where the barrels were and Nat was rolling one out to me when the farmer found us. I ran away. I thought Nat was behind me, but the old man sort of caught him. But he managed to get away and as he was running, the old man shot him. Got him in the arm. Nat had me pick the bits out in the school toilets the next morning. Nat wanted to get back at the old man and he wanted me to go with him. I didn't want to, but Nat said I would be letting him down if I didn't go and that we wouldn't be pals anymore.' He shrugged. 'So, I said I would.'

'What did you and Nathan do?' Matthew asked.

'On Monday morning, we got up early — he'd stayed at my house that night — and went out through my window. We got to the farm and unlocked the cowshed and left the farm gate open. Nat said the cows would get out and trample over everything and the old man would be mad.'

Matthew's heart sank. 'You let the cows out?'

Charlie nodded. 'That's all we did, I swear it. You believe me, don't you, Dad?'

Mr Woods studied his son's face for a long moment. Then he looked at Matthew. 'If that's what Charlie says he did, then that's what he did. He's a good boy, inspector.'

'Did you see Mr Clough that morning, Charlie?' Matthew asked.

Charlie shook his head. 'We didn't see anyone.'

Pinder made himself look busy as Matthew and Denham returned to the CID office. He watched Matthew as he strode straight past him without a glance and went into his office, slamming the door shut.

'Oi, Justin,' Pinder said in a low voice. 'What's up with him?'

Denham made a face. 'He just lost his murder suspects. The boys let the cows out at the farm. They didn't touch the farmer. Didn't even see him. And…' he dragged out the word as he picked up a newspaper from his desk, 'he's seen this.' He showed Pinder *The Chronicle*'s front page. The headline screamed TROUBLED SCHOOLBOYS HELD ON SUSPICION OF MURDER.

Pinder nodded. He'd seen the article for himself earlier that morning and had been worried at the inclusion of the boys' names. He'd made a point of telling Teddy he couldn't give him their names, but Teddy must have found out for himself, maybe from the milkman who had fingered Nathan Jowett. Remembering how Mullinger had reacted when he thought Mayhew had sold the crime scene photographs to the Press, Pinder was hoping no one would look at him for this latest leak.

Denham turned back to his desk and Pinder reached for the pile of post. He opened one envelope after another, his mind on the newspaper article, until he glanced down and saw a lavender-coloured envelope addressed to DI MATTHEW STANNARD. He glanced around, making sure no one was watching, then ripped the envelope open.

Dearest Matthew,

I just had to write to you again because you're the only person I can unburden myself to. I only wish I could talk to you in person. Then I would feel so much better, especially if you put your arms around me and held me tight. I'm so worried, Matthew darling, and I can't tell anyone. I feel only you would understand. Only you could save me. Would you save me, my darling? If I asked, would you do anything to protect me? I close my eyes and imagine you saying, 'Yes, my darling. I would do anything for you'. If only I could see you, tell you my fears. Maybe one day, my darling, I will pluck up the courage. And when I do, you must be kind. I know you will.

Your ever-loving, Henrietta.

Pinder made a face. Nothing saucy, nothing to make him laugh. Just a soppy old bag who fancied the inspector. He stuffed the letter back in the envelope and put it into his desk drawer before moving onto the next.

Barnes handed the coins to the barmaid and pushed the three pint mugs together to carry them to the table where Denham and Pinder were waiting. He set them down and took a seat.

'I really thought we had them.' Denham shook his head. 'I could have sworn they did it.'

'They were only kids, though,' Barnes said.

'You don't think kids can kill?' Pinder asked, eyebrows raised as he took a mouthful of his beer.

Barnes shrugged and stared down into his glass. 'The inspector looked miserable, didn't he?'

'Can you blame him?' Denham said. 'For a minute there, it looked like he had the case all sewn up and now he's back to square one.'

‘We should have asked him to the pub with us,’ Barnes said.

‘I did. But he said he was going to take another look around the farm.’

‘What’s he gone there for?’ Pinder said. ‘I already searched it.’

‘I don’t know, do I?’ Denham said irritably. ‘It’s what you do when you haven’t got any leads. Go back to the beginning and hope you get a new idea. I tell you, I wouldn’t like to be in his shoes and have to explain to Old Mouldy the case still isn’t solved.’

‘That’s what he gets paid for,’ Pinder said, leaning back in his chair and stretching out his legs. ‘If he didn’t want the hassle, he shouldn’t have gone for promotion.’

‘You’re all heart, you know that?’ Denham sneered.

Pinder made a face. ‘Don’t waste your sympathy on Stannard. He loves it. Couldn’t wait to come back, could he? Probably worried he was missing out on some juicy case. Now, if that was me, if I’d been hit on the bonce and got knocked out, I’d have milked it for all it was worth. I’d have had a month off. Told Old Mouldy I was hallucinating or something.’

‘Yeah, I expect you would,’ Barnes said, shaking his head in disgust.

‘You two make me sick. If I didn’t know better, I’d say you fancied Stannard as much as those women who write to him.’

Barnes and Denham both coloured and busied themselves with their glasses, not saying another word until they’d finished their drinks. Frank Greader, the landlord of The King George, came over to take their empty glasses.

‘All right, lads?’ he asked, the glasses clinking as he gathered them up. He got grunts in response. ‘What’s up?’

Barnes looked up at him. ‘We thought we had the killers of Mr Clough. Turned out we didn’t.’

‘Those boys didn’t do it, then?’

Denham shook his head. ‘No. They only let the cows out.’

‘So, who’s in the frame now?’

Barnes glanced nervously at Denham, conscious they shouldn't be talking about the case with civilians.

'We're following up various leads,' Denham lied.

Greader nodded. 'Like that bloke who was in here the other day?'

'What bloke?' Denham asked.

'A red-haired bloke,' Greader shrugged. 'Scar on his chin. I didn't like the look of him. Built like the proverbial he was, and he had a face like thunder when he walked in here.'

Denham met Barnes's eye. They were both thinking of Mrs Askey's mention of a red-haired man outside her house on Blackbird Lane. 'You didn't know him?' he asked.

Greader shook his head. 'Never seen him before. And he didn't seem the Craynebrook type, if you know what I mean?'

Denham wasn't sure he did know what the landlord meant, but he nodded anyway. 'And he was in here the night of the murder?'

Greader scratched his head. 'Not that night, no. A few nights before, I think it was.'

'Well,' Barnes frowned, 'what makes you think he had anything to do with the murder?'

'Because he trod manure in here,' Greader cried, gesturing at the carpet. 'Took Mabel ages to clean it up. We didn't smell it at first, but the next morning, when the room had been shut up all night, it stunk to high heaven.'

'And you didn't think to tell us this?' Barnes cried indignantly.

'Well,' Greader shrugged awkwardly, 'I didn't really think about it until now.'

'Would you recognise him if you saw him again?' Denham asked excitedly.

'I suppose so,' Greader shrugged.

Denham got out his notebook. 'You need to tell me everything you remember.'

Chapter Twenty-Five

Matthew turned the key in the lock and pushed open the farmhouse door. It swung on its hinges, making an eerie squealing noise. He held his breath as he listened, feeling his skin prickling in anticipation. He heard nothing and stepping inside, headed for the kitchen.

His eyes were drawn once again to the blood on the kitchen floor. Was this where Clough had been shot? He turned, looking around for some clue that this was so. The bullet had gone right through the arm, so if Clough had been shot in the kitchen, the bullet should be somewhere there.

Matthew examined the kitchen walls and door frame at shoulder height and found nothing. He stepped back out into the hall. It was dark there and so he ran his hands over the wall, letting his fingers do the looking. They soon found a small hole. He grabbed a knife from the kitchen, sticking the tip into the hole, and prised a bullet out of the wall. With a smile of satisfaction, he dropped it into his top jacket pocket, tapping it to make sure it was safely stowed.

Once more into the kitchen. This was where Clough had lived, he thought. This was where he had spent his time. Aside from the mess, the kitchen stank, not least because the remains of a fish and chip supper had been left on the table. Matthew folded the vinegar-stained newspaper around the food and looked around the kitchen for a bin. There was a filthy curtain hanging beneath the sink. The bin was probably behind it. He carried the parcel over and yanked back the curtain.

Matthew frowned. There was a bin there, but it was full, overflowing. Overflowing with bloodied cotton wool. He dropped the parcel onto the draining board and took the bin out, resting it on the edge of the sink. Pinder hadn't mentioned finding blood-stained cotton wool in his report. Matthew cursed him. Pinder had already missed the bullet in the wall, and now this. What else had he missed?

Matthew tipped the bin upside down, its contents falling onto the floor. He rooted through the rubbish, ignoring empty tobacco pouches and broken stale biscuits, and the usual rubbish found in any household bin. But then he found two halves of an envelope and picked them up. The front of the envelope simply bore the legend, 'Josiah'. No address. No stamp. This envelope had been hand-delivered. Matthew had heard only one person refer to Clough as Josiah. Taking out the two halves of the letter the envelope contained, Matthew looked first at the signature, confirming the letter was indeed written by Father Pettifer, then turned his gaze to the beginning.

Josiah,

It pains me to write this letter, but I cannot keep to myself how hurt I was by your attitude towards me this afternoon.

After all I've done for you over the years, that you could turn me away in my hour of need wounded me so very deeply. I have never expected thanks from you, nor indeed have thanks ever been forthcoming, but I would have liked to think that you felt some semblance of friendship towards me after all this time and that you would not deny me the first favour I ever asked of you.

It goes against my nature and against my vocation, but I now consider myself absolved of any duty towards you. You have made it clear to me that we are not friends and have never been, and that you do not possess even a shred of Christian kindness for someone who has done so much for you.

I will not visit you again. I will not enquire after you. I will, in short, have nothing more to do with you.

My hurt is joined by my anger at your callous treatment of me, and though it is not a Christian feeling, I cannot bring myself to think of you with anything but disappointment and, yes, even contempt.

May God forgive you for I cannot.

Stephen Pettifer, in sadness.

Matthew read the letter three times before putting all the pieces in the back of his notebook for safekeeping, taking out the photographs he had cut out of *The Chronicle* of the kitchen. He studied the picture, then compared it to the kitchen. It all looked the same.

Matthew frowned at the photograph as something caught his eye. One of the shelves looked as if something was missing from it. There was a gap between two tins when the rest of the shelf was stuffed. He went over to the shelf and saw there was a mark where something had stood. Had Teddy Welch taken something? he wondered. Matthew put the photograph back in his notebook and left the farmhouse to make his way to the rectory.

Matthew knocked on the rectory door, bouncing on the balls of his feet while he waited for it to be answered. He waited for perhaps a minute and knocked again. More time passed and still no response.

He stepped back and looked up at the windows. No curtains had been drawn, but no lights were on either.

'You looking for Father Pettifer?' a voice called.

Matthew looked up. A man was looking out at him from an upstairs window next door. 'Yes,' he replied. 'Is he in?'

'I saw him go out about an hour ago,' the man said. 'Don't know where. Can I help?'

Matthew held up his warrant card. 'Inspector Stannard, Craynebrook CID.'

A female head joined the other at the window. 'Oh, it's you again,' Mrs Gould said. 'It's the inspector I told you about, Bill.'

'Any idea when Father Pettifer will be back?' Matthew called up.

'No,' she said. 'But he's never long. Do you want to come in and wait?'

'That's very kind of you.'

'Wait there a mo.' Her head disappeared.

'She's coming down,' the man said and disappeared, too.

A moment later, their front door opened, and Mrs Gould waved Matthew inside. 'Go into the front room. Would you like tea?'

'If it's not too much trouble,' Matthew said, taking a seat on the squishy settee.

'It's no trouble at all,' she said and went out.

The man came in, hand held out. 'Bill Gould. You're that detective who's been in the 'paper?'

'That's me,' Matthew nodded.

'Is it the murder you want to see the vicar about?'

'Yes, it is.'

Mrs Gould came in with a tea tray and set it on the table. 'That was quick,' Matthew said, eyeing the shortbread biscuits hungrily.

'Lil always has a kettle on the boil,' Gould said proudly. 'He's here to talk to the vicar about the murder, Lil.' He raised his eyebrows at her as they both sat down.

'Did he have something to do with it?' Mrs Gould asked in a hushed voice as she handed Matthew a cup and saucer.

Matthew's curiosity was piqued. 'Why do you ask that?'

Mrs Gould glanced at her husband. 'Best tell him, love,' he urged.

'I'm not sure I should,' she said, offering Matthew a biscuit.

He took one. 'Tell me what, Mrs Gould?'

'It may be nothing.' Another glance at her husband, who nodded at her to continue. 'Well, it's just that he's been having money problems. I know because I've seen the Final Demand letters on his desk and heard the telephone calls. I weren't listening deliberately, I'll have you know.'

'I'm sure you weren't,' Matthew shook his head understandingly. 'Father Pettifer is being chased by creditors, is he?'

'People have been on at him for money. His sister, she lives up in the Cotswolds, I think, in a family cottage, but it's mortgaged from what I gather, and Father Pettifer's behind on the mortgage payments. And he hasn't paid me for weeks.'

'Tell him the rest, Lil,' Gould urged, prodding her elbow.

'But he's got money,' she burst out. 'I found a tin rammed full of bank notes when I was cleaning the other day, hidden under his study settee.' She crossed her arms in a huff. 'All that making out he didn't have it and us going short and worrying his sister like that. It isn't right.'

'And him a man of the cloth,' Gould shook his head at Matthew.

'You say the tin was hidden?' Matthew asked.

She nodded. 'If I hadn't shoved the broom under the settee, I would never have found it.'

'And tell him the other, love,' Gould said, jerking his head at Matthew.

Mrs Gould heaved a sigh. 'He was drinking the other night. He slept in his clothes in his study.'

'We supposed he passed out in there,' Gould said. 'I mean, him drinking so much he passes out. That ain't right for a vicar, is it?'

'I would never have believed it of him. I said to you, didn't I, Bill? I'd never have guessed he was a drinker.'

'You did,' Gould confirmed.

'You've never known him to be drunk before?' Matthew asked.

'I've never seen him touch the stuff,' Mrs Gould said. 'But it just goes to show, don't it? You never can tell.'

'What night was this?'

'It was the Sunday night. You came round the next morning and I had to get him out of his bedroom to talk to you.'

'I remember,' Matthew nodded, thinking back to his first meeting with Pettifer. The vicar had looked rough that morning, but he had put it down to him simply being old and weary, not that he had been hungover. 'And that's the first time you've ever known him to drink?'

They both nodded, then looked towards the window as there came the sound of a front door shutting with a bang.

'He's back,' Gould said.

Matthew drained his teacup, set it down on the table, and rose. 'You've been very helpful. Thank you.'

Mrs Gould followed Matthew out into the hall. 'You're not going to tell him what we've said, are you? Only I don't want any trouble.'

'Don't worry, Mrs Gould,' he said with a smile. 'I won't say a word.'

Matthew banged once more on the rectory front door and this time it was opened almost immediately.

Pettifer frowned at Matthew. 'Inspector?'

'I'd like a word with you, please, Father.'

'Could it not wait until tomorrow? It's been a busy morning, and I'd rather like my lunch—'

'I'm afraid it can't wait.'

'Oh, very well. Come in.' Pettifer gestured Matthew into the sitting room. 'I'd appreciate it if you could be brief.'

'I've been over at the farmhouse.' Matthew took out the ripped letter. 'And I found this.'

Pettifer's face paled as Matthew put the two halves together and showed him the front with his own writing upon it. 'That was a private letter, inspector. You have no right—'

'I have every right, Father,' Matthew interrupted. 'I'm conducting a murder investigation and nothing is private. Do you remember what you wrote?'

'Yes, I do.'

'Then can you explain what it refers to? What was the favour you asked of Mr Clough?'

Pettifer sat down in the armchair. 'I'd prefer not to say.'

'And I need an answer.'

'It has no bearing on the murder.'

'That's for me to determine. What was the favour?'

Pettifer's lips pursed, and he drummed his fingers on the arm of the chair.

'I've been told you were drinking on Sunday night,' Matthew said. 'The night Mr Clough was murdered. I've also been told that was an unusual thing for you to do. So, what led you to drink, Father?'

'This is intolerable.' Pettifer jumped up from the armchair. 'I will not stand here and have you question me like this. Please leave me alone.'

'Are you refusing to answer my questions?'

'I most certainly am.'

'Then I have no choice but to arrest you.'

Pettifer's mouth fell open. 'You can't do that.'

‘I can, and I will, unless you start cooperating.’

‘You are prying into my private affairs. I have every right to refuse to answer your unnecessary questions.’

‘Then, Father Pettifer, I’m arresting you on suspicion of murder.’

Chapter Twenty-Six

Matthew watched the police car drive off, taking Pettifer to the station. He had decided to remain behind to search the rectory. After Pinder's balls-up, Matthew wasn't inclined to trust it to anyone else. He found the OXO tin in the bookcase in Pettifer's study. The rolls of money Mrs Gould had spoken of were still inside. He also found a pair of black brogues with a dark stain on one of the soles. It looked like blood to Matthew.

He returned to the farmhouse and put the OXO tin in the gap on Clough's kitchen shelf. It fitted exactly. So did the shoe, the bloody footprint matching the outline of Pettifer's footwear. There was no doubt in Matthew's mind. Pettifer had been in the farmhouse after Clough had been shot. Had he also been there when Clough was murdered?

Matthew walked back to the station and into CID. He'd barely got through the door when Denham and Barnes rushed towards him.

'We may have something, sir,' Denham said. 'We were over at The King George for lunch. The landlord told us there had been a red-haired man in the pub that he hadn't liked the look of and who had trodden manure into the carpet.'

'When was this?' Matthew asked.

'The night of Tuesday the thirteenth. Mrs Askey said a red-haired man had gone down to the farm, if you remember.'

'The landlord didn't know this man?'

Barnes shook his head. 'He'd never seen him before and he didn't think he looked like he came from Craynebrook. He was rough-looking. Had a big scar on his chin and was built like a brick you-know-what.'

Matthew considered. 'Tuesday night. That's six days before Clough was killed. That fits the timeframe for the bruises he had on his body.'

'You mean this red-haired man could have been the one who beat Clough up? Then he went back on the Sunday and killed him?'

'Hold your horses, Barnes,' Matthew said. 'I've just arrested Father Pettifer on suspicion of murder.'

'The vicar?' Barnes cried.

Matthew nodded. 'I found a letter at the farm from Pettifer to Clough severing all ties with him because Clough had refused to do him a favour he'd asked. And his housekeeper says he was drunk on Sunday night and that was unusual. You know as well as I do that any unusual behaviour in a murder investigation is suspicious.' He told them about the OXO tin and shoes.

'So,' Denham's brow creased, 'he had a row with Clough, shot him and then killed him?'

'That I don't know,' Matthew said, and remembered the bullet in his pocket. He pulled it out and handed it to Barnes. 'I found that embedded in the hall just outside the kitchen door. I need you to get that to the lab. Find out what gun it came from.'

Denham was frowning. 'I thought Pinder searched the farmhouse. Why didn't he find the letter or the bullet?'

'That's a bloody good question, Denham,' Matthew agreed. 'Where is Pinder?'

'We left him at the pub, sir,' Barnes said, glancing warily at Denham. 'He's got another twenty minutes left on his lunch.'

Matthew nodded, not entirely sorry the detective constable was absent. He wasn't in the mood to deliver a reprimand. 'I want you in with me when we interview Pettifer, Denham.'

'Of course, sir.'

'What about the red-haired man, sir?' Barnes asked.

Matthew sighed, rubbing his forehead. 'Leave him for the moment. If Pettifer is the killer, it won't really matter who beat Clough up.'

'It's still a crime, sir,' Barnes said. He reddened as Matthew shot him a stern look. 'Sorry, sir. Not for me to say.'

'No, you're quite right, Barnes,' Matthew acknowledged. 'Look into it.'

'Yes, sir. Thank you, sir.' He turned as the CID door opened and Mullinger stormed in. Barnes and Denham stepped away, not wanting to be noticed.

'Is this right you've arrested a vicar, Stannard?' Mullinger demanded.

'Yes, sir,' Matthew said. 'I had no choice but to arrest him. I have reason to believe he's connected with the murder and he refused to answer my questions.'

'A vicar involved? I find that very hard to believe. Didn't you have him identify the body?'

'Yes, I did,' Matthew admitted.

'Well, why the devil did you allow that if you had your suspicions about him?'

'I didn't have any suspicions at the time, sir. New evidence has come to light only today.'

'What new evidence?'

'A very angry letter torn up and in the bin, written by Father Pettifer to Clough regarding a falling out they'd had, and a bullet found in the farmhouse's wall.'

'Both found at the farmhouse? But I thought the place had been searched on Monday? Why weren't they found then before you arranged the identification?'

'They were missed, sir,' Matthew said.

'Missed? How did you manage to miss them?'

'It wasn't Inspector Stannard's fault, sir,' Barnes interjected.

'Barnes!' Matthew said sharply and shook his head for the young man to keep quiet.

Mullinger glared at Barnes. 'It is an inspector's responsibility. As you will discover, should you ever reach the rank of inspector, Barnes.' He sniffed and turned to Matthew. 'Pettifer contacted the diocese when you brought him in and I've already had the bishop on the telephone. He is deeply concerned about Pettifer and has engaged a solicitor to sit in on your interview. I hope I need not tell you to ensure your conduct is above reproach.'

'No, sir,' Matthew said stiffly. 'You don't.'

'I'm very glad to hear it. I want to be kept fully updated regarding this vicar, Stannard. And pull your socks up, for God's sake.' Mullinger turned on his heel and strode out of CID.

'All right, Denham,' Matthew said, noticing the two younger detectives exchanging angry glances. 'Let's go and talk to the vicar.'

'Mr Palmer,' Matthew nodded to the solicitor sitting beside Pettifer in the interview room.

'It's good to see you again, inspector,' Joseph Palmer said.

'You've had time to talk to your client, I trust?'

'A very short time, but yes, I believe we've conferred all we need to.' Palmer glanced at Pettifer, who was sitting quietly, his chin upon his chest. 'Father Pettifer would like me to speak for him at this time.'

Matthew frowned. 'I'm not sure that's going to be possible. I have questions for him—'

'Yes,' Palmer held out a hand, 'I understand, but he would like me to tell you what happened on the night in question. It's not a confession,' he said as Matthew's eyebrows rose.

'Very well,' Matthew nodded. 'Please go on.'

Palmer pulled out a sheet of paper from a file before him on the table. 'Father Pettifer has been suffering from financial difficulties of late. He asked Josiah Clough to loan him some money. Mr Clough refused to help, which prompted the letter you found. The letter was written in a moment of great distress and on the spur of the moment.'

'That's not how it reads,' Matthew said. 'I believe it reads as if Father Pettifer gave his words a great deal of thought.'

'Nevertheless,' Palmer went on. 'He regrets the writing of the letter.'

'Especially as it gives him a motive for murder,' Denham said wryly.

Pettifer's eyes widened at this remark, his mouth formed an O, but he said nothing.

Palmer cleared his throat. 'My client once had a problem with alcohol. For many years, however, he hadn't touched a drink. But earlier that day, he had been given a bottle of whisky by a grateful parishioner and the stress he was under led him to take a drink and to continue drinking into the night. Not having been exposed to alcohol for many years, he quickly became intoxicated and rendered incapable. He, therefore, was not in a position to kill Mr Clough as you seem to think.' Palmer looked up from the paper. 'That is all my client has authorised me to say on his behalf, inspector.'

'I thank your client for his clarification,' Matthew said. 'However, I've searched the rectory.' He nodded at Denham, who reached beneath the table and lifted the pair of black shoes onto it. 'I found these.' Matthew turned the right shoe over to show the underside.

'You can see a stain on the sole. We'll need the lab to confirm it but I reckon that's blood.' Denham put the OXO tin next to the shoes. 'I also found this. It's filled with banknotes. They belonged to Mr Clough. I found the spot on his shelf where that tin used to sit.'

Pettifer stared at the shoes and the tin.

'How did the tin come into your possession, Father?' Matthew asked. 'How did blood get on your shoe?'

The vicar's chin wobbled. 'I do remember going to the farm-house that night,' he said, his voice barely above a whisper. 'I was going to tell him what I thought of him. The letter I'd written hadn't got all my anger towards him out of my system. But I didn't see Josiah. I know that. I went into the kitchen and I called to him, but I didn't get any answer. I saw the tin on the shelf. I knew there was money inside and I took it.' He closed his eyes. 'I must have been mad. I took it and I went home. I don't remember anything after that.'

He suddenly burst out crying, burying his face in his hands, and the other three men looked at each other in embarrassment.

'I think you ought to let my client rest, inspector,' Palmer said quietly. 'That is, if you intend to continue holding him?'

'Father Pettifer will remain in custody until he's in a fit state to resume the interview and while we make further enquiries,' Matthew said and gathered up his papers.

'What do you think, sir?' Denham asked as he and Matthew returned to CID. 'Did he do it?'

'I'm not sure,' Matthew said. 'The evidence is quite damning, but he doesn't seem the type.'

Denham deposited the shoes and OXO tin in an evidence box. 'I agree. An old man like him. You'd think Clough wouldn't have had any trouble defending himself against him.'

'Unless Clough was already wounded,' Matthew suggested. 'I want you to go through Pettifer's financial records. I didn't have time when I was there. Find out exactly how much money he owes and to whom. It may not have any bearing on the murder, but it would be good to know.'

'Right away, sir,' Denham said.

'And send Pinder in to me,' Matthew said, lighting a cigarette. He fell down into his chair and closed his eyes. Christ, he was tired.

'You wanted to see me, sir?'

Pinder was standing by his desk when Matthew opened his eyes. 'You searched the farmhouse on Monday.'

'Yes, sir.'

'You carried out a thorough search?'

'Yes, sir.'

'Then how did you come to miss the bullet lodged in the hall wall?'

Pinder frowned. 'I didn't see any bullet, sir.'

'What about the blood-soaked cotton wool in the bin under the sink? Or Father Pettifer's letter thrown away in there? There was no mention of those in your report.'

'I didn't see any bin, sir.'

'You said you did a thorough search.'

Pinder swallowed uneasily. 'I wasn't told to look out for any bullet, sir, or a letter.'

'You have to be told what to look for?' Matthew cried incredulously. 'A search is exactly that, Pinder. You search for anything that looks out of place or which could be relevant. You're trained to use your eyes and decide what looks unusual. You're trained to find evidence, for Christ's sake.'

'I thought I did that, sir.'

'You did nothing like that. Did you even bother to search at all or did you just wander through the house having a fag?'

'I searched, sir,' Pinder insisted.

Matthew glared up at him, his right hand clenching into a fist beneath the desk. 'You're on report, Pinder. Now, get back to work.'

Pinder went out, and Matthew heard him kick his chair around before falling into it. He reached into his desk drawer and took out the aspirin bottle. There was only one tablet left, and he swallowed it dry, tossing the empty bottle into his waste bin. He must remember to get some more, he told himself as he checked his watch. Half-past three. Visiting time at the hospital was four o'clock.

Matthew snatched his hat from off the stand and strode out of CID.

Sam Rudd lifted out the dry, withered flowers from the metal vase and threw them on the grass beside the gravestone. He turned the vase upside down, tipping out the filthy, smelly rainwater, and took it over to the standing pipe to refill it.

Putting the vase back in its place on the plinth, he filled it with the lilies that were already wilting and which he'd bought from the florist just inside the cemetery gates. He would have preferred to get a cheaper bunch from the flower stall in the market, but he hadn't had the time.

Sam stood back and surveyed the gravestone. Bird mess splattered the top of it and lichen was growing in the etched inscription. 'Sorry, Mum,' he murmured. 'I forgot to bring a cloth with me.'

He sighed, wishing his mother was still with him. Sam didn't have anyone he could talk to anymore. His older brother wasn't interested in him, caught up with problems of his own, and his father wasn't the listening type. It was no good telling his father how much he wanted to be a detective and how unfair it was that he wasn't being given the chance to prove himself. Sam knew if he tried to tell him how frustrated he felt, his father would tell him to stop whining and be grateful he had a job at all.

Sam closed his eyes and said a prayer for his mother, pressing two fingers to his lips, then tapping them on the gravestone. 'Bye for now, Mum,' he said, and turned away, heading for the way out.

His way out took him past a plot of land that bore the mounds of newly dug graves, and he glanced at the man standing beside one of them. As he watched, the man took off his flat cap and laid it against his breast, his lips moving as though he was talking. Sam looked away, not wanting to be nosy and spy on such a private moment.

Sam took a few more steps, then frowned and looked back. He watched as the man flipped his cap back onto his white-blond hair. He stared harder, then fumbled for his notebook that he always kept on him and flipped to the back, taking out a newspaper clipping showing Wilfred Gadd's mugshot.

His heart beat faster. It was him. Sam was sure. The man every copper in London was on the lookout for and he had found him. He could take him in. Even Old Mouldy would have to be impressed by that.

Sam put his notebook away and took a step towards Wilf. Then he stopped. He couldn't arrest Gadd while he was standing by his mother's grave. That wasn't right. He'd wait and follow him out. Then, when they were near the exit, he would arrest him. It would be better like that, anyway. The guard on the gate would be there to give him a hand and there would be a telephone in the gatehouse so he could call the station to come and get them.

He didn't have long to wait. Wilf stood over the grave for a few more minutes, then walked away, hands sunk deep in his pockets. Sam followed at a discreet distance, never losing sight of him. As the exit came into view, Sam's mouth became dry in anticipation of what he had to do. He quickly shortened the distance between him and Wilf, and when Wilf was only a few strides away from the gate, Sam ran towards him and laid a hand on his shoulder.

'I've got you, Gadd,' Sam said. 'You're under arrest—'

Wilf grabbed Sam's hand and crushed his fingers. Sam cried out in pain. Wilf brought his right arm up and landed a fist in his face. He stumbled away but managed to stay on his feet. His cheek was throbbing, and his first instinct was to put his palm to it, but he overrode that instinct, reaching out to grab Wilf's sleeve. His fingers locked around Wilf's wrist, and he tugged, but Wilf wasn't giving in. He struggled with Sam, kicking out, trying to knock his feet out from under him. He twisted his arm, forcing Sam to let go, and the next minute, Wilf had Sam in a bear hug, squeezing the breath out of him.

Out of the corner of his eye, Sam saw the gatekeeper standing in the stone doorway of the gatehouse, horror-struck by the sight before him.

'Help me,' Sam cried, but the gatekeeper didn't move.

Wilf squeezed even harder and the weight of his body forced Sam to his knees. Once he was down, Wilf took full advantage, shoving his face into the ground, then moving to kick him again and again. Sam tried to curl himself into a ball to protect himself, just wishing now Wilf would take his chance and run away. But Wilf continued to deliver blow after blow to Sam's vulnerable body.

Then Wilf's boot kicked him in the back of the head and Sam's world went mercifully dark.

Dickie was sitting up in bed when Matthew arrived.

'You're looking better,' Matthew said, pulling a chair up to the bed. 'Sorry I couldn't come yesterday.'

Dickie shook his head. 'I said you didn't have to. I know you've been busy?' Dickie reached to the bedside cabinet and held up *The Chronicle*. 'You got the boys who killed Clough?'

Matthew shook his head. 'That's out of date. I had to let them go. They didn't do it. All they did was unlock the cowshed door and leave the farm gate open so the cows would get out. They were getting back at Clough because he caught them trying to steal his beer and he shot one of them in the arm. A schoolboy prank, that was all.'

'So, you're no further along?'

'Actually, I've got another suspect in custody.'

'And who's that?'

'You know I can't tell you, Dickie.'

'Matthew,' Dickie cried in exasperation, 'who the hell am I going to tell, stuck in here?'

Matthew tugged at his earlobe and nodded. 'A vicar.'

'Not Father Pettifer?'

'You know him?'

'I've spoken with him plenty of times.' Dickie frowned at Matthew. 'Pettifer, a vicious killer? Are you sure?'

'Why is it so impossible to believe a man of the cloth can kill?' Matthew asked, irritated. 'No one is beyond killing, Dickie, given the right circumstances.'

'And what were his circumstances?'

'He desperately needed money and Clough had turned him down when he asked for a loan. He was under stress, feeling aggrieved, got very drunk and then…' He shrugged.

'And then?' Dickie pressed.

'He claims he didn't kill him, but we've got good evidence against him.'

'Well, I suppose you know what you're doing,' Dickie said doubtfully. 'But I am surprised.'

A nurse came over and offered tea to Dickie and Matthew. Dickie accepted for them both. Before she could go, Matthew turned to her.

'You don't have any aspirin you can let me have, do you?' he asked.

'We're not supposed to dispense any medicine without a doctor's approval.'

'Not even an aspirin? I can buy it at a chemist easily enough.'

The nurse shook her head. 'It's the rules, I'm afraid. I'll bring your tea.'

'Still suffering?' Dickie asked when she'd gone.

'Just this bloody headache,' Matthew said, rubbing at his left temple. 'I can't seem to shift it.'

'Any news on Gadd?'

'Nothing, so far as I've heard.'

'And how are you getting on at your sister's?'

'All right. Mum's getting a bit clingy, but that's nothing new. She was on at me the other night to get a flat near the pub. Can you imagine? She'd expect me for dinner every evening,' Matthew smiled. 'I know she means well. They all do.'

'But you'll be glad when Gadd's caught, all the same,' Dickie said understandingly.

'I miss my own place,' Matthew nodded.

'Well, hopefully it won't be too much longer before you can go back. Ah. There's Emma.'

Emma had entered the ward carrying a string shopping bag. She looked a little flustered. 'The bus was late,' she explained. 'Otherwise, I'd have been here ten minutes ago.'

'It's all right. Matthew's been keeping me company.'

'Mr Stannard,' Emma nodded.

'Mrs Waite,' Matthew returned and rose. 'I should—'

'No, don't go,' Dickie halted him. 'You haven't had your tea yet.'

'I don't want to intrude. I'm sure Mrs Waite would like you all to yourself.'

'Don't be daft,' Emma said. 'We've been married too long for that. And I know Dickie enjoys talking to you. You stay where you are.'

Matthew resumed his seat as the nurse brought over a tray with three cups and saucers of tea. 'I saw you arrive,' she said to Emma, explaining the extra teacup.

'You are a dear,' Emma said, taking a sip. 'Oh, I needed that.'

'One for you,' the nurse said, smiling at Matthew as she handed him a cup and saucer. 'And here.' She pushed two aspirin tablets into his hand. 'Just don't tell Matron.' Giving him a conspiratorial wink, she walked away.

Matthew stared at the aspirin, then felt Dickie's eyes upon him. He looked up to see his friend grinning.

'How do you do it?' Dickie asked in admiration.

The bell rang, signalling the end of the visiting hour, and Matthew rose. 'I better get back to the station,' he said, knowing Dickie and Emma should be allowed to say goodbye in private. 'I won't say I'll be in again tomorrow, just in case.'

'When you can,' Dickie said, raising a hand in farewell.

Matthew made his way out of the ward, seeing the nurse who had given him the aspirin hurrying towards him.

'I'm glad I caught you,' she said. 'I thought you'd want to know. I just heard a young man has been admitted to the hospital. He's been pretty badly beaten up. But apparently, he's a policeman. I thought he might be a friend of yours.'

'What's his name?' Matthew asked.

'Samuel Rudd. Do you know him?'

'Yes, I know him. Where is he?'

'Come with me.' She took him to where Rudd had been taken and pointed out the bed. 'You can stay only a few minutes,' she said and left him.

Matthew looked down at Rudd. His nose had been broken, and the top half of his face was one large bruise. A bandage had been wrapped around his head and Matthew could make out the edge of a red stain around the back. Two fingers on his left hand were also bandaged. He could only imagine what other injuries lay beneath the blankets. Rudd's eyes were closed, and Matthew wasn't sure whether he was asleep or unconscious. He got an answer a few moments later when Rudd's eyes fluttered open.

'Sir?' he croaked.

'Yes, Rudd,' Matthew said. 'I just heard what had happened. Who did this?'

'It was Gadd, sir. I saw him at the cemetery and tried to arrest him.'

'On your own?'

'I thought I could take him. But he was like a mad thing. I couldn't hold him. I'm sorry.'

'You were brave to even try.' Matthew actually thought the boy had been reckless, but Rudd didn't need to hear that.

Rudd's face crumpled a little. 'It won't look good on my record, though, will it? Mr Mullinger was here. He said I should have called it in and let Uniform arrest him.'

Matthew mentally cursed Mullinger; Rudd needed consolation, not criticism. 'Forget what he said, Rudd. There'll be nothing bad on your record. You're not to worry about anything. That's an order. You just rest. Is there anything you need?'

'Can you let my dad know I'm in here? I didn't want to ask Mr Mullinger.'

Mullinger should have thought of it himself, Matthew thought bitterly. 'I'll see to it,' he promised. Rudd was struggling to keep his eyes open. 'Get some sleep.'

Rudd's eyes had closed as soon as he finished his sentence and he left the ward. As he approached the entrance doors of the hospital, he saw Teddy Welch hurrying towards him.

'Inspector,' the reporter called, raising an arm to attract Matthew's attention.

'I'm busy,' Matthew said, not stopping.

'I heard Wilfred Gadd's attacked another policeman. Is that right?'

'No comment.'

'If it is true, that proves Gadd is still local, doesn't it? So, why haven't the police been able to catch him?'

'It's not for want of trying, Mr Welch.'

'Doesn't it bother you that your inability to catch Gadd is putting the public in danger?'

'I said I have no comment.'

'My readers are going to want to know what the police are doing.'

Matthew came to an abrupt halt. 'Your readers? Don't you think you're getting a bit above yourself?'

Teddy grinned. 'I don't think so. It's my stories that have pushed the newspaper's circulation up, inspector.'

Matthew shook his head. 'Have you been to see Mr Waite?'

Teddy seemed taken aback by the question. 'No,' he said. 'I've been busy.'

'So am I, Mr Welch. Too busy to waste any more time with you.' Matthew walked away, leaving Teddy staring after him.

'Have you heard about Rudd, sir?' Barnes asked as Matthew walked into CID.

'I've seen him,' Matthew said grimly. 'I was already at the hospital.'

'Are you not feeling well, sir?'

'I was visiting someone.'

'How is Sam?' Denham asked.

Matthew shook his head. 'Gadd beat him up pretty bad. Worse than he did to me.'

'Gadd must be a right nutter,' Barnes said angrily. 'Why the hell can't we find him?'

'Look,' Matthew said, understanding the young detective's anger but keen to get back on track, 'I know what's happened to Rudd is upsetting, but we can't let it distract us from the murder enquiry. Has Pettifer calmed down yet?'

Denham shook his head. 'His solicitor says he's still not fit to be questioned. He wants a doctor called.'

'Get him one,' Matthew said.

'But, sir,' Denham protested. 'He's just putting it on—'

'I'm not taking any chances, Denham. Not again. Get a doctor to look him over.' He turned to Barnes. 'Have you got anywhere with this red-haired man?'

Barnes brightened up. 'I think so, sir. Graydon Heath reckon he's a David Cotton. Apparently, Cotton's got a charge sheet as long as my arm. Petty theft, shoplifting. But he's also been done for illegal gambling and bare knuckle boxing, and they say he's very ready to use his fists. They're sending over a copy of his record.'

Matthew nodded and checked his wristwatch. 'I don't suppose there's anything more to be done tonight. After the doctor has seen Pettifer, Denham, put him in a cell. We'll talk to him again in the morning.'

'I don't think Mr Mullinger will like us keeping a vicar in a cell, sir,' Denham said carefully.

'I don't give a damn whether he likes it or not,' Matthew said sourly, ignoring Pinder as he came in, munching on a packet of biscuits. 'If you need me, I'll be at home.'

Chapter Twenty-Seven

Duggan rapped on the door and waved at Richard through the glass. Richard glanced at Roger sitting at the opposite desk.

'Let him in,' Roger said, and returned his gaze to his paperwork.

Richard rose and unlocked the door. Duggan smiled and stepped inside.

'I thought you might still be here,' he said, nodding awkwardly at Roger. 'It's been a while since we spoke, so I thought I'd pop over. See if you've settled in yet.'

'We're fine,' Richard said.

'Good, good.' Duggan swallowed and licked his dry lips. 'You heard the news? About the farmer, I mean?'

'Of course we heard,' Roger said, staring at him coolly across the office.

'Yes, of course you did. Silly me. But I thought it might mean good news for you. The farm will have to be sold now as there isn't any family to take it over. So, it's all worked out all right, in the end, hasn't it?'

'Is that what you think?' Roger said, glaring at him. 'It's nothing of the sort.'

'I don't underst—' Duggan tugged uneasily at his collar.

'There'll be a long delay,' Roger cut him off. 'A murder investigation is bound to hold up the sale. And if there's no family, the farm will go to the Crown and then it will be put up for auction. If we still want it, we'll have to compete with other developers. So, how is that good news?'

'Ah, I hadn't thought of all that.'

'But whatever happens, whether we get it in the end or not, there'll be no commission for you.'

'Oh no,' Duggan waved his hand, 'of course not. No, no, wouldn't expect it after all that's happened. But, er, in the future…?' He looked appealingly at Richard.

Richard glanced at Roger, who nodded almost imperceptibly. 'There may be other deals,' he said. 'But it would all depend.'

'On what?' Duggan hardly dared to ask.

'On how discreet you prove. You see, you arranged that beating up all on your own, didn't you? We wouldn't have agreed to that if you'd let us know that's what you were planning. But you see, if it comes out, if the police were to come calling on you, we wouldn't be pleased if you mentioned us.'

'Oh, there's no question of—'

'We don't want the police knocking on our door, wondering how involved we were.'

'I wouldn't, Richard,' Duggan said solemnly, putting his hand on his heart. 'I'm not expecting the police to find me — my man is as discreet as I am — but if they do, then, of course, my lips are sealed.' He turned to Roger. 'Not a word, I swear it.'

Satisfied, Roger rose from behind his desk and put his hands in his trouser pockets, a signal he wasn't about to offer Alfred his hand. 'Well, then, I daresay we can do business in the future, should the opportunity arise.'

'Excellent,' Duggan breathed again. 'Well, I shan't bother you any longer. I'm sure you're very busy.' He reached for the door and yanked it open. 'Good to see you both. Good evening.' He hurried away.

Richard watched him through the glass, then locked the door again. 'Was it enough, do you think?'

'To keep his mouth shut?' Roger said, joining his brother at the door and looking out. 'I should think so. He's a weasel.'

'I'm still worried.'

Roger shook his head. 'They've got those boys for it, Rich.'

'But what if—'

Roger grabbed his shoulders and turned Richard to face him. 'We deny everything. If it comes to it, you leave it to me.'

Richard sighed. 'Like always?'

Roger nodded. 'Like always.'

Edwards leaned over Teddy's typewriter, peering at what the young reporter had just written. 'Where are you getting all this?' he asked, incredulous.

Teddy chuckled. 'I've got an inside man, boss.'

'I worked that out. Who is it?'

'Did Mr Waite tell you who his sources were?'

Edwards grunted and sat down in Dickie's chair. He waved at the typewriter. 'You can prove all this, can't you?'

Teddy whirled on his chair to face the editor. 'The circulation's up, isn't it? The proprietor's pleased?'

'He's over the moon,' Edwards nodded ruefully. 'But we got letters about your pictures. There were plenty of readers who thought we'd gone too far printing them.'

'You don't want to pay any attention to those,' Teddy said, making a face. 'They're just people who have nothing better to do.'

'The pictures were grim.'

'You approved them,' Teddy reminded him.

Edwards grunted again. 'You didn't answer me. Have you got proof this is all true?'

'Proof is for the police. It's our job to get the story out. That's all our readers need from us.'

'You're sure they've arrested the vicar?'

'He's spending tonight in a police cell, boss.'

Edwards ran a hand over his bald head. 'I can hardly believe it. We got any pictures of him?'

'I found this one from when Dickie did a feature on him the other month.' Teddy showed him a slightly blurry image of Pettifer taken outside the church. 'It's a lousy pic. I expect Dickie took it. But it will have to do.'

Edwards frowned at Teddy's lack of respect, saying 'Dickie' instead of 'Mr Waite'. 'What about this copper beaten up by Gadd? Mullinger's been on the blower. Apparently, the police are offering a reward for information about Gadd now.'

'I was going to make it a separate article. Just a couple of paragraphs. If it had been Stannard who got beaten up again, I'd say we should make it the main feature, but it was only a constable no one's heard of, so there's no point. And I couldn't get any pictures of him in the hospital. A nurse threw me out.'

Good for her, Edwards thought. 'Did you see Dickie when you were there?'

Teddy had begun battering away at his typewriter, and he tutted at the interruption. 'Visiting hour was over by then. Anyway, he doesn't want to see me.'

'It's nice to have visitors when you're in hospital. And don't you think you owe him, Teddy?'

'Owe him what?'

'He's been teaching you ever since you started here,' Edwards cried. 'The trouble he's taken over you, the least you can do is pop by and see how he's doing.'

Teddy sighed, a bitter turn to his lips. 'He hasn't been teaching me. Dickie's held me back. Do this, do that, don't do this.' He shook his head. 'Best thing that could have happened to me was him being laid up. What?' he demanded as Edwards stared at him. 'It's true, and you know it.'

Edwards rose and shoved the chair in beneath the desk angrily. 'Time I was getting home to the missus.' He jabbed a finger at Teddy's copy. 'Make sure that goes to the press in plenty of time for the morning edition.'

'Don't you worry. It'll be there,' Teddy said, not looking up from his typewriter as Edwards stormed out of the office.

Chapter Twenty-Eight

Matthew was pacing up and down outside Mullinger's office. As soon as he'd stepped foot inside the station, he'd been told the superintendent wanted to see him and now he was being kept waiting while he finished his telephone call.

'I'm sure he won't be long, inspector,' Miss Halliwell said soothingly. 'Are you feeling better now?'

'Yes, thank you.'

'Because if there's anything I can do—'

She broke off as the door opened. 'Stannard,' Mullinger barked. 'Come in.'

Matthew stepped inside and closed the door. Mullinger didn't invite him to take a seat but strode over to his desk and threw a newspaper at him. It struck Matthew in the stomach and he only just caught it.

'We have a leak, Stannard,' Mullinger said as Matthew cast his eyes over *The Chronicle*'s front page. 'The public now knows you released those schoolboys and that we have the vicar in custody. I've just had the bishop shouting down the telephone at me. Actually shouting.' He banged the desktop. 'Who is it, Stannard?'

'I don't know, sir,' Matthew said, folding the newspaper and putting it on the desk.

'Why don't you know? You're supposed to know. What kind of investigation are you running?'

'Sir, I—'

'I don't want to hear any excuses,' Mullinger waved him silent. 'I want this leak found and dealt with. Is that clear?'

'Exactly when am I supposed to have the time to find the leak, sir?' Matthew snapped. 'I do have a murderer to catch.'

Mullinger glared at him. 'If you can't handle it, inspector, I can easily find someone who can. Is that what I should do?'

'No, sir,' Matthew said, swallowing down his anger. Had Mullinger forgotten he was supposed to be on light duties? 'I'll find out who it is.'

'I should think so.' Mullinger sat down heavily in his chair. 'And as for this murderer? The vicar?'

'The evidence points that way. I had to end the interview yesterday because he was feeling unwell.'

'I don't like it. The bishop feels it's highly unlikely Father Pettifer is involved.'

'With all due respect, sir, the bishop doesn't know what we know.'

'Were the vicar's fingerprints on the murder weapon?'

'No.'

'And this vicar is quite frail. He's in his seventies, isn't he?'

'I believe so.'

'Then is it likely he would have had the strength to kill this farmer? The farmer was in his late fifties and in robust health. An outdoors man. He would have been more than a match for an aged vicar, wounded or not.'

'That's true,' Matthew admitted. It had been bothering him, too.

'In that case, it will be better to err on the side of caution and release him.'

'I don't think that would be wise, sir. As I said, the evidence against him is strong. He has blood on his shoes and money that belonged to Clough.'

'I've read your report,' Mullinger said, referring to a file on his blotter. 'Your evidence points to him having been in Clough's kitchen and nowhere else. Clough was killed outside the farmhouse. Can you put this vicar at the actual scene of the murder?'

'No, but—'

'Or that he owns a gun?'

'No, sir.'

'So, he didn't shoot Clough?'

'I have no evidence for that as yet, sir, but—'

'Then release him. That's an order, Stannard. I won't have the Press claiming Craynebrook Police are hounding a vicar when there are far more likely candidates for you to investigate.' He tapped the report. 'Find this red-haired man. I'm sure you'll find he's your killer.'

Barnes looked around the office and leaned in closer to Denham. 'Who do you reckon it is?'

'Who do you think?' Denham glanced at Pinder's desk.

'Really?' Barnes's eyes widened.

Denham shrugged. 'Gary's always got more money than he should have. And he's got a big mouth.'

'But he wouldn't give all this information away, would he?' He pointed at Teddy's article.

'I don't think there's anything Gary wouldn't do, given half the chance.'

'Do you think the inspector suspects it's him?'

'I don't know.'

'Should we tell him?'

Denham shook his head. 'I'm staying out of it, and you should, too.'

'But what if Old Mouldy gets the idea it's one of us? I'm not going to take the blame for Gary.'

Denham put a finger to his lips as Pinder walked in.

'What are you two up to?' Pinder asked suspiciously, seeing them huddled together.

'Seen this?' Denham gave him the newspaper. 'Word is Old Mouldy's hitting the roof.'

'I saw it,' Pinder said, scanning the front page. 'Where do they get their information from, eh?' He handed the newspaper back to Denham. 'Where's the inspector?'

'Up with the Super,' Barnes said. 'We reckon he's giving him a hard time over this.'

Pinder fell down into his chair and put his feet up on the desk. 'I expect so,' he said with a smile.

Barnes's telephone rang. With a last glance at Denham, he picked it up. 'Craynebrook CID. DC Barnes speaking.'

'PS Baker here. Graydon Heath. I heard you were interested in David Cotton.'

'That's right. I haven't been able to get hold of him, though.'

'Then you're in luck. The night shift pulled him in for being drunk and disorderly. He's sitting in one of our cells as we speak.'

Pinder watched Matthew and Barnes leave the office, hearing their footsteps growing fainter. Denham had disappeared too and Pinder was all alone. No one to tell him what to do or have a go at him. He pulled open his top drawer and lifted his feet up onto it, leaning back in his chair and blowing the smoke from his cigarette up into the air to watch it collect around the yellowed lampshade.

His telephone rang. Tutting in annoyance, he snatched it up. 'What?' he barked.

'All right, all right,' Turkel said. 'You don't have to be like that.'

'What is it, sarge?'

'Is the inspector there?'

'He's gone out,' Pinder replied, and was about to hang up when Turkel said, 'Maybe you can help, Gary?'

'With what?'

'There's a lady in the waiting room asking to see him. Won't tell me what about, but I get the feeling she's going to be a pain if she doesn't see someone. So, do us a favour and talk to her, would you?'

Pinder sucked on his cigarette. 'What's she like?'

'Oh, she's nice,' Turkel said. 'Very classy. You'll like her.'

'I'll come down,' Pinder declared.

'I thought you might.' Turkel hung up.

Pinder ran a hand over his hair, adjusted his tie, and hurried down the stairs to the entrance lobby. He raised his eyebrows at Turkel standing behind the front desk, who smirked and nodded towards the door of the private waiting room. Pinder went in with a smile, which vanished when he saw the woman sitting at the table. She was nice, and classy, just like Turkel said, but though she was good-looking, she was a good-looking forty-something and far too old for Pinder's tastes. Turkel had been pulling his leg.

Her smile of similar expectation had also vanished when Pinder entered. 'You're not Inspector Stannard,' Hettie said, and he couldn't miss the note of disappointment in her voice.

'Inspector Stannard's out, madam,' he said, taking a seat. 'I'm DC Pinder. How can I help?'

'Oh,' Hettie sighed dramatically, 'I wanted to see Inspector Stannard. But if he's busy…' She gave Pinder a sideways look, then seemed to make up her mind and unclasped her handbag. He watched with reluctant interest as she drew out a rectangular cardboard box decorated with a ribbon. 'Would you see he gets this?'

Pinder took the box. 'What is it?'

She shrugged one shoulder coquettishly. 'Just a little something. Tell him I hope he likes it.' She snapped her handbag shut and rose.

'Is that all?' Pinder asked, twisting around in his seat as she opened the waiting room door.

Hettie smiled. 'Yes, that's all.'

'Who shall I say it's from?'

'Henrietta,' Hettie said, and Pinder realised this was the woman who had been writing to Matthew. 'I can rely on you to give it to him for me, can't I?'

'Yes, madam.'

'You're very sweet,' she said, and went out.

Pinder watched the door swing shut, then turned back to the table and pulled the ribbon off. Taking the lid off the box, he whistled when he saw what was inside. He took out the cigarette case, feeling the weight of it in his hand. Solid silver. It must have cost a fortune. He pressed the catch, and it opened to reveal a neat row of expensive-looking cigarettes.

Pinder turned to the door, stared at it for a few seconds, then returned his gaze to the cigarette case. He considered a moment longer, then slipped the cigarette case into his inside jacket pocket. 'Thank you very much, Henrietta. Don't mind if I do.'

The custody sergeant drew back the wicket on the cell door and Matthew stepped up to the hole and peered through. A man with bright red hair lying on the wooden bench lifted his head and stared back.

'That who you're after?' PS Baker asked.

'Could be,' Matthew nodded. 'I'd like to question him. Can I use an interview room?'

'I'll bring him to Interview Room 2. Make yourself comfortable in there.'

Matthew gestured to Barnes to follow. 'Well done for finding him,' he said to the young detective.

'Thank you, sir,' Barnes beamed. 'Is it right you've had to let Father Pettifer go?'

'The Superintendent's orders,' Matthew sighed as he pulled out a chair from the table in the interview room. 'He doesn't think the evidence points to him killing Clough, and he's had a bishop on his back about the arrest being in the newspaper.'

'So, is the vicar off the hook?'

'Not entirely.' Matthew lit a cigarette. 'Let's see what Mr Cotton has to say.'

The door opened and PS Baker pushed David Cotton into the room. 'Sit down, Davey, and behave,' he warned. 'You all right with him?'

'Fine, thank you,' Matthew replied, and Baker went out, closing the door. 'Mr Cotton, I'm DI Stannard, this is DC Barnes. We'd like to ask you some questions.'

Cotton sniffed. 'What about?'

'Craynebrook. You ever been there?'

'Might have passed through once or twice.'

'Been in The King George?'

'I go in lots of pubs. Can't remember all their names.'

'The landlord of The King George says you were in there on Tuesday of last week.'

'He knows me, then, does he? To say I was there?'

'You match the description.'

'Ah, well, if I match the description,' Cotton grinned at Barnes.

'Are you're saying you weren't there then?' Matthew asked.

'I ain't saying nothing, pal.'

'What about Blackbird Farm? You heard of that?'

Cotton shook his head.

Matthew took a puff of his cigarette and looked down at Cotton's massive hands. There was a pale band of skin around his forefinger. 'I hear you're handy with your fists, Mr Cotton. You box.'

Cotton balled his left hand into a fist and cupped it with his right proudly. 'Yeah, I like to box.'

'Bare knuckle, I'm told.'

'When I'm allowed to. I prefer it to wearing gloves.'

'You like a fight?'

'What if I do?'

'But only in the ring? Or do you use your talents outside as well?'

Cotton stopped grinning. 'What you getting at?'

Matthew had had enough of tiptoeing around. 'Did you beat up a Mr Clough at Blackbird Farm last week?'

Cotton's expression didn't change. There was no sign of guilt, no sign of anything to tell Matthew he was on the right track. Cotton folded his arms. 'I don't think I want to talk to you anymore, copper.'

'I doubt if you'll get anything out of Cotton if he's clammed up,' Baker said as he locked Cotton back in the cell. 'He's a pro. Knows if he keeps his mouth shut, there's not much we can do.'

Matthew nodded. 'I think you're right. You're charging him with the Disorderly Conduct, though?'

'Oh yes. He knows he's banged to rights on that. He's not bothering to deny it.'

'Can I see his personal effects? Just in case there's something of interest?'

'I got them here.' Baker brought a box out from beneath the booking-in desk and put it before Matthew.

'What are you looking for, sir?' Barnes asked as Matthew searched through the contents.

'Cotton's left-handed,' he said. 'Clough suffered bruising on the right-hand side of his face and body. And Cotton also had a ring mark on his left index finger. Ah.' He lifted a gold ring with a patterned flat plate out of the box and showed it to Barnes. 'I wonder if Dr Wallace could match this to the mark he found on Clough's cheekbone?'

'It's worth asking,' Barnes nodded. 'Something else, sir?' he asked as Matthew pulled another item out of the box.

'His wallet.' Matthew opened the large rear flap and his eyebrows rose. He took out the notes he'd found and counted them. 'There's fifteen pounds here in brand new five-pound notes. Where did Cotton get these?'

Baker shrugged. 'No idea.'

'He says he's unemployed, doesn't he?' Matthew said. 'So, how does he come to have brand new notes and this many?'

'I couldn't say, inspector,' Baker said a little testily. 'Maybe he stole them?'

Matthew stared at the notes.

'What are you thinking, sir?' Barnes asked.

'This looks more like payment than theft. We need to trace the serial numbers on these notes. Find out who they were issued to. I'm thinking David Cotton was paid to beat up Clough.'

Chapter Twenty-Nine

Lenny Gibbs sniffed as the tobacconist handed him his pouch of tobacco and wiped his nose with his sleeve. He glanced at the newspapers lying on the counter. He hadn't bought one since he'd spotted the article about the beaten detective and a similar, though smaller, headline caught his eye now. Lenny snatched the newspaper up and squinted at the paragraph beneath the headline POLICE CONSTABLE SAVAGELY BEATEN IN GRAVEYARD.

'You've got to pay for that, Lenny,' the tobacconist warned.

'All right, all right,' Lenny said, poking around in his cardigan pocket for a coin. He slammed it down on the counter with the palm of his hand. 'There you go,' he sneered, and shuffled out of the shop with the newspaper.

He read as he walked, causing people to step around him, but came to an abrupt halt when he read the article's last sentence. "Police are offering a reward of £100 for information on the whereabouts of Wilfred Gadd."

'A hundred quid,' he murmured, and found a bench to sit down on. Blimey, what he could do with a hundred notes in his hand. He nibbled his bottom lip. Mind you, he was getting money regular with Wilf giving him half of his takings. A long-term arrangement like they had might work better for him than a one-off payment, but then he shook his head. He didn't like having Wilf in the house, skulking up in his room all day. He was a nasty bleeder; Lenny didn't feel safe. He'd played it brave when he'd demanded money from Wilf, thinking the first copper had been a one-off, but now this. He glanced down at the newspaper again, his eyes fixing on the words "savagely beaten".

Lenny looked up, watching people going by, not one of them looking his way or coming over for a chat. If Wilf got it into his head to do him in, no one would know. He'd be lying there with his head bashed in, brains all over the floor, for days, maybe weeks. Until he started to rot and a neighbour complained about the smell, and then.... Lenny shuddered. No, he didn't want that to happen. And besides, someone was bound to spot Wilf coming and going and tell the rozzers. Why should they have the money and not him? The police would come and arrest him for having Wilf in the house. Harbouring a criminal, wasn't it? Or aiding and abetting? One of those, anyway. Well, he wasn't going to prison for Wilf, not when he could have a hundred quid in his hand for turning the rotter in.

He stared at the telephone box a few yards away while he smoked one of his roll-ups. Then, decision made, he got up and crossed to the box. He told the operator to connect him to Crayne-brook Police Station. When the line connected and a voice asked how he could help, Lenny licked his dry lips and said, 'I've got information about Wilfred Gadd.'

This was met with a 'Yes, sir?' that sounded bored. Weren't they grateful for the information? Lenny thought angrily.

'Well? What about the reward?' he demanded.

'If your information proves correct, sir, you'll get paid,' the speaker assured him.

'How do I know that?'

A heavy sigh. 'You're talking to the police, sir. We don't lie.'

Lenny couldn't help himself. He laughed down the line, and the voice at the other end said, 'I'm hanging up now.'

'No, no,' Lenny shouted. 'Don't do that. I know where he is. Just put me through to whoever I should talk to.'

'You can tell me, sir, and I'll take your details.'

'And then I'll get the money?'

'As I said, sir.'

'I suppose I'll just have to trust you, won't I?' Lenny said. 'All right, then. Wilfred Gadd is staying at my house.' He gave the address. 'Come and get him sharpish. And don't forget my money.'

Lenny hung up and left the telephone box, making his way back to the house. He was closing the front door when Wilf came clumping down the stairs.

'Been out?' Wilf asked.

'Went out to get some baccy,' Lenny said, alarmed to see Wilf up so early. He normally didn't stir until noon.

'You got the 'paper there?' Wilf pointed to the newspaper under Lenny's arm. 'Let's have a look.'

Lenny glanced down and clamped his arm tighter against his body. 'I haven't read it meself yet. You can have it after, if you like.'

Wilf shook his head and held out his hand. 'I just want a quick look.'

Lenny stared at Wilf's hand, considered, then forced a smile on his face and handed it over. 'All right. Put it on the stairs when you're done.'

He hurried into the kitchen and banged the kettle down on the gas ring. Turning to the kitchen table for the teapot, Lenny froze. Wilf was standing in the doorway, newspaper in front of him, but looking at Lenny.

'There's a reward for information about me,' Wilf said.

'Is there?' Lenny said, his voice cracking.

'You didn't see?'

'I told you, I haven't had a chance to read it yet.' He laughed nervously. 'How much they offering?'

'A hundred pounds. Tasty sum, ain't it?'

'Nice to know what you're worth.' Lenny swallowed and pointed at the teapot. 'Fancy a cuppa?'

Wilf stepped into the kitchen and threw the newspaper on the table. 'What's up, Lenny?'

'Up? Nothing. Why?'

'You ain't never offered me tea before.'

Lenny shrugged. 'It's 'cause you're standing there, ain't it? If you don't want one…'

Both men stared at each other.

'You rang them, didn't you?' Wilf said after a long moment.

'Rang who?'

'The police. You've told them I'm here.'

'Don't be daft. I wouldn't do that to you.'

'How long have I got?'

'I ain't called no one, Wilf. I swear. Look, hand on heart.' Lenny's gaze dropped to the kitchen table as Wilf picked up the rolling pin he'd left there after making himself a steak and kidney pudding the night before. 'Now, come on, Wilf. Don't do anything silly. I ain't told no one nothing.' He backed away, raising his arms across his face. 'WILF!' he screamed. 'NO! NO!'

Lund was in the office when Matthew and Barnes got back to Craynebrook.

'Have you heard?' Lund asked as Matthew came in.

'Heard what?'

'We got a tip-off about Gadd's whereabouts. A dump over in Fitton Gate.'

Matthew stared at Lund. 'He's been that close all this time? So, has he been brought in?'

Lund shook his head. 'Uniform get there, no answer. Next-door neighbour says she heard shouting. Screaming, more like. So, they break the door down and they find the bloke who called in the tip on the kitchen floor with his head bashed in.'

A lead weight landed in Matthew's stomach. 'Dead?'

'As a doornail. And no sign of Gadd. Witnesses say they saw a man matching his description running down the street with a holdall a few minutes before our lot arrived.'

Matthew sank into his chair and took out his cigarettes. He lit one, throwing the match at his ashtray and missing. He didn't even notice. 'Jesus,' he breathed.

'Looks like you and Rudd were the lucky ones, doesn't it?'

'Who was the man who alerted us?'

Lund consulted his blotter. 'Small-time crook by the name of Lenny Gibbs.'

'Poor sod.'

'Don't waste your sympathy. Now, you listen to me, Stannard. You've been stupid, carrying on the way you have been as if you're not in any danger. But Gadd's killed now, and I don't think he's going to stop until he's got you. So, you bloody watch yourself, you hear me? And if you do see him, you don't give him a chance. None of this gentlemanly conduct of yours. You hit him where it hurts and you slap the cuffs on him. Are you listening to me, Stannard?'

'I'm listening,' Matthew yelled, slamming his hand down on his desk.

'You better,' Lund grunted. He sat down at his desk. 'Where have you been?'

'Over to Graydon Heath. We may have identified one of the men the witnesses told us about.'

'I heard you've released the vicar. So, he's out of the frame?'

Matthew stabbed his cigarette out savagely in the ashtray, picking up the stray match and throwing it into the ash. 'He's still a suspect. I was ordered to release him.'

'Old Mouldy sticking his oar in again?'

Matthew nodded.

'Well, at least you've got other leads to follow up. That'll keep you busy.' Lund looked across at Matthew and shook his head. 'Concentrate on finding your killer, Stannard. Let others worry about Gadd.'

Matthew lit another cigarette. 'That's easy for you to say.'

'Where have you been?' Verity cried as Hettie breezed into her hallway. She slammed the front door shut and turned on her sister. 'You were supposed to be here an hour ago.'

'I went shopping on the high street,' Hettie said with a bewildered shake of her head. 'Why? What's the matter?'

Verity grabbed her wrist and dragged her into the sitting room, Hettie's heels clicking on the parquet flooring. She snatched a newspaper from the arm of the sofa and thrust it at Hettie. 'They've let the boys go.'

Hettie's mouth fell open and her frantic eyes scanned the front page. 'But they did it,' she cried and fell onto the sofa. 'Why? Why would he let them go?'

'How do I know?' Verity ran her hand through her hair, dislodging some pins. She shoved them back in angrily. 'Wait? What do you mean? Why would *he* let them go?'

'Well, Matthew, of course,' Hettie said, as if it was obvious. 'The detective in charge.'

Verity frowned at her. 'Matthew?' Then she sighed and shook her head. 'Oh, Hettie. What have you done?'

Hettie threw the newspaper aside. 'I haven't done anything, Verity.'

'Don't give me that. Why are you calling this detective by his first name?'

'I wrote to him, if you must know,' Hettie said. 'Just to say how sorry I was he got hurt. That's all.'

'Hettie, if you've started all that again—'

'It's none of your business.'

'Don't you care anything for Roger?'

Hettie sniffed and tears came into her eyes. 'How can you say such a thing? Of course I care.'

'Then why do you do these things? Haven't you hurt us all enough?'

Hettie burst out crying and buried her face in a cushion. 'You're so mean to me,' she said between sobs. 'Going on about me and Matthew when I have all these other things to worry about.'

'When *you* have other things to worry about?' Verity cried, incredulous. Her breath was coming fast, and she glared down at her sister. 'Get out,' she said, her voice hard.

Hettie looked up at her. 'What?'

'I said get out. I don't want you here. You selfish, ungrateful cow.'

'Verity!'

Verity grabbed Hettie's arm and pulled her off the sofa. Hettie hit at her feebly, begging to be released, but Verity dragged her sister back to the front door and threw her out. 'I can't look at you at the moment. Just leave me alone, Hettie.' She slammed the door, leaving her sister sobbing and bewildered on the front step.

The police car pulled up at the kerb on Graydon Heath High Street and Matthew looked up at the sign above the door. It read Duggan Sales and Lettings, and this was where the bank notes in Cotton's wallet had come from. It seemed an unlikely address to have an association with David Cotton.

A young man at a desk was speaking with a middle-aged couple to the left of the door, showing them pieces of paper and scribbling notes in a notebook. He was too involved to pay Matthew and

Barnes much notice, but a bored secretary looked up from filing her nails when they walked in.

'Good morning,' she said mechanically. 'Can I help you?'

Matthew showed her his warrant card and introduced himself and Barnes. 'We'd like to see Mr Duggan, please.'

The couple and the young man turned to look at them, then returned to their own matter. A mixture of curiosity and alarm on her face, the secretary glanced towards the rear of the office, where a door bore the legend ALFRED DUGGAN.

'Mr Duggan's just on a call with a client,' she said. 'If you'd wait here a moment, I'll tell him you're here.' She rose, smoothing her skirt over her thighs as she walked towards the rear office. She knocked, and Matthew heard a telephone receiver drop into a cradle and a voice say, 'Come'. The secretary went in, closing the door behind her. There was a murmur of conversation, then a male voice cried, 'Police?'

Matthew glanced at Barnes. 'Someone doesn't sound pleased we're here.'

'No, sir,' Barnes agreed. He peered at a stand showing local houses for sale. 'The price of some of these. They're almost as high as Craynebrook.'

The office door opened, and the secretary came out, followed by Alfred buttoning up his jacket. Matthew noted his appearance – suit, bald head, moustache – and thought this could be one of Mrs Askey's businessmen.

'Good afternoon,' Alfred said, looking from Matthew to Barnes. 'My secretary says you're from the police?'

'That's right,' Matthew nodded. 'We'd like to have a word.'

'Of course. Won't you come into my office?' he gestured them towards the rear, smiling at the couple to suggest nothing was wrong. 'Please sit down,' he said, closing the door. 'So, what is this about?'

'We're making enquiries into the murder at Blackbird Farm,' Matthew began. 'You may have read about it in the newspaper.'

'Er, no,' Alfred shook his head. 'I don't believe I did.'

'A farmer was killed, rather viciously, on Sunday night.'

'Really? How awful. But what has that to do with me?'

'Do you know a Mr David Cotton?'

Alfred scratched his ear. 'No, I've never heard that name.'

'You've never had any dealings with him? He doesn't work for you?'

'No, inspector. I don't know him. Who is he?'

'Mr Cotton is currently under arrest at Graydon Heath Police Station for an unrelated offence. But he had in his possession several new bank notes that were issued by the bank to you. We wonder how he came to have them?'

'I really have no idea.'

'You wouldn't have given them to him?'

'Really, inspector. How can I have given him bank notes if I don't know the man?'

'I see,' Matthew nodded and studied him for a long moment, watching Alfred grew hot beneath his glare. 'Do you know Craynebrook at all, Mr Duggan? Do you have any business there?'

'I know it, and yes, I have sold the odd property there.' Alfred smiled. 'Not as much as I'd like. Craynebrook is a very desirable location. But most of my business is here in Graydon Heath.'

'Is your business entirely residential?'

'It forms the bulk of my business, but I also deal in the occasional commercial premises. Leasing shops, that sort of thing.'

'What about farms?'

'Farms?'

'Yes. Would you ever buy or sell a farm, for instance?'

Alfred gave a little laugh. 'Agriculture is not something I know anything about, inspector.'

'So you've never heard of Blackbird Farm?'

'No, I don't believe I have.'

'Or Mr Josiah Clough?'

Alfred shook his head.

'Where were you on Sunday night, Mr Duggan?'

'Me? Sunday night?' Alfred snatched up his fountain pen and fiddled with it. 'I can't think why you're asking, but I was at home. Yes. At home.' He laughed as Matthew and Barnes continued to stare at him. 'You can ask my wife if you don't believe me.'

Matthew nodded and rose. 'Thank you for your time, Mr Duggan.'

'Of course. I'm only sorry I wasn't able to help.' Alfred saw them out, watching them get into the car through the office window.

'What do you think, sir?' Barnes asked, turning round to face Matthew from the passenger seat.

Matthew lit a cigarette and opened the back window. 'I think he's knows Cotton and Blackbird Farm. Let's get back to the station and see what more we can find out about Mr Alfred Duggan.'

'This was put through the door.' Turkel held out a lavender-coloured envelope to Pinder. 'For the inspector.'

Pinder took it. 'I'll see he gets it.'

'Ta.' Turkel dug into his tunic pocket and pulled out a brown envelope. He jiggled it beneath Pinder's nose and it made a clinking noise.

'What's that?' Pinder asked.

'We're doing a collection for Sam. We've all put in downstairs.'

Pinder pushed the brown envelope away. 'I'm broke.'

'Oh, come on, Gary, you can spare a bob or two. The poor sod's laid up in hospital.'

'It was his own fault. He shouldn't have gone after Gadd like that without any help.'

'You don't mean that,' Turkel said.

Pinder looked up at him, unapologetic. 'I do. He should have left Gadd well enough alone and called it in. That's what I would have done. I wouldn't have tried nabbing him on me own, not knowing what he's capable of.'

'He was doing his duty,' Turkel said angrily.

'Who was?' Denham asked as he entered CID.

'Sam,' Turkel said, looking at Pinder with disgust. 'But Gary here seems to think he should have left him alone.'

Pinder grinned. 'I'm just telling it like it is.'

'Is that for Sam?' Denham pointed at the envelope.

Turkel nodded, and Denham dug into his trouser pocket and pulled out a handful of coins. He dropped them into the envelope.

'Cheers,' Turkel said. 'Nice to know you're not all heartless bastards up here.' He went out, glowering at Pinder.

'Didn't you put anything in?' Denham asked.

'No, I didn't,' Pinder said. 'I ain't got money to waste on idiots.'

Denham shook his head. 'You're unbelievable,' he said and sat down at his desk, his back to Pinder.

Pinder made sure he wasn't watching, then opened the lavender-coloured envelope and read the letter inside.

My darling Matthew,

I hope you liked the cigarette case.

I didn't mean to write to you again so soon, but I have to see you. I thought everything was all right, but it isn't and only you can help me. I don't want to come to the station — you never seem to be there! — but if you can't meet me anywhere else, then I will and I won't leave until I see you.

If you can meet me, then please let me know by putting an advert in The Chronicle tomorrow saying when and where. Let it be soon, my darling. I need you.

Yours forever,

Henrietta

'Bugger,' Pinder muttered under his breath. If she came into the station and actually met Matthew, she'd know he never got the cigarette case and there'd be no end of trouble. He lit a cigarette, wondering what to do. Then an idea came to him and he got up, pulling on his jacket.

'You going out?' Denham asked.

'I need to check on something,' Pinder said, and hurried out before Denham could question him further.

Chapter Thirty

Barnes had turned up something interesting about Mr Alfred Duggan, and wanting to be on his own for a while, Matthew left the young detective looking into Cotton's background while he made a visit to Earlswood, just a few miles on from Graydon Heath.

Matthew climbed out of the police car and opened the door of Kempton's Hardware, a bell tinkling above his head. A woman carrying a basket looked at him expectantly to hold the door open for her and he stepped aside to let her exit, leaving him the only customer in the shop.

'Yes, sir?' the man behind the counter asked with a smile.

Matthew took out his warrant card and held it up. 'Craynebrook CID. Mr Kempton?'

'I'm Kempton,' the man said, watching Matthew warily as he replaced his card back in his pocket. 'What's the problem?'

'No problem. I just wanted to ask you about a complaint you made a couple of years ago to the Graydon Heath police. You claimed a Mr Alfred Duggan tried to intimidate you into selling this shop to him.'

'He did.'

'Can you tell me about that?'

The bell tinkled again, and both men turned to the door. Kempton shouted, 'Kenny?' and a boy emerged from behind a curtain at the back of the shop.

'Yes, Mr Kempton?'

'Serve this customer, please.' He gestured at the new arrival. 'Come in the back,' he said, and Matthew followed him behind the curtain into a storeroom.

Kempton pulled the curtain, closing them off from the shop. 'Duggan came in here one day, full of smiles, saying he wanted to buy the shop and the yard out the back. I'm one of the few shop-keepers on this street who actually owns their shop rather than leases it. And it's a big plot. I've had offers for it and turned 'em all down. But, you know, I'm getting on, thinking about the future, and when Duggan made his offer, I was tempted, I admit it. Between you and me, it was a bloody good offer, more than the others. So I said I'd think about it and went home and talked it over with the wife. Well, after a lot of back and forth, we decided not to sell. So, when Duggan came in again and asked for my decision, I told him no. All the smiles went then. He said I was making a mistake and that he already had plans for the land, giving me all the reasons why I should sell to him and trying to lay the guilt on thick by saying I had given him the impression I would go ahead. Now, I never said any such thing. All I said was that I would think about it. I didn't like the way he was acting, and I'll admit, I've got a short temper. I told him I'd had enough of him and to get out. Duggan got nasty then, saying I'd be sorry.' Kempton snorted a laugh. 'I've grown up with rougher men than him, so his threat didn't bother me. I put him right out of my head. Then a few days later, me and the missus are in bed upstairs and we hear a bloody loud crash and someone running off. I come down and find a brick's been put through the window.'

'You think that was Duggan?'

Kempton shrugged. 'I didn't see who it was. I get the window mended the following day. Go to bed. It happens again. And then Duggan shows up the day after. Says he heard we've had a bit of trouble and had it convinced us we should sell? Cheeky sod, I thought. I told him no, then went to the police to report him. Lot of good that did me.'

'The police report says there was no evidence Duggan was involved,' Matthew explained.

'Maybe not, but I know what's what. It was down to him, right enough.'

'Did he come back?'

Kempton shook his head. 'I didn't see him again. I reckon he got the message that I weren't going to roll over and decided not to bother anymore. So, why are you asking about him? I mean, my complaint's all over and done with.'

'Mr Duggan's name has come up in connection with an investigation.'

'Has he done the same thing to someone else?'

Matthew pulled the curtain back. 'That's what I'm trying to find out.'

Dr Wallace's office door was open and Matthew poked his head inside.

Wallace was standing by the window, glasses perched on the end of his nose, an open file in his hand. 'I saw you coming,' he said with a smile, nodding at the window.

'You got the ring?' Matthew asked.

'Yes, I got the ring.'

'And?'

Wallace pointed him to a chair. 'And although there isn't a unique design to match it to, I can say that the shape of the ring is a good match for the mark within the bruise on Mr Clough's cheek.'

'A good match?'

'If you want me to put a percentage on it, I'd say eighty. Not what you wanted to hear, I see?' he added at Matthew's disappointed expression.

'I'd prefer a hundred per cent,' Matthew admitted.

'Certainty is rarely possible in our line of work, inspector.'

'Eighty per cent will do.' Matthew held his hand out and Wallace returned the ring in its small brown envelope. 'Thanks.'

'Before you go,' Wallace halted him by the door. 'Come and sit back down, inspector.'

Matthew frowned. 'Why?'

Wallace raised a commanding eyebrow. 'Because I say so.' He patted the back of the chair Matthew had been sitting in.

Reluctantly, Matthew returned to the chair and watched Wallace as he opened a glass-fronted door in a cupboard against the wall.

'Of course,' Wallace said as he took out a flat box and put it on the desk, 'I'm used to working on corpses.' He took out a stethoscope. 'But I'm making an exception for you, inspector.'

'It's really not necessary, doctor,' Matthew sighed.

'I disagree,' Wallace said. 'You don't look well to my educated eyes. And if you don't want me to tell your superintendent you're unfit for duty, you'll let me have my way. Now, shirt open, if you please.'

Matthew pulled his tie loose and unbuttoned the top three buttons, holding the fabric aside while Wallace applied his stethoscope to his chest, wincing at its coldness. He followed the doctor's instructions, breathing in and out, and kept quiet. After a minute, Wallace withdrew.

'Well, that all sounds fine,' he said, putting the stethoscope back into its box.

'I said there was no need,' Matthew said, buttoning up his shirt.

Wallace put his hands either side of Matthew's head and tilted him back. He examined the wound where Wilf had struck him.

'That seems to be healing nicely.' He released Matthew's head and bent down. 'Follow my finger.' He drew his finger left and right, watching Matthew's eyes track it.

'Hmmm,' he said, and returned to his chair. 'How are you feeling in general? And don't lie to me.'

Matthew sighed. 'I get tired. I have headaches. But the doctor said I would for a few weeks.'

Wallace's eyes narrowed. 'How bad are the headaches?'

Matthew brushed some fluff from his knee. 'I have them most of the day.'

'Sharp or dull?'

'Dull. They're just there. In the background.'

'And are you taking anything for them?'

'Aspirin.'

'How many times a day?'

Matthew shrugged. 'I don't know.'

Wallace raised an eyebrow. 'You mean you've lost track?'

'Probably too many,' Matthew admitted. 'But they help.'

'You're looking very tired, inspector. I understand you're supposed to be on light duties. A murder investigation doesn't qualify as light.'

'I don't exactly have a choice, Dr Wallace,' Matthew pointed out. 'We're a small station. There's only me and Lund, and Lund's busy in court.'

'An inspector could be seconded from another station, surely?' Wallace suggested.

'I don't know,' Matthew muttered. 'Maybe. Look, Dr Wallace, I appreciate your concern, but frankly, my welfare isn't your business. I have a job to do.'

'That no one else can do as well as you?' Wallace asked as Matthew headed for the door. 'Is that what it is, inspector? You think you're indispensable?'

Matthew gave him a smile that was more of a grimace. 'Good evening, Dr Wallace.'

Barnes was waiting outside the mortuary for Matthew, leaning against the police car. Matthew told him what Dr Wallace had said about the ring, and Barnes confirmed that both Mrs Askey and Mr Greader had identified Cotton from his mugshot. Matthew ordered the driver to take them to Graydon Heath Police Station. He wanted another word with Cotton.

'What the bleeding hell am I still here for?' Cotton demanded as he was shown into the interview room. 'I've been charged for the Disorderly Conduct, so you've got to let me go.'

'We have a few more questions for you, Mr Cotton,' Matthew said. 'Sit down.'

Cotton dropped into the chair, folded his arms across his chest and glared at Matthew. 'I already told you I ain't got nothing to say.'

'You might feel like talking when you hear what we've found out.'

'Oh yeah? What's that?'

'You normally wear a ring on your left index finger, don't you, Mr Cotton?'

Cotton glanced down at his left hand. 'Yeah. So what?'

'So, what do you say if I tell you your ring left a mark on a dead man's cheek?'

Cotton's eyes narrowed. 'I don't know what you're talking about.'

'Then I'll explain. You remember I asked you about Craynebrook and Blackbird Farm last time we talked? You said you knew nothing about the farm.'

'I don't.'

'Your ring mark was found on the murdered farmer of Blackbird

Farm, Mr Josiah Clough. He had been beaten up a few days previously, suffering severe bruising to the right side of his face and body. The bruises were the result of blows delivered by a left-handed person with a ring on his index finger.' Matthew paused, watching Cotton. 'Still nothing to say, Mr Cotton?'

Cotton helped himself to a cigarette from Matthew's packet on the table. Barnes lit it for him at Matthew's nod.

'What about this, then?' Matthew went on. 'We have two witnesses who have conclusively identified you as being in The King George public house and on Blackbird Lane in Craynebrook.'

Cotton blew smoke in Matthew's face.

Matthew ignored it, not even prepared to give him the satisfaction of waving it away. 'When you were arrested for Disorderly Conduct, you had on your person fifteen pounds in brand new banknotes. Where did you get them?'

Cotton shrugged. 'Can't remember.'

'I know where you got them from. We traced them back to a Mr Alfred Duggan.' Matthew smiled. 'I see you know that name.'

'Yeah, I know Alfie,' Cotton said, knocking the cigarette against the ashtray. 'So what? Ain't no law against that.'

'He gave you the money?'

'What if he did?'

'Fifteen pounds? That's a lot of money, especially for someone who claims to be unemployed. Why did he give it to you?'

'We're pals.'

'Really? I wouldn't have thought you and Mr Duggan moved in the same circles.'

'You'd be surprised,' Cotton grinned.

'Where did you meet Duggan?' Matthew asked conversationally.

'I forget.'

'Try to remember.'

Cotton traced a figure of eight on the tabletop with his forefinger. 'Oh yeah. It was at the dogs.'

'Greyhound racing?'

'Yeah. Alfie likes a flutter.'

'Gambling acquaintances, then?'

'If you like.'

'Do any jobs for him? Cash in hand, no questions asked kind of jobs?'

'Now and then.'

'What kind of jobs?'

'This and that.'

'Fetching and carrying?'

'Yeah.'

'Putting bets on for him?'

'Yeah.'

'Throwing bricks through windows?'

Cotton's eyes hardened at Matthew.

'Did you put a couple of bricks through the windows of Kempton's Hardware in Earlswood when Duggan asked you to?' Matthew leaned forward. 'You see, I think you did. I think Mr Duggan paid you good money to do that. And he paid you good money to beat up Mr Clough, too. What do you think, Barnes?'

'I think you're right, sir,' Barnes said dutifully.

'What did you have to persuade Mr Clough to do?' Matthew went on. 'Did Mr Duggan have his eyes on the farm and Mr Clough didn't want to sell, so he sent you round to persuade him? Is that it?' His jaw tightened, irritated by Cotton's continued silence. 'Did you go back there Sunday night and finish the job off? Did you kill him?'

'Now, you wait a minute,' Cotton said, his fist curling beneath Matthew's chin. 'I ain't killed no one.'

'That's how it looks from where I'm sitting. I've got a dead man who took a beating from you. You left your mark on him and I can prove it. And I've got you with a lot more money than you should have to give you a motive for killing him.'

'No. You can't pin that on me.'

'You might be able to convince a judge it wasn't premeditated. You could be convicted for manslaughter, in which case you might do… what do you reckon?' Matthew turned to Barnes. 'Ten years?'

'At least, sir,' Barnes nodded. 'But there aren't many judges who will be so lenient, are there? Especially not once they've seen Mr Cotton's record.'

'You think they'd go for murder, then?' Matthew said. 'That means you're going to hang, Cotton.'

'I didn't kill him,' Cotton shouted.

'Then who did?' Matthew yelled back.

'I don't know.'

'Start talking, Mr Cotton, or I'm going to charge you with murder.'

'Look, I beat him up. But that's all I did. That's all I was paid for.'

'Paid by whom?'

Cotton took a deep breath. 'Duggan. He paid me twenty notes to beat the old man up and tell him he had to sell the farm. That was on Tuesday, Tuesday the thirteenth. I told Duggan what I'd done on the Wednesday. Now, you can check that because I went to his office to tell him. His secretary will remember, the toffee-nosed cow. She didn't want to let me in. You go and question Alfie. And you tell him I ain't going down for his murder.'

Chapter Thirty-One

The next morning, Matthew had Barnes invite Alfred Duggan to come to the station to help with their enquiries. Duggan didn't refuse. He did, however, call his solicitor to meet him at the station, and Matthew had to wait almost an hour before he sat down opposite Duggan in Interview Room 1. He had a feeling Duggan would respond with No Comment to all his questions, and he opened the interview already feeling it would be a waste of time.

'Thank you for coming in, Mr Duggan,' Matthew said, allowing Alfred the idea he had had a choice. 'Following our conversation yesterday, some new information has come to light.'

'What new information?' Alfred asked nervously.

'A complaint was made against you almost two years ago by a Mr Alec Kempton. Mr Kempton complained you used intimidation methods to persuade him to sell you his property.'

'That matter was investigated, inspector,' the solicitor said, marking off a line of text in his notebook. 'The police found no evidence of intimidation.'

'I'm aware the matter was dropped,' Matthew nodded. 'The reason we're interested in the accusation is because it sounds remarkably similar to what happened to Mr Clough at Blackbird Farm. Mr Kempton was made an offer by you which he refused. Mr Clough appears to have been made an offer which he refused. Mr Kempton claimed he was threatened by you and suffered damage to his property. Mr Clough ends up dead.'

'My client has already told you he had no dealings with Mr Clough.'

'We've spoken with a David Cotton,' Matthew went on. 'He claims your client paid him to throw bricks through Mr Kempton's shop windows. He also claims your client paid him to beat up Mr Clough.'

'He's lying,' Alfred burst out.

'Why would he lie?'

'I don't know. He's a criminal. It's second nature to him.'

'So, you do know him?'

Alfred's mouth opened and shut, bewildered. 'What?' he croaked.

'You said he's a criminal. How do you know that if you don't know him?'

'Well, I...' Alfred looked desperately at his solicitor. 'From what you said. Throwing bricks. It's the work of a criminal, isn't it? I don't know him.

'Can you explain how Mr Cotton had banknotes that were issued to you in his possession?'

'I've already told you, no. I've no idea.'

'Move on, inspector,' the solicitor said in a bored tone.

Matthew lit a cigarette. 'You claim you've never been to Blackbird Farm, Mr Duggan. Yet we have a witness who claims to have seen a man matching your description parking his car on Blackbird Lane and going into the farm on several occasions.'

'They can't have,' Alfred declared, folding his arms over his chest and shaking his head. 'I wasn't there and you can't prove I was.'

'We can clear it up if you'll agree to an identity parade,' Matthew suggested.

Alfred's eyes widened. He turned to his solicitor. 'They can't make me do that, can they?'

'Are you arresting my client, inspector?' the solicitor asked.

'Not yet.'

'Then you cannot compel my client to take part in an identity parade.'

'If he's adamant it wasn't him our witness claims to have seen, why should he refuse?' Matthew wondered.

The solicitor smiled. 'You're reaching, inspector. My client need not offer any explanation for his refusal.'

'It will make me look like a criminal,' Alfred cried.

The solicitor's eyes closed briefly in irritation at the interruption. 'Quite. Is this all you have, inspector? The accusation of a criminal? A vague description of a man who may or may not look like my client?'

Matthew was about to answer when the door opened and Denham poked his head inside the room.

'Sorry, sir,' he said. 'But I need a word.'

Matthew closed his file and rose. 'Excuse me a moment,' he said and went out with Denham into the corridor. 'What is it?'

'A man has come into the station,' Denham said. 'He found a revolver in his front garden. I've had a look at it and it's a Webley, sir, the same make of gun the bullet you found was fired from. And you won't believe it, but there's a name on it.'

'Has this been dusted?' Matthew asked Bissett, pointing at the gun lying on Denham's blotter.

Bissett nodded.

Matthew picked it up and turned the gun upside down and read the name on the engraved metal rectangle riveted to the bottom. He blinked a few times as black spots danced before his eyes. They focused, and he read, 'Thomas Henry Bagley. 1880-1919.'

'Years he served?' Denham suggested.

'Or birth and death. Anything on a Bagley locally?'

'Nothing in the telephone book. Pinder is checking the electoral register.'

Matthew shook his head. 'Just how many suspects are we going to get for this bloody murder?' Turning to Denham, he said, 'Find this Bagley. Barnes, let's get back to Duggan.'

The air of Interview Room 1 was thick with smoke. Duggan had a cigarette clamped between two fingers and he looked up worriedly as Barnes and Matthew returned.

'Mr Duggan,' Matthew said without any preamble, 'do you know a Thomas Henry Bagley?'

He saw Alfred start, then frown. 'No. No, I don't.'

'It seems to me you recognised the name?'

'I don't know any Thomas Henry Bagley,' Alfred insisted. 'Why?'

'Would you be willing to provide your fingerprints for elimination purposes?'

'I refer you to my previous statement about the identity parade, inspector,' the solicitor said. 'Unless and until you arrest my client, he is not under any obligation to provide you with his fingerprints. Now, as this is proving a rather redundant exercise, do you have any more questions for my client? If not, I am going to advise him to leave. He has business appointments this afternoon he is eager to get to.'

Matthew took a deep breath, considering. What did he have against Duggan? The word of a convicted criminal? Banknotes that in truth could have passed through a few hands before they got to Cotton? A previous accusation of intimidation that came to nothing? It wasn't enough.

'Your client is free to go,' he said, unable to resist adding, 'for the moment. Barnes, show Mr Duggan out.'

The nurse deposited a tea tray on Dickie's table, gave Matthew a smile and departed. 'I like it when you come,' Dickie said, reaching for his cup. 'I get biscuits.'

Matthew tipped two aspirin into his palm and swallowed them with the aid of his tea.

'Head still bad, is it?' Dickie asked, watching him.

'A bit,' Matthew said, biting into a biscuit and sinking back into the chair with a sigh.

'What's wrong, Matthew?'

'Nothing,' Matthew said, surprised by the question.

'Don't give me that. What's up?'

Matthew ran his hand over his forehead. 'I'm getting nowhere with this investigation. You were right, Dickie. I'm not up to it.'

'I didn't mean you weren't capable. Just that you needed a break from murders.'

'I'm having trouble concentrating,' Matthew admitted. 'I can't seem to work things out the way I used to. My head hurts all the time. I wake up with a headache. I go to bed with it. I'm so tired, Dickie, I can't think straight.' He heaved a deep breath. 'And I keep expecting to see Gadd everywhere I go. I can't shake the feeling he's just waiting to jump out at me. You heard about the man he killed?'

Dickie nodded. 'It was in the 'paper. That bloke's a nutter, Matthew. You're right to be worried.'

'Why the hell can't we find him?' Matthew threw his hands up. 'He's not that unnoticeable.'

'Gadd's clever. He knows how to hide.' He frowned. 'How is it at home?'

Matthew groaned. 'Mum and Georgie never leave me alone. I have no time to myself. It's driving me mad.'

'Then take me up on my offer,' Dickie said. 'Come and stay with me and Emma. It's got to be better for you.'

'I can't. They'd be hurt if I went somewhere else. And I wouldn't be happy imposing on your wife. She's going to have enough to do looking after you. No, I just have to put up with it until Gadd's caught.' He sighed, suddenly embarrassed about telling Dickie all his problems. 'Sorry. I shouldn't have bothered you with all this. Forget I said anything.'

'Well,' Dickie said with a forced laugh, 'at least, you're managing to have a bit of fun.'

'What do you mean?'

'You've got a lady friend.'

'I've got a what?'

'Come on,' Dickie grinned. 'There's no need to be coy.'

'Dickie, I've no idea what you're talking about,' Matthew insisted.

Dickie picked up his copy of *The Chronicle* from the bedside cabinet. 'Personals column. Fourth ad down,' Dickie said, raising his eyebrows at Matthew. '"Henrietta. Can't meet at moment. Please understand. One day soon. Yours, Matthew." So, who is Henrietta?'

Matthew held his hand out for the newspaper. 'Let me see that.' He read the advertisement for himself. 'I didn't put this in. It's nothing to do with me.'

'No?'

'No. I don't know any bloody Henrietta. And even if I did, I certainly wouldn't put an ad like that in the 'paper.'

'It sounds like something you'd write. It has just the right amount of chivalry,' Dickie teased.

Matthew tossed the newspaper onto the bed. 'I'm not the only Matthew in the world, you know.'

'It really isn't you?'

'It really isn't.'

'That's a shame. It would do you good.'

'What would?'

'A bit of How's-Your-Father,' Dickie winked. 'Take your mind off of things.'

'Pack it in, Dickie. If that's all you're going to talk about, I'm going.'

'All right, all right,' Dickie said, waving Matthew back into his chair. 'I was only joking, you touchy sod. Seriously, though, Matthew. If you feel this bad, you should get the doctor to sign you off for a bit. Take some more leave.'

'I can't do that. I've got a murder to solve,' Matthew cried.

'And you're not the only copper in London who can do it,' Dickie retorted. 'There are plenty of detectives at Scotland Yard who can take over if Lund's unavailable. I'm going to call Mr Mullinger and—'

'Don't you dare,' Matthew said, glaring at Dickie.

'But Matthew—'

'I mean it. I won't be signed off sick. I'm not giving Gadd the satisfaction.'

Chapter Thirty-Two

Matthew stepped out of the chemist, pocketing the bottle of aspirin he had bought, and took out his cigarettes. Cupping his hand around the flame of his match, he drew the smoke down and checked his watch. He had a few minutes before he needed to be in the station, and he found an empty bench just inside the park where he could smoke his cigarette in peace.

He watched people on the high street going about their business. Women dragging children along behind them, pushing prams, filling their shopping bags. Men with newspapers under their arms, lifting their hats to passers-by. None of them had his cares, Matthew thought with envy. None of them had to find a murderer or worry that he was going to be attacked any minute. He looked about him. Was Gadd here, watching him? he wondered, almost wishing he was. If Gadd made a move on him now, at least the waiting would be over.

Matthew shook his head and stubbed out his cigarette on the arm of the bench. There was no point thinking like that. He had to believe Gadd would be caught before he hurt anyone else and that his life would go back to normal.

His eyes followed a man with a ladder over his shoulder as he walked along the high street opposite. Window cleaner, perhaps, although he didn't have a bucket with him. Out of curiosity, Matthew continued to watch as the man leant the ladder against a shop, one that had been boarded up until the last week or so. He watched as the man stooped and sorted through a stack of painted boards leaning against the front, selecting one, then taking it with him as he climbed the ladder. He was putting up the shop sign, Matthew realised, as the man hammered the board into place. A large B and a small a. The man climbed down and selected another board and repeated the process. Small g, small l, small e.

Matthew sat up straight and peered, his eyes narrowing, holding his breath. One more trip down the ladder and back up again. Small y, large B, small ros. 'Bagley Bros,' he breathed out in astonishment and started up from the bench, hurrying out of the park and across the road, ignoring the car horn that blasted at him in anger. He stood in front of the shop as the last board was banged into place and read 'Bagley Bros. Building Co'. He looked at the remaining pile of boards. The last part of the sign to go up had revealed a Sales and Letting board that had been taken down. With a disbelieving shake of his head, Matthew read 'Duggan Sales and Lettings'.

He saw movement inside the shop. Opening the door, he went in.

'I'm afraid we're not open yet,' Richard said with a smile.

Matthew took out his warrant card and showed it to him. 'Can I take your name, please, sir?' Matthew asked.

The smile dropped from Richard's face. 'Richard Bagley. Is something wrong?' He turned as Roger came out of the room at the back. 'Police, Rog.'

'What's this about?' Roger asked, sending a warning glance to Richard.

'You've just moved in?' Matthew gestured at the boxes still on the floor.

'Yes, last week. We're opening on Monday. Is there a problem, Mr…?'

'Stannard,' Matthew said. 'Are you related to a Thomas Henry Bagley?'

'He was our father.'

'Was?'

'He's dead. Died in 1919 from the Spanish flu. Why are you asking?'

'Did he own a Webley revolver?'

'You've found it?' Roger asked.

'Found it?' Matthew echoed, taken aback by the response.

'Yes. It was stolen, or lost, we don't know which, during the move.'

Matthew's heart sank. He had been so hopeful he'd been on to something and now… 'When did you notice it was missing?'

'Oh, when was it, Richard? Tuesday? Wednesday?'

'Around then,' Richard nodded.

'You didn't report it stolen?' Matthew said.

'No,' Roger shook his head. 'I suppose we should have, but well, we've been busy.'

'Which of you had possession of it?'

'I did,' Richard said.

'Why bring a gun to an office?' Matthew wondered.

'Oh no, not here. At home. It was in one of the packing boxes for home and we're still going through those. That's why I didn't notice it was missing straightaway.'

'You've moved house as well?'

'Yes. We've moved to Craynebrook.'

'Look,' Roger said impatiently, waving Richard to be quiet. 'Have you found our father's gun or not?'

'Yes, Mr Bagley, it's been found,' Matthew nodded. 'It was found in the front garden of a house on Fountain Road and brought to us.'

‘Well, that’s excellent. At least we’ll get it back. When can we collect it?’

‘I’m afraid it’s not that simple,’ Matthew said. ‘The gun may have been used in a shooting.’

‘What?’ Richard cried. ‘You’re joking.’

‘Not at all. You may have read about the murder at Blackbird Farm?’ Another glance between the brothers, Matthew noted.

‘Briefly,’ Roger said. ‘We’ve been too busy to pay much attention to local news.’

‘I thought his throat was cut,’ Richard said. ‘I’m sure that’s what the newspaper said.’

‘He was also shot. So, if you’ve both handled the gun, I’m going to need you to come to the station.’

‘What for?’ Richard demanded.

‘To provide fingerprints,’ Matthew explained.

‘Well, of course our prints will be on the gun. It doesn’t mean we shot him.’

That was a rather odd thing to say, Matthew thought. ‘I’m not suggesting you did shoot him, Mr Bagley. We need your prints for elimination purposes. Do you have any objection?’

‘No, we don’t,’ Roger answered. ‘We’d be happy to provide our fingerprints, inspector.’

‘Good.’ Matthew pointed to the board, still leaning against the shop front outside. ‘I see you had dealings with Alfred Duggan.’

‘He arranged the lease of this unit, as well as our houses,’ Richard said.

‘You know him well?’

‘Only professionally. Why?’

Matthew ignored the question. ‘Why come to Craynebrook?’

‘It seems a nice place to be.’

‘With all the scandals and murders we’ve had lately? There’s many people who would avoid it like the plague.’

'Things like that don't bother us,' Roger said. 'We're good at spotting business opportunities.'

'Building opportunities?'

'That's the trade we're in, inspector. We're looking to grow our business and Craynebrook is ripe for that.'

'Really?' Matthew frowned. 'I would have thought the area's already pretty well built up.'

'You'd be surprised.'

'Would I?' He met Roger's eye and held it. Roger didn't blink or look away. 'Where were you before?'

'We were and still are in Balham, business-wise. This is effectively a temporary second branch. It will become our head office once we're settled.'

'So, you're still operating in Balham?'

'Yes. We keep our materials yard there. Timber, hardware.'

'But you live here now?'

'Correct.'

'Whereabouts?'

'St Jude's Avenue.'

'Ah,' Matthew smiled. 'The best street in Craynebrook.'

'So we were told,' Roger smiled back. But his smile dropped from his face as the door opened.

Matthew turned to see Verity standing in the open doorway. 'Good morning, madam,' he said. She nodded in reply, and he turned back to Roger and Richard. 'I'd appreciate it if you would come to the station at your earliest convenience today.'

'Yes, of course,' Roger nodded. 'As I said, we'll be happy to.'

'What was he doing here?' Verity asked when Matthew had gone.

Roger glanced at Richard, a warning not to speak. 'Our father's gun has been found. He came to tell us.'

'Your gun?' Verity glared at Richard. 'You didn't tell me it was missing?'

'I didn't know until the other day,' Richard shrugged.

'We assumed it got lost in the move,' Roger said. 'Or one of the removal men liked the look of it and took it. Anyway, he needs us to go to the station to provide a set of elimination prints.'

The door opened and Hettie came in. 'Who was that I saw leaving?' she asked.

'To eliminate you from what?' Verity demanded, ignoring her. 'For God's sake, Roger, what is going on?'

'Who was he?' Hettie insisted.

'He was a detective,' Richard said. 'Inspector Stannard.'

Hettie's hand went to her mouth. She looked fearfully at Roger. 'Why was he here?'

'Now look what you've done,' Roger muttered to Richard, going to his wife. 'It's nothing for you to worry about, my darling. It's just that the farmer who was killed the other day was also shot. Inspector Stannard thinks whoever took our father's gun may have used it to shoot him.'

'Oh, my Lord,' Hettie whimpered. 'Does he suspect you?'

'No,' Roger said laughingly. 'Nothing of the sort. Our fingerprints may be on the gun so he needs our prints to distinguish from any others that are on there. The killer's presumably. Although I would think a killer would have the sense to wear gloves. Wouldn't you, Rich?'

'What? Oh, yes, absolutely,' Richard nodded distractedly.

'But what if he thinks you had something to do with it?' Hettie whined, looking up into Roger's face.

'There's no reason he should,' Roger said, kissing her on the tip of her nose. 'You're not to worry. That's an order, Hettie. Rich and I will pop over to the police station and give them our prints and that will be the end of it.'

'I found the owner of the gun,' Matthew declared as he walked into CID.

Denham, Barnes and Pinder all had telephone receivers to their ears, and hastily finished their calls at Matthew's words.

'Who?' Denham asked, getting to his feet and following Matthew into his office.

'Father of Roger and Richard Bagley, recently moved to Craynebrook,' Matthew said, knowing he sounded rather smug at finding out this information. 'They own a building company with a new office on the high street and houses on St Jude's Avenue. They claim the gun was stolen or lost during their move here.'

'Claim, sir?' Barnes asked, eyebrows raised.

Matthew shrugged. 'It could be the truth, but they're associated with Alfred Duggan. He sold them their houses and arranged the lease of their office.' He shook his head. 'I think that's too many coincidences.'

'You think they're all involved in the murder?'

'Why not? Think about it. The Bagleys told me they're looking to expand their business, and that Craynebrook offers opportunities for development. Clough's sitting on a prime plot of land. Maybe they had their eyes on Blackbird Farm. Duggan, whatever he says, is ready to intimidate to get the land he wants, or to get the land his clients want. Clough won't agree to sell, so they threaten him. They argue, they fight. Clough ends up dead.'

'You say 'they', sir,' Denham said. 'Which one of them?'

Matthew slammed his drawer shut. 'I don't know. But the minute the Bagleys are here, I want to know.'

Matthew hurried down to the cells. The Bagleys had come in to give their fingerprints.

'Thank you for coming in so promptly, gentlemen,' he said.

'We'd like to get it over with,' Roger said, allowing Sergeant

Copley to take hold of his left hand and press each digit into the ink pad. 'Although, thinking about it, I don't remember touching my father's gun since we had the nameplate put on it and it was cleaned, so I'm not sure there's any point in taking my prints.'

'Just in case, then,' Matthew said.

'You will have them destroyed once you've eliminated them from your enquiry?' Richard demanded, watching as his brother's fingers left their imprint on the card. 'I won't have my prints kept in your files where I can be treated like any common criminal.'

'Of course, sir,' Matthew said.

'You're all done,' Copley said to Roger, giving him a cloth to wipe his fingers with. 'If you could come over?' he said to Richard.

Richard hesitated before taking Roger's place, Matthew noted. He also saw sweat on Richard's forehead. *What are you worried about?* he wondered.

'All done, inspector,' Copley announced as the last of Richard's digits was imprinted on the card.

'Good.' Matthew held his hand out for the cards. 'I'll see you out.'

Matthew returned to CID, his head banging inside his skull with each step on the stair. He saw Pinder sitting at his desk and held out the cards to him.

'Get these checked against the prints on file.'

Pinder took the cards and rose lazily to retrieve the prints from the file. Matthew lit a cigarette, his fifth of the morning, he noted. He really was smoking too much.

Barnes came over and handed him a mug of coffee. 'Got the prints all right, then?'

Matthew nodded, taking a sip of the coffee. He grimaced. Too much sugar, too much milk. Still it was hot. He closed his eyes, feeling himself swaying a little. *Sit down*, he told himself, *before you fall down.*

'Richard Bagley's prints match those on the gun, sir,' Pinder declared, bringing the card and the file's prints over and pointing out the similarities in the swirls.

Matthew opened his eyes and took both cards. He tried to make out the points Pinder had indicated, but his vision was too blurry. 'What about Roger?'

Pinder shook his head. 'No match, sir.'

'Right.' Matthew sighed and tapped his forehead gently. *Think*, he told himself. *What do you do next?*

'Are we going to question Richard Bagley, sir?' Barnes asked, glancing confusedly at Matthew.

'No,' Matthew said, realising he was making an exhibition of himself. 'Not until we can make a connection between him and Clough. Or between him and Duggan. I want you to look into the Bagleys' business. They come from Balham, so start there. See if there are any complaints lodged against them, like with Duggan.'

'I know what to do, sir,' Barnes said. 'Why don't you go and sit down for a bit?'

'I'm perfectly all right,' Matthew snapped as Barnes started swaying.

'Of course you are, sir,' Barnes said with a kindly smile. 'Just a bit tired, that's all.' He gently pushed Matthew towards his office and Matthew obeyed, going to his desk and sitting down. He leaned back in his chair and closed his eyes.

Barnes tiptoed out of Matthew's office and quietly closed the door.

'He's not right in the head.' Pinder peered through the window at Matthew. 'He shouldn't be here, if you ask me.'

'I'm not asking you,' Barnes said. 'Have you seen Inspector Lund?'

'He's in the canteen,' Pinder said, taking a magazine out of his drawer. 'What do you want him for?'

'None of your business,' Barnes snapped as he left the office. He found Lund sitting at one of the canteen tables, a plate of fish and chips before him. Barnes pulled out a chair and sat down.

'Yes?' Lund asked, raising an eyebrow at the presumption.

'Sorry to interrupt, sir,' Barnes said, 'but I wanted a word with you about the inspector.'

'Stannard? What about him?'

'I don't think he's well. I was just talking with him, and he didn't seem right, if you know what I mean. I made him go and sit down and he fell straight asleep.'

'So?' Lund shrugged. 'He's tired. It's not surprising. A murder investigation is always knackering.'

'I think it's more than that. He's normally so on the ball, isn't he? But just now… well, it was like he didn't know what he was doing.'

Lund put down his knife and fork. 'What do you want me to do about it?'

'Talk to the Super?' Barnes suggested. 'Maybe the inspector should be on sick leave still? I think he came back too early.'

'You want me to ask Old Mouldy for sick leave for Stannard when there's a murder to solve? You know what he's like. He'll just think Stannard's trying it on.'

'The inspector's not like that.'

'*I* know he's not. *You* know he's not.' Lund shook his head. 'I suppose I could have a word with the doctor. The Super would have to listen to him. But Stannard would have to agree to be re-examined and I can't see him doing that.'

'I'm worried something's going to happen to him, sir,' Barnes pressed. 'He's not himself.'

'All right, Barnes, your concerns are noted. I'll see what I can do.'

Chapter Thirty-Three

'This is lovely.' Verity smiled sweetly at Roger as the waiter poured the wine.

'I'm glad you like it,' Roger said, looking around the small restaurant. 'Richard found this place. I would never have known it was here. He's good at that sort of thing.'

'Oh yes,' Verity sighed, 'your brother's very good at that.'

Roger took a mouthful of wine. 'How was your church meeting?'

'Quite sad, really. The vicar said how sorry he was to see me go.' She smiled ruefully. 'I told him I was too.'

'Verity,' Roger groaned.

She held up her hands. 'I know, I know. I'm not allowed to say so, but there it is. I can't help it.'

'I thought you liked Craynebrook. You seem to be settling in.'

'How would you know?' she shot back angrily, then closed her eyes and turned her head away. 'I'm sorry. I shouldn't take it out on you.'

He reached across the table and grabbed her hand. 'What's wrong?'

Verity looked down at his hand and curved her fingers around his. 'I just wish it could all be undone. The past few years. Actually, the past thirty years.'

'What do you mean?'

She lifted his hand up and cradled it. 'Don't you ever wonder what our lives would have been like if you and I had married? If Hettie hadn't come back from school that summer—'

Roger snatched his hand away. 'No, I never wonder.'

'But if she hadn't, we might have married and—'

'She did come back, and we didn't. There's no point going over all that. I wouldn't have it any other way.'

'My God.' Verity shook her head, her eyes narrowing at him across the table. 'After all the trouble she's caused you, after all the trouble she still causes, you don't regret falling in love with her.'

'Never,' he declared vehemently. 'Why are you so jealous of your sister?'

'Because she has you,' Verity cried, causing heads at neighbouring tables to turn in their direction.

'And you have Richard,' he reminded her in a low voice, his eyes warning her to keep her voice down. 'And whatever you say about her, you love Hettie just as much as I do.'

'As much as Richard does?' She raised a sarcastic eyebrow.

His jaw tightened. 'That's all been forgiven. And forgotten. I don't want to talk about it, Verity. I have enough to worry about as it is without you bringing that all up again.'

They fell silent for a few moments. Verity watched Roger as he pushed food around his plate. 'What are you worrying about? That policeman this morning?'

He nodded.

'But I thought that was all over? You gave him your fingerprints. You had nothing to do with what happened at the farm. Roger? Is there something you're not telling me?'

Roger sighed. 'Richard was there that night. He shot the farmer.'

Verity's mouth fell open. 'He did what?'

'He went there to frighten Clough with the gun, that's all. It was a silly, reckless idea, but you know what Richard's like. Anyway, there was a confrontation and a struggle and, somehow, the gun went off. The farmer was shot. Richard thought in the arm or the side.'

Verity frowned. 'But that's not how he died. His throat was cut. It said so in the newspaper.'

'I know, but the police may think that if Richard shot him, then he may have done the other, too. The detective, Stannard, he seemed very suspicious.' Roger sighed again. 'And we've lost the farm, whatever happens. '

'But I thought—,' Verity reached across the table and took his hand. 'I thought with the farmer dead, everything would be all right. You'd get the land.'

'If only it were that simple. It'll go to the Crown and then to auction and we might not be in a position to wait that long.'

'Roger, I'm so sorry.'

He squeezed her hand. 'I shouldn't have said anything. Stop,' he said with a laugh as her frown deepened and he pushed a frizzy red curl away from her cheek. 'I won't have you worrying.'

But the damage was done. Verity continued to frown.

'No, I really must be going. Go in to your mother.' Hettie pushed away the tiresome child clinging to her skirt and hurried down the garden path.

It had been such a tedious afternoon. What on earth had made her accept the invitation to tea? Mrs Livermore had seemed quite delightful when they were in the hairdressers together, and when she had invited Hettie to tea, Hettie had agreed with alacrity, not wanting to be alone in the house while Verity and Roger were returning to Balham. And, of course, she simply couldn't spend the evening with Richard. That would never have done, not after…

So, to tea with Mrs Livermore she had gone, hoping for an afternoon of companionable gossip in a well-appointed house, learning about Craynebrook's social life. What she had got instead was a fussily decorated, old-fashioned sitting room with the smell of boiled cabbage hanging in the air and the constant presence of Mrs Livermore's noisy children. So, there had been no talk of the scandal at the Empire Club, nor of the Craynebrook Strangler or indeed any talk of fashionable gatherings or what the ladies of Craynebrook were wearing, but of how dear little Robbie had fallen over at school and scraped his knee, of how ever-so-clever Jeanie was progressing with her piano lessons and how the youngest, the apple of her father's eye, Stella, was suffering with a cold and how Mrs Livermore hoped Hettie didn't find the child's running nose too off-putting.

Hettie had found it very off-putting, and she had tried not to look in the child's direction, but it had been so difficult to ignore the girl's perpetual sniffing. The visit had already lasted far longer than Hettie had intended, but she had made the mistake of telling Mrs Livermore Roger was staying in town for the night and her hostess had insisted she stay a little longer.

She had borne it for as long as she could, but even the emptiness of her new house had become preferable to another minute in the Livermore household and she had risen, insisting she mustn't take up any more of her hostess's time, heading for the front door before Mrs Livermore could voice a protest.

Being away from the noise and bustle of the Livermores, however, meant Hettie had time to think, and her thoughts weren't at all pleasant. Ever since that morning, when she had learned Matthew had been in the office, she had been frantic. Her first thought was that Matthew had come looking for her. Her second that he had gone to tell Roger his wife was writing to him and giving him presents. But there was none of that. Instead, there had been talk of fingerprints and of Roger and Richard going to the police station, and she had felt sick. Was Roger in trouble? Why did Matthew want his and Richard's fingerprints?

If only he'd agreed to meet her, she could have found out everything. Oh, why had he said he couldn't? He could have put all her fears to rest. Just a few words. *Don't worry, darling. I won't let anything happen to you.* And she could relax and not have to carry this awful burden, sure she would be found out.

Hettie sighed. Finding herself at the kerbside, she looked right and left and then glanced across to the other side of the road to The King George public house. Its large windows were brightly illuminated and every time the doors opened, the sound of conversation and laughter escaped. She looked at the large building wistfully. How she would have liked to go in, but women of her class simply didn't go into public houses, and certainly not alone. She giggled. How scandalous! Whatever would Roger say if she did, though? And Verity would be apoplectic.

She sighed again and was about to cross the road when her eyes caught sight of a figure heading for the pub's doors. Her breath caught in her throat. It was! It was Matthew, going into the pub.

Hettie hurried across the road and pressed her nose to the stained glass window, but the glass was too thick and mottled to allow her to see anything. She stamped her foot in frustration. He was in there. She could see him, talk to him. If only she dared. Hettie glanced around nervously, bit her lip, then yanked the door open and stepped inside.

Smoke and the smell of beer enveloped her, almost overwhelmed her. *So many people in here*, she thought as she tried to take in all there was to see: the press of bodies, the glint of glasses, the mirrors behind the optics, the gleam of polished wood. Then she realised people were staring, curious expressions on their faces, talking to their companions while looking her up and down. Hettie raised her chin to show she didn't care and searched for Matthew.

She found him, standing over to the left, a magazine in one hand, a pint of beer in the other, waiting for a man wearing an apron to finish wiping the table. Hettie saw him nod when the man had done and take a seat, putting his pint on a cardboard coaster and laying his magazine on the table. He hadn't even looked up. Hadn't even realised she was there.

'You looking for someone, my dear?'

Hettie gasped and whirled around at the words to find herself staring up into the round, ruby face of a middle-aged man in a three-piece suit. He was smiling at her in a way Hettie didn't like.

'Or is it my lucky night?' he added with a wink.

'I'm with someone,' she blurted out and backed away before hurrying over to Matthew. She knocked the table, and he grabbed hold of his glass, the beer swirling and threatening to spill, before looking up to see who had interrupted his reading.

'Hello, Matthew,' Hettie breathed, her heart fluttering. 'It's me.'

Matthew looked up at Hettie, swallowing down a sigh of irritation. *Can't I have just a few moments to myself?*

He was annoyed, and not just with this woman who had barged into his table, but with himself. To fall asleep at work! It was unforgivable and he could hardly believe he'd done it. He'd been shaken awake by Lund, who said he daren't leave him to sleep any longer as Old Mouldy would be coming up to CID, and there'd be trouble if he caught Matthew napping on the job. Matthew had nodded and tried to pull himself together, reaching for the files in his In tray, but Lund had put a hand on the pile and shook his head.

'Go home, Stannard,' he said. 'You're dead on your feet. And don't come in tomorrow. Have Sunday off. You're owed it.'

There was something in Lund's voice that told Matthew not to argue, and he'd grabbed his hat and thanked his fellow inspector, not even asking the junior detectives what progress they'd made with the Bagleys. He didn't have the energy to care; he was, as Lund had said, dead on his feet. But he hadn't been able to face going home straightaway, so he'd made his way to the pub, wanting to have a beer and a read of his cricket magazine in peace. And now this bloody woman had spoiled all that.

'Hello?' he said.

'May I?' she asked, gesturing at the stool opposite him and sitting before he could answer. She looked back over her shoulder. 'Sorry. There was a man…' She shook her auburn hair, eyes closed. She opened them and smiled at him. 'Aren't you going to buy me a drink?'

Matthew was so shocked by the question, he found himself asking her what she wanted. She told him and he crossed to the bar, bringing her back a brandy and setting it before her. He sat back down and watched her with curiosity as she cupped the round glass and took a sip.

'That's better,' she said, setting the glass down. 'Oh, you don't look pleased to see me. I know, I know. You said we couldn't meet, but oh Matthew, I do so need to talk to you.'

'Madam,' Matthew began, thoroughly confused, 'I don't—'

'Madam?' she cried. 'Don't call me that, please.'

'What should I call you?'

'Henrietta,' she said, reaching across the table to grab his hand.

He pulled it away. 'There's some sort of mistake. I think you're confusing me with someone else.'

She drew back. 'Why are you being like this? Are you angry with me?'

'Madam,' he said as patiently as he could manage, 'I'm off duty. If you need to speak to the police, the station is just on the other side of the park.'

'I don't need the police. I need *you.* Oh,' she groaned, 'I'm making a mess of this. Matthew, please. Be kind to me. I've been so worried.'

Matthew's head was throbbing. He didn't need this nonsense. He rolled up his magazine and stuffed it into his pocket. 'I'm sorry. I can't help.' He rose from the table, leaving his pint untouched, but she jumped up and barred his way, pressing her body against his.

'Don't leave me,' she whispered, putting her arms around his neck. 'I love you.'

'For Christ's sake,' he snarled, yanking her arms away. People were staring. 'Get your hands off me.'

She cried out, and he saw her eyes grow wet. Oh God, that was all he needed, this mad woman crying in front of everyone. He pushed past her, trying to ignore the laughter as he went, and burst out of the doors onto the pavement. He closed his eyes as his head swam, and he took several deep breaths to steady himself.

'Why are you treating me like this?'

Matthew whirled around. Hettie had followed him out. 'What is it you want?'

'I just want you to be nice to me,' she whined, and reached out both hands to cup his face.

He grabbed her wrists again and shoved her away. She stumbled backwards, her chest heaving, staring at him in horror. Matthew felt ashamed for being so rough, but he couldn't bring himself to apologise. 'You leave me alone,' he said, seeing a bus approaching the stop over the road. He turned away, crossing the road and climbing on board as it pulled up.

Matthew sank down into a seat, determined not to look out of the window to see what the woman was doing. *Drive off*, he urged the bus driver. *Drive off before she can get on.*

'Are you all right, young man?' an old woman on the other side of the bus asked worriedly.

'Yes, thank you,' he said with a nod. He smiled wanly. 'I've just had a really bad day.'

Chapter Thirty-Four

Bishop Lancey bent down to the letterbox and lifted the flap. Peering in, he saw movement at the end of the hall, near the kitchen door. 'Stephen? I know you're in there. I can see you. Please let me in.' He let the flap drop and waited, conscious the Goulds were staring out of their front-room window. *Let them stare*, he thought a little uncharitably. *If it wasn't for them telling tales, none of this would have happened.*

He heard the latch lift and the front door opened a fraction. Pettifer's face appeared in the crack and Lancey was shocked. The vicar hadn't shaved for what looked like days and the flesh of his face was hanging from him like a bloodhound's jowls.

'Please let me in,' Lancey said in a kindly voice and was relieved when the door opened wide enough for him to step inside. A rank odour filled his nostrils as Pettifer leaned past him to close the door. The vicar hadn't been washing, either.

'What do you want?' Pettifer asked, not looking at him.

'To see how you are,' Lancey explained. 'You've not been performing the services and you're turning away all callers, by all accounts. People are worried about you, Stephen.'

‘What people?’

‘The Goulds, for one,’ Lancey said. ‘Your friends in the church. I expect many of your parishioners are wondering why they haven’t seen you.’

‘I can’t face them,’ Pettifer muttered. ‘Not after what I’ve done.’

‘Now, now, old chap,’ Lancey said, taking hold of the vicar’s skinny arm. ‘Don’t talk like that. Everyone makes mistakes.’

Pettifer shook his head. ‘It was unforgivable.’

Lancey cleared his throat. ‘Let’s sit down and have a chat, shall we? See what we can do about all this.’

‘There’s nothing to be done. I’ve betrayed the trust my flock had in me. I betrayed Josiah. I’ve betrayed God.’

‘Now, I won’t have this,’ Lancey said sternly. ‘This is self-pity. It’s not manly, and it’s not justified, Stephen. If anyone’s to blame, then it’s me. I should have been more understanding of your trouble when you came to me. I let you down, Stephen, and for that, I am truly sorry. Now, I’m here, hoping to make amends. Will you let me try to help you?’

‘Isn’t it too late?’ Pettifer said, but Lancey heard a note of hope in his voice.

Lancey smiled. ‘It’s never too late.’

Fred watched Matthew as he entered the pavilion and disappeared from view. He frowned and turned to Georgie, sitting on the grass beside Matthew’s deckchair.

‘What’s up with him today?’

Georgie shrugged. ‘I don’t know. I asked if he was all right earlier and he bit my head off.’

‘He had the right hump when he came home last night,’ Fred said, taking a swig from his bottle of ginger beer. ‘I was going to ask him to give me a hand behind the bar, but I thought he’d put the customers off with a face like he had. Is it because he's not playing today?'

Georgie shook his head. 'He decided not to play. Said his headache was too bad. I think it's work, Fred. This murder investigation, and Gadd still being free. It's playing on his mind. I know it is.'

'Has he said something, then?'

'He doesn't have to. I've heard him at night.' Georgie checked Matthew wasn't on his way back and leaned closer to Fred. 'He has nightmares. Wakes up in a sweat. He thinks I don't know, but I've seen and heard him.'

'Blimey,' Fred said, shocked. 'That don't sound like Matt. Maybe we ought to get him to go back to the doc?'

'He won't go,' Georgie sighed. 'Mattie won't have it that's he taken on too much. I mean, going back to work so soon after the attack, and having a murder to deal with, too. It's too much for him. I don't see why that other inspector can't investigate it.'

'Because they know Matt's better,' Fred suggested with a shrug. 'Let's face it. If you had a detective who had caught three murderers on the trot, you're not going to let one who hasn't caught any investigate, are you?'

'It's not fair,' Georgie said angrily, pulling up blades of grass. 'It's going to kill Mattie, all this worry.'

'I don't suppose there's anything we can do about it,' Fred said, delving into the small picnic hamper Pat had made up for them and pulling out a Scotch egg. 'Best not say anything to Matt when he comes back. You know what he's like. Doesn't like anyone to interfere.'

Alfred bounced on the balls of his feet as he waited for his knock to be answered. He was feeling better than he had for days. The police hadn't been to see him again, which meant they didn't really have anything on him, regardless of what that detective thought or tried to make out. His solicitor had told him the same thing. He was a good chap, knew his stuff. He'd got him out of a hole.

He smiled as the door opened. 'Richard!' he cried.

'What the hell are you doing here?' Richard said, poking his head out of the door and looking right and left down the street. 'Get in before someone sees you.' He grabbed Alfred's lapel and pulled him inside, slamming the door shut.

'Richard, really,' Alfred said, straightening his jacket. 'What's the matter?'

'What's the matter?' Richard echoed. 'After what you've done, you've got the cheek to ask me what's the matter?'

'What have I done?'

'Only brought the police to our door, that's all.'

'The police?' Alfred gasped. 'But I didn't breathe a word, Richard. I swear.'

'They came to the office.'

'Who did?'

'A detective. My brother and I had to go down to the station yesterday and give them our fingerprints. What the hell did you tell them?'

'Nothing. I had my solicitor with me and he told me to say No Comment, so that's what I did. And it worked. They had to let me go because they had nothing on me.'

'You swear to me, Duggan, you told them nothing about me and Roger?'

Alfred held up his hand. 'I swear. I promised you I wouldn't, and I didn't. I can keep my mouth shut, Richard. I don't understand how they got on to you.'

Richard sighed and shook his head. 'Maybe it doesn't matter. What are you here for, anyway?'

'I just thought I'd come round, see if there was anything I could help you with?'

'You don't give up, do you?'

'You said—'

'I know what I said. But not now. Not until this whole thing has blown over. You mustn't come round here again. Not to the office, either. Just in case.' He reached for the latch. 'You understand?'

'Of course I understand,' Alfred said, forcing a smile. 'I'm sorry I came round today, but I just thought…' He stepped towards the door. 'When it's all over, then?'

'Yes,' Richard said as Alfred stepped down onto the front step. He shut the door before Alfred could say another word.

'Will there be anything else, madam?' Daisy asked as she cleared away the tea things. 'Madam?'

'What?' Hettie stared up at the maid in confusion. 'Oh no, that's all. Thank you, Daisy.'

'Have you finished with my scrapbook, madam?' Daisy asked. 'It's fine if you haven't, but I have some more cuttings I'd like to paste in if you have.'

Hettie pulled the scrapbook out from behind the sofa cushion and laid it on her lap. 'Not quite finished, Daisy, if you don't mind.'

'Very good, madam,' Daisy said, and went out.

Hettie had heard the note of irritation in Daisy's voice and knew the maid would dearly liked to have had her scrapbook returned, but she wasn't ready to give it up just yet. She turned the pages, her heart heaving every time she saw a photograph of Matthew.

She had rushed home last night after her meeting with him, tears streaming from her eyes, so very glad Roger wasn't home to see her, and shut herself in her bedroom. Why had he treated her that way? She couldn't understand it. Matthew had been angry with her and she hadn't done anything to deserve it. Hettie knew she had surprised him, maybe even embarrassed him. Men didn't like women showing affection in public and she should have behaved better. But to push her away, not once but twice, the second when they were outside and no one was looking. It wasn't fair. It was mean.

Why were men so cruel? What had she ever done that men should treat her so badly?

She flipped the pages angrily. There Matthew was again, being lauded and praised for doing such a good job as a policeman. But what about him as a gentleman? No, there was nothing in the newspapers about that. There couldn't be. Matthew wasn't a gentleman. He was working class, and she supposed she shouldn't have expected more from him.

Hettie slammed the scrapbook shut. Daisy could have it back, after all. She didn't want to look at it anymore. Her lips pursed. All the time she had wasted on Matthew, all the love she had poured out into her letters, even giving him a very expensive present, and he had thrown it all back in her face. He shouldn't be allowed to get away with it.

Chapter Thirty-Five

Matthew climbed the front steps to the station entrance wearily, feeling for perhaps the first time in his career that he really didn't want to go into work. He wasn't doing his job properly. Never before would he have taken a day off while investigating a murder, and he was worried he had lost interest in the job. What would he do if he wasn't a policeman? He had no talent for anything else, and though he knew Pat and Fred wouldn't see him on the dole, he shuddered at the thought of having to work behind the bar at the pub.

He pulled the door open and headed straight for the stairs to CID. Before he could get there, Turkel leaned over the front desk to get his attention.

'Yes, sergeant?' Matthew said, waiting for the inevitable summons to the top floor.

'Mr Mullinger wanted to see you as soon as you came in, sir.'

Matthew nodded to Turkel. He took the stairs to the top floor slowly, in no hurry to see the superintendent, who either wanted an update on the murder investigation or wanted to give him a bollocking for taking the day off.

'Morning, Miss Halliwell,' he said as he reached the top step. 'Mr Mullinger wants to see me.'

'You're to go straight in, inspector,' she said stiffly, not giving him her usual smile.

'Thank you,' he said, a little taken aback by the omission. He rapped on the superintendent's door and opened it without waiting for a response. He was surprised to see Lund sitting in one of the visitor chairs. 'You wanted to see me, sir?'

'Yes, Stannard,' Mullinger said and pointed at the empty chair beside Lund. 'Sit down.'

Matthew obeyed, sensing something was wrong. He raised an eyebrow at Lund in query, but Lund looked away.

'I'm afraid a rather serious matter has arisen, Stannard,' Mullinger said. 'A complaint has been made against you.'

Matthew's head throbbed. What the hell was this now? 'Against me? For what?'

Mullinger's neck flushed purple. 'A woman claims you molested her on Saturday evening.'

'Henrietta?' Matthew cried. He knew at once he should have kept his mouth shut. Mullinger's eyebrows rose and his eyes met Lund's.

'So, you do know this woman?'

'No, I don't know her. Of her. She came up to my table in the pub and started talking to me.'

'What about?' Lund asked.

Matthew shook his head. 'Some nonsense about me telling her we couldn't meet and her needing to talk to me. She just went on and on, and I couldn't get rid of her. So I left.'

'Alone?'

'Yes, alone. But she followed me out.'

'And then what?'

'Then nothing. I told her to leave me alone and got the bus home.'

'You didn't touch her?' Mullinger asked.

'Of course I didn't!' Matthew cried indignantly. Mullinger glanced at Lund. 'What?'

'She claims you grabbed her and pushed up her against the wall,' Lund said. 'Held her there while you molested her.'

Matthew felt blood rushing into his face. 'I didn't touch her,' he said, barely able to get the words out.

'She has bruises on her wrists,' Mullinger said.

'Finger marks,' Lund added.

Matthew closed his eyes and rubbed his forehead. 'She threw her arms around my neck and wouldn't let go. I may have taken hold of her to push her away.'

'You said you didn't touch her,' Mullinger said.

'I meant I didn't molest her, sir.'

'Why would she say you did?'

'I have no idea.'

'And you hadn't met this woman before?' Lund asked.

'I'd never seen her before Saturday.'

'But she knew who you were,' Mullinger pointed out.

'That's easily explained, sir,' Lund said. 'Stannard's been in the 'papers enough. And women have been writing to him ever since the attack.'

'Have they?' Mullinger raised an eyebrow. 'I wasn't aware of that.'

'It was nothing to bother you with. But some of the letters were pretty racy.' He turned to Matthew. 'Could she have been one of those?'

'I suppose so. I didn't read the letters.'

'We've got them on file,' Lund said to Mullinger. 'I'll go through them. See if I can find anything from a Henrietta.'

'Very good,' Mullinger nodded. 'Now, Stannard, obviously this complaint has to be investigated and ordinarily, I would be duty-bound to suspend you for the duration—'

'No, sir, you can't do that,' Matthew begged.

'Indeed, I can't,' Mullinger said stiffly, annoyed at being interrupted. 'Not with the Clough murder still outstanding and Lund having to deal with this. So, you will confine your activities to the murder investigation. You will not interfere with Lund's enquiries. Is that clear?'

Matthew nodded miserably. 'Yes, sir.'

Mullinger watched the door close and waited a few moments until he was sure Matthew had gone. 'Well, what do you think?'

Lund shook his head. 'I can't believe he touched her, sir. Not Stannard.'

'He admitted grabbing hold of her.'

'Not in the way she claims. I can believe he grabbed hold of her to get rid of her, but not for a bit of the other.'

'Why would she make it up?'

Lund shrugged. 'I don't know. People do all sorts of strange things.'

'And yet....' Mullinger pushed out his lips and shook his head.

'And yet what, sir?'

'We can't ignore the possibility the complaint is true.'

'Which is why we're looking into it,' Lund pointed out. 'I'm saying I think it's going to turn out he didn't molest her.'

'Perhaps, but let's consider that knock on the head. I agree with you. Before that, I would have thought Stannard was the last man to be accused of mistreating a woman, but the attack may have done something to his brain—'

'You're not serious?' Lund snorted, but then he thought of his conversation with Barnes, when the young detective had expressed concern about Matthew not being himself. Was there something in what Mullinger was saying?

'We are not doctors, Lund,' Mullinger went on. 'Who's to say what damage a blow to the head can do? And what about these letters you say he received? Racy?'

'Stannard's a good-looking bloke, sir. Women go funny around him.'

'Funny?' Mullinger didn't understand.

'They like him, sir. I've seen it.' He jerked his thumb towards the door. 'Miss Halliwell goes weak at the knees every time he walks in the room.'

Mullinger stared at the door, aghast. 'Does she?'

'And the women who wrote to him weren't shy about what they were offering him.'

'Really? I had no idea women could be so…' Mullinger searched for the right word, 'forward. Well, maybe Stannard took advantage, then. He is a single man, after all.' He banged his hand on the desk. 'This is all we need. If this gets into the newspapers… Well, if it does, I shan't hesitate to make an example of Stannard. The public must be able to feel they can trust us.'

Lund's eyes narrowed. 'Can we make sure he's guilty before you go throwing him to the wolves, sir?'

Mullinger drew himself up. 'Of course, Lund. I'm hoping you find this complaint to be false. But if he is guilty, then I'll have him off the Force before he can blink.'

Lund got to his feet. 'I understand you, sir. All too well, in fact.'

Barnes tapped Denham on the shoulder and Denham turned, telephone at his ear, brow creasing. He held up a finger to tell Barnes to wait, then finished his call. 'What is it?' he said, setting the receiver into the cradle.

'Have you heard about the inspector?' Barnes said in a low voice.

'Heard what?'

'There's been a complaint against him. A woman's complained he had a go at her.'

'You what?' Denham shook his head. 'Nah. The inspector's polite as anything with civilians. Too polite if you ask me.'

'I don't mean she says he was rude to her,' Barnes said impatiently. He glanced around the office and leant in closer. 'She says he molested her.'

Denham stared at him. 'You're having me on.'

'I'm not. Sergeant Copley just told me. The woman came in yesterday to make the complaint.'

'How does Copley know?'

'Mavis told him. She overheard it all. He's well pleased. You know she likes the inspector. Well, she's gone off him now and Copley's back in favour.'

'I don't believe it. Stannard wouldn't.'

'What are you two whispering about?' Pinder was leaning back in his chair, looking at them through narrowed eyes. 'You up to something?'

'We're not up to anything, Gary,' Barnes said, straightening.

'Well, spit it out, then.'

'Some woman's accused Stannard of molesting her,' Denham said.

Pinder laughed. 'You're kidding?'

'It's not funny, Gary,' Barnes chided.

'I think it's bloody hilarious. The old dog.'

'You can't believe he did it?' Denham asked.

'Why not? He's a bloke, ain't he? She was probably asking for it and then changed her mind. You know what tarts are like. I wonder if it was one of those old bags who wrote to him? They were up for a bit of the other, weren't they? Probably thought he was on a promise.'

'Don't let on that you've heard about it,' Barnes said uncomfortably. 'No one's supposed to know.'

Pinder grinned. 'Are you kidding? I'm going to enjoy this. Mr High-and-Mighty Stannard gets his comeuppance at last. Just goes to show, he can play the gent, but when it comes down to it, he's just the same as any of us.'

Matthew jumped as the door to the Gents was flung open. He closed his eyes, holding his breath.

'Stannard?' Lund called. 'You in here?'

'Just a minute,' he said from behind the cubicle door.

'Get out here. There's no point hiding.'

Matthew yanked the chain and unlocked the door. 'I'm not hiding,' he lied, and brushed past Lund to wash his hands.

'Look, sunshine,' Lund said, catching his eye in the mirror. 'I'm not happy about this either. I don't want to investigate you. It's not my idea of fun.'

'My heart bleeds for you.'

'You going to pack this in?' Lund said angrily, grabbing Matthew's shoulder and spinning him around to face him. 'I'm on your side, you silly sod, though God knows why.'

'You don't think I did it?' Matthew asked, surprised.

'Of course I bloody don't.'

'You could have said so to Mullinger.'

'I did say so after you'd gone,' Lund shot back. 'But I've still got to look into it, haven't I? Now, are you going to cooperate with me so we can get this cleared up and go back to what we're good at?'

Matthew drew in a deep breath and nodded.

'Good. So, I'm going to need a full statement from you of exactly what happened on Saturday night. The lot. Don't leave anything out. I don't care how embarrassing you think it is. I need to know everything.'

'Everyone's going to know,' Matthew sighed, shaking his head.

'Yeah, I'm afraid so. You can't keep a secret in this place.'

'Even Miss Halliwell gave me the cold shoulder.'

'Don't you worry about her. You get your statement written and given to me, and then you just worry about solving your murder. You let me sort this mess out. Right?'

Matthew nodded. 'Right.'

Matthew followed Lund into CID, knowing he had to carry on as if nothing had happened. He knew they all knew in CID; he could tell as soon as he walked in. Barnes and Denham looked hastily away, Bissett glanced up from beneath lowered lids, and Pinder had a smug grin on his face. Oh yes, they knew all right, and Matthew's cheeks burnt with shame.

He sat down at his desk and busied himself with writing his statement for Lund. He struggled to remember everything Henrietta had said and did, and struggled even harder to remember his own words and actions. It was all something of a blur, but he set it down as well as he could and handed it to Lund.

'Ta,' Lund said, taking it. 'This is everything?'

Matthew nodded, staring at the statement.

'You can leave it with me now. Go on. Get on with your murder.'

Matthew went to the door and called Barnes into the office. 'What have you found out about the Bagleys?' he said, resuming his seat at the desk and lighting a cigarette.

'Perfectly respectable building firm, sir,' Barnes said. 'Established in Balham before the war. Did quite well afterwards, getting council grants to build social housing. But they seemed to go off that idea about four years ago when they began building projects a bit further out, Surrey and Middlesex, for the middle classes. Semis and that.'

'Nothing untoward?' Matthew asked.

'Not that I've been able to find, sir.'

'Any connection with Duggan before this Craynebrook move?'

Barnes shook his head. 'Nothing. And in regards to Duggan, his wife confirms he was at home on the night Clough was killed. I also got confirmation from the Duggan maid and the next-door neighbour who saw Duggan going into his garden shed around nine o'clock.'

'Anything on the gun?'

'It's at the lab. We're still waiting to find out if the bullet you found at the farm was fired by that gun. The lab warned it could take a week or two to get a result.'

'Great,' Matthew muttered.

'Sorry, sir,' Barnes said.

'What about the removal men? Have you talked to them?'

'Not yet, sir.'

'Give me the address. I'll do it.'

'I can do it, sir,' Barnes protested.

'Just give me the damn address, Barnes!'

'Don't take it out on others, Stannard,' Lund said quietly as Barnes rushed out to his desk.

'Here you are, sir,' Barnes said, coming back and handing Matthew a slip of paper.

Matthew took it. 'Thank you. Sorry for just now, Barnes. I'm a bit tired.'

'Of course, sir. Do you want me to come with you?'

'No, you stay here and carry on with whatever you're doing.' Matthew rose and grabbed his hat. 'Be back later,' he said, hurrying out of CID.

'It's not true, is it, sir?' Barnes asked when the door had closed. 'What's being said?'

‘It’s none of your business, Barnes,’ Lund said, re-reading Matthew’s statement.

‘It’s just I can’t believe it. Not him.’

‘You got cloth ears or what?’ Lund went to the shelf and took down the file with the letters Matthew had received. When he turned back, Pinder had come in and was leaning against the doorjamb.

‘You talking about Stannard?’ he asked.

‘That’s Inspector Stannard to you, Pinder,’ Lund said sternly, throwing the file on his desk and resuming his seat.

‘Only if he don’t get thrown out of the Force for trying to have his wicked way,’ Pinder grinned.

‘Could you try not to enjoy it quite so much?’ Lund asked as Barnes ducked out.

Pinder looked over his shoulder to the outer office before closing the door. ‘He did it, you know?’

Lund frowned up at him. ‘And how do you know that?’

Pinder pulled a rolled-up newspaper from his back trouser pocket and put it before Lund on the blotter. ‘Read that.’

Lund squinted at the advert. ‘“Henrietta. Can’t meet at moment. Please understand. One day soon. Yours, Matthew.” Bloody hell.’

‘That proves it, don’t it?’

‘Haven’t you got work to do?’ Lund said, waving him out of the office.

Pinder slouched out, and Lund watched him fall into his chair with a self-satisfied air. He looked back at the advertisement and shook his head. ‘You bloody fool, Stannard.’

Chapter Thirty-Six

Matthew was back at Bagley Bros. Building Co., knocking on the door and seeing Richard stiffen as he answered it.

'Yes, inspector?' he said, not inviting Matthew in.

'I'd like another word, please, Mr Bagley.'

Richard sighed and stepped aside to allow him to enter. 'I had hoped we'd seen the last of you.'

'I'm the proverbial bad penny.'

'Yes, you are.' Richard shoved his hands in his trouser pockets. 'Well?'

'We've confirmed your fingerprints are on your father's gun—'

'Which they would be.'

'And we're waiting to see if the bullet recovered from the farm was shot from your gun.'

'Right.'

'And I've spoken with your removal men,' Matthew said, pointing to a chair. Richard nodded, and he sat down. 'They claim to have no knowledge of your gun being in one of the boxes they moved and all the men deny taking it.'

'Well, they would, wouldn't they?'

'I'm at a loss what their motive would be in killing Clough.'

'Don't ask me,' Richard cried in exasperation. 'And besides, I didn't say they definitely took it. I said the gun must have gone missing during the move. For all I know, someone took it from a box while the back of the van was open. I suppose it could have been anyone.'

'That leaves the field rather open.'

'And I'm afraid that's your problem. Now, if you don't mind, inspector, I've got a great deal to do.' He held his hand out towards the door.

'Where were you on the night of Sunday the eighteenth?'

Richard's arm fell to his side. 'What?'

'Do you need me to repeat the question?'

'I don't think I care for your tone, inspector.'

'If I could have an answer, Mr Bagley?'

'I was at home.'

'From what time?'

'I was there all day. We'd only just moved in. There was a lot to do.'

'Is there anyone who can confirm you were at home?'

'My wife,' Richard said after a moment. 'She'll confirm it.'

'And where will I find your wife at this hour?'

'I'm not sure. She may be at home. She may be out. Look. Do you really need to bother her? I've told you where I was. Surely my word is good enough? I'm not some hobble-de-hoy, you know?'

'I'm afraid I must have it confirmed.'

'Why must you? I had nothing to do with Clough. If the cantankerous old fool got himself killed, it's nothing to do with me.'

'Cantankerous?' Matthew said, raising an eyebrow.

'What?' Richard said, staring at Matthew.

'You called Mr Clough cantankerous.'

'Did I?'

'You did. I thought you didn't know him?'

'I didn't,' Richard said, running his hand through his hair, messing it up.

'It's an oddly personal way to describe someone you don't know.'

Richard moved to the door and pulled it open. 'If there's nothing else, inspector…'

'I'll be speaking to your wife, Mr Bagley,' Matthew promised as he left.

Lund opened the door to *The Chronicle*'s main office and nodded at the secretary, who peered at him over the top of her spectacles.

'Yes? Can I help you?' she asked, her fingers poised above her typewriter keys.

Lund showed her his warrant card, and she stared at him in surprise. 'I want to ask you about an advert in your Personals column from the twenty-third of May.' He showed her the copy of the newspaper Pinder had given him. 'The fourth ad down.'

She read it. 'What about it?'

'How did you get the wording for the ad? Did someone come in and dictate it or what?'

Without a word, the secretary rose and went over to a bank of wooden filing cabinets against the wall. She pulled a drawer out and rifled through the files inside, pulling one out and carrying it back to the desk. 'Yes. Here it is.' She pulled out a sheet of paper. 'That one came in by post.'

'Who wrote it? Who was it from?'

'There wasn't a name.'

Lund frowned. 'Is that usual?'

'Oh yes,' the secretary nodded. 'Some people value anonymity. They don't want all their little secrets out in the open.' She looked again at the ad. 'But there is a name. See? It says Matthew.'

‘Yeah, I know that,’ Lund nodded. ‘You charge for the ads, I take it?’

‘Of course.’

‘So, how was this one paid for?’

‘There was payment in the envelope.’

Lund tutted. ‘So there’s no way of knowing who sent it?’

‘I’m afraid not, inspector.’ She broke off and looked over Lund’s shoulder.

Lund turned to see Edwards standing in his office doorway.

‘Hello, inspector,’ Edwards said. ‘What brings you here?’

‘Just making an enquiry, Mr Edwards.’

‘You want to put an ad in the ’paper?’

‘Not quite.’ Lund nodded a thank you to the secretary and left the office without another word.

‘What was he after?’ Edwards asked.

The secretary told him.

‘What’s his interest in that?’ Edwards wondered, looking at the text. ‘Matthew.’

‘Do you know who that is, Mr Edwards?’

Edwards narrowed his eyes and stared at the door Lund had gone through, thinking. ‘Maybe.’

Roger burst into the office. ‘Was that the inspector I saw leaving?’ he panted.

‘Yes,’ Richard said, kicking the leg of the nearest desk. ‘He’s asking where I was the night Clough was killed. I told him I was at home all day and he’s going to speak to Verity. Jesus, Rog, what do we do?’

Roger snatched up the telephone and instructed the operator. He tapped the desktop frantically while he waited for his ring to be answered. ‘Verity?… Yes, it’s me… Listen, Verity. You’re going to be getting a visit from a police inspector shortly…. Yes, that one.

He's going to ask you where Richard was on the...?' He put his hand over the mouthpiece and raised his eyebrows at Richard.

'Sunday the eighteenth,' Richard whispered.

'Sunday the eighteenth.' Roger repeated. 'Now, that's the first Sunday we were here in Craynebrook... Yes... Now, just tell him Richard was at home all day, will you?... You know why... Will you do that, please?... Yes?... Well, see you later, then... Yes, yes. Bye.' He hung up. 'That's sorted.'

'You told her she knew why,' Richard said worriedly. 'Have you told her what I did?'

Roger nodded. 'But she's a good girl. She'll back us up.'

'And will that be enough to get him off my back?'

Roger sighed. 'I hope so, Rich.'

Frank Greader ran his damp cloth over the countertop, looking up as the door to the pub opened. 'Hello, Ray,' he greeted Lund as he walked in. 'Haven't seen you for a while. What'll it be?'

Lund shook his head. 'I'm not here for a drink.' He noticed the barmaid a few feet away and the other patrons looking at him with interest. 'I want a word in private, Frank.'

'Come through to the back.' He lifted the flap in the bar and Lund stepped through. 'What's up?'

'It's about Saturday night. You were here?'

'I'm always here Saturday night.'

'Did Inspector Stannard come in?'

'Yeah. He came in early. I cleared a table for him.'

'Was he on his own?'

'Well, he came in alone. A woman went over to him about five minutes later.'

Lund nodded. 'Was he expecting her?'

Greader frowned. 'I couldn't say. He didn't look as if he was. I mean, he had a magazine out and he was reading.'

'What was the woman like?'

'Posh,' Greader said without hesitation. 'Turned a few heads, I can tell you.'

'Was she with anyone?'

'No, that was the thing. Women like her don't generally come into a pub at all, let alone without a fella. I did think maybe she needed help or something and I was going to go and ask her if she was all right, but then she went over to the inspector and that was that.'

'Did you see what happened?'

'What do you mean, what happened?'

'Well, how he greeted her? If they looked friendly?'

'Why are you asking this, Ray?'

'It's important, Frank. Please.'

Greader folded his arms and frowned as he concentrated. 'I think he was surprised. And as for friendly, well…' he shrugged. 'He bought her a drink, so I suppose they must have been.'

'He bought her a drink?'

'Yeah. Brandy, I think.'

Lund shook his head. 'Then what?'

'Ray, I was busy. I weren't watching them all the time. I didn't see.'

'What you did see,' he pressed.

'Well, there was a scene. She threw her arms around his neck and he sort of pushed her away. He looked angry about it.'

'He pushed her away?'

Greader nodded. 'Embarrassed, I think. Then he went out, and she followed him.'

'Did you see what happened outside?'

'Course I didn't. So, go on. Tell me why you're asking.'

'I can't,' Lund said. 'It's confidential.'

'Is the inspector in trouble?'

'He might be. Keep it to yourself, though, Frank.'

Greader nodded. 'Mum's the word.'

Verity opened the front door and Matthew's eyes narrowed as he realised he'd seen her before. Then it hit him. She'd come into the Bagleys' office when he'd first met Roger and Richard.

'Yes?' she said, raising a plucked eyebrow.

'Mrs Richard Bagley?' Matthew asked, showing her his warrant card. 'Could I come in, please?'

She stared for a long moment at his warrant card, then nodded and stepped backwards to open the door for him. 'Is this about my husband?' she asked, closing the door and turning to him.

Matthew nodded. 'I've just been at the office on the high street.'

'Really? Is there a problem? I thought now you had his fingerprints, that would be an end of it?'

'I just need your husband's whereabouts confirmed for the night of Sunday the eighteenth. Can you tell me where he was?'

'Of course,' she said. 'He was here.'

'From what time?'

'All day. We were unpacking. Why do you need to know where he was?'

'Because of the murder.'

'Which he had nothing to do with.'

'That's yet to be determined.'

'You suspect my husband?'

'He's on my list of suspects, yes.'

'I see,' Verity nodded.

Not an indignant cry that to suspect her husband of murder was ridiculous; not an assertion that he was being insulting by saying so; just an 'I see'. Matthew found her reaction more than a little odd. 'Were you aware your husband's gun was missing?' he asked.

'Not until he told me.'

'What do you think happened to it?'

'I really have no idea.'

'Your husband thinks it was stolen by the removal men.'

'Yes, perhaps.'

'I imagine it's rather upsetting to learn your husband's gun was used to shoot a man?'

Verity's mouth curved a little. 'I haven't really given it any thought, inspector.'

'You didn't know Mr Clough?'

'No, I didn't know him.'

'Did your husband?'

'I don't believe so.'

'What do you know of your husband's business?'

'Nothing. Richard knows I'm not interested in business, so he doesn't bore me with it.'

Matthew looked around the hall. 'I was here before with the previous owners.'

'Oh? Friends of yours?'

There was a hint of surprise in her voice, he noted. A man of Matthew's class wasn't supposed to be friends with people who could afford a house on St Jude's Avenue. He shook his head. 'Police business. The previous owners of this house were the Fairbanks. Mr Fairbank was murdered.' Matthew watched her carefully, but there was no change of expression.

'So I understand,' Verity said. 'But not in this house.'

'I believe Alfred Duggan acquired this house for you?'

Verity smiled. 'Again, inspector, you ask me a question of which I have no knowledge. My husband arranged the purchase.'

'But surely, Mr Duggan showed you around before you bought it?'

'I didn't see it before Richard bought it,' she sighed. 'The first time I was in this house was the day we moved in. Does that answer your question because I have things to do?'

Matthew had had enough of her coolness. He was ready to leave. ‘I think so, Mrs Bagley. Thank you for your time.’

Verity opened the door. He glanced down at the console tables on either side, noting the photograph on the left-hand one of Roger and Richard standing outside what looked like a timber yard, both men looking considerably younger, before turning to the one on the right. His breath caught in his throat.

‘What is it?’ Verity asked sharply, following his gaze.

‘That woman,’ he said, snatching up the frame and pointing.

‘That’s my sister,’ Verity said, frowning at him. ‘Why?’

‘Your sister is Henrietta?’ Matthew asked, staring at her in astonishment.

‘Yes.’ Verity’s eyes narrowed. ‘Why? Do you know her?’

Chapter Thirty-Seven

Lund rang the doorbell of No. 13 St Jude's Avenue, the address Henrietta had given when she made her complaint. The door opened and Daisy smiled at him.

He showed his warrant card. 'I'd like to see your mistress.'

Daisy's eyes widened. 'Is she expecting you?'

'I doubt it,' Lund said, stepping inside.

'Then if you would like to wait, I'll tell her you're here. The master and mistress are having their luncheon.'

'Tell her I don't have time to wait on her leisure,' Lund called after her as she went into a room, closing the door to. He heard the murmur of voices; a man's voice saying, 'Oh, this is ridiculous,' and a woman's saying, 'What, here?' Then the door was yanked open, and a man strode out.

'This is unacceptable, inspector. We are having our lunch.'

Lund was unfazed by Roger's bluster. 'There's no need to disturb you, sir, if you'd rather carry on eating. I'm here to see your wife.'

Roger was taken aback. 'Why do you want to see my wife?'

Lund looked past him to the doorway where Hettie was peering out. 'Your wife knows why.'

Roger turned to Hettie. 'What is all this? Darling?'

'If I could have a word?' Lund said to Hettie.

'Come into the sitting room,' Hettie said, avoiding her husband's eye. 'Not you, darling. You finish your lunch. I know you want to get back to the office.'

'The hell I will. What does this policeman have to do with you?' Roger demanded.

'Oh, it's nothing, really,' she said, glaring a little at Lund. She ushered him towards the opposite door.

Roger followed her and Lund into the sitting room. 'What's going on?'

'Oh,' she cried, her hand going to her face. 'I didn't want to involve you.' She turned on Lund. 'You really shouldn't have come here.'

'Needs must, I'm afraid,' Lund said unapologetically and took a seat on the sofa.

Roger stared at his effrontery, then turned to Hettie. 'Involve me in what? Are you in some kind of trouble?'

Hettie sank onto the other sofa. 'What do you want to talk about, inspector?'

'I take it you haven't told your husband about the complaint you've made?' Lund said, taking out his notebook and licking the tip of his pencil.

'A complaint?' Roger cried.

'Your wife came to the police station yesterday afternoon to complain that Inspector Stannard molested her on Saturday night,' Lund said.

'He what?' Roger roared.

'Darling, please don't shout,' Hettie said, covering her ears.

'What did he do? Did he hurt you? Where was this? Why didn't you tell me?'

'If I could get a word in edgeways, sir?' Lund said. 'Madam, I have to inform you that Inspector Stannard denies molesting you.'

'Well, he would deny it, wouldn't he?' Hettie thrust out her arms and tugged at her sleeves. 'But I didn't do these to myself.'

Roger gave a small cry and gently took hold of her hands. 'He made those?'

'Yes, he did,' Hettie said defiantly.

'He doesn't deny that he grabbed hold of you,' Lund said. 'But he claims it was only after you threw your arms around him and made a scene in public. He grabbed you to make you let go of him.'

'Oh, really,' she said, blushing, quite nicely, Lund thought. He wouldn't blame Matthew for fancying her. 'That's quite ridiculous.'

Lund took the lavender-coloured envelope out of his pocket and unfolded the letter. He passed it to her. 'Did you write that letter to Inspector Stannard?'

She glanced at it before handing it back. 'Yes, I did. I read about him in the newspaper and was concerned for him.'

'Let me see that,' Roger demanded.

'No,' Hettie cried, but Lund had already handed it over.

'It's quite a provocative letter for a woman to send to a man she doesn't know, I'm sure you'll agree,' Lund said.

Roger stared at Hettie for a long moment, then gave the letter back to Lund. 'I don't agree. My wife offered her sympathy to the inspector in perfectly respectable language. If you read more into it than that, then I'm afraid that says more about you than it does about her. My wife is a very compassionate woman.'

'Oh, I'm sure,' Lund grinned, putting the letter back in his pocket.

Hettie was incensed by his sarcasm. 'I felt sorry for him,' she cried indignantly, 'and I read in the newspaper that he doesn't have anyone to look after him. That's why I thought he'd like my present.'

'Your present?' Lund asked.

'The cigarette case.'

Matthew hadn't mentioned a cigarette case. Lund swallowed down his irritation. 'I've spoken with people at the pub. They say Inspector Stannard was surprised to see you.'

'Yes, he was.'

'You hadn't arranged to meet?'

'No, of course not.'

'I'm only asking because of this ad in the newspaper.' He showed her *The Chronicle*. 'That suggests you'd asked to meet and he'd said no.'

'Well, I don't know,' she said, giving the paper back to him. 'Maybe. I can't remember.'

'So, you followed him into the pub?'

'I saw him across the road and thought I'd pop in.'

'You went into a pub? Alone?' Roger asked, aghast.

Hettie closed her eyes and didn't answer.

'I'm sorry, madam, but you have to appreciate how this looks. You write to Inspector Stannard offering him your sympathy,' Lund said with a raised eyebrow, 'and you follow him into a public house, which isn't the kind of place a lady of your class should really be in. Witnesses state you threw yourself at him and he rebuffed you, so you followed him out of the pub. It seems to me you've been the one doing all the chasing.'

'What the hell are you suggesting, inspector?' Roger said.

'I'm not suggesting anything. I'm stating the facts as I've found them. Your wife's been chasing after Inspector Stannard all this time.'

'He hurt me,' Hettie jumped off the sofa and screeched at Lund. 'Whether I chased after him or not, he had no right to hurt me. Darling? You believe me, don't you?'

'Of course I do,' Roger assured her, taking hold of her shoulders and pushing her back down onto the sofa. He pointed a finger at Lund. 'I know what this is. You're covering up for him. He's one of your own and you all stick together. So, you're keen to show him not at fault. Well, I won't have my wife treated this way. If you think we're going to drop this complaint, you've got another thing coming. We're going to make sure he gets what's coming to him.'

Lund put his notebook away and got to his feet. 'If you say so, sir. There's no need to see me out.'

The doorbell rang and Roger heard Daisy answer it. Heard too Richard's voice asking where Roger was and Verity greeting the maid. He went to the door.

'In here,' he said, jerking his head at Richard.

Richard and Verity came into the sitting room. 'Verity confirmed—' Richard broke off as he caught sight of Hettie on the sofa. 'What's wrong?'

Hettie's face crumpled, and she put her handkerchief to her eyes. 'Don't tell them,' she begged Roger.

'Tell us what?' Richard asked, looking from Hettie to Roger.

'I have to, darling,' Roger said. 'We've had another policeman here.'

'Oh, for Christ's sake,' Richard cried. 'They're not going to leave us alone, are they?'

'It wasn't about the gun. Hettie made a complaint to them yesterday.' He winced as Hettie's cries grew louder. 'About that Inspector Stannard.'

'Oh, no, don't tell me,' Verity said despairingly. 'She's accused him of something, hasn't she?'

'He molested me,' Hettie shrieked at her. 'So, I told on him.'

'For heaven's sake, Hettie.' Verity threw her handbag onto the sofa, only just missing hitting her sister. 'Not this again.'

'Verity,' Roger said with a sigh.

'You don't believe her, do you?' Verity cried incredulously. 'Please tell me you don't.'

'If Hettie says he molested her, then I believe her,' Roger said defiantly.

Verity stared at him, then turned to Richard. 'And you?'

Richard looked uncomfortable and shuffled his feet. 'If that's what she says happened—'

Verity shook her head at them both. 'You're pathetic, both of you.'

'Verity, that's enough,' Richard snarled.

'Oh, shut up, Verity,' she mocked. 'Keep quiet, Verity. Don't say anything unkind about Hettie, Verity.'

'Stop! Stop!' Hettie screeched. She pushed Verity out of the way and ran from the room.

'Now look what you've done,' Roger said, starting after her. He had reached the bottom of the stairs when he heard a door slam upstairs and sighed. Coming back, he closed the door and glared at Verity. 'Why did you have to say all that?'

'Because it's true, even if you're happy to pretend it isn't. You know as well as I do that most of what comes out of Hettie's mouth is a lie or at best a gross exaggeration. How can you keep on defending her when she causes so much trouble?'

'Because she's my wife.'

'A wife who goes after every man who takes her fancy,' Verity retorted, shooting an angry glance at Richard. Richard coloured and turned away, pouring himself a drink from the decanter on the sideboard.

'There are bruises on her wrists where he grabbed her,' Roger said, trying to keep his temper under control.

'Which she probably made herself,' Verity scoffed.

'Hettie wouldn't do that.'

'Oh, God, Roger. You have no idea what Hettie is capable of.'

They fell silent, both glaring at each other, both too angry to speak any further.

'You know, Rog,' Richard said quietly, breaking the silence. 'This could be good for us.'

'How?' Roger said disbelievingly.

'Think about it,' Richard said. 'If this Inspector Stannard's facing a complaint from Hettie, then if he comes after us again, we can say it's because of that. He's getting his own back, trying to clear himself by making us appear guilty.'

Roger nodded. 'Yes, maybe it will work in our favour.'

'So, you don't believe her,' Verity said, smiling bitterly. 'Despite everything you've said, you know she's lying about him touching her.'

'I don't care what you think of me, Verity,' Roger said. 'But we must back up her story. If for no better reason than it gets the police off Richard's back. Even you must want that.'

Verity studied him and her husband coolly. 'I'm going home.'

Matthew found Lund in the canteen. He pulled out a chair and sat down.

'Can I eat in peace, please?' Lund said, stuffing chips into his mouth.

'Henrietta is Henrietta Bagley,' Matthew said, leaning in close.

Lund frowned at him. 'Foster,' he corrected. 'Henrietta Foster.'

'No,' Matthew shook his head. 'I've seen a photo of her with her sister, Verity Bagley. Henrietta is married to Roger Bagley.'

Lund's eyebrows rose. 'She must have given me a false name, then. Maybe her maiden name? That makes sense. She didn't want her husband to know about the complaint.' He munched on his chips. 'Aren't the Bagleys the fellas you're looking into?'

'Yes,' Matthew cried desperately, drawing glances from the other policemen in the canteen. 'That's what I'm telling you. Henrietta's brother-in-law might be involved in the murder. It was his gun that almost certainly shot Clough. Her husband might be involved, too.'

'You're investigating them as suspects?'

'Of course I am.'

'Then you're going to have to stop.'

Matthew drew back. 'I'm what?'

'You heard me,' Lund said, sprinkling salt on his chips. 'There's a conflict of interest with the complaint.'

'But don't you see?' Matthew pleaded. 'That's why she made the complaint.'

Lund shook his head. 'I don't get it.'

'Because I'm on to something. I must be.'

'Or it's just a coincidence.'

'You can't believe that.'

'I believe you're best off staying away from the Bagleys.'

'They're suspects in my murder case, Lund. I can't stay away from them.'

Lund groaned. 'You just won't listen, will you?' He looked around the canteen as Matthew had done and lowered his voice. 'I've found a few things out about you and this Henrietta. Things you didn't tell me. Things you didn't include in your statement.'

Matthew frowned. 'What things?'

'Like how you put an ad in the newspaper to her? Like how you bought her a drink in the pub?' Lund raised his eyebrows at Matthew. 'Like how she gave you a cigarette case as a present?'

'I didn't put that ad in.'

'Oh, you didn't put it in, but you do know about it?'

'I saw it, but it wasn't me, Lund. I didn't do it. And as for the drink…' Matthew threw up his hands. 'She asked for one. I didn't think. I just got it for her.'

'And the cigarette case?'

Matthew shook his head. 'I don't know anything about a cigarette case.'

'She says she gave you a cigarette case as a present.'

'She didn't. I don't have a case. My cigarettes are always kept in the packet they came in.'

'Why would she lie about that?' Lund wondered.

'Why is she lying about anything?' Matthew said sourly. 'Are you saying you don't believe me now?'

'I'm not saying that,' Lund retorted. 'I'm saying it doesn't look good. And if you keep on at this brother-in-law of hers, it's going to look worse. So, do yourself a favour, Stannard, and look elsewhere for your killer.'

Roger had expected the bedroom door to be locked, but when he tried the handle, it moved and the door opened. He poked his head inside and saw Hettie lying curled up on the bed.

'Hettie darling,' he said, going in and closing the door behind him.

Hettie sniffed. 'If you're going to shout at me—'

'No, no,' he said, sitting on the edge of the bed and putting a hand on her hip.

She turned red, puffy eyes on him. 'You're not angry with me?'

Roger sighed. 'Of course not. I just wish you'd told me what happened. And what you were going to do.'

Hettie sat up. 'He did do these,' she said, showing her bruises. 'I didn't make that part up.'

He took hold of her hands and kissed her wrists. 'He had no right to hurt you. But why did you have to follow him into the pub, Hettie?'

'I wanted to talk to him. I was so worried, Roger. I thought he would help me.'

'Help you with what? What have you been worrying about?'

She bit her bottom lip and took a deep breath. 'I wasn't going to tell you. But I went to the farm that night.'

The pub door opened and Pinder waved at Teddy Welch as he came in. Teddy made his way over to Pinder's table and sat down.

'You're late,' Pinder said.

'I got held up,' Teddy said, setting his camera on the seat beside him. 'So, you got something for me?'

Pinder glanced towards the bar where Frank Greader was talking with another customer. 'It's going to cost you.'

'It always does,' Teddy said, reaching into his pocket and putting two pound notes on the table.

Pinder snatched them up and quickly put them in his pocket. He shook his head. 'More than that.'

'You what?' Teddy laughed. 'No chance.'

'What I've got is worth more than that,' Pinder insisted, staring hard into Teddy's eyes.

Teddy's smiled vanished. He leant his elbows on the table and leaned closer. 'You serious?'

'Deadly,' Pinder said. 'A fiver.'

Teddy hesitated for another ten seconds, then took three more notes out of his pocket and laid them on the table. 'It better be good, Gary.'

Pinder, happy now he had his money, grinned and took a mouthful of his bitter. 'Oh, it's good, Teddy. You listen to this.'

Chapter Thirty-Eight

Mullinger skipped up the stairs and beamed at Miss Halliwell, already at her desk. 'Good morning, Miss Halliwell. And how are you this morning?'

'I'm very well, Mr Mullinger,' she said, a little taken aback by the unusual question.

'Good. Excellent.' Mullinger held up his left arm, the paper-wrapped parcel he'd been carrying draping over her typewriter. 'Hang this up for me, please.'

She rose and slid the parcel from his arm, hanging it on the hatstand behind her desk.

'It's my dress uniform,' Mullinger explained when she didn't ask. 'I'll be out all afternoon, so cancel any appointments.'

'Going somewhere nice?'

'Lunch at the Guild Hall. I've been invited by the Assistant Chief Commissioner himself.'

'Oh, I say,' she said with a girlish jiggle of shoulders that was entirely for his benefit.

Satisfied with her reaction, Mullinger smiled. 'Coffee, when you're ready, Miss Halliwell. And let's have some of those shortbread biscuits.'

He hummed as he went into his office, tossing his cap gaily onto the edge of his desk and twiddling the rod to open his blinds. He peered out of the window. Even the banal view of the street outside filled him with pleasure this morning.

The invitation for the function had come out of the blue just after seven-thirty that morning. To think he had cursed when his telephone rang, imagining it would be the station expecting him to deal with some emergency those lazy beggars under him couldn't manage themselves. He had been a little curt with the woman who had asked if he was Superintendent Howard Mullinger, he remembered. 'Yes, yes,' he'd said. Then she'd told him she was calling from the office of the DAC and he'd held his breath. What trouble had he got himself into now?

But then had come the invitation and his expression had turned from worry to delight. Yes, of course, he would be delighted to attend, he told the woman, wondering if his dress uniform was clean and pressed. He expected it would do even if it hadn't because he was under no illusion his presence had been sought for its own sake. Some other chap had dropped out and he was needed to make up the numbers, so he would be bound to be below the salt. That didn't bother him. An invitation from the DAC was not something to turn one's nose up at. It was an opportunity to introduce himself properly to the other top brass. They didn't know Howard Mullinger, but he was determined they would by the time the lunch was over. He just had to make a good impression, that was all. And he could do that. Oh yes, he could do that standing on his head.

The door opened and Miss Halliwell came in with his coffee, two shortbread biscuits balanced precariously in the saucer in one hand and a stack of newspapers in the other.

'Your coffee, Mr Mullinger,' she said, setting the cup down by the blotter. 'And the newspapers.'

He took them from her, just to help her out, for she was struggling with their weight, and dropped them onto the blotter.

Miss Halliwell took up his small wooden desk calendar and turned the wooden rod to set it to the correct date. 'Will that be all?' she asked, putting it back down.

'Yes, yes, thank you,' Mullinger said, reaching for a biscuit and taking a bite, his eyes already scanning the front of *The Times*.

He flipped the newspaper forward to reveal the front page of *The Daily Mail* beneath. A rather more lurid headline, he noted, but undoubtedly more interesting, though he would never had admitted so to anyone else. The *Mail* was flipped forward to reveal *The Chronicle*, and Mullinger's brow creased.

He pulled *The Chronicle* out and laid it on top. He coughed as biscuit crumbs caught in his throat.

'MISS HALLIWELL!' he spluttered, spitting crumbs all over his shirt front.

Dickie was home, and ensconced in his front room before the fireplace that Emma had insisted on lighting for him even though he was quite warm, swaddled in blankets as he was. He didn't argue, sensing that to do so would be interpreted as a snub, and allowed Emma to fuss around him.

He wished he could go back to work. All thoughts of leaving *The Chronicle* had vanished in the days since his operation. He missed it, rather desperately, he realised, and was despondent when he considered the next two weeks of enforced domesticity before him. Edwards would visit, he supposed, and that would break up the monotony. Maybe even Matthew if he got the chance. He would have gone for a walk if Emma would allow it, but she was worried he'd tear his stitches and end up back in the hospital, and she'd told him to stay in the house and sit still. *Like an obedient dog*, he thought a little resentfully.

Emma bustled in with a tray, which she put down on his lap. 'There's your breakfast,' she said needlessly, for Dickie could see for himself the boiled egg and toast. 'I'm going out for a couple of hours, but I'll be back for your dinner. Will you be all right?'

'I'll be fine,' Dickie nodded, picking up the teaspoon and banging the back of it against the egg.

She went into the hall, and he heard her pulling on her coat. The letterbox flapped, and there was the sound of thuds, louder than the noise ordinary letters would make. Emma tutted, and Dickie called out, 'If those are the 'papers, I'll have them in here.'

She came in. 'How much are all these costing us?' she demanded, dropping at least eight newspapers onto the table beside him.

'I need to know what's happening,' he said. 'I'm out of the game, Emma. I need to know what the competition's up to.'

She stuffed her hat on her head. 'You're supposed to be resting,' she chided. 'I'm off. See you later.' She banged the front door behind her.

Dickie finished his egg and toast, then lifted the tray off his lap, and grunting with the effort and the tug of his stitches, set it on the floor by his feet. Lifting the newspapers onto his lap, he searched through for *The Chronicle*, sliding it out and holding it aloft.

'Bloody hell,' he cried as he read the front-page headline.

'There you go, Mrs Berry,' Georgie said, handing the sausages in their paper wrapping over the counter. He dropped her payment into the till and shoved the drawer back so vigorously, the bell tinged.

He sighed and rubbed his stiff fingers. That was the worst thing about working in a butchers — the cold. Georgie was always cold when he was at work. He always had a sniffle.

Georgie glanced up at the clock above the wall as another customer came in. A few more minutes and he could take his break. The customer asked for liver, and Georgie lifted the slippery, dark-brown organ onto the chopping board and cut off the required amount, plopping it down on the paper and wrapping it up.

Mr Bennett came out from the back as the customer left, a newspaper in his hands. 'You seen this?' he asked.

'Seen what?' Georgie said.

'It's about your brother.' Mr Bennett turned the newspaper around so Georgie could see the front page. Georgie read the headline, which blared FAMOUS DETECTIVE MOLESTS WOMAN, and his stomach lurched.

Bennett turned the newspaper back to face him and read. '"Craynebrook's most renowned detective, Inspector Matthew Stannard, has been accused of sexually molesting a woman, this reporter has been informed. The incident took place on Saturday night at The King George public house in Craynebrook, where the inspector was seen to be drinking heavily. Witnesses—"'

Georgie snatched the newspaper from his hands and read the article for himself, his heart thumping harder with each word.

'It's not true,' he said, shaking his head in disbelief. 'Mattie didn't do that.'

'It's in the 'paper,' Mr Bennett pointed out.

'But my brother wouldn't do that.'

'You know what they say, Georgie. There's no smoke without fire. Must say, though, it's a bit of a comedown for him, ain't it? I wonder what your mum'll say when she reads it. She's always coming in here, saying how wonderful her Mattie is.' He laughed. 'Don't expect she'll be saying that today.'

Georgie threw the newspaper on the floor. 'You shut up,' he roared. 'My brother's a decent man.'

Mr Bennett's amusement vanished. 'You watch your mouth, Georgie. You're not too big for a clipped ear, you know.'

'Don't you talk about my brother like that.'

'I'll talk about him any way I like. This is my shop and if I say he did it, he did it.'

'You say anything bad about Mattie and I'll punch your lights out,' Georgie threatened.

'Oh yeah? A mummy's boy, like you? You couldn't fight your way out of a paper bag.'

'I'll show you if you say anything else about Mattie,' Georgie promised, his fists curling at his sides.

'Tried to get his end away, didn't he? Probably thought he could have any woman he liked, him being in the 'papers all the time, blowing his own trumpet. Come a cropper now, though, ain't he? The 'papers know what's what. They've found him out, all right.'

Georgie lunged for Bennett, grabbing him by the lapels and shoving him up against the counter. The till wobbled on its table and Bennett stretched out both arms to steady himself.

'I warned you,' Georgie roared in his face, dabbling his skin with spittle. He brought his knee up and thrust it into Bennett's ample belly. Bennett grunted in pain and expelled sour air into Georgie's face.

The bell above the door tinkled and Georgie jerked around to see Miss Jacobs standing in the open doorway, her petite mouth forming a perfect O. He shoved the butcher aside. Mr Bennett fell onto his hands and knees and scrabbled in the sawdust on the floor, trying to get away. Pushing past Miss Jacobs, Georgie ran out of the shop.

Wincing with each step, Dickie climbed the stairs up to *The Chronicle*'s office and threw open the door.

The secretary looked up, and her eyes widened in surprise. 'Mr Waite. What are you doing here?'

Dickie scowled and walked past her into Edwards' office. He

threw his copy of the newspaper onto the editor's desk. 'What the bloody hell do you think you're doing, Bill?'

Edwards raised an eyebrow, his mouth set hard. 'It's news, Dickie, whether we like it or not.'

'That's not news. That's scandal.'

'It's a legitimate story. A much-lauded police officer stands accused—'

'It's bollocks,' Dickie spat. 'Stannard didn't do it.'

'You know that for a fact, do you?' Edwards countered, lighting a cigarette.

'I know him. He's not that kind of man.'

'Every man's that kind of man given half the chance. And we're duty-bound to report it. He's in the public eye and the public has a right to know the truth.'

'You call this rumour-mongering the truth?' Dickie snatched up the newspaper from Edwards' desk. '"…has been accused… inspector seen to be drinking heavily… the detective indecently molested the lady after arranging an assignation… trading on his fame to secure her compliance… the famed Inspector Stannard found conquest was not so easy and forced his attentions upon the lady up against the wall of the public house, just yards from other patrons…"' Dickie made a noise of disgust. 'The pub's on the high street's corner with windows all around. There are no walls he could have shoved her against.'

'You're splitting hairs, Dickie,' Edwards said.

'And as for the language,' Dickie cried, cutting him off. 'This article assumes Stannard's guilty. You couldn't write a more biased article if you tried. Where's the other side of the story, Bill? Whatever happened to innocent until proven guilty?'

'Do you want me to show you the circulation figures?' Edwards demanded, pulling a sheet of paper from a stack on his desk. 'We're selling copies all over London, not just locally—'

'Bugger the sales,' Dickie roared. 'You're ruining a man's reputation.'

'I'm saving the 'paper,' Edwards bellowed back, his breath coming fast. 'Face it, Dickie, if we don't change, if we don't write this kind of rubbish, we're going to be left behind.'

'Saving the 'paper?' Dickie scoffed. 'You're saving yourself. You don't want us reporting this filth any more than I do. You're just too much of a coward to admit it.'

'You're out of line, Dickie,' Edwards said, shaking his finger at him. 'And I—'

'What's going on?'

Dickie turned to see Teddy standing in the doorway, his hands in his trouser pockets.

'Who gave you this story about Stannard?' Dickie asked, holding up the newspaper, his lips curling at the sight of the young reporter.

'Ah, you've seen it.' Teddy grinned. 'It's a belter, isn't it?'

'I asked you who gave it to you.'

'I have my sources.'

'It's got to be a copper at Craynebrook,' Dickie said, his eyes narrowing. When Teddy's lips twisted in irritation, he knew he was right. 'It's Gary Pinder, isn't it?'

Teddy drew his hand out of his pocket and wagged a finger at Dickie. 'A good reporter never reveals his sources, Mr Waite. You taught me that.'

'You're not a good reporter, Teddy,' Dickie snarled. 'You should be ashamed of yourself for writing this trash.'

The grin vanished from Teddy's face. 'You're just jealous.'

'Jealous?' Dickie repeated, incredulous.

'Yeah. You're out of date, Dickie. No one wants to read your old-hat prose anymore. They want to read me. I'm giving the public what they want.'

‘Teddy,’ Edwards said warningly. ‘You remember who you’re talking to.’

Teddy snorted and looked Dickie up and down contemptuously. ‘A has-been, that’s what.’ He grinned again and pursed his lips. Whistling, he sauntered over to his desk.

‘You don’t want to pay any attention to him, Dickie,’ Edwards said, as Dickie watched Teddy through the window. ‘You know what the young are like these days. All mouth. No respect for their elders.’

The office door was suddenly thrown open, banging against the wall and making the secretary cried out in alarm.

‘What is it now?’ Edwards growled.

‘That’s Georgie,’ Dickie cried, recognising the dark-haired young man through the window.

‘Where is he?’ Georgie demanded of the secretary.

‘Who?’ she cried.

‘Teddy Welch.’

‘I’m Teddy Welch,’ Teddy said, adding with a wink at Dickie, ‘*The Chronicle*’s top reporter.’

Georgie crossed the office in three strides and grabbed Teddy. He drew back his arm.

‘Bloody hell,’ Dickie cried, and hurried out of Edwards’s office as Georgie’s fist connected with Teddy’s jaw. Teddy went flying, banging into his desk and collapsing in a heap on the floor.

‘Georgie, no,’ Dickie yelled as Georgie bent over and grabbed Teddy’s lapels, yanking him to his feet and drawing his arm back again. He grabbed Georgie’s arm and held on tight. Georgie whipped his head around and Dickie saw a fury on his face he hadn’t thought the sensitive young man capable of.

‘Let me go,’ Georgie roared and tugged his arm out of Dickie’s feeble hold.

But Dickie’s intervention had given Teddy an opportunity to

wrench himself free from Georgie's grasp. He twisted away and put the desk between him and his attacker.

Even angrier now at being thwarted, Georgie picked up a pencil pot from the desk and hurled it at him. Teddy ducked, so Georgie grabbed the telephone and threw that. It struck Teddy hard on the shoulder and he cried out in pain. Georgie grabbed the heavy typewriter from Teddy's desk with both hands and lifted it above his head.

'Put it down, Georgie, for Christ's sake,' Dickie yelled.

'STOP!' a deep, authoritative voice shouted, and Dickie turned to see a blue-coated giant standing behind him. The secretary was behind him, trying to catch her breath. Dickie realised she must have rushed out into the street and found a policeman.

The command had worked. Georgie had turned too, the typewriter held frozen above his head.

'Don't be silly, lad,' the police constable said. 'Put it down before you hurt yourself.'

Georgie's breath was coming quick and shallow, and he lowered the typewriter onto the desk. 'He's a bastard,' he cried as the constable put a hand around his elbow and turned him away from Teddy. Dickie saw that Georgie's rage had burnt itself out and now the boy he knew had returned, a boy whose face was crumpling as tears filled his eyes.

'Come on, lad,' the constable said. 'Let's get you down the station.'

'Do you have to, constable?' Dickie asked. 'He'll be all right now.'

'I've got to take him in, sir.'

'And I'm pressing charges,' Teddy declared. 'He nearly killed me.'

'You'll need to come down the station, sir, and make a statement,' the constable said to Teddy.

'Bloody right, I will,' Teddy declared.

Dickie sighed. 'I'll come too.'

Lund threw *The Chronicle* onto Matthew's desk. 'You've made the front page again, sunshine.'

Matthew stared in horror at the headline. 'Oh, Christ,' he muttered, feeling sick. 'How the hell do they know?'

Lund glanced through the partition window. He studied Barnes and Denham, both at their desks and both pretending not to read the newspaper they had on their laps. At Bissett, who never read the newspapers and might not even know about the article. And Pinder, who was smoking a cigarette, looking more than a little pleased with himself.

'Mullinger's going to hit the roof,' he said, pulling open his drawer and taking out his striped paper bag of boiled sweets and popping one into his mouth. 'If I were you, I'd make myself scarce.'

'I can't believe this is happening,' Matthew said, putting his head in his hands. His telephone rang, and he stared at it for a long moment before snatching it up and sighing, 'Stannard.'

'Matthew?'

'I can't talk now, Dickie,' Matthew said and made to hang up.

'Listen to me,' Dickie instructed, and Matthew put the receiver back to his ear. 'It's about Georgie. He's been arrested, Matthew. I think you ought to get down here.'

Chapter Thirty-Nine

'Where is he?' Matthew asked Dickie as he burst into the entrance lobby of the police station and saw his friend sitting on a bench.

'In the back,' Dickie said, getting up with a grunt. 'Being charged.'

'What happened?'

'Georgie came into the office and started on Teddy. Got a punch in, then started throwing things. He was about to throw a typewriter at him when the copper came in.'

'Why the hell—?' Matthew cried.

'He saw the newspaper.'

Matthew groaned and fell down onto the bench. 'This is all I need.'

Dickie stared down at him. 'What's going on with you, Matthew?'

Matthew fell back against the wall and looked up at him. 'You've read it, haven't you? Then you know.'

'I know it's not true. That's why I was at the office, telling Edwards so. Georgie didn't know about the complaint?'

'I haven't told my family about it.'

'Why not?'

'Because I'm humiliated enough without them knowing.'

'But you didn't do it.'

'How do you know I didn't?' Matthew challenged him.

Dickie held his gaze. 'Because I know you.'

The custody area door opened, and a uniformed constable led Georgie out. Matthew rose. The brothers' eyes met. He turned away without a word and walked out of the station.

'Come on, Georgie,' Dickie said kindly and steered the young man towards the door.

Matthew was sitting on a wall a little further down the road, smoking a cigarette, when Dickie and Georgie found him.

He glared at Georgie. 'What did you think you were doing?'

'That Welch shouldn't have written those things about you,' Georgie said. Matthew leapt up from the wall. 'How is this helping, Georgie? How?' he yelled, drawing the attention of passers-by.

'I just thought I should get him for you,' Georgie said. 'I wanted to help.'

'Dear God. I need your kind of help like a hole in the head.'

'All right, Matthew,' Dickie said. 'You've made your point.'

Matthew squeezed his eyes shut. His headache was back with a vengeance and the sunlight was piercing his eyes.

'I'm sorry, Mattie,' Georgie said, head down, shoulders hunched, like a dog expecting to be hit.

'What have you been charged with?' Matthew asked.

'Assault,' Georgie said. 'I've got to go up before a magistrate. Will I go to prison?'

'Of course you won't,' Matthew snapped. 'You'll be fined. But you'll have a record, Georgie. That's going to look good for me, isn't it? A brother with a criminal record.'

'Matthew,' Dickie chided. 'Georgie didn't mean all this. He was upset, worried about you.'

But Matthew didn't want to hear it. 'You better get back to work,' he said.

'I can't go back,' Georgie said.

'Why can't you?' Matthew's eyes narrowed at Georgie's expression. 'Oh God, what did you do?'

'Mr Bennett was saying you did it,' Georgie burst out. 'He said there's no smoke without fire and how upset Mum will be when she finds out what was in the newspaper. I wanted him to shut up.'

'Did you hit him, Georgie?'

Georgie frowned. 'I think I kneed him in the stomach. Not hard, Mattie, not really. But I can't go back there.'

Matthew sank back onto the wall. 'So, you've beaten up two men, got yourself arrested and lost your job. That's not bad for a morning's work, Georgie.' He sucked hard on his cigarette and shook his head. 'Go home.'

'Can you come with me?' Georgie asked quietly.

'I've got work to do,' Matthew said and turned his head away.

'He'll see you later, Georgie,' Dickie assured him with a smile. 'Go on. Go home.' He watched Georgie walk away. 'You were a bit hard on him, Matthew.'

'I don't want to hear it, Dickie,' Matthew warned.

Sighing, Dickie sat down next to him. 'So, what's being done about this accusation?'

'Lund's looking into it.'

'Who is this woman?'

'Henrietta Bagley.'

Dickie frowned. 'The same Henrietta the ad in the paper was to?'

'I suppose so. I didn't put that ad in. I told you that.'

'Someone did.'

'Obviously.'

'Who?'

Matthew sighed. 'I've no idea.'

'So, what happened? Come on, you can tell me.'

'She followed me into the pub on Saturday night, talked a load of nonsense about how she needed to talk to me and how worried she'd been. I told her I couldn't deal with whatever it was, told her to go to the station and tried to leave. She threw her arms around me and clung on like a limpet. I shoved her away. Maybe I was a little too rough, I don't know, I was angry. I walked out of the pub. She came out after me and tried it on again. I left her there, got on the bus and went home. The next thing I know, she's made a complaint against me claiming I molested her.'

'A woman scorned, eh?'

Matthew looked at him. 'You think that's what it is?'

'Sounds like it to me,' Dickie shrugged.

'I thought it had something to do with her brother-in-law.'

'You've lost me.'

'Oh, of course, you don't know. We're still waiting for the lab to confirm it, but I think her brother-in-law, Richard Bagley, owned the gun that shot Clough. I think he's involved in the murder.' Matthew shrugged. 'And now, Lund says I have to leave the Bagleys alone. That there's a conflict of interests. They can claim harassment if I try to investigate them.'

'Have you got any other suspects?'

'None nearly as good as Richard Bagley. The vicar has a motive and the opportunity, but I can't see him killing Clough, not with a spade to the throat. He's too weak for that. There is an estate agent, but his wife says he was home and I have nothing to prove that alibi false. Which leaves Richard Bagley. But his wife also says he was home. So, there's nothing I can do.'

'Unless you ignore Lund?' Dickie suggested.

Matthew threw his cigarette on the pavement and crushed it with his shoe. 'And get into more trouble?'

'What more trouble can you get into?' Dickie grinned, elbowing him in the ribs. 'I reckon the best thing you can do is to do your job. If it takes you where you're told not to go, so be it.'

'That'll get me the sack, Dickie.'

'You might be out of the Force anyway if this complaint doesn't go away. Have you thought of that?'

'Of course I have,' Matthew snapped. 'Maybe it will be better if I just resign?'

'You don't really think that, do you?'

Matthew shrugged. 'I don't know what I think anymore.'

Dickie shook his head. 'Don't resign, Matthew. If you do, she wins and Craynebrook will have lost the best copper it's had. And now, I'm off, before I really get overly sentimental and embarrass myself.' He rose and buttoned up his coat. 'If you want my advice, and I know you don't, but I'm going to give it to you, anyway, do your job, Matthew. And I'll do mine.'

Mullinger lifted his glass to his lips and took a sip of the wine. He wasn't used to drinking at lunchtime, and he was feeling more than a little light-headed. He would have liked to switch to water, not trusting himself to say what he was supposed to say to make a good impression, but he didn't think that would go down too well with his lunch companions, who were knocking back the wine with careless gusto.

A man at the far end of the table spoke. 'I disagree, Butler. The Press is an absolute menace.'

'They can be useful, Alford,' Butler said. 'An appeal in a newspaper—'

'Brings out all the loonies,' Alford cut in. 'How much time is wasted following false leads? Answer me that.'

Butler nodded. 'I admit there are drawbacks, but the fact is the Press needs us and we need the Press. Don't you agree, Campbell?'

DAC Campbell, the man who had issued Mullinger his invitation, nodded as he set down his wineglass. 'I've found them a vital resource. But it does depend on the newspaper. The broadsheets can be trusted to report the facts, but I'm afraid the tabloids play fast and loose with them. In fact, I saw an instance of sloppy reporting only this morning.' He turned to Mullinger. 'In your neck of the woods, I believe, Mullinger. *The Chronicle*?'

'Er, yes,' Mullinger nodded, conscious of all his fellow diners' eyes upon him. '*The Chronicle* is local to Craynebrook.'

'The front-page article,' Campbell pressed. 'I take it you saw it?'

'Yes, yes, I did.'

'What are you doing about it?'

Mullinger stared at him. 'I'm sorry? Doing about it?'

'What is this story, Campbell?' Butler asked.

'The article claims one of Mullinger's men has been accused of molesting a woman. Now, the accusation may be valid, I can't say, but the language used is biased, to say the least.' He turned once more to Mullinger. 'I assume you've made a complaint to the editor?'

Mullinger opened his mouth, then closed it again. What should he say to this?

'Speak up, man,' Butler cried.

'No,' Mullinger said, 'I haven't.'

'You haven't?' Campbell said.

'I didn't think it was my place. Freedom of the Press and all that.'

'Does the accusation have any foundation?' Alford asked.

'It's being looked into,' Mullinger nodded, pleased to be able to say so.

'But you must know it's not true?' Campbell said irritably. 'Stannard would never molest a woman.'

'Stannard?' Butler queried. 'Why do I know that name, Campbell?'

'He was the officer who caught the Marsh Murderer. And two more killers in just the last few months. Isn't that correct, Mullinger?'

'Yes, yes, quite correct,' Mullinger said.

'Oh, that fellow.' Butler waggled a finger. 'Isn't he the chap there was that funny story about at your place?'

'What story, Butler?' a man next to Mullinger asked.

Butler chuckled. 'It's all coming back to me. There was a woman in Campbell's division who had a penchant for the uniform. She used to call the station, oh, once a week or so, claiming she'd heard a prowler in her garden or some such. The station would send a constable round, and she'd open the door wearing nothing more than her chemise. This woman would tell the constable he needed to have a good look around the house and garden to make sure there wasn't an intruder. So, he'd do that, then go back to her and she'd offer him a drink, and a great deal more.' He waggled his eyebrows. 'You can imagine.'

His listeners laughed, and he carried on.

'The lads would take it in turns to go round there, have a bit of fun with her, and be back on patrol within the hour. Isn't that right, Campbell?'

'I'm afraid so,' Campbell nodded.

'Well, her usual call came in and it was Stannard's turn to attend. So, the sergeant sends him round, telling him to enjoy himself when he gets there, and Stannard knocks on her door. She answers, practically in her birthday suit, and goes through the routine. Stannard looks around, can't find any sign of an intruder, and goes to leave, refusing her offer of a drink. "I'm on duty, madam," he says. So, she tells him not to be so silly and doesn't he know what he's there for? He works out there wasn't any prowler and that she only made the call to get a bit of the other and do you know what Stannard did?' He leaned forward and looked around the table impishly, his eyes sparkling. 'Arrested her for wasting police time!'

He roared with laughter, and the rest of the table followed suit. All except Campbell and Mullinger, who both managed only a polite smile.

'Well, quite,' Campbell said, as the laughter ebbed away. 'That's the kind of man Stannard is, so I find it hard to believe he would assault a woman. You must be of the same opinion, Mullinger?'

'Well,' Mullinger said, shifting uncomfortably on his chair, 'as I said, another officer is looking into the allegation.'

'But Stannard has denied it?' Campbell pressed.

'Emphatically.'

'Then his denial would be good enough for me, and I'm sure it is for you. I trust he has your complete support and that you will be talking to the newspaper concerned?' Campbell eyed Mullinger sternly.

So, this was why the DAC had invited him to lunch, to make sure he was supporting bloody Stannard. DAC Campbell was poking his nose in again, just like he had when Mullinger had wanted to transfer Stannard after the Empire Club killings.

Mullinger swallowed down the lump in his throat and nodded at Campbell. 'Absolutely, sir.'

The sitting-room door opened and Hettie looked up from her magazine. 'Yes, Daisy. What is it?'

'Excuse me, madam,' Daisy said, 'but there's a man asking to see you.'

'Who is he? Does he have a card?'

'No card, madam, but he said he's from *The Chronicle*.'

'The newspaper? But what does he want with me?'

Teddy poked his head around the door and smiled at Hettie. 'Good afternoon, Mrs Bagley. I thought you might like to tell your side of the story about what happened between you and Inspector Stannard?'

'Oh, no,' Hettie said, dropping her stockinged feet to the floor. 'I couldn't do that.'

'But my readers want to know,' Teddy said, coming further into the room. 'They want to know the woman behind the story.'

'But I'm not anything special.'

Teddy gave her a deprecating smile. 'I think you're being too modest, Mrs Bagley. A beautiful lady like you is very special.'

Hettie's cheeks rounded in pleasure. 'Won't you sit down, Mr…?'

'Welch,' Teddy said, taking a seat beside her on the sofa. 'Teddy Welch.'

'You're very young to be a reporter, Mr Welch,' Hettie said, waving Daisy away.

'I'm older than I look.' Teddy lifted the camera strap over his head and set it on the coffee table. Then he took out his notebook and pencil and looked expectantly at Hettie.

'Well,' she said with a coquettish, one-shouldered shrug, 'where do you want to start?'

Dickie picked up the telephone receiver and asked the operator to connect him to the office of the *Balham Recorder*. He'd returned home after his chat with Matthew and had been on the telephone ever since, calling his contacts in the trade, hoping to get some background history on the Bagleys. So far, he'd got nothing. The local rag in Balham was his last resort.

'Yes, hello,' he said when the line connected, 'my name's Dickie Waite. I'm a reporter on *The Chronicle* and I'd like to speak with your chief reporter, please.' He drummed his fingers on the table as he waited, his mind turning over the events of the morning. He wasn't sure who to feel more sorry for, Georgie or Matthew.

Dickie understood Matthew's frustration with his brother, but he understood Georgie's anger, too. A voice at the other end of the line broke into his thoughts with a 'Hello?'

'Yes, hello,' Dickie said again, and introduced himself. 'This is a bit of a long shot, but I wonder if you know anything about a family called the Bagleys?' His eyes widened. 'You do?' He picked up his pencil and began scribbling as the voice talked. He listened for a while before asking, 'But you don't know where he is now?… I see… No, that's been extremely helpful… Yes… thank you so much. Goodbye.' He hung up the receiver and grinned as he read over his notes. A long shot it might have been, but he'd come up trumps. He was getting the old feeling back, the old feeling of a good investigative reporter.

'Now, this, Mr Teddy Welch,' he said, imagining the young man standing before him, 'is what being a reporter is all about.'

Matthew heard voices as he climbed the stairs. They were muted, low, and they all sounded concerned. He took a deep breath as he entered the sitting room, knowing he had to face his family sooner or later. Four worried faces turned in his direction.

Pat got up from the settee and, without a word, put her arms around him and drew him into a tight embrace. Over her shoulder, Matthew saw Amanda crying, Fred frowning and Georgie staring at the floor.

'You've heard, then?' Matthew said, pulling away from Pat.

'We saw it in the newspaper,' Pat said, kissing his cheek.

'I didn't do it.'

She tutted loudly. 'As if you need to say that. Of course you didn't. Come and sit down.' Pat pulled him onto the settee and sat down next to him, clutching his hand. 'Mum wants to wring that cow's neck.'

Amanda nodded vigorously, wiping her red-tipped nose with a

handkerchief. 'I hope she rots in hell for telling such lies about you.'

Matthew smiled gratefully at his mother.

'Why didn't you tell us, Matt?' Fred asked, perching on the arm of Amanda's armchair.

Matthew shrugged. 'I was embarrassed.'

'You've got no reason to be embarrassed,' Pat chided. 'Not with us.'

'I've been publicly humiliated, Pat,' Matthew said. 'Everyone knows and everyone believes it.'

Fred shook his head. 'No one who really knows you will believe it. But who is she?'

'I think she was one of the women who wrote to me after my attack.'

'Wrote to you saying what?'

Matthew's blush deepened. He looked up at Fred and understanding passed between them.

'Oh, I see,' Fred said.

'What?' Pat demanded.

'Nothing, love,' Fred said, shaking his head at her not to ask again. 'So, what happens now?'

'Lund's looking into it. But at the end of the day, it'll be my word against hers and she's got the bruises to prove I got angry.'

'What bruises, Mattie?' Pat asked.

'I pushed her away when she threw herself at me. I got hold of her wrists and I think I was a little rough with her. I was angry. I wasn't thinking.'

He knew Pat and Fred were exchanging glances above his head and knew how it sounded. Why had he been so rough?

'And then Georgie goes and puts his boot in,' Fred sighed.

'Don't you have a go at Georgie,' Amanda snapped, surprising everyone. 'At least he tried to stand up for Mattie. What have you done, Fred Harris?'

'What can I do?' Fred protested.

Amanda turned her head pointedly away.

'Well,' Pat sighed, letting go of Matthew's hand and rising, 'there's no point going on about this. What's done is done. Tea will be ready soon and we're going to sit down and not think anymore about it. Right?'

She received a few affirmative murmurs and nods, then bustled off into the kitchen, where she proceeded to bang everything she could get her hands on.

'I'm going to get changed,' Matthew said, getting up and going into the bedroom.

Fred followed him in and closed the door. 'How much trouble are you really in, Matt?'

Matthew flopped onto the bed, waking Bella, who yawned and meowed at the same time and stretched before settling back to sleep. 'If Lund can't prove I didn't do it, then I could be thrown off the Force.'

'Bloody women. All this because you turned her down. How did the 'papers know about it?'

'Someone at the station must have told them.'

'One of your colleagues would do that to you?'

'People will do anything if there's money in it.'

'I suppose so.' Fred watched Matthew as he leaned back against the wall. 'How's your head these days, Matt?'

Matthew opened one eye and looked at him. 'Hurts like hell, if you must know.'

'You should see the doc.'

'I should do a lot of things, Fred. Like resign.'

Fred gasped. 'You're not going to do that, are you?'

'I'd rather resign than get thrown out of the Force.'

'But this Lund fella will find you not guilty of molesting her.'

'He might, he might not. But even if he does, mud always sticks.'

'You shouldn't do anything hasty, Matt,' Fred said. 'Let's see how this enquiry thing turns out before you make a decision. You listening?' he added when Matthew didn't reply.

'I heard you,' Matthew nodded.

'But you're not agreeing with me,' Fred noticed. He sighed heavily. 'Look, you're your own man. If you want to resign, you resign, but I think you'll be mad to do it just yet. But if you do, I want you to know you don't need to worry about getting a job straight away. You can stay here as long as you need to and you can work behind the bar until you get something better.'

'Thanks, Fred,' Matthew said miserably.

'That's all right.' Fred patted Matthew's arm. 'Why don't you have a nap? We'll call you when tea's ready.' He went out, closing the door behind him.

Matthew reached down to the end of the bed and grabbed Bella. She protested with an indignant mew, but he shuffled down the bed and plonked her on his chest, stroking her vigorously. She settled, her head just below his chin, and Matthew laid his head on the pillow and tried to sleep.

Chapter Forty

The bus was jolting Matthew, making his brain knock painfully against his skull. Despite his best efforts, he hadn't been able to sleep and had spent the early hours of the morning sitting up in bed with Pat's writing case on his lap, penning his resignation letter and trying not to wake Georgie. That letter was in his inside jacket pocket and he meant to hand-deliver it to Mullinger as soon as he got to the station.

He tried to nap, leaning his head against the glass, but the constant motion was not the soporific he hoped for and he gave up, glancing around the bus. His attention was caught by a man reading a newspaper in the seat on the other side. He squinted to read the headline and his head throbbed even harder. The man looked up as the bus pulled into the kerb and rose, tossing the newspaper on the seat before exiting.

Matthew snatched it up. DETECTIVE'S VICTIM SPEAKS OUT ran the headline, and the article was accompanied by a head-shot of Hettie. Relieved there wasn't a photograph of him, Matthew took a quick look around the bus to make sure no one was watching and read the article.

The woman at the centre of the scandal involving famed detective, Inspector Matthew Stannard, has spoken out about her ordeal. The lady, Mrs Henrietta Bagley, told this reporter of how the detective used his position of authority to attempt to seduce the attractive Mrs Bagley, and when she proved insusceptible to his charms, attempted to force himself upon her.

Like many other members of the public, Mrs Bagley had written to Inspector Stannard to express her concern and condolences to him after he was brutally attacked by the notorious burglar, Wilfred Gadd, as well as sending him a present of a silver cigarette case. Although police officers are not allowed to accept gifts or gratuities, Inspector Stannard kept the case and subsequently took advantage of Mrs Bagley's compassionate nature to satisfy his own carnal lusts.

In conversation with this reporter, Mrs Bagley spoke of how she and her husband, and her sister and brother-in-law, have only recently moved from Balham to Craynebrook, believing it to be a reputable and desirable area. Mrs Bagley's husband, Roger Bagley, and brother-in-law, Richard Bagley, have opened a second branch of Bagley Bros. Building Co. on Craynebrook High Street following their success with the business in Balham.

"Roger and Richard had big plans for Craynebrook," said Mrs Bagley proudly, "but unfortunately, those have had to be put on hold for the time being. We thought Craynebrook was a nice place to live, but it seems to be full of murderers."

Mrs Bagley was, of course, referring to the spate of murders Craynebrook has suffered in recent months, namely the Empire Club killings and the attacks of the Craynebrook Strangler, as well as the recent murder of Josiah Clough at Blackbird Farm. Coincidentally, Detective Inspector Stannard solved both the former murders and is currently investigating the Blackbird Farm killing.

Asked if the murders and the indecent attack against her have made her regret moving from Balham to Craynebrook, Mrs Bagley admitted they have. "Things have not gone as I hoped," she said. "The farmer's murder has made things difficult for my husband's business, and I don't feel safe in Craynebrook with Inspector Stannard around. He's an influential man with people to protect him. I'm just a weak woman who trusts too much."

'Lying bitch,' Matthew muttered, a little too loudly, for the woman sitting in front turned around and glared at him. 'Sorry,' he said, returning his gaze to the article.

He reread the article, trying to ignore the lies told about him, and focusing on what Hettie had actually been quoted as saying. Something was niggling at him. What had she said? Roger and Richard had had big plans for Craynebrook, but that they had had to be put on hold. Not because of her complaint against him, Matthew noted, because the very next sentence was referring to all the murders. And later she said Clough's murder had made things difficult for her husband. He shook his head. Hettie was all but saying Bagley Bros. had intended to buy Blackbird Farm. There could be no other meaning. But how could he prove that?

One word in the article caught his eye. Plans. Of course. What an idiot he'd been. If Bagley Bros had been so sure they were going to get Blackbird Farm, chances were they had commissioned an architect to draw up building plans.

I've got to find those plans, Matthew thought, angry he hadn't thought of it before. He rang the bell. 'Stop the bus,' he cried, showing the driver his warrant card.

The driver pulled into the kerb, and Matthew jumped down

from the bus. He wasn't going to the station. He needed to get to Balham.

'Next,' the nurse called, and Dickie pushed himself up from the chair and followed her into an examination room.

A white-coated man was sitting at a desk by the window. Dickie judged him to be in his early forties. He was handsome, urbane. He looked up and gave Dickie a tired smile. 'Do come and sit down,' he said.

The accent was clipped, polished. Very different from the working-class accents Dickie had heard while he'd been in the waiting room. The language too — the 'do come' — was unusual for this area of East London, and Dickie wondered if Dr Aidan Bostock ever felt out of place in the Free Hospital.

'Thank you,' he said, taking the seat Bostock offered.

Bostock nodded at the nurse she could go, and he consulted the brief note he had before him. 'I understand you've recently been operated on, Mr Waite?' he said.

'Yes, for appendicitis.'

'I see. And the operation went smoothly?'

'As far as I know.'

'You were discharged when?'

'Monday morning.'

'And you're up and about already? I must say, that's really not advisable. You could tear your stitches. I imagine you're in some pain?'

'A bit,' Dickie admitted. 'But nothing I can't cope with. I'm going to have to ask you to forgive me for this, but I'm not here to talk about myself. I'd like to talk to you about Henrietta Bagley.'

The colour drained from Bostock's face. 'Who the devil are you?'

'I'm a reporter,' Dickie said, knowing the next few seconds were going to be difficult.

Bostock jumped to his feet. 'Get out. Get out at once,' he cried. 'This is intolerable.'

'I'm not here to hound you, Dr Bostock,' Dickie said, holding up a hand in a plea for patience. 'In fact, I'm hoping you can help me. I'm not here to get an interview for my 'paper. It's purely personal. Please.'

Hesitatingly, Bostock resumed his seat. 'Help you how?'

Dickie pulled *The Chronicle* out of his pocket and put it on the desk before Bostock. Bostock read Teddy's article, then looked up at Dickie. He didn't say a word.

'You see,' Dickie said when Bostock didn't say a word, 'DI Matthew Stannard is a friend of mine and I know he didn't molest Henrietta Bagley. From all I've heard about you, you didn't either.'

Bostock slumped in his chair. 'Henrietta Bagley accused me of molesting her during a medical consultation. Her husband reported me to the British Medical Council. There was an enquiry and I was cleared of the charge.' He gave a bitter laugh and shook his head. 'Cleared, but still ruined.'

'You had your own practice?'

'I did, and it was doing very nicely until Henrietta Bagley became my patient.'

'I need to know everything.'

Bostock made a face. 'I don't want my life in the newspaper all over again, Mr Waite.'

'It won't be,' Dickie assured him.

'I have your word?'

'You do. Please. Tell me.'

Bostock nodded. 'Henrietta Bagley developed a fixation on me. She would make appointments, claim imaginary illnesses, anything to see me. I suspected she had taken a liking to me and made sure my nurse was always in the room when she was there, or that the secretary was in earshot.'

'To protect yourself?'

'Yes. That sort of thing, that kind of obsession, can happen with female patients. When I realised it was getting out of hand and what she was building up to, I told her it had to stop. I said any sort of relationship other than a doctor/patient relationship was out of the question and that it would be better if she found herself another doctor, as I wasn't prepared to see her anymore. She was furious. Said I'd got her entirely wrong. That I was being presumptuous. She burst into tears, hit out at me and ran from my surgery. The next thing I know, I get a visit from a BMC representative telling me her husband has made a complaint against me.'

'How were you able to prove your innocence?'

'My nurse and secretary were able to tell the board at the BMC what they had witnessed, the flirtation on her part, and fortunately for me, the threat Henrietta Bagley had thrown at me before she left.'

'What threat was that?'

'That I couldn't treat her that way and expect to get away with it.' He nodded. 'I was very lucky she had been heard to say that otherwise I dread to think what might have happened. The BMC dismissed the complaint. Even so, my practice was ruined. Once it got in the local rag that I was under investigation, my patients left in droves. I had to sell the practice, at a loss, sell our house, find another job. I ended up here. I very nearly lost my wife. All because of Henrietta Bagley being a vindictive bitch. Hell hath no fury.' He glanced down at the newspaper. 'And she's still up to her old tricks.'

'You say her husband filed a complaint against you, not Henrietta Bagley?'

'He made the complaint. Unwillingly, I suspect.'

'Why do you say that?'

Bostock folded his arms across his chest and sighed. 'Roger Bagley was never able to meet my eye, Mr Waite. I believe he knew his wife had made it all up.'

'You think he knew she was lying about you?'

'Just a feeling. She'd confided in me that she'd had an affair with her brother-in-law. I didn't realise it at the time, but her brother-in-law is also her husband's brother and her sister's husband.' He laughed, shaking his head. 'And yet, they all stood by her and supported her. That family is as tight as a drum. And Roger Bagley is the most devoted husband I've ever seen. I suspect he does everything and anything Henrietta wants.'

'Even support her in a lie?'

'You don't believe me?'

Dickie shook his head. 'I just don't know if a man would allow another man's reputation to be ruined based on a lie.'

'Then you have a naïve view of human nature, Mr Waite. Some people will do anything to protect those they love.'

A middle-aged man came into the office, five document files beneath his arm. 'I'm Maurice Fry, the office manager,' he said. 'You're from the police, I'm told?'

'DI Stannard,' Matthew nodded. 'Craynebrook CID. I'd like to ask you some questions.'

Fry deposited the files on a desk. 'What about?'

'Do you know a Craynebrook farmer by the name of Josiah Clough?'

Fry shook his head. 'I don't know anyone in Craynebrook. Well, except for the Bagleys, now they're there.'

Matthew looked around the room that had empty shelves and uncluttered desks. 'They've opened an office on Craynebrook High Street. Does that mean this office is closing down?'

'It will be, eventually,' Fry sighed and pointed to a stack of boxes beneath the window. 'What you see there will be moved to the new office. They're the current jobs. A lot of the old paperwork has been put into storage or destroyed if it was no more use. And the building yard administration is going to be handled on site now, so some paperwork has gone over there. That's where I'll be from now on. No longer in a comfortable office, but in a cubby hole attached to the building yard. Yes, twenty years with the Bagleys, working my way up as office manager, and now I'm going to be working out of a shed.'

Matthew nodded sympathetically. 'Could you not have moved to Craynebrook?'

'Oh, it's not so easy for me to up sticks and move across London, inspector. And besides,' Fry drew himself up, 'I wasn't asked. I'm needed to oversee the building yard, apparently. That's all I'm good for.'

'I don't believe there's a Bagley's building yard in Craynebrook?'

'Oh no. It's not that kind of setup. The Craynebrook office is for show, you see. Plush office, the owners of the firm there to greet prospective clients. A head office, I suppose. That's what that's for.'

'The Bagleys want to go up in the world?'

Fry rolled his eyes. 'Oh yes. They've been on about that for months. And I suppose there were other reasons for the move.'

'Such as?'

Fry hesitated, but then shook his head. 'Not my place to say. But what do you want from me? You don't think I had anything to do with this murder, do you?'

Matthew smiled. 'You haven't heard of Clough, but what about Blackbird Farm? Have you heard of that?'

Fry frowned and glanced at the document files. 'Not Farm. Estate.'

'Blackbird Estate?' Matthew said, his heart beating faster. 'What's that?'

Fry shifted uncomfortably. 'I'm not sure I should say.'

'This is a murder enquiry,' Matthew reminded him. 'If there is something you can tell me, Mr Fry, then it's important you do so.'

Fry considered for a long moment, then nodded at the files. 'Mr Bagley came here yesterday. I wasn't expecting him and he was in a foul mood. He was looking for files to take back with him to Craynebrook. He couldn't find them and he was getting uptight. I said it was possible they'd been taken over to the yard by mistake and that I'd look for them. Well, I went to the yard and had a root around and found them. I'm going to send them on to him today.'

'What plans was he after?'

'The plans for Blackbird Estate. I'd seen it when I was packing up and thought it was an old job that came to nothing because I'd never heard of it. And it's my job to know. All building projects should be put in front of me so I can budget for them. This one hadn't been.'

'Can I take a look?' Matthew pointed at the files.

Fry frowned. 'I suppose I should ask if you have a warrant.'

'I don't,' Matthew admitted. *Please don't make me get one*, he mentally begged. 'It is a murder I'm investigating, Mr Fry. I need all the help I can get to find the killer, and the answer may be in that file.'

Fry looked at the document file for another long moment. 'Oh, take it,' he said, turning away. 'I'm not paid enough to get into trouble with the police.'

Matthew grabbed at the files, searching through until he found one labelled 'Blackbird Estate'. He pulled out the plans eagerly and examined them. There was a site plan showing five detached houses. Five other plans followed, each one detailing a different house. Left in the file was a yellowed, tatty-looking plan, and Matthew took this out and unfolded it. His breath caught in his throat as he stared at the original blueprint for the plot of land marked as Blackbird Farm.

'Are they what you're looking for, inspector?' Fry asked.

'Oh yes,' Matthew said, putting the plans back into the file file. 'These are exactly what I'm looking for.'

Lund kicked open the door to the station's lobby and glared at Dickie sitting on the bench by the far wall. 'I don't have anything for the Press, Waite,' he said as Dickie hurried over to him.

'This isn't for the 'paper,' Dickie said. 'Look, inspector, I don't want to talk to you any more than you want to talk to me, but I'm told Inspector Stannard's out. But trust me, this is important. You'll want to hear it.'

Lund narrowed his eyes at Dickie. 'Come upstairs.'

'I'd rather go somewhere more private.' Dickie pointed to the private waiting room door behind him. 'In there?'

Lund nodded and followed Dickie into the room. 'This is all rather cloak and dagger,' he said, pulling out a chair and sitting down.

Dickie did the same. 'You've got too many ears up in CID.'

'What you saying?' Lund demanded.

'You know what I'm saying,' Dickie said, undeterred by his brusqueness. 'You've got a leak in CID. And,' he added as Lund looked away, 'I reckon you know who it is.'

'That's none of your business, Waite,' Lund said. 'And I'm a busy man, so spit out what you've got so I can get on.'

'You're looking into the allegation against Stannard, right?'

'How'd you know that?'

'I just know,' Dickie said dismissively. 'Can I ask how far you've got?'

'No, you bloody can't.'

Dickie sighed. 'Can I ask if you think Stannard's innocent at least? Come on, inspector, give me that.'

'Why do you care?'

Dickie sat back in the chair. 'Stannard's a friend,' he said after a long moment, knowing Matthew wouldn't want their friendship to be known. 'And I don't think he touched her, at least, not in the way she claims.'

'A friend, eh?'

'That's right.'

Lund drummed his fingers on the table while he studied Dickie. 'All right. No, I don't think he did it. Proving it might be difficult.'

'But it is just her word against his?'

Lund nodded.

'I think you should look at these.' Dickie pulled a roll of papers from his pocket and laid them out on the table. 'These are copies of the *Balham Gazette* from early last year. Henrietta Bagley accused Dr Bostock of sexually molesting her. The BMC cleared him of the charge. You've got the whole story in these papers.'

Lund leaned forward and looked over the papers. 'How did you find out about this?'

'I'm a reporter, Lund. I made a few telephone calls,' Dickie said, feeling more than a little pleased with himself. 'And I've spoken with Dr Bostock. He's working at a training hospital in East London. Quite the comedown from his previous address.'

'You said he was found not guilty?'

'He was, but the damage was done. Now, I don't want the same thing to happen to Stannard. Do you?'

'Does Stannard know you've got these?'

Dickie shook his head. 'Matthew doesn't know anything about it. I decided to look into it. To be honest, inspector, this is something you should have turned up for yourself.'

'I've been busy,' Lund said angrily.

'Good thing I've had time on my hands, then, isn't it?' Dickie tapped the papers. 'She's done it before, inspector. Stannard didn't do it.'

'Can I keep these?' Lund asked.

‘Please do,’ Dickie nodded and Lund gathered the papers up. ‘But can I make a suggestion?’

‘What?’

‘Keep it to yourself for the moment? Just in case your leak thinks of causing more trouble?’

Lund pursed his lips, then nodded. ‘Will do.’

Chapter Forty-One

Matthew threw open the door of Duggan Sales and Letting and strode past the secretary flapping her hands at him all the way to the back of the office.

'You can't go in there,' he heard her cry as he threw open Alfred's door.

Alfred jumped up. 'I'm not speaking to you without my solicitor,' he said, holding out his hand and coming around the desk to force Matthew out.

Matthew held up the plan of Blackbird Farm and Alfred's face paled. 'Your business card, Mr Duggan,' Matthew said, pointing to the item paper-clipped to the top of the plan. 'You want to tell me now you don't have any interest in Blackbird Farm?'

Alfred's shoulders sagged, and he sloped back to his chair. He leant his elbows on the desk and put his head in his hands. Matthew sat down in the visitor's chair.

'Do I have to take you to the station, Mr Duggan?' he asked.

'Please don't,' Alfred muttered.

'Then talk to me here.' Matthew laid the plan across Alfred's desk. 'You've written on your business card, "This is just what you're looking for, if we can get the farmer to sell."'

Alfred lifted his head and pulled the card out from under the paperclip. 'I'd forgotten I wrote this,' he said, shaking his head.

'You are in business with the Bagleys?'

'To be honest, inspector, I don't know anymore. I have a feeling they've dropped me.'

'Why?'

'I couldn't deliver,' he shrugged. 'I promised I'd get them the farm and, in the end, Clough refused to sell.'

'So, what happened?' Matthew asked. 'Cotton?'

Alfred nodded. 'I sent him to persuade Clough, but he still wouldn't sell. I told Richard Bagley I couldn't make the deal. And that's the end of it, inspector. I did nothing more.'

Matthew noted Alfred had emphasised the 'I'. 'So, *you* did nothing more, but what did the Bagleys do?'

'I don't know,' Alfred said. 'Honestly, I don't. But I do know Richard was furious about the deal falling through.'

'Furious enough to kill?'

Alfred shrugged. 'For all I know. Are you going to charge me?' he asked miserably.

Matthew considered. 'I need you to make a statement about the farm, Clough and your involvement with the Bagleys. You do that, and there may be no need to charge you with anything.'

'Really?' Alfred's eyes widened in hope.

'Will you make a statement?' Matthew asked.

Alfred sighed in relief. 'I will.'

Matthew strode into his office and closed the door.

'Where have you been?' Lund demanded.

'Balham,' Matthew said. 'Look at these.'

'Just a mo. I've got something to tell you.'

'It can wait.' Matthew spread the Blackbird Farm plan on Lund's desk, moving the inspector's afternoon snack of tea and cake. 'I found this at the Bagleys' Balham office. Roger Bagley had been looking for it, probably to dispose of it. You see what it is?'

Lund peered at the box in the bottom right-hand corner Matthew was pointing at. 'Blackbird Farm.'

'The Bagleys claim they had no interest in Blackbird Farm. And Alfred Duggan has admitted he was trying to get Clough to sell the farm, acting as intermediary between him and the Bagleys.' Matthew stepped back, biting his bottom lip, watching as Lund picked up the statement and read it. 'Well?' he cried, unable to wait any longer.

'All right,' Lund nodded. 'I agree. The Bagleys are involved.'

Matthew grabbed the file on Clough from his In tray and opened it.'

'What are you looking for, Stannard?' Lund asked.

'Just double-checking those prints. We've got both Roger's and Richard's.'

'I thought Pinder checked them,' Lund said. 'Richard's prints are only on the gun.'

'I just want to check,' Matthew persisted, grabbing the magnifying glass from the shelf behind him and poring over the prints.

'Do you want to know what I've got to tell you?' Lund asked.

'Wait,' Matthew said. 'Let me do this.'

Lund tutted and leaned back in his chair, folding his arms over his chest, watching Matthew as he worked back and forth. He frowned when Matthew started. 'What is it?'

Matthew stared at him. 'Roger's prints are on the spade.' He shook his head. 'Double-check for me, Lund. I don't trust my eyes.'

Lund clambered out of his chair and snatched the magnifying glass from Matthew's hand. He bent over the desk, comparing Roger's fingerprints with the prints found on the shaft of the murder weapon. 'You're right.' He threw the glass down and yanked the door open. 'Pinder. Get in here.'

Pinder came in. 'What's up?' he asked.

'You checked the Bagleys' prints against those on file, didn't you?' Lund demanded.

'Yeah,' Pinder frowned. 'Richard Bagley's were on the gun.'

'What about the spade?'

'What about the spade?' he shrugged.

'You did check the Bagleys' prints against the fingerprints found on the shaft of the spade?'

'No one told me to,' he protested.

'For Christ's sake,' Matthew muttered.

'No one told you to?' Lund roared. 'You're a bloody detective, Pinder. If you check prints, you check prints against everything.'

'Why all the fuss?' Pinder asked.

'The fuss is because Roger Bagley's prints are on the bloody murder weapon.' Lund waved him savagely away. 'Get out of my sight.'

Pinder went out, slamming the door behind him. Matthew had fallen into his chair, feeling suddenly tired.

'Unbelievable,' Lund said, shaking his head. 'We could have had him days ago if it wasn't for that idiot.' He narrowed his eyes at Matthew. 'You feeling all right?'

'I'm tired,' Matthew said, rubbing his forehead. 'I've not been sleeping.'

'Well, I've got some news for you that should make you feel better,' Lund said, going back to his desk and picking up the paperwork Dickie had given him. 'I reckon you're in the clear on the molestation complaint.'

Matthew looked up, staring at him. 'How?'

'You've got your friend Dickie Waite to thank,' Lund said. 'He did a bit of digging. Found out that Henrietta Bagley accused her doctor of molesting her. She made a complaint, same thing she's done to you. It all came to nothing. Turns out she'd tried it on with this doctor and he rejected her. Same with you. She is, old son, a woman scorned.' He handed Matthew the paperwork.

'Dickie found all this?' Matthew asked as he read.

'Yep. Told me I should have found it,' Lund said, adding ruefully, 'and he's right. I should have done. So, that's good news, isn't it? Her complaint won't hold any water. Not now it can be proven she's got a history of making this sort of complaint.'

'Thank God,' Matthew breathed, sinking back in his chair and resting his head on the back. He closed his eyes, feeling the tension drain away from him.

'You look done in, Stannard,' Lund said, reaching for his hat. 'Stay there. I'll bring the Bagleys in.'

'I should do it,' Matthew said, jerking upright. 'It's my case.'

Lund shook his head. 'Until it's official that the complaint's a load of nonsense, it's best if you stay out of it. It's all right. You can trust me to do it right.'

Matthew had been pacing CID for the last half hour since Lund had left, taking Denham and Barnes with him. Pinder had made himself scarce and Matthew was glad. He wasn't sure if he would have been able to keep his temper if the detective constable had remained in the office.

He hated the waiting, even though he knew Lund was right in making him stay behind. He felt little satisfaction in finding the proof the Bagleys had been lying about Blackbird Farm. All he felt was relief he would be cleared of the accusation that he had molested Henrietta Bagley. If it hadn't been for Dickie… He owed his friend a very large drink indeed.

Matthew stubbed out his cigarette as he heard footsteps on the stairs outside the door. Lund came in a moment later.

'They're in the interview rooms,' he said.

‘Did they say anything?’ Matthew asked.

‘Only that they wanted their solicitors,’ Lund replied unhappily. He threw his hat on the desk. ‘I bloody hate solicitors. The wives were there. That Henrietta was crying. The other one said we were just getting back at them because of you.’

‘What did you say?’

‘That you were in the clear. Told them we knew all about the doctor back in Balham.’ Lund grinned with pleasure. ‘That wiped the smiles off their faces, I can tell you.’

Matthew felt a surge of satisfaction. ‘I want to sit in on the interviews with you.’

‘No,’ Lund said, as if he’d expected Matthew to ask. ‘Absolutely not.’

‘Just sitting in, Lund. You’ll be leading the interviews.’

‘No. I’m not having it. You’re too involved—’

‘You know I’m innocent.’

‘I know you are. But if they’ve got smart-aleck lawyers with them, they’ll have a field day if you’re in the interviews. If we end up charging the Bagleys, by the time their case gets to court, they’ll be claiming police harassment and all sorts of things and everything we’ve got on them will be taken to bits. So, don’t me ask again. I’m doing the interviews and that’s that.’

Matthew fell into his chair with a sigh. ‘You know what questions to ask?’

‘I’m not a bloody idiot, Stannard.’

‘I didn’t mean that. It’s just I know the case better than you.’

‘Fine. Write down the questions you want me to ask and I’ll make sure I’ll ask them. But you’re not coming in with me.’

It hadn’t taken long for the Bagleys’ solicitors to arrive at the station and Lund hadn’t wasted any time. He’d told Matthew he was interviewing Richard first, believing Richard was the weaker of the two brothers and therefore more likely to crack. Matthew hadn't disagreed.

Richard was looking very nervous as Lund and Denham sat down at the interview table. His hand shook as he lit a cigarette and he took short drags, his eyes darting from Lund to Denham.

'You understand why you're here, Mr Bagley?' Lund asked, opening his file and seeing Matthew had put a list of questions inside.

'Yes,' Richard said. 'And you've no right to—'

'We've every right,' Lund cut him off. 'You see, we've had the results back from our laboratory and they confirm the bullet that shot Mr Clough was fired from your gun.'

'What if it was?' Richard shrugged. 'I told you my gun had been stolen.'

'Yes, you did tell us that. Convenient, wasn't it? A gun that's used to shoot someone being stolen by an unknown thief.'

'If you say so.'

'And your fingerprints are the only prints on the gun.'

'As it's my gun, my prints would be on it,' Richard said, as if Lund was being stupid. 'Presumably, whoever shot the farmer wore gloves.'

'That's not a bad idea,' Lund nodded, 'but if that were the case, then your prints would be smudged. But they're not. They're perfectly clear. You fired your gun. You shot Clough.'

Richard took a drag of his cigarette. 'Why would I shoot him?'

'Because he'd done you over on a deal. He wasn't going to sell you the farm, was he? And you couldn't have that. Not after all the money you'd sunk into getting it. Did you mean to shoot him or did you just get carried away?'

Richard didn't answer.

'Because it messed it all up even more, didn't it?' Lund went on. 'If you'd left him alive, he might have come to us and reported you.

There would have been a scandal and that wouldn't have been good for business. So, he had to be shut up for good.'

'I didn't kill him.'

'No. Roger did that.'

'What?' Richard said, startled by the remark.

'You told your brother what you'd done,' Lund explained, 'and he cleared up for you. That's what big brothers are for.'

'Roger didn't kill him,' Richard said.

'His prints are on the murder weapon.'

'No, they can't be. We were together after…' He broke off and stared at Lund.

Lund raised his eyebrows. 'After what, Mr Bagley?'

'Nothing,' Richard said, swallowing nervously.

'It will look better in court, you know,' Lund said, annoyed because he felt he'd almost had Richard.

'What will?'

'Admitting your guilt. Because I'm going to charge you with the shooting, Mr Bagley. Judges like men who admit their guilt rather than go to the time and expense of a trial. Get a lenient judge, you might not even go to prison. It all depends on how you behave now. Cooperate now and I promise, it'll be easier for you.'

It took barely a minute for Richard to work out what was best for him. He shuffled forward in his chair, putting both forearms on the table, keeping his head down.

'All right. I'll tell you,' he said. 'I did shoot him. The gun wasn't stolen. I went to the farm that night to frighten him. That's all I meant to do. But he came at me, tried to grab the gun, and it went off. I don't even know which of us pulled the trigger. He was bleeding, but he was alive when I left, I swear it.'

'What time was this?' Lund asked.

'It was after nine. I don't know exactly.'

'What did you do with the gun?'

'I threw it away on the way home. I panicked. I was worried about being caught with it.'

'You went home?'

'Yes. No, not exactly. I went to Roger. I told him what had happened.'

Lund licked his lips, knowing he had to tread carefully now. 'And?'

Richard shrugged. 'And he calmed me down. Told me not to do anything else stupid. We had a few drinks and smoked a cigar.'

Lund frowned. 'How long were you together?'

'A couple of hours. Until our wives came back around eleven, I think it was. They'd been to a cocktail party at Lady Cantor's.'

'Oh, very nice. And when the ladies came back, you went home?'

'Yes. My wife and I went straight to bed.'

'That's everything, is it?'

Richard met Lund's eye. 'Yes. I admit I shot Clough but I didn't kill him. And neither did Roger.'

'Well?' Matthew demanded as Lund and Denham came into CID.

'Richard's admitted to shooting Clough,' Lund grinned, gesturing for Denham to give Matthew the notes he'd taken during the interview.

Matthew quickly scanned them. 'But not to killing him?'

'No,' Lund admitted with a sigh. 'And I think he's telling the truth about that. I reckon Roger finished Clough off.'

'But he claims he and Roger were together until eleven.'

Lund nodded. 'Yeah. Until their wives came home from some party. It doesn't stop Roger going out afterwards and killing Clough. You don't have an exact time of death for Clough, so it could have been any time after eleven. If Richard went to bed like he said, he can't alibi his brother, can he? And it wouldn't surprise me Roger keeping it to himself that he was going to the farm to finish Clough off. Let's face it, Richard's a bit of an idiot. If he hadn't thrown the gun away, we'd probably never have got on to him. ' He clapped his hands at Denham who was leaning against the doorframe, yawning. 'Wakey, wakey, Denham. We're going to have a chat with Roger.'

Lund walked into Interview Room 2 and sat down. 'Right, Mr Bagley. You've got your solicitor, so we're all ready to start chatting. So, why'd you kill Clough?'

'I didn't,' Roger said, glaring at Lund. 'I've already told you I didn't know the man.'

'Yeah, you did tell us that. You also told us Bagley Bros. had no interest in Blackbird Farm.'

'We don't.'

'So, what are we to make of this?' Lund laid the plan of Blackbird Farm on the table before Roger. The veins on Roger's neck stood out as he looked at it. 'That's a plan of Blackbird Farm. You recognise it, Mr Bagley?'

'No, I don't believe I do,' Roger said, reaching into his pocket for his cigarette case.

'That's odd. It was found at your office in Balham. An employee of yours, a Mr Maurice Fry, confirms it belongs to you.'

'Mr Fry's mistaken.'

'He's ready to swear to it. And then there's this.' Lund put Duggan's business card on top of the plan. 'As you can read for yourself, Mr Duggan has written, "This is just what you're looking for, if we can get the farmer to sell." That was paper-clipped to the plan. So, what we have here is a plan of Blackbird Farm and an estate agent's declaration that it's just what you're looking for. The only problem was the farmer.'

Roger blew out a plume of smoke. 'It's nothing to do with me.'

'There were other plans in the file. Individual plans for five houses to be built on what you've called the Blackbird Estate. Bit of a coincidence, wouldn't you say?'

Roger shrugged at Lund. 'No comment.'

Lund put down another sheet of paper. 'We have here a sworn statement from Mr Alfred Duggan, who confirms he was acting as intermediary between you and Mr Clough for the purchase of Blackbird Farm. What do you have to say to that, Mr Bagley?'

Roger looked down at Alfred's statement. His jaw tightened. 'No comment.'

Lund slapped Roger's bank statements on the table. 'We've searched your house and found these. Your finances are well in the red, aren't they, Mr Bagley?'

'Moving is an expensive business, inspector.'

'But it's not just the move to Craynebrook that's put you into the red. It's the legal fees you had to pay for your wife's complaint against Dr Bostock. And that was all for nothing, wasn't it? Once it came out what lies your wife had been telling about him. So, it's the move, the legal fees and the money you've laid out for building materials. Why have you been spending so much on that?'

'A building firm can't build without materials. I would have thought that was obvious.'

'But you told my colleague you don't have any big projects on at the moment because you've been preoccupied with the move to Craynebrook. And Mr Fry in Balham has confirmed that no further materials are required for your current building works. At least, nothing on this scale. So, I ask again, why the excessive stocking up on materials?' Lund waited, but no answer came. 'Nothing to say, Mr Bagley? Then how about this for an answer? You laid out such a lot of money for materials because you expected to have a very big building project right here in Craynebrook.' He tapped the building plans. 'At Blackbird Farm, in fact. According to these plans, you were going to build five houses on the land the farm takes up.'

'No comment.'

'And everything was rosy. You sold your houses, bought bigger ones here in Craynebrook, opened a new office and then Clough turns around and says he's not selling the farm. Which means you and your brother find yourselves up shit creek. So, what do you do? Take it on the chin? Look around for another plot of land? Or do you make Clough sell? Yeah, that's the answer. Get heavy. Alfred Duggan sends one of his thugs round to persuade Clough, but that doesn't work. So, your brother goes to the farm with his gun to scare Clough into selling.'

'My brother didn't shoot Clough.'

'Oh yeah? Then why has he just told us he did?'

Matthew was going through Denham's notes. Something was niggling at him. Something Richard had said, or maybe Lund? He wasn't sure.

He moved Denham's notes to the side and picked up his pen, making a list of all the facts on his blotter.

1. Richard shot Clough after 9 p.m., most likely around 9.30 p.m. when Mrs Askey had heard the shot she complained to Turkel about.

2. Richard had thrown the gun away on the way back to St Jude's Avenue.

3. He and Roger had been together until around 11 p.m. when their wives returned home from a cocktail party given by Lady Cantor.

4. Richard had gone to bed and not left his house again.

Matthew circled point three and grabbed the telephone directory from the shelf behind him. He flipped the pages to the Cs, running his finger down the columns until he found the Cantor name.

Picking up the telephone receiver, he gave the number to the operator and when the line connected, asked to speak to Lady Cantor. A few minutes later, he hung up the receiver and studied his notes. Hettie and Verity had left Lady Cantor's just after ten o'clock. Lady Cantor remembered because she had thought it rather early. Lady Cantor's house was on The Avenue, a ten-minute walk at most from St Jude's Avenue. So, why had it taken them so long to get home?

Matthew turned back to the file, flicking slowly through the pages. His eyes fell on the witness statement Mrs Askey had given him on the morning of the nineteenth. He pulled it out and reread it.

'You bloody fool,' he chided himself, and rose, grabbing his hat and striding out of CID.

Roger stared at Lund. 'You're lying.'

Lund shook his head. 'We've got it in writing. He'll be signing a statement as soon as it's written up. He's told us he went to you after shooting Clough, and after throwing the gun away, and you two were together until eleven when your wives came home. You got rid of Richard, then you went to the farm and finished Clough off.'

'That's ridiculous. I didn't go anywhere that night.'

'So, how did your prints get on the murder weapon?' Lund asked.

Roger stared at him. 'What?'

Lund grinned. 'Your prints are on the shaft of the spade that was used to slice open Clough's throat. If you didn't kill him with it, how did your prints get there?'

'I don't know,' Roger said, flustered. 'I don't believe you. You're making it up.'

Lund put two sets of prints in front of him. One was the set Roger had supplied at Matthew's request; the other were the prints taken from the murder weapon.

'Those marks,' Lund said, pointing with his pencil at the swirls Matthew had ringed, 'are a match.'

Roger stared at the prints. He glanced at his solicitor, who was frowning at them ominously.

'Let me sum up what we've got against you,' Lund said. 'We have a sworn statement from Alfred Duggan saying you were trying to buy Blackbird Farm from Mr Clough and that he was refusing to sell. We have plans showing what you intended to build on the land once the farm was yours. We have bank statements that show your company is in debt because of building materials you've bought for a building project that doesn't yet exist. We have your brother confessing to shooting Clough and going to you immediately after. And we have your prints on the murder weapon. I'd say that's more than enough to charge you with murder, Mr Bagley.'

'I think I need a few minutes with my client, inspector,' the solicitor said.

Lund swallowed down a sigh. 'If you must.'

He and Denham left Roger and his solicitor in the interview room and returned to CID.

'Where's Stannard?' Lund asked Bissett, sitting at his desk.

'I don't know, sir,' Bissett said. 'He took off like a whippet up a drainpipe about fifteen minutes ago. Didn't say a word. Took Barnes with him.'

Lund wandered into the inspectors' office and studied Matthew's desk. He saw the open Clough file and Matthew's blotter with point three ringed. 'What are you up to?' he muttered.

Chapter Forty-Two

Matthew banged on the door, bouncing on the balls of his feet in impatience for his knock to be answered. He banged again, and the door opened.

'What's all the noise?' Mrs Askey demanded fiercely. 'Oh, it's you. What do you want?'

'I'm sorry to bother you at this time of night, Mrs Askey, but I need to ask you something.'

'You better come in, then,' she said, gesturing Matthew and Barnes into the front room. 'Sit down.'

Both men sat. Matthew took out a folded piece of paper from his pocket. 'When we first spoke, you said you had girls singing and dancing outside your house. When was that?'

'The night when I called your lot to complain about him shooting.'

'What time that night did you see the girls?'

She frowned. 'It was later, I think.'

'After your telephone call? How long after?'

'An hour, maybe. Why?'

'You called them girls. Are you sure they were young?'

'Well, I thought they were. I mean, grown women don't go along the street singing and dancing, do they? But now you're making me think about it, they weren't dressed young. You know what young girls are like nowadays, showing all they've got. Well, they weren't like that. They were dressed proper.'

'So, they were older,' Matthew said. 'How old?'

'Ooh, I don't know. Thirties, forties, maybe. She sounded middle-aged when she called out, anyway.'

'When who called out?'

'The one who tried to get the other one to be quiet. Pot calling the kettle black that was.'

'She called out? What did she say?'

'Betty. The other one was running down the lane and she shouted after her.'

'You're sure it was Betty?' Matthew licked his dry lips. 'Could it have been Hettie?'

Mrs Askey frowned. 'I suppose it might have been Hettie. They sound the same, don't they?'

Matthew felt a surge of satisfaction. 'Now, I need you to think very carefully, Mrs Askey. This is vital. Did they go down towards the farm?'

'They went that way,' she nodded. 'Then they was quiet for a bit, then one of them shouted out after the other and I heard running.'

'Both of them running?'

'No, just the one. I heard the running and the other one shout out.'

'What did the other one do?'

'I don't know. I didn't see her.'

'You didn't see her follow after the other woman?'

'No. I waited to see her, but she didn't come past, and I went back to bed.' She held up a finger. 'I did hear heels walking past about fifteen minutes later. So that was probably her, weren't it?'

Matthew nodded and put the paper back in his pocket. 'Thank you, Mrs Askey,' he said and rose, Barnes doing the same.

She followed them into the hall. 'I'm surprised you're still with the police. I read what you did in the 'paper.'

Barnes turned on her. 'Inspector Stannard didn't do anything, Mrs Askey. He's innocent.'

'Oh yeah?' she said, raising an scornful eyebrow. 'They all say that, don't they?'

'My client wishes to make a statement,' the solicitor said as Lund and Denham returned to the interview room.

'I'm listening,' Lund said.

Roger took a deep breath. 'I did not kill Josiah Clough. It is true, however, that we had been hoping to buy the farm and land from him and he turned us down. It was a blow. We had invested a great deal of money in the expectation that we would get the farm. Alfred Duggan, without our knowledge, sent someone to threaten Clough. That didn't work and Richard took matters into his own hands, again without my prior knowledge. I deny emphatically that either of us killed Clough.'

'Why are your prints on the murder weapon?' Lund asked.

'Richard and I went to see Clough the day before he was killed. I wanted to talk to him, try to make him see reason. He was angry and abusive, and he threatened me with a spade. I grabbed it from him. That's the only explanation I can give for my prints being on it.'

'My client also has a witness to his whereabouts on Sunday evening,' the solicitor added.

'Oh yeah?' Lund said. 'That's convenient. Who?'

'A neighbour across the road from our house,' Roger said, ignoring the sarcasm. 'I remembered late that the dustbins would be emptied on the Monday morning and I hadn't put the rubbish out. I took the bags out just after my wife came home and put them in the dustbin. My neighbour was doing the same, and we spoke briefly to each other. You can ask him. He'll confirm that.'

'We will,' Lund assured him. 'But that doesn't prove you didn't go out later.'

'I didn't,' Roger said with a sigh. 'I went to bed with my wife.'

'Right. Well, we'll check with your neighbour,' Lund says, nodding to Denham to rise. 'In the meantime, you'll go back in the cell.'

'I'll have to leave it to you to make the arrests, Barnes,' Matthew said as they waited for their knock to be answered.

'But the complaint's all cleared up now, isn't it, sir?' Barnes asked.

Matthew shook his head. 'Not officially. And we need to do everything above board.'

'Righty ho, sir,' Barnes said, holding up his warrant card as Daisy opened the door. 'Police to see Mrs Bagley.'

Daisy's eyes widened as Matthew followed Barnes inside. 'Inspector Stannard,' she said. 'Do you remember me?'

Matthew frowned at her, trying to recall her name. She did look familiar, but…

'Daisy Evans,' Daisy said, putting a hand to her chest. 'I used to work here for the Ballantynes.'

'Of course,' Matthew said, nodding. 'I remember. And now you're working for the Bagleys?'

'Yeah.' She made a face. 'Out of the frying pan and into the fire.'

Before Matthew could ask her what she meant by that, a voice called down from above.

'Daisy, who is it?'

Matthew recognised Henrietta Bagley. He nodded at Barnes.

'Could you come down please, Mrs Bagley?' Barnes called up into the stairwell.

'Who are you?'

Barnes held up his warrant card. 'Police.'

'Police?' Hettie screeched, and Matthew heard running and a door being slammed.

'She's gone into the bedroom, sir,' Barnes said.

'Miss Evans,' Matthew said. 'Kindly inform Mrs Bagley that if she doesn't come down, DC Barnes here will break down the door and put her in handcuffs.'

Daisy's eyes widened. 'You wouldn't really do that, would you?'

'Oh yes, I would,' Matthew said with not some little satisfaction.

Daisy hurried up the stairs and Matthew heard her knocking on the door and telling Hettie what he had said. He heard Hettie screaming at her to go away and didn't open the door.

'Go on,' Matthew said to Barnes, and Barnes took the stairs two at a time.

Matthew heard Barnes warn Hettie was he about to do, then the thud as the detective constable put his shoulder to the door.

'What's going on?' a female voice behind him demanded.

Matthew turned to see Verity at the open front door. She glared at him, then looked up towards the first-floor landing.

'Your sister has locked herself in her bedroom rather than talk to us, Mrs Bagley,' Matthew explained. 'Perhaps you could convince her to cooperate?'

'What do you want to talk to her about?' she asked, jumping at another thud from upstairs.

'The murder of Josiah Clough,' Matthew said, watching Verity's expression carefully. She was very controlled, he thought, as the only sign his words had shocked her was a slight tightening of her jaw.

'I can't think why you want to speak to Hettie. Aren't our husbands enough for you?'

'I want to speak to you, too.'

'Me?'

Another thud.

'It would be better if my colleague doesn't have to break the door down.'

Verity hurried up the stairs. 'Hettie? It's me. Open the door.'

There followed a brief exchange, but Matthew heard the door open. Barnes said, 'Come with me, madam,' and the party of four came down the stairs. Daisy was wide-eyed in astonishment at the back, staring from Hettie and Verity to Matthew.

Hettie's eyes were on Matthew as she came down the stairs, clutching Verity. 'I didn't mean to do it,' she said in a cracked voice.

'Quiet, Hettie,' Verity said, glaring at Matthew. 'Don't say another word.'

'Read them their rights, Barnes, and put them in the car,' Matthew said.

Barnes pushed them out onto the path. Matthew watched them go with a sense of satisfaction he knew he shouldn't feel. He remembered what Daisy had said and turned to the maid.

'What did you mean earlier about out of the frying pan and into the fire?'

Daisy was staring out of the front door as Barnes bundled Hettie and Verity into the back of the police car. 'They're an odd lot, that's all,' she said. 'I've wondered if madam's a bit funny in the head, the way she talks sometimes. Mr Bagley's nice. He's besotted with her, but he lets her get away with murder.'

That's an ironic choice of words, Matthew thought. 'In what way?' he asked.

Daisy coloured. 'I read about what she said you did in the newspaper. When I read it, I thought it couldn't be true. I remembered how nice you were to me when Mr Ballantyne was killed. And then, I heard them talking.'

'Who talking?'

'Mr Bagley and his brother and madam's sister.' She nodded towards the car. 'They knew she was making it up about you. And I thought that ain't right. If they know she's lying, they should say so.' She looked down at her feet. 'I suppose I should have said something, but my mum said I shouldn't get involved. I'm sorry.'

'That's all right,' Matthew said with a smile. 'Thank you for believing in me.'

Daisy beamed at him. 'Oh, I never doubted you, inspector.' She glanced again at the car. 'What have they done?'

'Have you ever heard them talking about Josiah Clough or Blackbird Farm?' Matthew asked.

'You don't think they had something to do with his murder, do you?'

Matthew shrugged.

'No, I never heard them talking about him,' she said, her brow creasing. 'Is it me?' she asked him quietly.

'Is what you?' Matthew asked, not understanding.

'Am I jinxed or something? First the Ballantynes, now them?'

Matthew shook his head. 'It's nothing to do with you, Miss Evans. If anyone's jinxed, it's me.'

'And where have you been?' Lund demanded as he caught sight of Matthew in CID.

Matthew took a deep breath, knowing Lund was going to explode. 'I've arrested the wives,' he said.

Lund stared at him. 'You've done what?'

'Hear me out,' Matthew pleaded.

'I don't need to. I've got Roger Bagley admitting to being at the farm, wanting to buy it, and knowing his brother shot Clough.'

'But he denies killing him,' Denham pointed out, earning a silencing glare from Lund.

'He did it,' Lund insisted. 'Him and his brother.'

'I'm not so sure,' Matthew said.

Lund clapped a hand to his forehead. 'Stone me. You were the one who said it was them.'

'I reread Mrs Askey's statement,' Matthew explained. 'I don't know how I missed it, but she mentioned girls singing and dancing outside her house. Except they weren't girls. They were women. Hettie and Verity.'

'So what?'

'So what?' Matthew cried. 'They were at the farm the night Clough was murdered!'

'All right, smart arse. Why would the women kill Clough?'

'I don't know,' Matthew admitted.

Lund put his hands on his hips. 'Be honest. Is this you getting your own back?'

'No, it isn't,' Matthew said through gritted teeth. 'They're involved, Lund. Barnes, back me up on this. What did Henrietta Bagley do the moment we got to the house?'

'Ran away and locked herself in her room, sir,' Barnes said. 'And when she came out, she said she didn't mean to do it.'

'Now tell me that doesn't sound like a guilty woman?' Matthew demanded.

Lund chewed on the inside of his cheek. 'She could have meant you,' he said. 'She didn't mean to lie about you.'

Matthew sighed. He hadn't considered that.

'All right,' Lund said after a long moment. 'I'll question the women. Have they asked for a solicitor?'

Matthew shook his head.

'Then don't you bloody offer them one,' Lund warned Matthew. 'This case is doing my head in and I want it over with by tonight.'

Chapter Forty-Three

'Now then, Mrs Bagley,' Lund said, 'why don't you tell me everything? Get it off your chest?'

Hettie was sniffing into a sodden handkerchief. Mascara had run down her cheeks and her nose was bright red at the tip. 'It was an accident,' she whimpered. 'I didn't mean to kill him.'

'Josiah Clough?' Lund asked.

She nodded. 'I went to the farm to have a look at it, that's all. I wasn't expecting him to be walking around at that time of night.'

Lund swallowed down an irritated sigh. Stannard was bloody right, after all. 'What happened?'

'He shouted at me,' she cried, her tone indignant. 'Said I was trespassing. I knew I was, but… well, he didn't have to shout at me, did he? I said he shouldn't talk to me like that, that he didn't need to be so rude and that my husband would teach him to mind his manners. He wanted to know who my husband was, and I told him, and that seemed to make him even angrier. He started shouting how he was sick of us and how he was going to have the law on us, and oh, all sorts of things. Swearing at me. Waving his arms around. I just wanted to get away and tried to get past him, but my shoes got stuck in the mud and I stumbled and fell against him. He grabbed me. We struggled, and I fell to the ground. He was towering over me and I was so frightened. There was a spade leaning against the fence and I grabbed it and swung it at him. I don't really know what happened. I just remember the blood running down his face. He was crying out in pain, cursing at me, and I got up and I ran. It was self-defence. He was going to hurt me. He would have killed me if I hadn't hit him with the spade.'

'If you hadn't killed him with the spade,' Lund corrected.

'I didn't mean to kill him,' she said, wiping her nose. 'I didn't think I even hit him that hard.'

'And your sister? What part did she play?'

'Verity came with me to the farm. She didn't want to go in like I did, so she waited at the farm gate.'

'She wasn't with you when you hit Clough?'

Hettie shook her head. 'No. If she had gone in with me like I wanted her to, it would never have happened. So, really, it's all Verity's fault.'

'She's coughed,' Lund declared. 'Henrietta Bagley killed Clough.'

Matthew could hardly believe it. He held out his hand for Denham's notes. 'She confessed just like that?'

'What can I say? I'm a brilliant interviewer. So, we'll charge Richard with owning an unlicensed gun and for shooting Clough, and Henrietta for the murder. Roger and Verity are free to go. And we can all go down the pub and celebrate.' He groaned as he looked at Matthew. 'What is it now?'

'Oh, nothing,' Matthew said, shaking his head and frowning.

Lund waggled his fingers. 'Come on. Out with it.'

'It's this bit here.' Matthew pointed to part of Hettie's confession. 'She said she swung the spade and remembers the blood running down his face.'

'Yeah, so?'

'That would be the injury above his eye.'

Lund nodded. 'Then she swung it again and got him across the throat.'

'But she doesn't say that,' Matthew persisted. 'She said she ran after the first blow.'

'So, she's missed out a bit. Blimey, that's not difficult with a brain like hers. She's not playing with a full deck, Stannard. You know that.'

'I know,' Matthew nodded, still frowning.

Lund snatched the notes from his hand and slapped them down on the desk. 'Don't go making things difficult,' he warned. 'We've got a confession and it's good enough for me. She was there, she hit him, he died. End of story. Right?' He leaned in closer and glared at Matthew. 'Right?'

Matthew drew in a deep breath. 'Right,' he said.

'Thank Christ for that,' Lund muttered. 'Come on. Let's release the others. There's a pint at The King George with my name on it and you're buying.'

Matthew thought he'd never seen a man look so broken as Roger Bagley when Lund told him his wife had confessed to murdering Clough. Roger had protested it wasn't true, that his wife had a habit of making things up, that she didn't know what she was saying. When that hadn't moved Lund, he'd declared he'd killed Clough and insisted they let Hettie go free.

Lund wasn't having any of it, and pushed Roger down the corridor that led to the station lobby, Matthew following a pace or two behind.

Verity was waiting for him in the lobby. She jumped up from the bench when they entered and rushed to Roger.

‘My God, you look terrible,’ she said, grabbing his hand and stroking his face. ‘Are you all right?’

‘They’re keeping Hettie,’ he said, staring blankly into her face.

‘I know,’ she nodded.

‘They think she killed Clough.’

Verity sighed. ‘She did, Roger.’

He frowned. ‘You knew?’

‘She told me.’

‘Why didn’t you tell me?’

‘There was nothing you could do, Roger.’

‘I could have taken her away. Protected her.’

‘Again?’ she said, shaking her head. ‘How many times have you had to protect her, Roger?’

‘She’s my wife, Verity. That’s what I’m supposed to do. I’m supposed to look after her.’

‘Oh, God, Roger, she doesn’t deserve you,’ Verity groaned, drawing away. ‘How can you still love her? After all she’s done.’ She pointed at Matthew. ‘He was just the latest man she took a fancy to. Dr Bostock, her piano teacher, your own damn brother. And how many before them, Roger? How many?’

‘Verity!’ Roger cried, pain evident on his face. ‘You know Hettie can’t help the way she is.’

‘You always make excuses for her. Well, I’m glad she’s going to hang.’ Verity’s chest was heaving with fury and indignation.

Matthew stared at her, and it suddenly all made sense. ‘It was you,’ he said to Verity. ‘You killed Clough.’

‘What’s that?’ Lund said, looking from Matthew to Verity.

‘That’s right, isn’t it?’ Matthew went on. ‘Your sister ran away after hitting Clough on the forehead, and you stayed behind and went into the farm.’

‘But her sister’s confessed,’ Lund cried in exasperation. ‘Why would she do that if she hadn’t done him in?’

Matthew stared at Verity. ‘You let your sister think she killed

Clough, didn't you? Henrietta hit him, striking him on the forehead, then ran away, past you waiting at the farm gate. She was probably in a panic, and you called out — that was what Mrs Askey heard — but she didn't stop and you didn't go after her. Instead, you went into the farm, maybe to see what had scared her so much, and you found Clough injured, blood in his eyes, unable to defend himself. This was the man who had caused Roger and Richard so much trouble and he was at your mercy. You picked up the spade and you swung it, slicing his neck open. Then you left. The next morning Clough's body is found and your sister thinks she killed him and you don't tell her any different.'

'Why?' Lund demanded. 'Why would she do that?'

'Because she hates her,' Matthew suggested. 'Because her sister's the one who gets all the attention and always has.' He glanced at Roger. 'Because Henrietta had you while Verity had to make do with Richard.'

'Verity,' Roger cried, 'it's not true, is it? You wouldn't do that.'

Verity didn't answer him. She kept her hard, flinty gaze on Matthew.

Matthew went on. 'And with Richard charged with the shooting and Hettie with the murder, you finally have Roger all to herself. That's right, isn't it?'

Roger grabbed Verity, forcing her to look at him. 'Is it true?' he begged.

Verity stared at him for a long moment, then her face creased and tears tumbled from her eyes. 'All these years, Roger,' she sobbed, 'when you and I could have been together if it hadn't been for her.'

'You would let your own sister hang?' Roger said, incredulous.

Verity drew back. 'She's done worse to me. She's ruined my life. Hettie took you from me, and then she took Richard, too. She's taken everything of mine all our lives.'

'Wait a minute,' Lund said, pointing at Verity. 'Are you saying you killed Clough?'

'Of course it was me,' she screeched. 'You think my sister would ever have had the courage to do what I did?'

Lund's mouth opened in astonishment.

Matthew put a hand on Verity's shoulder and said, 'Verity Bagley, I'm arresting you for the murder of Josiah Clough.'

'This case beats everything,' Lund said as he sank down into his chair. 'We get the brothers on one thing after another, then you point the finger at Henrietta and we get a confession. Then, as we're letting Roger go, you get the one person we never suspected to admit she killed him all along. Which means,' he said with a groan, 'you solved the case. Not me.'

'You got Richard to confess. You got Roger to talk,' Matthew said, perching on the windowsill and lighting a cigarette.

'I suppose I did,' Lund nodded. 'Still, you just had to have the last word, didn't you?'

There was no malice in his words, and Matthew smiled in answer. 'Are you writing the report or am I?'

'I was going to say you can do it, but I'll only have the missus moaning at me for being so late home. And besides, you look done in. Go on, go home and get some sleep. You're going to have a big day tomorrow, explaining all what's happened to Mullinger and getting the story straight for the 'papers.'

'The 'papers?'

'Mullinger's been on to the proprietor of *The Chronicle*. Given him a right earful for printing unsubstantiated rumours and naming names before arrests were made. He's threatened to sue the newspaper for libel. When I show him Henrietta's admission that she made it all up, he'll be insisting on a full retraction and apology from them. Everyone will know you were and always have been an angel, Stannard. Ain't that nice?' Movement in the outer office caught Lund's eye, and he saw Pinder walk in.

'It'll be very nice,' Matthew agreed, sliding off the windowsill and grabbing his hat. 'Thanks.'

'What for?'

He shrugged. 'You know.'

'You ain't getting soppy on me, are you, Stannard? Because I'm not having any of that.'

Matthew smiled. 'I'll see you tomorrow,' he said, and headed out of CID.

Pinder put his head around Lund's office door. 'Heard you got a result, guv?'

'Stannard got the result,' Lund said.

Pinder nodded. 'And got himself off an indecent assault charge while he's at it.'

Lund leaned back in his chair and played with his tie. 'Despite your best efforts to make it stick.'

Pinder's mouth twitched. 'Guv?'

'Why'd you do it, Gary? Why'd you set Stannard up like that?'

The detective tried to smile, but his eyes betrayed his apprehension. 'What you on about?'

'You planted the story in *The Chronicle* about the complaint against him. You put the ad in the newspaper. And you helped yourself to the silver cigarette case Henrietta bought Stannard as a present. He never even saw it. And don't bother lying to me. Turkel told me he'd called you down to talk with Henrietta Bagley and that you took her into the private waiting room. You two were alone in there. I bet that's when she gave you the cigarette case expecting you to give it to Stannard. But you thought you'd have it for yourself, didn't you? And no one would ever know.'

Pinder straightened. 'It was a joke, that's all. Just a bit of fun.'

'Some joke.'

'Well, there's no harm done, is there? The complaint's been dropped. Everyone will know he didn't do it. So, what's the problem?'

'The problem,' Lund sighed, 'is I know what you did and soon Old Mouldy's going to know because I'm going to tell him. And I can't see him finding it as funny as you do.' He rose and headed for the door. Pinder backed hastily away to let him pass. 'If I were you, Gary, I'd start clearing out my desk because you ain't going to be here much longer.'

Chapter Forty-Four

Matthew stepped down from the bus, feeling his legs tremble beneath him. He'd been kept on his feet by adrenaline for the past twelve hours, but during the journey home, he'd barely been able to keep his eyes open. All he wanted to do was crawl into bed and sleep for eight hours straight.

He turned the corner to The Fiddlers Retreat and checked his watch when he saw all the lights were out. It was gone closing time, but he was still surprised Fred had closed up so soon. He hoped he hadn't locked the door. Matthew pushed at it and was glad when it opened.

He stepped into the dark, walking slowly to avoid barging into the furniture, and made his way to the flap in the bar counter. He took a step behind the counter and nearly fell over something on the floor. He fumbled for the light switch and turned it on.

'Fred!' he cried, and bent down to his brother-in-law lying face down on the floor. He put two fingers to his neck and felt for a pulse. He found it, strong and steady, and Matthew heaved a sigh of relief. But it was short-lived as his mind turned to the rest of his family.

He mounted the stairs as quietly as he could, dreading what he might see when he reached the top. As he reached the landing, he saw a light on in the sitting room, but he heard nothing. Tiptoeing to the door, he pushed it slowly open and stepped inside.

His breath caught in his throat. Pat was on the floor in the far corner of the room, her knees drawn up to her chin, her wrists and ankles bound with ropes. Her face was a dark red, her nose running and her cheeks streaked with tears. Her puffy eyes met his in a silent appeal for help.

Amanda was in her armchair, her bony, white hands clutching the arms, her knees held tight together. Her face was white and taut, her bright blue eyes wide and staring. She'd been crying too. A hand was on her left shoulder, holding her in place, and a cosh was held to her head.

'Found you, didn't I?' Wilf crowed, showing his yellow tombstone teeth.

'You leave them alone,' Matthew said. 'Your problem's with me, not with them.'

Wilf shook his head. 'You killed my ma. Now, you're going to watch as I kill yours.'

Amanda whimpered and the sound made Matthew feel sick. Sick and angrier than he'd ever felt in his life. Not stopping to think, he lunged, grabbing the hand that held the cosh and twisting the arm back.

Wilf cried out, more in anger than in pain, and brought round his other hand to punch Matthew in the side of the head. But it was a feeble blow, and though it made Matthew's ear ring, it didn't stop him from putting all his weight forward and forcing Wilf backwards.

The armchair toppled with them, Amanda having scrambled out of it as soon as she could, and Matthew lost his hold of Wilf. Wilf punched and caught him in the neck, making Matthew gasp, but he got another hold on Wilf's wrist and forced him to the floor. Wilf, growling like an animal, kicked anywhere he could, and Matthew took the kicks to his legs and ankles, knowing if he relinquished his hold on Wilf, he might lose the fight.

He moved his body to cover more of Wilf and stop his legs from kicking. Still holding one wrist, Matthew drew back his arm and punched Wilf in the face. Pain shot through his knuckles as they made contact with bone, but Matthew didn't care, for he had heard a cry of pain from Wilf and revelled in it. He punched him again and again, sometimes making contact, sometimes hitting the carpet as Wilf twisted away beneath him.

And then he lost hold of Wilf's wrist. Wilf's arms clamped around Matthew's chest and squeezed. Matthew could hardly breathe. He pushed away from Wilf, but Wilf turned with him, forcing Matthew onto his back until Wilf was on top of him, holding him down. Matthew kicked out, knocking against the tumbled armchair and tipping a side table over. Wilf pushed himself up, sinking back onto his haunches, straddling Matthew, and put his hands around his neck. He squeezed again and Matthew's head felt as if his skull was about to split in two. His vision darkened, and he felt himself growing weaker. His brain screamed, 'No', that he couldn't let it happen. He grabbed Wilf's wrists and tried to pull them from his neck, but Wilf was holding on so tight and all Matthew's strength was gone. *This is it*, he thought. *Wilf's going to kill Mum and Pat, and probably Fred and Georgie as well, and it will be all my fault.*

And then suddenly, Wilf's hands were gone from his throat and Wilf was no longer straddling him. Matthew coughed and gasped for breath, his hand going instinctively to his bruised throat as he struggled to sit up.

He blinked, forcing his eyes to focus, and saw Georgie, with his arms hooked around and beneath Wilf's from behind, forcing him face down on the floor and putting a knee in the small of Wilf's back.

Making sure Wilf could not move, Georgie unhooked one arm and grabbed a brass Buddha that had fallen to the floor during their struggle and whacked it across the back of Wilf's head. Wilf gave a grunt and lay still. Georgie, panting with the exertion, held the Buddha aloft, ready to deliver another blow.

'It's all right, Georgie,' Matthew gasped, and Georgie looked across at him with shock on his face.

'Have I killed him?' he asked, horrified.

Matthew crawled over to Wilf and put his fingers to his neck. He shook his head. 'He's out.'

Georgie dropped the Buddha from shaking hands and it bounced noisily on the floor. He manoeuvred himself off Wilf's prone body and fell onto his backside, shocked by what he'd done.

'Mum?' Matthew called.

'Here,' came her weak reply and Matthew saw her cowering against Pat in the corner of the room. He crawled over to her and pulled her to him. She sobbed against his chest and he kissed the top of her head fiercely. With his free hand, he cupped Pat's face and his eyes asked a silent question. She pressed her cheek against his palm and nodded that she was all right.

'Sit up, Mum,' Matthew croaked, and she did, leaving him free to untie Pat. As he pulled the gag out of her mouth, she cried, 'Fred?'

'He's downstairs,' Matthew said. 'He's knocked out, but he'll be all right.'

Pat clambered to her feet and rushed unsteadily out. A few moments later, he heard her cry out Fred's name again and her loud crying.

'Georgie.' Matthew tossed the ropes across to his brother. 'Tie him up, ankles and wrists. Then call the police and tell them we need an ambulance, too.'

Georgie did as Matthew said. 'Are you all right, Mattie?' he asked as he got to his feet.

Matthew nodded, though he felt far from all right. 'Make the calls and then bring up some brandy for Mum.'

'I will,' Georgie said and headed for the door.

'And Georgie,' Matthew halted him.

'Yeah?'

Matthew leaned back against the wall and smiled at him. 'Well done.'

Georgie beamed at him and hurried out to make the calls.

Matthew drew Amanda to his chest once again and closed his eyes. 'It's all right now, Mum. It's over.'

Also by C. K. Harewood

Under Cover of Darkness

(exclusive to subscribers)

The Empire Club Murders

Echoes of a Murder

Scan the QR code to find out more at
www.ckharewood.com